"Do you want to hold him?"

Connor stretched out his arms and leaned toward Gage.

Gage scooted his chair back. "I'll try."

Connor babbled an unintelligible sound and kicked one leg against Skye's hip while leaning farther out of her grasp. He wasn't old enough to use words yet, but she understood his body language. She gently passed him to Gage.

Skye avoided eye contact and moved past him to the kitchen, wishing there was a wall or a cabinet or anything to block her view of Gage, cautiously holding Connor like he was the most fragile thing in the world. A telltale flutter in her midsection made her deliberately turn away and take her sweet time rummaging in the pantry for a container of the puffed rice snacks Connor loved.

That was the last thing she needed—succumbing to the image of this strong, competent man riding in like some fairy-tale hero to rescue the damsel in distress.

She wasn't in distress. Okay, maybe she had a little bit going on in her life, but she didn't need him to rescue her.

His Easter Baby

Heidi McCahan

&

Lois Richer

2 Uplifting Stories

Their Baby Blessing and *A Baby by Easter*

LOVE INSPIRED
INSPIRATIONAL ROMANCE

LOVE INSPIRED®
INSPIRATIONAL ROMANCE

ISBN-13: 978-1-335-62188-7

His Easter Baby

Copyright © 2023 by Harlequin Enterprises ULC

Their Baby Blessing
First published in 2019. This edition published in 2023.
Copyright © 2019 by Heidi Blankenship

A Baby by Easter
First published in 2011. This edition published in 2023.
Copyright © 2011 by Lois M. Richer

Recycling programs
for this product may
not exist in your area.

For questions and comments about the quality of this book, please contact us at CustomerService@Harlequin.com.

Love Inspired
22 Adelaide St. West, 41st Floor
Toronto, Ontario M5H 4E3, Canada
www.LoveInspired.com

Printed in U.S.A.

CONTENTS

Heidi McCahan is a Pacific Northwest girl at heart, but now resides in North Carolina with her husband and three boys. When she isn't writing inspirational romance novels, Heidi can usually be found reading a book, enjoying a cup of coffee and avoiding the laundry pile. She's also a huge fan of dark chocolate and her adorable goldendoodle, Finn. She enjoys connecting with readers, so please visit her website, heidimccahan.com.

Books by Heidi McCahan

Love Inspired

Home to Hearts Bay

An Alaskan Secret
The Twins' Alaskan Adventure

The Firefighter's Twins
Their Baby Blessing
An Unexpected Arrangement
The Bull Rider's Fresh Start

Visit the Author Profile page at LoveInspired.com.

THEIR BABY BLESSING

Heidi McCahan

Commit thy works unto the Lord,
and thy thoughts shall be established.
—*Proverbs* 16:3

To my Colorado family:
although we don't see each other often,
I'm thankful for the moments when our paths intersect.
Much love to all of you.

Chapter One

She shouldn't have said yes.

Seated at a table next to the window, Skye Tomlinson cupped both hands around her disposable coffee cup and scanned the parking lot outside Common Grounds for a man who might be Gage Westbrook. What was she thinking—meeting a total stranger for coffee? And after only a brief exchange of direct messages on social media, too. What if he'd fabricated his whole story? Maybe this was an elaborate scheme he'd plotted to—

Relax. Not every man was out to manipulate women for their own personal gain.

Skye took a sip of her skinny hazelnut latte, desperate for comfort as the painful memories of her ex-boyfriend threatened to resurface. He'd controlled her, mocking her need for independence. Then made her feel like nothing. Over and over. While his harsh words no longer played on an endless loop in her head, she still carefully guarded tender emotional wounds. And loathed her own foolishness at ever believing he genuinely loved her.

Stop. You're safe here. A quick glance around the newest coffee shop in Merritt's Crossing revealed two of her mother's friends sitting in the overstuffed chairs by the fireplace. More familiar faces lingered around tables, savoring the warm and inviting atmosphere on a blustery Sunday afternoon. She was confident any of these folks would come to her aid if she needed them.

Although she'd snooped around Gage's social media profile—or tried to anyway—he hadn't made many details available to her prying eyes. His profile picture featured a submarine, and his cover photo was a sunset over the Florida coast. On the upside, she'd asked her brother who worked at the local sheriff's department to run a quick check, and he'd come back squeaky-clean.

Despite Gage's spotless record, she was still apprehensive about meeting him. But he said he knew about baby Connor, and that he had sensitive information about the birth father. Maybe that meant he also knew more details about where Skye's cousin McKenna might be, so Skye couldn't afford not to hear what he had to say. Because as much as she adored the sweet eleven-month-old who'd been left in her care more than a month ago, it was time for McKenna to come back, step up and be Connor's mom.

While Skye hated the convoluted family feud that no doubt influenced her cousin's dangerous and heart-breaking life choices—and wrestled with her own guilt over not doing enough to help resolve it—she couldn't be Connor's permanent legal guardian. If she was honest, she didn't *want* to be his guardian. A temporary leave from her pharmaceutical sales position in Denver to come home to Merritt's Crossing and help her widowed mother while she recovered from knee surgery was manageable. Keeping the family furniture store afloat proved daunting, but Skye could handle it until Mom was back on her feet. Literally.

But motherhood? Though a noble endeavor, it wasn't part of her carefully orchestrated plans. Kids were fine for her friends, and she'd love it if her brothers married and started families someday, but she wasn't interested in raising Connor or having children. It wasn't just the day-to-day tasks of meeting Connor's needs and finding adequate child care, although juggling both responsibilities felt overwhelming. Caring for him threatened the self-reliance she'd worked so hard to gain. What was worse, with each passing day, Skye worried more and more that McKenna might not ever show up. The thought of parenting Connor on her own and managing a career planted an icy ball of dread in her stomach. She couldn't stand the thought of the precious baby boy going to foster care, though.

Common Grounds's front door opened, and a blast of frigid air accompanied a tall, broad-shouldered man wearing a dark green winter jacket and black knit hat. Her breath caught. Was that Gage? Although he'd worn exactly what he'd promised in his message so she could easily identify him, she wasn't prepared for his impressive physical appearance. The words *devastatingly handsome* darted through her mind.

Flustered by her reaction to his arrival, she willed the butterflies flitting through her abdomen to settle down while she let her eyes travel—just for a second—from his angular, clean-shaven jaw to his dark-washed jeans and what appeared to be new hiking boots. Interesting choice for a Colorado winter. Maybe he wasn't from around here?

The pleasant hum of conversation faltered as he removed his hat and surveyed the coffee shop. When his gaze landed on Skye and he strode toward her table, she felt the weight of every curious stare in the room. She squirmed, pressing her spine against the rungs of her ladder-back chair, while her legs itched to stand and carry her to the safety of her car outside. If she was quick, she could brush past him. Offer a hasty excuse and cancel their meeting.

He stopped beside her, his fingers twisting his hat in his hands. She forced herself to meet his gaze. The flicker of uncertainty in his hazel eyes gave her pause. Was he nervous?

"Skye?"

She managed to find her voice. "Yes?"

"Gage Westbrook."

Skye clasped his outstretched hand, groaning inwardly as she realized the contrast between his cool skin and her clammy palm. "Nice to meet you," she mumbled and quickly pulled her hand away.

"It's nice to meet you, too." He gestured toward the counter behind him. "Mind if I grab a cup of coffee?"

His smooth voice and impeccable manners—not to mention those captivating eyes flecked with hints of gold—derailed her intentions. Any thought of getting up and leaving had vanished.

"Skye?"

Warmth heated her skin. "No, I—I don't mind. The coffee here's great."

"I'll be right back."

While Mr. Handsome-Hazel-Eyes strode to the counter, Skye avoided eye contact with anyone else in the room and pulled her phone from her purse. Her brother

Drew had agreed to stay with Connor this afternoon while she met with Gage, and Mom went to church and then to lunch with a friend. Although Drew said he was willing to help, his lack of experience with babies put her on edge. Connor wasn't easy to care for. Would Drew be able to handle him?

Sure enough, two text messages waited for her. The first asking if they were out of diapers, and the second requested tips for coping with a fussy baby who refused to nap. She winced. Poor Drew. He wouldn't volunteer the next time she needed help. She sent a quick response and then set her phone down in front of her so she wouldn't miss another text.

A few minutes later, Gage slid into the seat across from her and set a steaming mug of black coffee on the table. He unzipped his jacket and draped it across the empty chair beside him. His aqua-blue sweater emphasized his muscular arms and shoulders, and Skye forced herself to avert her gaze. Gage settled in his chair and quickly smoothed his hand through his close-cropped sandy-blond hair.

"Thank you for meeting with me." His smile revealed straight white teeth and Skye's heart blipped double time. "I'm sure my message seemed odd."

Skye cradled her coffee again and strong-armed her thoughts into submission. Handsome or not, Gage was still a stranger, and she was only meeting with him to see if he could help her get what she wanted—a permanent guardian for Connor. "You said you found me because my cousin McKenna Tomlinson posted a picture online of the two of us at Christmas with her baby, Connor. It's unnerving, although not surprising, since she posted a lot of photos that day. The part I can't figure out is your connection to McKenna. I'd ask her my-self, but she left town right after the holidays."

"I was afraid that might be the case." Gage frowned. "Do you know where she went?"

"Hard to say. She's…complicated. Last text I re-ceived said she'd made some friends in Wichita." Skye picked at the cardboard sleeve on her cup. "I was hop-ing she'd reconnect with her mom, who lives in Kan-sas City now, but there's really no way to predict what McKenna might do next."

Not that McKenna's mother would bother to call if McKenna showed up in Kansas City anyway. Aunt Willa stopped speaking to Skye and the rest of their extended family a long time ago. The familiar regret over their long-standing feud made Skye's heart ache.

"And her baby?"

Gage's question pulled her back to the present. Her scalp prickled with uncertainty. "Before I say more about Connor, I'd like to know why you're asking. Who are you?"

"McKenna's boyfriend, Ryan, is—was—my best friend." Gage reached inside his jacket pocket and then slid a photograph across the table. "We were stationed in San Diego with the navy, and that's where he met McKenna."

"Oh." Skye examined the picture of Gage and a blond-haired, blue-eyed man standing on the beach, wearing shorts and T-shirts and grinning at the cam-era, with the ocean in the background. Ryan. Skye didn't know much about the guy with Gage, other than McKenna claimed he was Connor's father. McKenna's stories had always seemed a bit convoluted, though. It was reassuring to meet someone who could fill in some of the gaps, especially anything about Connor's father.

"I'm not sure what happened after San Diego," Gage said. "Ryan couldn't stop talking about her, but then we got our orders to transfer to Florida and he asked her to move there."

"She didn't, did she?"

Gage shook his head. "Ryan said he talked to her all the time and tried to convince her to change her mind, even offered her money to help cover the expenses. Then she told him she was pregnant, and he..." Gage looked away, and a muscle in his jaw knotted.

"He what?"

Gage dragged his gaze to meet hers. "He died before he could see her again or meet Connor."

"Oh no." Skye's stomach plummeted. "I'm so sorry. I—I had no idea. She never told me that part." No wonder Connor's father hadn't come forward to help. Questions pinged in her brain, and she wanted to ask more, but the sheen in Gage's eyes made her keep quiet.

"When did she come back to Merritt's Crossing?" His voice was shaky as he tucked the photo away.

"First she showed up at my apartment in Denver right before Thanksgiving, with Connor in his car seat, a backpack and five dollars to her name." Skye shivered at the memory. "I still don't know how she got to Denver from California with a newborn. Frankly, I was afraid to ask."

"So she and Connor lived with you?"

"I let them stay with me for a couple of days because I knew she didn't have anywhere else to go. We'd both lost so much, and it was nice to have family around, you know?" She clamped her mouth closed before she revealed details about her family's struggles. What was it about him that made her want to share information so freely?

"Where is Connor now?"

"My mom let McKenna and Connor move in with her in November. He's been staying with my mother and me since McKenna left in January, although my mom is recovering from knee-replacement surgery, and I'm trying to keep the furniture store open..." She trailed off. Again with too much information. *Stop.*

Gage studied her. "Sounds like a lot for one person to handle."

"I've managed so far, although it's been really hectic. As long as Connor doesn't get kicked out of the church's child care program, then it's all good." And given the program director's recent warning about Connor's behavior, that was definitely a possibility. She forced a wobbly smile. "I hope."

"Here's the thing. I made a promise to Ryan before he died." He worked his jaw before continuing.

A niggling in Skye's chest forced her to stiffen. "What kind of promise?"

"I told Ryan that I'd take care of his child, and I intend to keep my word."

What did he mean—*take care of his child*? She clenched her fists in her lap. "I don't understand. What are you—"

He held up his palm to silence her. "This sounds ridiculous, I'm sure, and I don't blame you for being skeptical, but—"

"*Skeptical* doesn't even begin to describe how I'm feeling." Skye linked her arms across her chest. "Why would I believe anything you tell me?"

Irritation flashed in his eyes. "Because Ryan was like a brother to me. I can assure you he had every intention of being involved in Connor's life."

Skye's throat tightened at the raw emotion in his voice.

"I—I want to do for Connor what Ryan can't." He cleared his throat. "I'd like to see him on a regular basis."

This was crazy. She didn't know this man, and he wasn't even related to Connor. Did she really look that gullible? "I'm afraid that's out of the question."

Gage was not giving up. He'd come so close to finding Connor, only to encounter an unexpected obstacle—Skye Tomlinson. She was not only determined, but incredibly attractive. Her pink cheeks, long dark curls and pale blue eyes fringed with dark lashes all conspired against him and threatened to distract him from his critical mission.

Focus.

He couldn't afford to blow his one chance and based on the way she was glaring at him, he estimated she was about three seconds from getting up and leaving.

"I'm sorry I've upset you." He softened his tone. "Is there anything I can say to change your mind?"

Something unreadable flickered in her gaze and vanished.

"Why are you here? I—I heard what you said about the promise to your friend, but do you really expect me to believe that you came all the way from Florida to find the baby he'd never met?"

The doubt in her voice pricked at him. What was wrong with a man keeping his word? Gage sipped his coffee and weighed his response. To be perfectly honest, he'd do anything to assuage the guilt he carried from watching helplessly while Ryan succumbed to the flames, knowing he could've saved him if only he'd followed the correct protocol.

No. Not now. He squeezed his eyes shut and battled back the mental images from that horrific day. Tomorrow was the one-year anniversary of the accident that killed his best friend, and he still had nightmares.

Setting his mug down, he met Skye's gaze again. "After eight years in the navy, I decided to not reenlist. I'm almost finished with my online certification to become a wind energy technician, and the program's director told me he places most new graduates with companies in eastern Colorado or Wyoming."

"Ah." Skye nodded. "Alta Vista Energy just opened a new wind farm not far from here."

"I start my on-the-job training with them on Friday."

"Did you move to Merritt's Crossing hoping you'd find McKenna? Seems like a huge risk."

"I moved here because it offers the best chance at starting my second career, and the only time McKenna and I communicated, she mentioned she was trying to move back home. While your cousin sounds unpredictable, she shared a lot on social media up until a couple months ago. All of her recent posts were from this part of Colorado, so I assumed this was home."

Skye's gaze narrowed. "When did you talk to McKenna?"

"Just after Ryan's funeral. She wasn't there, and I was worried, so I sent her a text."

"But you've never heard from her again?"

"No." Gage leaned back in his chair. "She's ignored

all my messages. I started looking for her as soon as I moved here, though. My first stop was a diner on the interstate near Limon because McKenna had posted that she worked there."

Skye scrunched up her nose in a way Gage found incredibly adorable. "Yeah, that job didn't last long. McKenna's not meant to be a waitress."

"That's what the owner told me. She also mentioned your family's furniture business here, and that someone might have more info if I stopped by the store. Honestly, I thought it was better to reach out online first. In case you didn't—"

Skye's phone buzzed on the table between them, interrupting his explanation. Her gaze toggled between him and the phone.

"Do you want to get that?" he asked.

"It's just a text. I'll read it later."

Six more notifications chimed in quick succession. He felt his mouth twitch but suppressed his smile. "Are you sure?"

"I'd better look. My babysitter is the only one who sends blasts of texts like that."

He waited while she studied the screen.

"Oh no." The appealing shade of pink on her cheeks faded to a pale white. "I can't believe this."

"Everything okay?"

She set the phone down. "Connor's babysitter just gave her notice. Her husband is being transferred to Phoenix, and she leaves on Saturday to look for a house there."

"I thought you said Connor was in day care at a church?"

Her hand trembled as she massaged her brow with

well-manicured fingertips. "He is, but just two mornings a week because he's having issues."

"What kind of issues?"

"Biting." Skye heaved a sigh. "It's happened twice. Once more and they'll ask him to leave. That's why I hired a sitter for the other three days, hoping that if he wasn't around other kids quite so much, he'd get the one-on-one attention he seems to need."

"What will you do without a regular babysitter?"

"I—I don't know." She stared out the window.

A possible solution formed in his head. He hesitated. Given her earlier reaction, how would she respond if he mentioned he had a flexible afternoon schedule since most of his training could be completed in the mornings?

"I'm already on thin ice with the church's child care director. She thinks I shouldn't be Connor's guardian, that he'd be better off in a two-parent home. Anyway, if he bites another child again, I'm worried she'll use it as an excuse to call social services."

Not on his watch. Gage's heart fisted. "No." He wouldn't let that happen.

Skye flinched.

The single word came out more forceful than he'd intended. "I—I'm sorry." He held up both palms in surrender. "Please, don't let it come to that."

Skye's voice lowered to a whisper. "People talk. Look at how you found out about me from someone in Limon. Word will get out that I'm not able to care for him well enough and—"

"Skye." Gage's hand shot out and blanketed hers. "Let me help you. Please."

Her eyes widened, and she stiffened at his touch.

Startled by the warmth that zinged up his arm, he scrambled to form a coherent thought. "I have afternoons free. Maybe some mornings, too. I can watch Connor as much or as little as you need."

The words tumbled out before he could stop them.

She stared at him. An awkward silence filled the space between them, and he suddenly regretted his bold offer. What if he scared her off?

Finally, the rumble of the espresso machine broke through the quiet, and she tugged her hand free. "I can't ask you to do that."

"You didn't ask. I offered."

She frowned. "Do you have any experience with babies?"

"I can learn." It was a weak argument. She'd probably say no for sure now. He held his breath. *Please say yes. Please say yes.*

"I—I don't know. I can't afford to risk Connor's safety with someone who lacks experience."

His gut cinched tighter and he leaned forward, fighting to keep his tone even. "And I can't go back on my word to my best friend. Give me two hours with Connor and let me prove to you that I can handle taking care of him."

She sighed and shrugged into her coat. "Come over for dinner tomorrow. I'll introduce you to my mother and Connor. We'll see how it goes."

Seriously? Relief washed over him. "What time?"

"Five thirty. I'll message you our address." She stood and reached for her purse. "See you then."

"Yeah. Great." His shock limited him to monosyllabic responses. "See you then," he called over his shoulder as her boots *click-click-clicked* across the hardwood floor behind him.

He'd done it. Somehow he'd convinced Skye to let him meet Connor. A smile tugged at his mouth and he pumped the air with his fist.

Through the window, he watched Skye jog toward her car as thick wet snowflakes fell from a gray sky. She was intense. And beautiful. He purged the observation from his thoughts. Nope. Not going there. He had one mission right now, and it didn't include flirting with a pretty brunette. Besides, he wasn't "relationship material." The last woman he'd dated in Florida had solidified that when she'd called him emotionally unavailable.

Gage gritted his teeth. He had his binge-drinking mother and absentee father to thank for that. And he knew firsthand how tough some foster homes could be. Maybe that was why he found Skye's loyalty to her own family both intriguing and intimidating.

He reached for his phone to check McKenna's social media for an update.

Still nothing. Gage sighed and revisited her older posts, landing on an image of McKenna holding Connor on her lap.

Man, Ryan would be so proud of his son. He hated that Ryan never had a chance to meet the baby before the accident.

"I'm going to look out for him. I won't let you down. I promise," Gage whispered, swallowing against the tightness in his throat. He didn't know yet how he would fulfill that promise specifically—looking out for an almost one-year-old—but it didn't lessen his resolve. He knew all too well the heartache of growing up without a dad, and he couldn't rest until he was certain Connor was safe. Loved. Being a part of Connor's life was about so much more than keeping a promise to Ryan.

When Gage was a child, other adults had enabled his mother's reckless behavior. He never wanted Connor to experience the pain and hopelessness of that kind of betrayal from the very people who were supposed to protect him. And he'd do whatever it took to make that happen.

Chapter Two

She shouldn't have invited Gage over.

A dull ache throbbed at Skye's temples, and she'd snapped at Mom more than once this afternoon. The thought of allowing a man they'd just met into their home—into Connor's life—sent a shiver down her spine. She hurried to fix dinner in Mom's kitchen, while Connor sat at her feet, babbling as he pulled every single plastic container out of the bottom cabinet drawer.

Caught off guard by Gage's bold offer at the coffee shop yesterday, and still reeling from her babysitter's sudden resignation, she'd relented too easily. Her healthy suspicion of strangers had inconveniently vanished, and now, in less than ten minutes, he'd be at the door and she'd have to come up with a compelling reason why she didn't need his help. His desire to keep his promise to his friend was honorable and all, but she had to consider Connor's safety, too. What did she really know about Gage?

"There has to be another option," she muttered, sidestepping Connor to fish the salad-serving tongs out of the drawer.

"Honey, are you all right?" Mom sat at the oval table in the breakfast nook, slicing tomatoes for the garden salad. "You've been talking to yourself all afternoon."

"Yep. Fine. I've just got a lot to think about." Skye skirted the L-shaped counter and set the tongs beside the salad bowl in front of Mom, then quickly pivoted away. She felt her mother's concerned gaze following her as she turned off the Crock-Pot. Gage and her child care issues paled in comparison to the furniture store's financial issues she'd stumbled across today. Dad had left a much more convoluted mess than Skye had originally thought. How in the world would she ever bring that up? Mom had endured so much already.

"That's a real shame about Bethany and her family moving to Phoenix," Mom said. "She was a wonderful babysitter."

"I wish she could've given more notice." Skye pulled a stack of plates from the cabinet and carried them to the table. "Her timing is the worst."

"Maybe God has something better in mind. For her and for you." Mom's gentle smile and trite observations made Skye bristle.

"You don't believe that's true."

"I didn't say that." Skye swiped her palm across her forehead and turned away to grab napkins and silverware. "It's just… Never mind."

Hurt filled Mom's brown eyes.

Skye clamped her mouth closed, conscious of poking holes in Mom's beliefs. Even though they were once her beliefs, too, she sure had a lot of doubts lately about what God must have in mind for her. For McKenna and Connor, too.

"I'm worried. I—I don't know what we're going to do without Bethany."

Without a lot of things. Skye kept her lengthy list of worries to herself while she struggled to tamp down the anxious feelings twisting her up inside. If the business was in worse shape financially than she'd thought, and she had to hire a full-time babysitter for Connor while she tried to save the furniture store, her own personal savings account would dwindle quickly. Both of her brothers said they were committed to helping, but neither of them were prepared to financially support Mom, either.

"We've certainly endured quite a few surprises lately," Mom said quietly.

Connor squealed and banged two plastic measuring cups together, then held one out for her, accompanied by a toothy smile. Grateful his outburst might've saved her from discussing her waning faith, Skye leaned over and smoothed a wisp of his pale blond hair across his forehead.

"No, thanks. That's for you." When she pulled away without taking the measuring cup, his blue eyes filled with tears and his expression crumpled.

While his cries grew louder, Skye quickly glanced at the timer beside the oven. In two minutes, the rolls needed to come out. The stew in the Crock-Pot was ready, but there weren't drinks in the glasses yet, and she hadn't prepared anything for Connor to eat. Still so much to do before Gage arrived, and Mom wasn't mobile enough to carry hot dishes to the table. Letting him sit there and cry wasn't okay, either.

"C'mon, let's move to the living room and play with some trucks. Your favorite." She scooped him up and carried him into the living room, where his toys were still scattered across the beige carpet.

"Anything I can do?" Mom asked.

"I've got it." Skye set him on the floor and pushed a plastic truck and some blocks toward him, but Connor only screamed louder, while his face deepened to a shade of pink she hadn't seen before in his previous tantrums.

"Wow." Skye glanced at Mom over her shoulder. "He's really angry."

"He'll calm down in a minute." Her mom braced against the table and pushed to a stand. "Let me—"

"No, don't get up." Skye hurried to her side and grasped her elbow. "I said I've got it. What do you need?"

"Honey, Dr. Bradley said I'm supposed to be walking short distances." Mom raised her voice to be heard above Connor's wailing. "There's no reason for me to sit here while you wear yourself out. I can at least carry a few things to the table."

Skye opened her mouth to argue, but the timer rang, reminding her that if she had any hope of getting the meal on the table, she'd have to relent and let her mother help a little bit.

"All right. I'll set the table while you get the rolls out of the oven."

"Deal." Mom patted Skye's arm and then moved slowly toward the kitchen.

"Oh, look at this." Skye brought Connor a bright-colored shape sorter from the toy bin beside the sofa, and thankfully he dialed back his cries to a pathetic whimper. While he examined the plastic shapes inside the rectangular box, Skye hurried to put plates and silverware on the table.

A few minutes later, the doorbell rang. *No.* A jolt of adrenaline zinged through her. She wasn't ready. She tucked a strand of hair that had escaped her ponytail behind her ear and glanced at her plaid button-down shirt and favorite skinny jeans. She'd meant to change before Gage—

Wait. Why did it matter how she looked? A relationship with him apart from their shared interest in Connor wasn't even on her radar.

She opened the door and Gage stood on the other side. His sandy-blond hair gleamed in the light from the porch, and the skin beside his hazel eyes crinkled when he smiled. A stunning smile that she was working hard not to stare at right now.

"Hey." That voice. Deep. Confident. Smooth. How could one simple word make her heart pound so easily?

Great. While most normal humans might return his casual greeting, Skye couldn't find her words. Or ignore Gage's shoulders, which seemed broader than she remembered. Or was it the green winter jacket that added bulk? Instead of speaking, all she could think about was how that shade of green emphasized the flecks in his eyes and—

"Skye?" Gage's brow arched. "You did say five thirty, didn't you?"

"Yeah, hi. Sorry, I was, uh…" *Just thinking about your amazing shoulders and gorgeous eyes.*

Oh brother. Warmth rushed to her face. "Please, come in."

She stepped back and pulled the door wide, while another wave of anxiety washed over her. Was she doing the right thing—allowing Gage to meet Connor? He'd been through so much in his first year of life. Introducing another stranger, even one with the best of intentions, made her uneasy.

The aroma of something delicious—soup, maybe—enveloped Gage as he toed off his boots inside the Tomlinsons' front door. Definitely smelled more appealing than the canned chili he'd planned to fix for himself.

"Thanks for coming." Skye took his jacket, and his heart skittered at the way those pink lips of hers curved into a tentative smile.

He quickly banished those thoughts. "No problem."

"Hello, you must be Gage." A petite woman with salt-and-pepper curls and wearing black pants and a red blouse walked slowly from the kitchen to the nearby table, her eyes focused on a small basket balanced precariously in her hands.

"That's my mother, Rhonda Tomlinson," Skye said.

Before Gage could respond, Connor squealed so loud that Skye winced. "That's Connor's way of welcoming you."

Gage glanced at the little boy sitting in the middle of the living room floor, and his breath hitched. He'd recognize those blue eyes anywhere. They were a carbon copy of Ryan's. He swallowed hard and glanced at Skye again. "Mind if I say hello?"

"Please do." Something undecipherable flashed across Skye's features. "Dinner will be ready in a minute."

Gage approached slowly and sank onto the beige shag carpet. "What's up, little dude?"

Connor stared at him, wide-eyed, then babbled a

string of unintelligible words while offering Gage an orange plastic dump truck.

"Thanks." Gage gently took the truck and drove it across the carpet and up Connor's leg, while making the appropriate truck noises.

Connor giggled and playfully pushed Gage's hand away.

Gage's heart expanded at the bubbly sound of Connor's laugh, and he drove the truck along Connor's gray sweatpants again, making him laugh louder. This time Gage laughed right along with him, and they repeated the cycle. He quickly surveyed his surroundings—casual furnishings, floral curtains framing the windows, and shelves nearby lined with books and knickknacks indicated the Tomlinsons lived comfortably but didn't seem pretentious.

Feeling the weight of their stares, Gage glanced up to see Mrs. Tomlinson and Skye watching him, their mouths open.

Uh-oh. What had he done? "What's wrong?"

"Nothing's wrong. It's amazing." Skye's smooth brow furrowed. "We just haven't heard him laugh that much before."

Oh. Gage shifted his focus back to Connor. How sad. "He's got a great laugh. I'd want to hear more, too."

While Skye and her mother put dishes on the table, Connor offered Gage more of his toys, coupled with enthusiastic sounds, and Gage admired each car, plastic tool and rattle.

"I hate to interrupt the fun," Skye said, "but dinner is ready."

"All right." Gage stood, and Connor's lower lip wobbled.

Oh no. Gage hesitated. He'd made the kid cry already.

Connor's expression crumpled, and he stretched both arms toward Gage as if asking to be held. What should he do? He'd made his promise to Ryan without ever spending much time around children. Especially babies.

Gage shot Skye a panicked look.

Skye gave him a sympathetic smile. "That means he likes you and wants to keep playing. Why don't you sit down, and I'll put Connor in his high chair?"

So this crying was good? "Let's eat, bud." Gage angled his head toward the dining room table. Connor's response was a painful cry that knifed at Gage's heart. He groaned inwardly at his ignorant assumption that such a young child would make the transition to his high chair without complaint. Man, he had a lot to learn if he was going to make good on his commitment. What if Skye realized how inexperienced he was and refused to let him spend time with Connor?

Mrs. Tomlinson had already sat down. Gage waited until Skye had scooped Connor up and carried him to his high chair. The little boy arched his back and screeched, making it difficult for Skye to secure the harness and buckles.

"Wow." Gage grimaced. He might not be able to talk, but he'd made his preferences quite clear.

"He keeps us on our toes." Mrs. Tomlinson shook her head while Skye finally buckled Connor in and latched the white plastic tray in place. She straightened, her cheeks flushed, and claimed her place across from Gage.

"He'll calm down in a minute." Skye reached for her napkin. "Would you like to ask the blessing, Mom?"

Connor cried the whole time Mrs. Tomlinson prayed, drowning out most of what she said.

When she'd finished, Gage surveyed the meal. A basket of dinner rolls, green salad and a generous helping of beef stew in his bowl made his mouth water. He glanced at Connor. "Are you ready to eat?"

Connor paused his tirade long enough to consider Gage's question.

"Can he have some bread?" Gage asked Skye. He really had no idea what babies Connor's age could eat.

"Sure. If he throws it, he may not have any more, though." Skye fired a warning glance in Connor's direction.

"Got it." No roll tossing at the table. Although it did sound a little fun.

Gage took a roll from the basket and pinched a small bite to share with Connor. "Here." He set it on the tray. "This bread looks yummy." His voice sounded goofy. And when was the last time he'd used the word *yummy*? He didn't dare look Skye's way.

Connor picked up the bread and popped it in his mouth.

Then his blue eyes widened, and he pointed toward the basket of rolls, while he bounced up and down against the high chair's vinyl cushion.

"Is it okay if he has more?" Gage asked.

Skye nodded, and he split another roll into chunks and handed it over. Connor gobbled it down as quickly as he could.

While Gage had anticipated the conversation might revolve around his reasons for moving to Merritt's Crossing, there wasn't much time to formulate a complete sentence. Once Connor realized Gage was willing to share from his plate, the little boy ate like he was a bottomless pit. Between putting food on the tray and trying to finish his own meal, dinner was almost over, and they hadn't had a chance to talk at all.

"You wouldn't know it by the way he's eating, but I promise we feed him on a regular basis. Or at least we try to." Mrs. Tomlinson scraped her own bowl clean. "Maybe you're our secret weapon, Gage."

"I don't know about that." Gage speared a bite of meat with his fork. "He's definitely got an appetite tonight."

A few minutes later, Connor shoved the chunks of carrots aside and rubbed his eyes with his fist.

"Yikes." Skye pushed back her chair. "I think he's about to melt down. Let me get him cleaned up before he rubs food in his hair."

"Is that usually what happens?" Gage asked.

"Sometimes." Mrs. Tomlinson chuckled. "We're not always great at figuring out when he's had enough."

Skye returned from the sink with a dishcloth in her hand. "I hadn't planned on giving him a bath tonight." She quickly wiped his fingers and his face while he did his best to squirm away.

Gage stifled a laugh. This kid had a strong will. Reminded him a lot of Ryan. The comparison felt like a gut punch, and his amusement vanished.

"Are you okay?" Mrs. Tomlinson reached over and patted Gage's arm. "You look sad all of a sudden."

How much to share? He'd already told Skye he wanted to be involved in Connor's life. Gage rubbed his fingertips along his jaw. "I hate that Ryan didn't get a chance to meet his son, you know?"

Mrs. Tomlinson's eyes filled with empathy. "We

wish things were different, too. I'm sure Skye told you we don't know if McKenna will return. Maybe God brought you into our lives for a reason."

"Mom—" Skye shot her mother a warning glance.

"It's true, whether you choose to believe it or not." Mrs. Tomlinson frowned at her daughter. "We don't know if she'll come back. What if she doesn't? Gage's connection to Connor's father isn't a coincidence."

Skye lowered Connor to the floor. He quickly crawled across the carpet to the toys he'd played with before dinner.

Gage tried to assess Skye's reaction to her mother's feelings. She seemed like she had a lot going on in her life. He didn't dare ask, but did she really plan on caring for Connor on her own if his mother wasn't willing or able to care for him?

"Like I said yesterday, I'm finishing my certification through the wind energy technician program at the community college. I'll start the hands-on training soon, and until I'm placed in a full-time position, I have a flexible schedule."

"See?" Mrs. Tomlinson beamed at her daughter. "A flexible schedule. That's exactly what we need."

Skye sank into her chair. Uncertainty was written all over her face. She sighed. "Can you come over tomorrow afternoon? From three to five thirty?"

"Absolutely."

"Okay. I'll leave a list of instructions for you. Mom will be here, too, just in case."

Gage ducked his head and suppressed a smile. Her subtext was not lost on him. *Just in case you're a lousy babysitter.*

"Now that we have that worked out, how about dessert?" Mrs. Tomlinson asked.

"I think I'll pass." Gage pushed back his chair and stood. "I still have some unpacking to do, and a test to study for."

"Oh, I'm sorry to hear that." Mrs. Tomlinson frowned. "Would you like to take some brownies home? Or maybe the leftover stew?"

"No, thank you." He didn't want to overstay his welcome. Skye's body language indicated she wasn't thrilled about what just happened, and he wanted to go before she changed her mind about tomorrow. "It was delicious, though."

"I'll walk you out." Skye crossed to the front door, pausing to pick Connor up and wedge him on her hip. He immediately gave her a sleepy smile and grabbed a chunk of her ponytail in his chubby fist.

She gently extracted her hair from Connor's hand and pressed a gentle kiss to his forehead.

Gage looked away and jammed his feet into his boots. So she wasn't a total ice queen. Maybe she was too stressed and overwhelmed. Or just not a fan of him dropping into her life unannounced? She'd mentioned her concerns about someone calling social services. Did she think he was going to try to take Connor from her?

Something told him now was not the time to offer reassurances. He put on his jacket and paused, one hand on the doorknob, and dared to look at her one more time. "Thanks for giving me a chance."

"Don't let me down."

Wow. Okay. "See you soon."

"Good night."

He stepped out onto the porch and pulled the door

closed behind him. Staring up into the night sky, his breath puffing in little white clouds, he silently offered a prayer for guidance.

I'm off to a shaky start here, Lord.

When he set out to find McKenna and her baby, he never anticipated meeting Skye. And no matter how hard he tried, he couldn't ignore his initial attraction to her. Not that it mattered. She was downright frigid tonight and clearly didn't like strangers, no matter how honorable their intentions. She'd probably only asked for his help because her mom coaxed her and she was desperate. But he couldn't let her attitude discourage him. He owed it to Ryan to keep his promise.

Chapter Three

Please, please let this be the one.

Skye folded her hands behind her back and pasted on a polite smile. Her customers, Mr. and Mrs. Crawford, circled the eight-piece dining room set in the furniture's showroom for the third time, their brows furrowed.

"What do you think, sweetheart?" Mr. Crawford clapped his hand on his wife's shoulder, while he jangled his loose change with his hand in his other pocket. Skye held her breath, waiting for Mrs. Crawford to answer.

"I just can't make up my mind. Do you think we can all fit around it for Easter? We're hosting this year."

Yes, of course. Skye dug her fingernails into her palm to keep from blurting out a response. She'd actually never visited the Crawfords' home and had no idea how much space they had in their dining room, but the store's dismal sales—almost nonexistent this month—could really use a boost.

"It might be a tight squeeze, especially with the credenza, too, but I'm sure we can make it work." Mr. Crawford gave Skye a reassuring smile, the lines on his weathered face crinkling around his eyes.

She widened her smile, while the tension between her shoulders knotted tighter. Mrs. Crawford did not seem convinced.

"We really love the bedroom set we purchased from your daddy some years ago," Mrs. Crawford said, running her hand over the oak tabletop. "Now that our son and his wife moved to Fort Collins and took our dining room table and chairs, I'd really like something that will accommodate him and his wife, and of course, any future grandchildren, if our daughter ever gets married…" She trailed off and stepped back as if to gain a better perspective.

"I'm glad you've enjoyed your bedroom set." Skye kept her tone warm. Optimistic. "We always appreciate loyal customers."

"Your father was a great guy." Mr. Crawford's gaze filled with empathy. "We had a good time coaching your brother's Little League team together all those years. How's your mom doing?"

Skye swallowed hard, surprised by the emotion unexpectedly rising at the mention of her father's good works in Merritt's Crossing. "Mom's getting by. I guess you heard she's had knee replacement surgery. The recovery's tougher than we expected."

"I can imagine." Mr. Crawford glanced at his wife, the change in his pocket jangling a little louder. "What do you say, hon? Is this the one or—"

Skye's phone rang, and she froze. Ignore it? What if it was McKenna? But taking the call meant stepping away from the customers, and she hated for them to think they weren't important. Quite the opposite, really.

"Go ahead and answer that if you need to, dear." Mrs. Crawford smiled politely. "We don't mind."

"I'll just be a minute." Skye crossed the showroom in quick strides to the antique rolltop desk that served as the home base when she couldn't be in the tiny back office. Business cards, a work space for her laptop and a vase of pink carnations with a sprig of baby's breath decorated the well-worn surface. Her phone's screen lit up with the church's number in the caller ID. *Oh no.* Her stomach dropped. Connor.

"H-hello?" she said, unable to keep the tremor from her voice.

"Hello, Skye, this is Betty Sanders over at the church. How are you?"

Skye squeezed her eyes shut. A call from the child care director wasn't a good thing. "I'm fine, Mrs. Sanders. How can I help you?"

"We've run into a bit of an issue with Connor this morning. Do you have a few minutes to chat?"

Skye opened her eyes and glanced over her shoulder. Mr. and Mrs. Crawford stood close together near the dining room set, talking quietly. At least they hadn't left. Yet. "What happened?"

"I'm afraid he bit another child on the arm. As we've already discussed, biting is a cause for concern. Since it's happened two other times, we're going to have to ask you to leave the Mom's Morning Out program."

No, no, no. Skye pressed her hand to her cheek. "I'm sure you're aware Connor's had a lot to deal with lately, with his mom…out of town for a while. I mean, he's not even one yet. Isn't there a chance he's just trying to express his frustration—"

"Skye, we can't allow him to bite. It's not fair to the other children."

"But he isn't trying to be aggressive. He's never bitten me or my mom or anyone outside the nursery. How do you know he wasn't provoked?" She knew she was pushing her limit with Mrs. Sanders, but she couldn't help but try. The Mom's Morning Out program was her child care lifeline. Without it, she had nothing. Well, nothing except Gage.

"I can assure you he was not provoked," Mrs. Sanders said, her tone icy. "As the director, I have a responsibility to provide a safe and nurturing environment for all who attend. While it's a real shame about Connor's abandonment, I'm not going to excuse his unacceptable behavior."

Skye bristled at the older woman's harsh, judgmental tone. She bit her lip and glanced at her customers again.

Mr. and Mrs. Crawford were already halfway to the store's front door. "We'll be back," they whispered.

No! She wanted to run ahead and plant herself in their path, maybe even offer them a discount off the full price. At this point, she wasn't above begging them to reconsider. She really couldn't afford to lose this sale.

"Skye?" Mrs. Sanders's voice grated on her nerves. "Are you still there?"

"Yes, I just—"

"I'll need you to come pick Connor up immediately."

"What?" Skye glanced at the oversize wooden clock mounted on the wall, the hands on the distressed finish inching toward eleven o'clock. "I usually don't pick him up until twelve fifteen."

"Perhaps I wasn't explicit enough. He's being removed from the program. Permanently. I expect to see you here in the next fifteen minutes."

"But—"

There was no point arguing. Mrs. Sanders had already ended the call. Skye pulled the phone away from her ear and stared at it in disbelief. This couldn't be happening. What was she going to do with an eleven-month-old in a furniture store? Sure, she could set up the portable crib to keep him contained in the back room, but he wouldn't be content there for more than a few minutes. And he'd never take a nap there, either.

Oh, McKenna. What have you done?

With Connor's first birthday coming up in a few days, surely her cousin would come home in time to celebrate?

Tears stung her eyes, but Skye refused to fall apart right now. She didn't have time for a meltdown, and she wouldn't give Mrs. Sanders the satisfaction of seeing her cry. After hastily scrawling a note indicating the store's unexpected closure due to a family emergency, she taped it to the glass door on her way out. This was one more reason why sales had to improve—she needed the income to hire additional help.

Another storm had blown in, and fresh snow blanketed the sidewalk in front of the store. She made a mental note to ask Drew to stop by and shovel it after work. Again. Ducking her chin against the flakes swirling around her, Skye trudged to her car parked behind the store, the reality of her circumstances weighting her steps.

A mother who could barely walk, an abandoned baby without a babysitter and her family's floundering furniture business, not to mention zero resolutions within her grasp.

What about Gage?

She pushed out a laugh at the ridiculous notion. They barely knew anything about him, and he hadn't even spent a single minute alone with Connor. How could he possibly be the answer to her problems?

Gage eased his truck into the Tomlinsons' driveway and turned off the ignition, wishing he could do the same for the anxiety wreaking havoc on his insides. Man, he hadn't felt this nervous since his first week at sea on the submarine. Sure, he and Connor got along great last night, but they hadn't been alone. He'd only played with a couple of toys and shared some food at dinner. Skye did most of the work, and she'd intervened when Connor threw a fit.

What if he totally messed this up?

An ache formed in his chest. Yesterday marked one year since Ryan died. He glanced at the picture wedged on his dashboard, the one of him and Ryan on the beach in San Diego that he'd shared with Skye at the coffee shop. After their meeting, he'd tucked the dog-eared photo inside one of the few books he owned, but this morning he'd mustered the courage to retrieve the picture and tuck it into the corner of his dash—a frequent reminder spurring him on to keep his promise.

Pocketing his keys, he climbed out of the truck and slammed the door. Although the snow had stopped falling, several inches coated the driveway, a sedan parked in front of the garage and the steps leading up to the Tomlinsons' modest rambler. Should he offer to shovel while he was here? Or maybe Skye wanted to take care of that herself, too.

He climbed the steps and the door swung open before he could knock or ring the bell.

"Hey," Skye greeted him, looking as though she'd stepped out of a corporate boardroom in a long gray dress belted at the waist and stylish black boots. His gaze flitted from her hair piled in a messy bun on top of her head, to her red-rimmed eyes and blotchy cheeks. Had she been crying? His chest tightened. Did something happen to Connor?

"Are you all right?"

"Come on in." She stepped back, ignoring his question. "I didn't want you to ring the bell. Connor's still taking a nap."

Gage stood in the foyer and quickly surveyed his surroundings. The house was quiet, and he didn't want to do anything that might upset her more. He was also afraid to ask why she wasn't at the furniture store. Maybe she'd decided she didn't trust him being there without her supervision after all.

"My mom will be home from her physical therapy appointment soon." Skye crossed to the table in the breakfast nook, where a can of soda and a bag of chips sat between a laptop and a large calendar. Did she have another job she hadn't mentioned? He shifted from one foot to the other, and kept his coat and his boots on, worried that one wrong move might earn him an icy stare.

She slumped into the chair with a sigh, then shot him a look, her smooth brow furrowed. "Why are you just standing there?"

"I'm waiting for my orders."

"What?"

"My orders. You look stressed. Or busy. Maybe both. If you need to get some work done, I'd be glad to shovel the driveway or something until Connor wakes up."

"You don't work for me." She massaged her forehead

with her fingertips. "I'm not going to ask you to shovel my driveway. Or boss you around."

Okay. He ducked his head to hide the smile tugging at the corners of his mouth. This was probably not the best time to mention that she'd been bossy since the first second they'd met. He took his time unlacing his boots and hanging his jacket on the rack near the door. How long did a baby sleep anyway? Hopefully not much longer. Gage needed Connor to wake up and save him from Skye and her fragile mood.

He padded in his socks toward the table and slowly eased into the chair across from her. He wasn't good with females and tears. No matter how hard he tried, he always seemed to say the wrong thing. Did she want to talk about it? She sure didn't seem like she wanted his help. While he racked his brain for something safe to say, her phone chimed, and she pounced on it. She swiped at the screen, her eyes quickly scanning, and then she flung the phone back on the table in disgust.

Oh boy. Gage wiped his sweaty palms on the legs of his jeans and braced for a fresh wave of tears.

"Perfect. Just perfect." She glared daggers at the phone and shook her head. "I can't believe this is happening."

"Do you want to talk about it?"

"Connor got kicked out of the church day care today."

Well. That explained a few things. "Why?"

"Bit another child. Third offense. They made me pick him up early." Her eyes brimmed with tears. "I don't know what I'm going to do," she whispered.

Please, please don't cry. Gage's knee bounced up and down under the table, and he scrambled for a pragmatic solution to get in front of her impending meltdown. "Can you appeal the decision?"

"Tried that. The senior pastor just texted me and said the director of the program has the final say." Skye reached for her phone again. "I really need to find someone who can watch Connor on a consistent basis. Most of the time he still takes two naps, so it's just a few hours each day—and only until Mom gets some of her mobility back. I've called everyone I can think of, though."

You haven't asked me. Gage clamped his mouth shut. What would she say if he offered?

She frowned, shaking her head as she scrolled some more. "Mom wants me to hire someone to manage the store so I can stay with Connor, but we just don't have any wiggle room in the budget…" She heaved another sigh. "And I don't have the heart to tell her about our financial situation right now, on top of everything else she's dealing with."

Her troubled gaze toggled to him. "Sorry to dump all this on you. Probably way more than you wanted to know."

Not true. He did want to know because he honestly wanted to help, and although the sheen of moisture in her beautiful blue eyes had subsided, he was going to tread lightly. She seemed guarded—suspicious, even— of his intentions. He really didn't want to blow his chance at being in Connor's life, or risk ignoring his pledge to Ryan. And what if word got out of Connor's situation and someone called social services?

Adrenaline slammed into him at the mental images that scenario conjured.

She narrowed her eyes. "What are you thinking?"

He shifted in his chair. *Here goes nothing.* "I—I know you're in a bind, and I totally get that you might have issues with accepting help from strangers—"

"I do not."

Really? Gage silently cocked an eyebrow.

She ducked her chin. "Okay, maybe a little."

"My schedule is flexible until I start the practical portion of my training, and I'd be glad to stay with Connor whenever you need me to."

She picked at her thumbnail and avoided his gaze. "I don't think that's a good idea."

"Why not?"

The sound of Connor crying came through the baby monitor resting on the kitchen counter nearby.

Lousy timing, kiddo. Gage studied her, hoping she wouldn't use that as an opportune time to escape the conversation.

"I'd better get him." Skye's phone chimed again, and she picked it up, glanced at the screen, then pushed to her feet and hurried down the hallway.

"Skye—"

She didn't turn back, and a minute later, he listened through the monitor as she spoke to Connor and his crying ceased.

Gage tipped his head back and stared at the ceiling. No, he didn't have any experience with babies. Or children at all, really. His brief stints in and out of temporary foster care placement had left a scar, though, and he couldn't fathom letting Connor grow up without consistent, stable male role models.

He smoothed his hand over his close-cropped hair and silently prayed for the words to change Skye's mind. Ryan was the closest thing to a brother he'd ever had and being a part of Connor's world was the only way Gage could express his gratitude for the bond they'd shared.

No, no, no. Skye's fingers trembled as she knelt on the floor beside Connor, trying to keep him from wiggling out of reach while she changed his diaper.

While Gage's story about his connection with Ryan seemed legitimate, and the photo he shared lined up with what little McKenna had shared about Connor's father, was Gage really the solution to her babysitting needs? What if she accepted his offer and he decided it wasn't for him? He said he was committed to being involved in Connor's life, but did he even know what that meant? She'd never forgive herself if Connor was hurt because she'd made a hasty decision. The wounds were still raw from the last time she'd allowed herself to be vulnerable. Suffering the consequences of her poor decisions was one thing, but what if her choices impacted an innocent child, too?

The thought made her stomach churn.

Out in the living room, she heard the front door open and Mom exchanging greetings with Gage. Connor's eyes followed her as she tossed the diaper in the trash. She pushed to her feet, eager to get back to the other room before Gage had a chance to woo her mother. Connor sucked loudly on his thumb while she lifted him off the floor. "Let's get a snack, sweet pea."

She strode down the hallway with Connor in her arms. Mom and Gage sat at the table, talking quietly. What had she missed? Fatigue lined Mom's face, and Skye cringed inwardly. Although she was probably trying to be a good sport and chat with Gage, Mom normally went straight to the couch and elevated her leg after physical therapy.

"Hi, Mom. How was your appointment?"

Mom gave her a tired smile and reached over to give Connor's leg a gentle squeeze. "It was all right. My therapist pushed me hard."

"Would you mind holding him while I fix his snack?" Skye hovered near Mom's shoulder. She hated to ask her to do anything extra, but maybe Connor wouldn't cry if he snuggled with Mom.

"For a minute." She stifled a yawn. "I'm fading fast. Might need a nap before dinner."

Connor stretched out his arms and leaned toward Gage.

"Do you want to hold him?" Skye couldn't keep the surprise from her voice.

Gage scooted his chair back. "I'll try."

Connor babbled an unintelligible sound and kicked one leg against Skye's hip, while leaning farther out of her grasp. He wasn't old enough to use words yet, but she understood his body language. She gently passed him to Gage, acutely aware of the warmth of Gage's fingers brushing against hers.

Skye avoided eye contact and moved past him to the kitchen, wishing there was a wall or a cabinet or anything to block her view of Gage, with his powder blue long-sleeve shirt hugging the defined curves of his muscular arms, cautiously holding Connor like he was the most fragile thing in the world. A telltale flutter in her midsection made her deliberately turn away and take her sweet time rummaging in the pantry for a container of the puffed-rice snacks Connor loved.

That was the last thing she needed—succumbing to

the image of this strong, competent man riding in like some fairy-tale hero to rescue the damsel in distress.

She wasn't in distress. Okay, maybe she had a little bit going on in her life, but she didn't need him to rescue her.

"Gage was just telling me he might be the solution to your child care dilemma," Mom said, her tone hinting that she was completely on board with the idea.

The round metal container slipped from Skye's hands and rolled across the hardwood. Blood pounded in her ears as she chased after it. Gage was watching her—she could feel the weight of those gorgeous hazel eyes tracking her. Did he sense her apprehension?

She straightened, just in time to catch Connor looking up at Gage, his little hand exploring his face, and his pudgy cheeks scrunched in an adoring smile.

Oh brother. Don't tell me you're captivated, too.

"We didn't get a chance to discuss it."

Mom shot her a look. "What's to discuss? You need someone consistent and reliable, with flexibility in their schedule. And I'll be here to advise Gage on what to do."

But what about long-term? What kind of impact would Gage's role in Connor's life have? She bit her lip and stole another glance at Connor. He babbled and cooed, his fingers meandering around Gage's angular jaw. When Gage mimicked a playful bite toward Connor's hand, the little boy's belly laugh made Skye's breath catch.

Mom caught her staring and arched a brow as if to say, *See?*

Skye averted her gaze and poured the rice puffs into a small plastic bowl, then carried it to the table.

"I know you wanted Connor to spend time with other children, but given his history with biting, and as long as he's still taking two naps, maybe keeping him here is the best thing for now. Gage can come by for a few hours. Between the two of us, we—"

"All right." Exasperated, Skye cut her off. "Point taken."

Connor stopped jabbering and stared at her, his lower lip pooched out. Gage and Mom both glanced at her, eyes wide.

"I'm sorry." She softened her tone as she set the bowl on the table in front of Gage and Connor. "That sounded harsh."

An awkward silence blanketed them, and she returned to the kitchen to put some water in a sippy cup for Connor, her face flaming. Again. She only wanted to do what was best for Connor, but now she felt like the irrational one. How did that happen?

"I think what Skye is trying to convey is that we weren't really prepared for any of this," Mom said. "McKenna has always been wild and impulsive, but she didn't give us any indication that she planned to leave him. Once she settled in here, she seemed content. But now that she's gone, we want to make sure we do the right thing. Between caring for Connor, the store and my surgery… This is a lot for us to handle."

Skye felt the tension in her shoulders loosen. There. *Ditto*, she wanted to say, but that sounded ridiculously inadequate. Not to mention childish. Gage probably thought she was a mess.

"I totally get it." Gage's deep voice was filled with empathy. Compassion. "It's a radical idea, me coming here, claiming a connection to this child and offering to help. I don't blame you for being skeptical. I'm glad you're questioning my intentions."

This time it was Skye's turn to stare in disbelief. "You are?"

"Absolutely. You can't be too careful." Gage shifted Connor to the crook of his opposite arm. "Let me assure you, again, that I want what's best for my friend's son, too."

"Of course you do." Her mother reached over and patted his hand. "I'm going to leave you two to iron out the details. I'm beat."

While Mom stood and slowly worked her way down the hall toward her bedroom, Skye tried to offer Connor the sippy cup, but he pushed her hand away and reached for more of his snack. She sighed and left the cup on the table before circling around to her chair and the calendar she'd abandoned earlier. "Aunt Linda just texted me and said she'd help in a pinch, so I have the next few days covered. How soon can you start?"

"How about next week?"

She hesitated, then picked up her pencil. "Sure, next week is…fine. Is one to five in the afternoon okay?"

"Sounds great."

She wrote his name and the time on the calendar. "And how about after that?"

"How far out would you like to schedule?"

Her stomach churned as her pencil hovered over the calendar. Were they really doing this? Had she just agreed to let Gage watch Connor as often as he wanted? "H-how about Tuesday, Wednesday and Thursday afternoons from one to five for now?"

"Perfect." She heard the smile in his voice and dragged her gaze to meet his. She wasn't at all prepared for the gratitude she'd find in those gold-flecked eyes.

"Thank you for giving me a chance to honor my word." His voice was gritty, emotional this time. "I won't let you down."

"Good." Uncertainty still weighed heavily as she quickly looked away and wrote his name on the dates they'd agreed on. A chance to honor his word? Yes. Not a permanent place in their lives, though. Sure, he'd looked super attractive holding Connor safely in his arms, but clearly it had muddled her thinking. No matter how much Gage's attentiveness toward Connor tugged at her heartstrings, she had to maintain firm boundaries. Strong men like Gage only used their power to control women, and she wouldn't allow herself to fall for him.

Chapter Four

Gage quickly anchored the metal carabiners of his harness straps to the safety rails along the platform's perimeter, then stood up. Cold air filled his lungs and he pivoted slowly, admiring the snow-covered wheat fields checkering the landscape in every direction. Despite the additional weight of his equipment, the view from the top of the wind turbine was worth the effort. A brilliant blue sky—a particular shade he'd heard was unique to Colorado—stretched overhead, and the late-afternoon sun made the moisture on the giant white blades glisten.

"Not a bad first climb, right?" Dane, one of his new partners for today's orientation, glanced back over his shoulder and grinned, arms stretched wide.

"Can't complain." Gage couldn't manage much more than a two-word reply. While he'd thought he'd maintained his physical fitness since he left the navy, his aching muscles protested from the three-hundred-foot climb. Clearly, he still had some work to do in the gym.

"Let's check on this beacon." Max, their team leader, summoned them to the red light nearby that was supposed to blink constantly, alerting approaching aircraft.

Gage complied, taking tentative steps toward Max. He might've spent weeks at sea living in a submarine in the depths of the ocean, but wearing a harness tethered to a tower in the middle of miles of farmland made his mouth dry and legs jittery. The height didn't seem to be the problem. He'd always loved the advantage of seeing the world from this perspective. Maybe it was the apprehension of working with a partner again that had his insides twisted in knots. Squashing thoughts of Ryan, he slowed his breathing and followed Max's and Dane's instructions. At least they were working in a team of three. Safety in numbers, right?

"The first day's always a tough one. Relax." Max offered Gage a reassuring smile. "You'll get the hang of it."

"Hope so." Did his lack of confidence seem that obvious? He hadn't had any trouble with his online courses, and he'd assumed starting the hands-on training would be less demanding than anything he'd experienced in the military. But after spending several hours with Max and Dane examining the interior portions of the turbine, his head felt like it was going to explode. The biting wind buffeting them, combined with the odd sensation of his harness and straps shadowing his every move, brought a whole new meaning to the phrase *on-the-job training*.

"This is a straightforward repair." Dane handed Max the new lightbulb. "We'll have this changed out in no time."

Gage squatted beside them and focused on Max's careful instruction, trying to memorize all the details he and Dane noted. An hour later, they had the new bulb installed, the cover in place and their tools packed up.

"Let's go, boys. It's quitting time." Max led the way toward the hatch.

They unlatched from the rail, then lowered themselves through the narrow opening and reconnected their harnesses to the pulley system inside the tower. Dane started the descent first, followed by Gage, while Max went last to make sure the hatch was closed properly.

Gage's heavy boots squeaked on the rungs and sweat trickled along his spine as he climbed down the ladder. Why wasn't this easier than going up? Dane and Max bantered back and forth, their words echoing off the walls of the tower. Gage trained his gaze on the next rung and kept quiet.

A few blessed minutes later, his feet touched the solid concrete floor.

"Well done." Max clapped him on the shoulder. "Let's celebrate your first trip to the top with the boys over at Angie's. They've got a Friday night special that's hard to beat. What do you think?"

Gage hesitated.

"C'mon, man," Dane urged. "It's like a rite of passage for all the trainees."

Gage stepped out of his harness and stalled for more time to respond. He wasn't about to admit he was wiped out. After the stress of his full day of orientation and climbing the tower in the cold, all he wanted to do was sleep until noon tomorrow. Dane and Max seemed like the kind of guys who'd give him a hard time about that, though. Besides, he'd missed the camaraderie of hanging out with other men—the harmless teasing, casual conversation, the inside jokes that made him feel like part of a group.

"Yeah, that sounds good." He smiled, then quickly stowed his gear and climbed inside the company truck.

Max drove while Dane rode in the passenger seat, and Gage sat behind Dane in the truck's extended cab. They made small talk on the drive back to Alta Vista's offices, and Gage felt the tension in his weary shoulders slowly release. Warmth from the truck's heater chased away the bone-deep chill, too.

Once Max parked near the maintenance garage, they unloaded their gear and tools inside.

"You know the way to the diner?" Dane stopped inside the garage doorway, jangling his keys in his hand.

Gage nodded. "Across the street from the furniture store, right?"

Dane grinned. "That's the one. By the way, if you need anything for your new place, I highly recommend Tomlinson's." He released a long whistle. "Skye Tomlinson is running the place right now, and she is easy on the eyes. Know what I mean?"

Gage gritted his teeth. He knew exactly what he meant. "Thanks for the tip. See you in a few." He turned and strode toward his own truck. Dane's comment bothered him more than it should. He was right—Skye was a beautiful woman. Was it the tone that pricked at him? Or the knowledge that Dane had noticed and didn't mind sharing his observations?

He started the engine and followed Max's and Dane's vehicles out of the parking lot, his headlights bouncing across the snowbanks lining the road. A light snow started falling, and he turned on the wipers to clear his windshield.

Why did he care what Dane thought? Gage barely knew Skye. They were two adults forging a friendship and keeping Connor's best interests as their shared focus. It wasn't like he had any interest in dating her.

Did he?

Connor flung another french fry onto the floor of the diner and followed it up with a defiant glare.

Skye wanted to scream. Why had she agreed to bring Mom to her book club in Angie's meeting room? The outing had seemed simple at first, and her mom had looked forward to it all week. They hadn't considered how Connor might react, though.

"No throwing food, remember?" Skye tried to keep her voice even while she gave him her most pointed stare.

His lower lip pooched out, and he made a throwing motion even though his hand was empty.

What a stinker. She bit her lip and glanced away. Another family with three young children sat at a booth nearby. None of the kids were flinging their food on the floor. The adults looked like they were actually having a conversation. They made it look so easy. She was not cut out for this parenting business.

She stabbed a forkful of Cobb salad and checked her phone for new text messages. Nothing. She'd already sent one desperate plea for reinforcements—first to her best friend, Laramie, and then to her brother Drew. Laramie had declined because she had a new puppy to train, but Drew said he'd be by soon.

The door to Angie's Diner swung open, ushering in a blast of cold air along with three guys wearing heavy winter jackets. They paused and stomped the snow off their boots on the mat in the entryway. The first was older and she didn't recognize him, but the second looked familiar—he'd stopped by the store at least once, although she didn't recall his name. The door swung shut behind the third man, and her breath caught as she recognized Gage. He glanced her way and their eyes met, sending a jolt of electricity ricocheting through her.

Connor chose that exact moment to swivel in his high chair and survey the new arrivals, too.

Uh-oh. Skye braced for his reaction once he saw Gage. Just as she feared, Connor pointed and squealed so loud most of the folks in the restaurant turned to see what all the fuss was about.

An embarrassing heat flushed Skye's skin as Gage spoke briefly to his friends before making his way toward her.

"Hey." He stopped beside their table and smiled, making her pulse stutter while Connor took his screeching to a whole new level. "What's up, buddy?"

Connor offered him a soggy fry.

Gage laughed and politely declined. "No, thanks. You can keep it."

The weight of every curious stare in the restaurant made Skye want to crawl under the table. This scene unfolding would give the whole town something to talk about.

Gage shifted his gaze back to her. "Your mom doing all right?"

"Yeah, she's meeting with her book club in the back room." Skye angled her head toward the far end of the restaurant. "I had the crazy idea that I could fly solo with this one tonight."

"Aw, I'm sure he's a great wingman." Gage shoved

his hands in his pockets. "I better catch up with the guys. See you next week?"

"Oh, I meant to ask you—would you like to come over on Sunday afternoon? We're having a small party for Connor at four. It's his birthday."

Surprise flickered in Gage's eyes. "Yeah. Of course."

"Perfect." She smiled, relieved he hadn't objected. "See you then."

"Catch you later, dude." Gage waved and walked away.

Connor's gaze tracked him, and then his expression crumpled and he burst into tears.

Not again. Panic welled as Skye tried to counteract his meltdown. She reached for a packet of crackers from the container in the center of the table and ripped it open.

"Here. Want to try a cracker?"

He batted it from her hand while his face deepened to a shade of dark pink. Wow, he was angry.

She tried offering him his sippy cup of apple juice mixed with water, but he pushed that away, too. Her appetite had waned, so she slid her plate aside and reached over to unbuckle Connor's straps. Maybe if she held him, he'd calm down. If that didn't help, she'd have to interrupt Mom's meeting and get them both in the car somehow.

"Need a hand?"

Skye glanced up as Drew slid into the chair opposite hers.

"I've never been so happy to see you in my life." She lifted Connor from his chair and handed him to her brother. "Here."

"Connor, my man. What's the problem?" Drew gently suspended Connor in the air and made a silly face.

Startled, Connor paused his tirade and reached for the bill of Drew's navy-blue-and-orange Broncos cap.

"Are you a Broncos fan?" Drew pulled Connor close and let him grab the edge of the hat. "You'll fit right in around here."

Skye slumped in her chair and took a long sip of her iced tea. How could one little person's temper tantrum ruffle her feathers so easily?

Maybe this has nothing to do with Connor.

She crunched on a piece of ice and dismissed the idea as quickly as it pinged through her mind. Her frazzled state had nothing to do with seeing Gage.

"Who was that you were speaking to before I got here?" Drew asked, his gaze roaming the restaurant behind her.

"Gage Westbrook. He's the guy I told you about— Connor's dad's friend."

"That's right. I ran his background check. Squeaky-clean. Does he still want to spend time with Connor?" Drew shifted his attention back to Connor and puffed out his cheeks while crossing his eyes, which made the little boy giggle and squeeze Drew's face between his hands.

"He already has."

"Really." Drew pulled back from Connor's grasp and studied her. "How's that going?"

She shrugged. "He had dinner with us, and he played with Connor. I guess it went well."

"Seriously?"

She sighed. "Yes. Seriously. Why?"

"No reason."

His line of questioning made her uneasy. What had he heard? "You seem surprised. What are you not telling me?"

"Nothing."

"Drew. If there's something I need to know, please—"

"Skye, relax. I'm just making conversation." Drew braced Connor against his shoulder and patted his back awkwardly. "What else is he doing, besides hanging out with you?"

"We're not *hanging out*." Skye glared at him. "I'm at the store when he's with Mom and Connor."

"Right." Drew waggled his eyebrows. "Would you hang out if he asked?"

"Don't make me sorry I invited you here." She balled up her paper napkin and flung it at him.

He easily deflected it. "Ha. You begged me."

She sighed and braced her chin on her hand. "You're right. Connor was wearing me out. Next time I'll ask Mom to find a friend to bring her to book club."

"Speaking of Mom, how do you think she's doing?"

"With her knee? As well as can be expected. I think she'll be able to live independently by the time I go back to Denver."

Drew frowned. "Possibly."

"What's wrong? You look worried."

"Even though it's only February, I'm wondering what your long-term plan is with this little guy, that's all."

She leaned across the table and lowered her voice. "I can't stay here forever. That was never the plan. I'm going back to my job right after Easter."

"That's less than two months from now. What will happen to Connor?"

"Maybe I'll take him with me and enroll him in a day care close to my apartment."

Drew's brow furrowed. "Are you sure? That's a huge commitment."

Her stomach twisted in an anxious knot. "I'm not sure, but we don't have a lot of other options. What if McKenna doesn't come back?"

His cheeseburger sat like a rock in his stomach. Nothing against Angie's Diner—the appetizers, burger and fries he'd ordered all tasted great. The reason for his discomfort had everything to do with the man sitting across from Skye on the other side of the restaurant, with Connor snuggled happily in his lap, while she leaned across the table, clearly engaged in meaningful conversation. The whole scenario aggravated him. And he hated to admit it.

"So how do you know Skye?"

Dane's pointed question rammed into Gage's careful introspection. He reached for his soda to keep his gaze from wandering her way again. "I'm a friend of the family's."

"Is that right?" Dane's lips twitched. "Small world."

"How so?"

Dane shrugged and helped himself to one of Gage's fries. "'Cause you haven't quit staring at her since we sat down, it must be—"

"I'm not staring."

"What would you call it, then?"

Gage's scalp prickled. "The baby was making a scene. I felt bad for her."

"Why don't you offer to help her out?" Dane glanced over his shoulder, then back at Gage, and feigned a sad expression. "Oh. Too bad. Somebody beat you to it."

Gage bit back a terse reply. Dane didn't mean any harm. This was tame compared to some of the razzing he'd endured from his navy buddies. He still wasn't going to tell Dane why he cared about Connor. Or Skye.

"Judging by the way you're not staring, I'm guessing you're single?" Dane asked.

Gage nodded and reached for his soda. "You?"

"Yep."

Shocker. Gage drained the last of his soda and set the plastic cup down.

"What made you leave the navy?"

He scrubbed his fingers along his jaw while he caught a glimpse of Skye's new friend kissing the top of Connor's head. Gage's chest tightened. Who *was* that guy? Dragging his gaze back to meet Dane's, he forced himself to sound casual. "I didn't feel the need to reenlist, and this seemed like the right time to try something new."

"Huh. Did you like it?" Dane rattled the ice in his own cup, then flagged the waitress down for a refill.

"Most of the time." He had enjoyed his years in the service. Even the mundane routines when they were in port, struggling through another physical fitness test or filling out paperwork—he'd thrived on the order and clear expectations. But when he'd made a selfish decision that ultimately cost his best friend his life, he'd suddenly loathed his role.

No need to go there tonight. That wasn't exactly something he wanted to reveal, especially if he wanted a permanent job with Alta Vista.

Max sat to Gage's left, swapping stories with a few other guys who'd joined them. They didn't seem to be in a hurry to finish their meals and go home. He stifled a sigh and tried to focus on what Max was talking about. He didn't want to leave before Skye anyway, or he'd have to walk past her table to get to the door. Part of him wanted to see how long her mystery man stuck around.

Dane must've given up on interrogating him, because he shifted his attention to the guy next to him, and before long they were engaged in a lengthy debate about the Rockies baseball team and their prospects for spring training. Normally Gage could hold his own in a conversation about professional sports, but tonight he was way too distracted.

And mad at himself for his acute awareness of Skye's presence. What happened to just being acquaintances with a common goal? In less than an hour he'd already caved on his resolve not to care. The guy holding Connor smiled and even though her back was to him, Gage imagined Skye revealing that beautiful smile of hers. He grabbed his cup and crunched on another mouthful of ice.

Dane shot him an amused look, but Gage ignored him and deliberately shifted in his seat toward Max. If he didn't pay attention to what was happening at Skye's table, maybe he'd have some hope of reining in his irrational thoughts.

A few minutes later, a group of ladies emerged from the back room, laughing as they moved at a slow pace to keep up with one woman using a walker. Mrs. Tomlinson. The parking lot outside was slick. Should she be using a walker to get to the car?

Oh brother. *Stop caring, remember?* He palmed the back of his neck. Full of opinions about what was best for Skye's family, when he really had no business getting involved. They were taking great care of Connor, and minus a few tantrums, he seemed to be thriving.

Why couldn't he leave well enough alone?

Mrs. Tomlinson made her way to Skye's table. Based on her wide smile and the way her hand touched the shoulder of Skye's mystery man, she was thrilled to see him. So they knew each other well. Interesting. Gage couldn't help but watch as Skye stood, lifted Connor into her arms and fumbled with putting his knit hat and jacket on. Mrs. Tomlinson moved toward the door of the diner, while Skye trailed behind, struggling to hold on to a wiggly Connor while shouldering the diaper bag, too.

The man walked behind her, then hurried to open the door for Mrs. Tomlinson. When he pressed his hand to Skye's back and gently guided her outside, Gage's stomach clenched in an ugly knot.

While it wasn't any of his business who Skye dated, Gage wasn't going to let just any guy get close to Connor without asking questions. If Gage was going to keep his promise to Ryan, didn't he owe it to his best friend to inquire about who was allowed into Connor's world?

Chapter Five

"You have polished those blinds to perfection. What gives?" Laramie Chambers, Skye's best friend, sat on Mom's living room floor wrapping Connor's birthday gifts.

"Nothing." Skye swabbed her microfiber cloth across the next row of cream-colored faux wood blinds. "Don't most people clean house before guests come over?"

"This is a birthday party for a one-year-old. You've known all the guests for most of your life. I don't think they'll notice—or care—if there's a little bit of dust."

"I'll notice."

The subtle crinkling of wrapping paper followed by the crisp slice of the scissors answered back. Laramie was too kind to say what she was thinking. She'd been her closest friend since seventh grade and was quite skilled at recognizing Skye's coping strategies.

Laramie was right—they'd intentionally planned a small, low-key gathering so as not to overwhelm Connor. There was still one guest in particular she was concerned about—one she hardly knew at all. That was what was driving her compulsion to clean, because that was what she did when she was worked up—created order out of chaos. It soothed her. So what if most women their age didn't spend their Saturday nights dusting their mother's blinds? Most twentysomething single women she knew didn't have a widowed mother reading quietly in bed down the hall, or someone else's baby asleep in a crib in the next room.

Satisfied the blinds were cleansed of all dust particles, she moved on to purging the wooden coffee table of extra magazines and junk mail. Her thoughts wandered to all the Saturday nights she'd spent out to dinner with friends at one of the trendy restaurants downtown or enjoying a musical at the theater. Lazy weekends doing whatever she wanted and taking her time to prepare for the coming workweek. Since Connor had upended every area of her life, she'd surprisingly spent very little time thinking about the vibrant social life she'd left behind. Her conversation with Drew at the diner last night had her second-guessing her future, though. Could she return to Denver with Connor in tow? What would happen when she severed the bond already forming between Gage and Connor?

"Want to tell me what's really bothering you?"

No. Yes. Skye heaved a sigh and sank onto the couch, a stack of magazines in her hands. "I wish I hadn't told Gage about Connor's party."

Laramie glanced up from the gift she'd just wrapped, her long platinum hair woven in a fishbone-style braid dangling over her shoulder. Her pencil-thin brows tented over her wide-set green eyes. "Told him or invited him? There's a difference, you know."

"Invited. Sort of." She tipped her head back and

stared at the ceiling. "It just slipped out before I could think about what I was saying."

"That's rather out of character for you, isn't it?" Laramie's voice carried a teasing lilt.

"I know," Skye groaned. "What am I going to do?"

"About…"

"Gage. Here." Skye pushed to her feet, abandoning the magazines on the couch cushions. "More than I want him to be."

There. She'd said it. Somehow honesty had done little to ease the familiar anxiety snaring her in its grasp. She crossed to the fireplace and collected the plastic Little People Connor had abandoned on the brick hearth before bath time, then swept them into the woven basket doubling as toy storage.

"I'm confused," Laramie said. "You don't want him here at all, or just not at Connor's party?"

"Letting him watch Connor, even for a few hours a day, was a difficult decision. It was so unexpected, the way he showed up, claiming this connection to Connor. Then when we saw him at the diner, Connor was giving me a fit, and I—I thought he might be happier if Gage was here for the party tomorrow."

Oh brother. It sounded even more ridiculous when she said it out loud.

"So what are you worried about? Sounds like a thoughtful gesture to me." Laramie slapped a green bow on the gift wrapped in green-and-yellow paper with a tractor pattern. "Do you think it's going to be awkward or something?"

"I'm just—" Skye gnawed on her thumbnail. "What if Connor gets too attached to him?"

Understanding flashed across Laramie's features, as

though the proverbial lightbulb had illuminated in her mind. "Connor? Or you?"

Skye shot her a pointed look. "This isn't about me."

"Are you sure about that?"

"Positive."

Mostly.

Sure, he was handsome and if she wasn't careful, those hazel eyes might be her undoing, but she could handle herself. She frequently crossed paths with attractive men when she called on physicians at their offices to pitch a new pharmaceutical product. Keeping Gage at arm's length wasn't an issue.

It was Connor she was worried about. Everything about his life was one big holding pattern. Including Gage. What happened when he started working full-time? Or if McKenna came back and undid all the stability she and Mom had worked hard to establish for Connor? In her effort to help, was she only causing more harm long-term by allowing another person into Connor's world who might not stick around?

"Connor is very young, and he's been through a lot but he's also resilient." Laramie drew her knees to her chest and wrapped her arms around them. "I've worked with a few kids at school who endured childhood trauma and are delightful, well-adjusted teenagers."

Skye valued Laramie's opinion. After growing up in Merritt's Crossing, then coming back after college to teach language arts at the high school and coach volleyball, Laramie had more insight into the resiliency of kids than she did. Still, worry niggled at Skye like a foe she couldn't conquer.

"I—I want some reassurance that this isn't going

to wreck him." She stacked the wrapped gifts on the hearth.

"Have you prayed about it?"

No. She swallowed back a snarky response and avoided Laramie's gaze.

"Skye—"

"I know." She held up both palms in self-defense. "You don't need to go there. I've heard it all before."

"Maybe you need to hear it again," Laramie said gently. "Listen, I know you've had a rough time lately. Between a difficult breakup and all your family has endured, I don't blame you for being anxious about the future. Or having trust issues."

Skye's limbs itched with the need to move, and her gaze darted around the room for something else to clean. To straighten. While she welcomed her bestie's advice on almost anything, the trajectory of her insight into Skye's now-dormant relationship with the Lord was most certainly not welcome.

Laramie didn't understand.

"I know what you're thinking," Laramie said, "and you're partially right—I don't fully understand what it's like to have dated a controlling man."

"You're right, that's exactly what I was thinking." Skye spotted a neglected animal cracker under the recliner in the corner and knelt to retrieve it. Short of leaving the room, she couldn't ignore the rest of what Laramie had to say, though. She sank back on her heels and forced herself to look at her friend.

"I know God loves me, Lare. He is all that He claims to be in His word." Her voice wobbled. "But sometimes I just can't figure out what He is doing. My dad was not a perfect man, but why was he killed in a terrible accident? And Connor—he's just a baby. Why does he have to grow up without a father? And why did my uncle—"

"Wait." This time Laramie held up her hand to interrupt, her eyes coated in a fresh sheen of moisture. "We are not alone in our struggles. God is with us for every horrible second."

Emotion tightened Skye's throat. Slowly, she shook her head. "I don't believe that's true."

"God is big enough to handle your doubts and your questions," Laramie said. "Don't be afraid to bring them to Him."

She turned away, intent on finishing her clean sweep of the cozy living room, while she willed fresh tears not to fall. God did still love her, but He seemed to have forgotten her and her family. Just like her dad's shortcomings had caused an ongoing dispute. That was why it was up to her to make sure Connor's needs were met. He didn't have a father, either, and she'd do everything in her power to protect him.

After church and an epic shopping trip to the big-box store on the interstate, Gage returned to his apartment with groceries and three bags full of gifts for Connor. Once the groceries were put away, he moved to the living room and spread his haul across the glass-topped industrial metal coffee table. A stuffed elephant, four books, a container of small rubber ducks for the tub and one large red plastic barn.

Yeah, he might've gone a little overboard. Skye would not be happy with him if he showed up with his arms full of gifts.

He winced at the mental image of her flashing him a disapproving look. Not that he wanted her to be displeased, but standing in the toy aisle, all he could think about was how much he wished Ryan was there to celebrate Connor's first birthday, so he'd loaded everything into the shopping cart.

Rubbing his hand across his jaw, he tried to narrow his selection to one gift. It wasn't easy, but he eventually picked the red plastic barn. When he'd visited for dinner, he'd noticed a small container with a half-dozen rubber farm animals. Maybe as Connor became more mobile, he'd progress to playing with the animals and the barn together.

Gage tucked the rest of the gifts back into the bags along with the receipt and stowed them in his coat closet. He'd return them on his next trip. At the store, he'd also spent a ridiculous amount of time in the wrapping paper section, temporarily paralyzed by the options. Honestly, the whole process of wrapping a gift felt daunting. He didn't have much experience. Once or twice as a child, he'd done enough chores for a neighbor to scrounge together a few bucks to buy his mom a gift. Even then, he'd had to make do with a brown paper grocery bag, markers and tape he'd "borrowed" from school to wrap it.

The hazy memory provoked an unexpected ache of loneliness. His mom had done the best she could—he knew that now. But her addiction often overpowered her, and people let her get by with flimsy excuses and empty promises. The ache in his chest deepened at the painful memories of all the birthdays that passed uncelebrated. No cake, no ice cream and definitely no gifts adorned with festive wrapping paper.

On one particular birthday, he'd rushed from his bed in their double-wide trailer, his bare feet skimming across the grungy shag carpeting, hoping with everything in his nine-year-old self that she'd remembered. That this birthday would be different.

Mom had stood at the counter in their tiny kitchen, wearing her faded bathrobe and smoking a cigarette. Only a bright yellow Mylar balloon with a smiley face waited for him.

Hey, baby. Happy birthday.

If he closed his eyes, he could still hear her raspy voice. Still feel the remnant of the hurt and disappointment. Man, he'd wanted to pop that stupid balloon.

He'd spent the next three birthdays in different foster care homes, and by the time he and Mom were reunited, he'd known to keep his expectations low. Dad was out of the picture, and he had learned the hard way that he couldn't count on her, either.

Gage stood and crossed to the closet again, retrieved the new stuffed elephant and carried it back to the living room. As long as he was around, Connor would never experience a birthday like that. What was wrong with a little excessive giving? The poor kid didn't have a mom or a dad. Surely Skye would understand if he brought something on behalf of Ryan.

Skye.

He couldn't ignore all the ways she'd crept into his thoughts since he'd seen her and Connor with that guy at the diner. He'd probably be at the birthday party today, too. Gage gritted his teeth and reached for the gift bags and tissue paper he'd bought instead of wrapping paper. Even though he didn't have a right to care about who she spent time with, it bothered him that they'd looked so comfortable together. It bothered him even more that she'd managed to get under his skin and make him jealous.

He groaned and ripped the plastic off the tissue paper. *Get a grip, dude.* Skye was not interested in hearing his opinions about what was best for Connor.

While he'd given himself that same pep talk multiple times, the message didn't seem to be sinking in. Or else he was too stubborn to admit he'd have to accept that other people—other men—would be involved in Connor's life, as well.

But he didn't have to like it.

The first sheet of fragile paper tore in his big hands, and he crumpled it in disgust and tossed it on the cream-colored carpet. Wasn't there a YouTube video for this? He picked up his phone and scrolled until he found help in the form of a video tutorial. Somehow the woman made it look effortless.

Finally, he'd wrestled the tissue paper and gifts into both bags, and it was time to leave.

Outside, wisps of feathery clouds were brushed against a pale blue sky and sunlight reflected off the white snowbanks. He set both gift bags gently on the passenger seat and started his truck. Again, his gaze landed on Ryan, staring back at him from the photograph. Grief tinged with remorse crept in, and Gage hunched forward, pressing his forehead against the steering wheel.

This was really happening—Connor's first birthday. Without Ryan or McKenna.

If you hadn't been so careless, maybe things would be different.

The harsh words knifed at him. Even though he'd conjured them on his own, they stung as if spoken aloud. It was true. His actions had deprived a sweet baby of ever knowing his father. There weren't enough birthday presents in the world to make up for that. The weight of the guilt almost made him want to go back inside and skip the whole thing. His throat constricted, and he swallowed hard, determined to gain control of his emotions.

He couldn't stay home. Not just because he had gifts to bring. Ryan would want him to be at Connor's party.

Gage straightened, whispered a prayer for strength and made the short drive to the Tomlinsons' neighborhood. As he approached their house, he counted five vehicles parked on the street, although none looked familiar. Easing his truck to the curb, he turned off the engine and stared at the front door. Man, he wasn't great at parties. The small talk, standing around and balancing a plate of food, trying to pretend he was having a good time—anxiety rippled through him.

C'mon. Don't be a wimp. You've got this.

He grabbed the gifts, climbed out of his truck and strode toward the front porch. Honoring his promise to Ryan meant participating in Connor's major life events, even if that made him uncomfortable. He wiped his clammy palm on his jeans and then knocked softly, in case Connor was still napping. When the door swung open, he expected Skye, but a vaguely familiar guy greeted him on the other side.

"Hey, come on in. You must be Gage." He grinned and stepped back. "Skye's told me a lot about you. I'm Drew, by the way."

The guy from the diner. Great. Jealousy slithered in and took up residence. He forced a cool smile and shook Drew's hand, trying to mentally smother the ugly emotions. He hated the thought of competing for Connor's attention, and even worse, he hated acknowledging that he was jealous of another guy being involved in Connor's life. It was going to be a long party.

Skye dunked the glass mixing bowl in the hot soapy water and reached for the sponge.

She needed a minute. A minute to scrub something until it sparkled. A minute away from Gage and his big shoulders and hazel eyes and smooth voice that kept reeling her toward him like an invisible thread.

Gage had arrived at Connor's party less than fifteen minutes ago, and already she was hiding in the kitchen, stalling while Drew chatted him up.

Honestly, what was she—twelve? Her skin flushed at the thought of her family and friends watching her try to ignore him for the rest of the evening.

Through the kitchen window, headlights illuminated the gathering darkness as a car approached and then slowed at the end of the driveway. Skye sucked in a breath and the bowl slid from her hands, landing in the dishwater with a clunk.

McKenna?

All day, Skye kept a close watch on her phone, flinching with every chime and notification. Wouldn't McKenna at least acknowledge her son's first birthday? No calls, texts or instant messages had arrived yet. Skye had scrolled through McKenna's social media accounts, too, but her cousin hadn't posted anything.

The car sped up and disappeared around the corner.

Deflated, Skye released a breath and leaned against the counter. A hollow ache filled her chest. She hadn't realized until this moment how much hope she'd invested in McKenna coming back in time for Connor's birthday.

"Everything okay?" Gage's deep voice enveloped her.

"Trying to clean up a little before we serve dinner." She tried for a smile, but it wobbled and did not go unnoticed.

A ridge formed in his normally flawless brow. "Anything I can do to help?"

In his gray sweater with the sleeves pushed up to reveal chiseled forearms, and his athletic frame filling the space between the counter's edge and the wall, her pulse ratcheted up a notch.

Quick! Assign him a task.

But her mouth was dry, and her eyes wandered from his gold-flecked gaze to the hint of a five o'clock shadow hugging his jawline—

"Skye?" His eyes searched her face. Without warning, he reached up and gently grazed her cheek with the pad of his thumb. For a hot second, she longed to lean into his touch. The warmth of his gaze pulled her in, making her forget how much it had cost her the last time she'd let down her guard.

Warning bells chimed in her head and she quickly stepped back.

"Sorry." He shoved his hands in the back pockets of his jeans. "You had soap on your face."

"I—I need to make sure my brother brought his camera." It was a lame excuse, and only half-true, but she had to put some space between the two of them. She let her gaze dart around the kitchen, avoiding eye contact.

"Your brother?"

"The guy who answered the door. Didn't he introduce himself?" She lifted a platter of deviled eggs from the counter and willed Gage to move out of her way.

"Yeah, I just…didn't make the connection." His smile was tight as he reached for the platter. "Can I carry that for you?"

"Put it on the table, next to the coleslaw." Instantly, she regretted the bossiness in her tone. "Please." She tacked on the word as an afterthought, flung halfheartedly toward his retreating back. Even in dark-washed jeans and a sweater, Gage's impressive stature—no doubt honed from his years in the navy—was hard to ignore. Since he couldn't see her, and she was blocked from her family's line of sight as well, Skye allowed herself to admire him—just for a second.

Until he pivoted and caught her staring.

Busted. He arched one eyebrow and then set the deviled eggs on the table.

She slipped around the corner and into the living room, where Uncle Milt and Aunt Linda had just arrived. She'd never been so happy to see her mother's sister and her husband.

"Thank you so much for coming," Skye said as Aunt Linda carried a large casserole pan toward the dining room table. "I've been thinking about your barbecued pulled pork all day."

"We wouldn't miss it, sweetie." Aunt Linda lowered the pan to the table, then glanced around the room. "Now, where is that adorable baby?"

Right on cue, Connor giggled, drawing the attention of everyone in the room. In his blue jeans and red T-shirt, he sat in the middle of the floor, babbling happily to Skye's younger brother, Jack. Much to her surprise, he'd decided to come to the party after all. Mom had been convinced he'd find a reason not to. In his crisp, white button-down with the pearl snaps, Wrangler jeans and cowboy boots, he looked…good. As if he'd tried to impress someone. But who?

Skye glanced to the sofa where Laramie sat between her parents, her gaze riveted on Jack, as well. Huh. Interesting. They'd definitely have a few things to discuss later.

Connor held out a red bow he'd managed to rip from one of his gifts prematurely, and Jack took it, then set it gently on Connor's head. When it slid off, more belly laughs ensued.

"Oh my." Aunt Linda smiled and propped her hands on her ample hips. "Isn't he the cutest thing? You must be having the time of your life taking care of him."

Skye opened her mouth to respond but swallowed back the harsh words before they spilled out.

No. She wasn't having a good time. Connor had a lot of needs and she struggled to meet them. This wasn't what she'd signed up for when she'd agreed to come home and help. This boy belonged with a mother and father who loved him and knew what to do when he seemed to cry for no reason at all. But Connor had already lost his father, and his mother… Could her cousin ever be a dependable caregiver?

Skye pushed the nagging doubts away. She had a house full of people to tend to.

The pleasant hum of conversation filtered through the cozy space, and the aroma of Aunt Linda's barbecued pork made her stomach growl.

Connor's exuberant chatter drew her attention, and she glanced at him, still sitting on the floor surrounded by presents. He lifted both arms toward Gage. Skye's breath hitched. Now, that was one gesture she did understand—he wanted Gage.

"What's up, buddy? Need some help?" Gage's arm brushed against hers as he moved past her and joined Connor and Jack on the floor. While she'd stood there, overanalyzing her struggles with Connor, somehow Gage had moved closer without her noticing. Her traitorous abdomen dispensed another batch of butterflies as she watched Gage and Connor interact.

"Hey, everyone, we're going to let Connor open his presents before we eat," Skye said, quickly granting permission. She could only imagine his disappointment if they asked him to wait any longer.

Connor crawled into Gage's lap, and then Gage handed him a present and helped him rip off the paper. Everyone expressed their approval while Gage encouraged Connor to open the next gift. Skye's heart expanded in her chest. They were really cute together. She grabbed her phone and sank to the floor nearby, eager to capture the moment with a photo. Maybe she'd get to share the image with McKenna someday.

When the presents were opened, Gage glanced at Skye for direction. "What next?"

"Let me ask my uncle Milt to say the blessing." She pushed to her feet and tugged on her uncle's chambray sleeve. "Uncle Milt, will you please pray so we can eat?"

"Of course." Uncle Milt's weathered skin wrinkled as he grinned, and his pale blue eyes flitted toward Gage. "First, how about you introduce us to your beau?"

All eyes swung in her direction and an expectant silence blanketed the room.

"Right. I mean, no, he's—he's not—" Flustered, she

glanced at Gage. He wore a smile that rivaled Uncle Milt's. Clearly, he was enjoying watching her squirm.

Cheeks flaming, she forced a smile and addressed the rest of the group. "Thank you for coming to Connor's party, everyone. This is our new friend, Gage Westbrook. He moved here to finish his certification to become a wind energy technician. We just met recently because he happens to be a good friend of Connor's father. Now Uncle Milt is going to pray, and then we can eat."

There. A brief introduction that clarified his status as definitively in the friend zone. Where he belonged.

Gage's afternoon with Connor wasn't going as well as he'd hoped.

Connor sat beside him on the living room floor, his lower lip protruding while he rubbed both chubby fists against his eyes. He hadn't napped nearly as long as Skye's detailed notes said he should. Mrs. Tomlinson had warned him before she'd retreated to her room for her own nap that Connor might be a little grumpy.

"Do you want to play with your new toys?" Gage slid the red plastic barn across the carpet toward Connor.

He pushed it away and started to fuss.

Oh boy. Gage gritted his teeth and looked around for the collection of colorful rubber animals he'd noticed the first night he'd stopped by. He found them in a basket nearby and dumped them on the carpet.

"Do you like cows?" Gage gently walked the black-and-white cow up Connor's leg. "Moo."

Connor amped up the tears, his face darkening from pink to red as he scooted out of Gage's reach.

"Okay, that's a negative on the farm animals." Gage

quickly put them away. Man, this was a big change from the birthday party, when Connor acted like Gage could do no wrong. Anxiety hummed in his veins and he looked around for an option that might soothe the baby.

Thankfully Mrs. Tomlinson had changed Connor's diaper when he woke up, so scratch that from the list of reasons Connor kept crying. He reached for an orange dump truck with a gray plastic rock in the back.

"Check this out, Connor." Gage drove it across the carpet and tried to make an authentic engine noise.

Connor just wailed louder.

"You're right, that sound I made was pretty lame." Gage angled the truck toward the fireplace and set it on the hearth. He palmed the back of his neck. Why was he so bad at this?

Turning, he reached for Connor and scooped him awkwardly into his arms. "Come here, little dude. What's the matter?"

Tears clung to Connor's eyelashes and moisture dampened his cheeks. Gage's heart fisted as Connor drew a ragged breath, then continued to cry. There had to be something that would help calm him. Gage stood slowly and walked toward the sliding glass door beside the dining room table.

"Let's look out the window." Maybe a peek outside might distract him? Gage shifted Connor in his arms so he could see the backyard. Remnants of snow from the last storm still lingered on the ground, and the cloudy gray sky hinted there was more winter weather to come. A few birds and squirrels scampered about.

"Look at the squirrels, Connor." Gage pressed his finger to the glass. "Do you see them?"

Connor stopped crying and his big blue eyes widened as he made a few sounds Gage couldn't interpret.

"What else do you see?" Gage gently patted Connor's back, wishing he could take him outside. The green one-piece outfit Connor wore had long sleeves, but he only had socks on and Gage had no idea where his jacket and shoes might be. If Mrs. Tomlinson had managed to sleep through all the crying, he didn't want to disturb her to ask.

There was so much comfort in fresh air, though. Or maybe just the change in perspective helped. Memories of his own childhood flooded back, reminding him of the times he'd slipped outside in a desperate attempt to escape the anxiety and fear of his parents' neglect and, later, his latest temporary foster care placement.

Connor babbled another string of unintelligible sounds, pulling Gage back to the present.

"I know. There's a lot to look at, isn't there?" He didn't really know how to talk to a one-year-old, and he felt a little silly at the moment. If his comments kept the crying to a minimum, though, he'd keep chatting.

Connor pointed toward the yard, then glanced at Gage and smiled. The tension in Gage's shoulders loosened. His frustration over the crying was no match for that innocent blue-eyed stare and toothy grin. Or the sweet scent that accompanied Connor. Gage smiled back, and Connor responded by resting his head against Gage's shoulder and heaving a deep sigh.

Gage's breath hitched. He wasn't quite prepared for the sudden display of affection. Thoughts of Ryan invaded, and he willed the tightness in his throat to go away. He couldn't bring his friend back, but he'd do everything in his power to build a relationship with Ryan's son.

Gage shifted and glanced at the clock on the wall. Three fifteen. Skye's instructions mentioned an afternoon snack of dry cereal and a sippy cup of apple juice. He didn't relish the thought of ruining the peaceful moment, but he knew better than to ignore her expectations. Especially on his first day with Connor.

"Are you ready for a snack?" Gage asked as he turned toward the high chair nearby.

Connor raised his head and looked around. No crying yet. That was good, right? Gage gently lowered him into the chair, buckled the straps and then adjusted the tray, just like he'd watched Skye do at dinner last week. There. Nothing to it.

Feeling more confident, he hurried to get the plastic container with the dry cereal and the cup of juice while Connor entertained himself by clapping his hands, then squealing with delight.

A few minutes later, Connor happily munched on his Cheerios, while Gage sat at the table and stifled a yawn. Sleep had eluded him last night, and he'd tossed and turned, snapshots of his evening spent at Connor's party still playing on an endless loop in his mind. Two days had passed. He should have powered through these convoluted emotions by now. Skye, her close-knit family, the bittersweet experience of celebrating Connor's birthday while pretending not to notice he didn't have any parents had churned him up inside. Made him do things he normally wouldn't—like touching her cheek when he'd found her alone in the kitchen.

Probably shouldn't have done that.

Someone or something must've hurt her deeply, because she'd skittered away as quickly as possible. He didn't imagine the chemistry arcing between them, though, and he couldn't ignore his own sense of relief once he figured out the guy from the diner was her brother.

He'd tried to speak with Skye privately—to let her know he hadn't meant to overstep her boundaries—but celebrating Connor took center stage for the rest of the evening. Although he'd stuck around to help clean up, her boisterous family and friends made meaningful conversation difficult. He shook his head, still smiling at the mischievous gleam in her uncle's eyes, and the ways her brothers provoked her for their own amusement. The party made him both envious and terrified at the same time. Skye and her family finished each other's sentences and dished out plenty of good-natured ribbing, yet their long history together and commitment to one another gave him the urge to run. It was too much. Too much intensity. Too much loyalty. Even if they weren't all related, the guests at the party lived in a densely woven web of connection and shared experience.

His status as an outsider was painfully obvious. Yet his desperate longing to keep his promise to Ryan and now to Connor, and his changing feelings for Skye, had kept him at the party. And motivated him to give his very best effort while caring for the little boy. If he was honest, he longed to be included, to build those rock-solid relationships, but his years in foster care made it difficult to trust people. Would he ever be able to have a family of his own and not live in fear of abandonment?

Chapter Six

Early Wednesday morning, Gage poured the contents of his smoothie from the blender into a tall plastic cup, then jabbed a straw into the thick mixture and took a sip. Meh. Not his best work. Wasting food was practically a criminal offense in his opinion, so he'd drink it anyway.

The laminate floor was cold against his bare feet as he crossed to his kitchen table and sat down in front of his laptop. It wasn't even 6 a.m., and he'd already subjected himself to a punishing workout in his apartment complex's fitness center, showered and made breakfast—all in a desperate attempt to avoid the email sitting unread in his inbox.

Somewhere around four this morning, he'd woken up, plagued with doubt about whether or not he was doing the right thing—dropping into Connor's life like this. Yesterday afternoon got off to a rocky start, but then Connor snuggled up close, and the surge of affection blindsided Gage.

Maybe this was just the same old fear taunting him. It wasn't a surprise when his ex-girlfriend told him he was emotionally unavailable. But that didn't make it any easier to hear.

Or admit that she was right. He didn't want to be alone forever. Yet the unpredictability of these big emotions did scare him because he knew how much it hurt when relationships fell apart. Connor's ability to sneak past his defenses, as well as his unmistakable attraction toward Skye, left him feeling vulnerable. And he didn't like it. Not one bit.

Frustrated, he'd reached for his phone to find a podcast or some music to help him fall back asleep when a message from Ryan's parents unexpectedly greeted him. Although he'd tried to pretend he hadn't seen it, the sickening lurch in his gut had propelled him out of bed and kept him in perpetual motion. Resistance was futile, though. He couldn't avoid it much longer. His heart rate quickened as his finger hovered over the keyboard, poised to open the message.

Dear Gage,
We hope this message finds you well and thriving. Gerald and I are getting by, although time has not healed all wounds, as they say. We still can't believe he is gone. I'm writing to you in hopes that you can help us sort out a troubling development. It has come to our attention that Ryan has a son. This wasn't something he'd disclosed to us. As you can imagine, we are both shocked and saddened to learn of our only grandchild in this manner. When you have a few minutes, would you please give us a call? You are one of our limited sources of information, and we'd desperately like to know more about this baby and where he might be.
Sincerely,
Gerald and Irene Simmons

Blood pounded in his ears as Gage pushed to his feet, eager to get away from his laptop. They didn't know? How was that possible? He strode to the window in the living room and stared out into the early-morning sky streaked in rich shades of orange, proclaiming the sun's imminent arrival.

Ryan had talked about his parents often, and his all-American experience in the affluent Chicago suburbs was the exact opposite of Gage's erratic childhood in Texas. Although Gage had only seen Gerald and Irene twice, once when they visited briefly in San Diego and again at Ryan's funeral, their love and devotion to their only child was obvious. While Ryan had described them as quite conservative, Gage assumed Ryan had eventually disclosed his relationship with McKenna and even told them about Connor.

She didn't come to the funeral. He mentally connected the dots. That might explain one reason why they weren't aware. While Ryan might not have told his parents about McKenna or her pregnancy, they had the right to know more about their only grandchild.

Gage scrubbed his palm across his face. Worse than the knowledge that Gerald and Irene were just now finding out about Connor was the realization that he'd have to tell Skye. What if she was happy about locating more of Connor's relatives? Would she advocate for Connor to go and live with his grandparents?

Stop.

He drew a deep breath and forced himself not to overreact. Gerald and Irene only wanted more information, and he needed to do the right thing and answer promptly.

Gage turned away from the window and went back

to the kitchen table and his laptop. His fingers trembled as he typed his response confirming Connor's existence and where he lived. While Gage wanted what was best for Connor, which was a permanent home with two loving parents, the possibility of the little boy getting caught in the volatile process of finding a forever family lodged an icy ball in Gage's gut. He remembered well the heartache of his own uncertain childhood and didn't want Connor to suffer the same way.

Oh, the crying.

She'd tried everything. Nothing helped Connor feel better. Poor little guy. He seemed miserable. Skye paced the short hallway between the bedrooms and the living room, the distraught baby nestled against her shoulder. Her arms ached from holding him, but when she tried to put him back in his crib, he screamed louder.

They'd walked endless loops around the house, from the kitchen and dining room, then back down the short hallway. Judging by the light glowing from behind the living room drapes, morning wasn't far away. Fatigue made her limbs feel heavy. What she wouldn't give to lie down and sleep. He'd started crying around 2 a.m. and hadn't really stopped.

She pressed her hand to his forehead again. "Oh, you still feel too warm." She'd already given him the last dose of fever-reducing medicine left in the tiny bottle. Why wasn't it helping? And how was she supposed to know if he needed a different medication?

Her chest tightened at the harsh reminder of all she had to learn about caring for someone so small and helpless. If he didn't settle down in the next few minutes, she'd call the pediatrician. Even though the office didn't open until nine, she could still leave a message.

Connor paused and drew a deep breath.

Skye stopped walking and leaned away from him to study his cherubic face. His eyelids drooped slightly and then he jammed his thumb in his mouth. Skye held her breath. Was his fever breaking? He nuzzled his cheek against her shoulder again, and a few seconds later, she felt his body relax.

"Finally," she whispered and resumed her slow path toward the living room. She was tempted to put him down in his crib, but feared he'd only wake up and start crying all over again. It'd be better to keep him in motion until she was certain he'd fallen asleep.

Mom's bedroom door opened, and Skye turned slowly.

Mom hesitated in the doorway, tightened the sash on her light blue robe, then moved toward Skye, pushing the silver walker in front of her.

"I'm sorry," Skye whispered. "I was hoping he wouldn't bother you."

"I was awake anyway." Mom raked one hand through her short salt-and-pepper curls. "What's the matter?"

"He has a fever." Skye's gaze traveled to Mom's knee. "Why aren't you sleeping well? Is your knee bothering you?"

"My knee feels all right. I haven't slept well since your dad died." She offered a weak smile. "Not used to sleeping alone, I guess."

"I'm sorry to hear that." Skye resumed her gentle swaying, while her chest ached at the mention of Dad. He'd been gone a little over a year. After more than thirty years of marriage, it was understandable that

Mom hadn't adjusted to his absence. They were all still feeling the pain his loss inflicted.

"Want some coffee?" Mom steered her walker toward the kitchen.

"Please." Skye followed her, gently shifting Connor in her arms. Although her back and arms screamed for relief, the pleasant sound of his even breathing motivated her to keep holding him. She'd do whatever it took to keep him asleep for as long as possible.

"I have that appointment with my surgeon today at nine," Mom said. "Want me to call and reschedule?"

Oh no. Skye winced. She'd forgotten. "No, I—I can take you."

Mom's brown eyes flitted to Connor. "With a sick child?"

"We don't really have a choice. You need to keep that appointment. How about Drew or Jack?"

"Drew is on highway patrol today, and Jack is likely swamped. One of his IT clients had a security breach."

"He can't spare two hours to take you to the doctor?"

Her mother continued scooping coffee into the coffee maker.

Skye clamped her mouth shut. Drew was helpful when he wasn't working as a sheriff's deputy, but other than Connor's birthday party, Jack had only stopped by to visit once since their mom's surgery. He lived less than an hour away, and he conveniently found plenty of reasons to keep busy. Mom said it was his coping strategy. Coming to the house reminded him too much of Dad.

Frustrated, she heaved a sigh, which prompted a pathetic whimper from Connor. Skye stiffened, then rubbed his back gently and made a soft shushing noise like her mother had taught her.

"Gage seems nice." Mom shot her a hopeful glance. "We could ask him."

"Mom." Skye tried to keep the irritation from her voice. "We aren't going to ask Gage to drive you to the doctor's office."

"Why not?"

"Because he's already helping us this afternoon. Besides, I'm supposed to open the store at ten, so asking him to drive you doesn't solve my child care problem."

"Honey, it's all right if the store doesn't open on time. Or at all. Things happen. Most folks will understand."

Skye bit back a sharp answer. Wasn't Dad honest with her about the store's precarious finances? Why didn't Mom realize they couldn't afford to lose any sales?

"I'm still not asking him to drive you to your appointment. What about Aunt Linda? She said she'd be glad to help you."

"I don't mind calling her, although she lives farther away than Gage. We'll be cutting it close if I have to wait for her to get ready and then come over."

Skye refused to back down. "Why don't you call her right now? I'll stay home with Connor until Gage gets here and then open the store late."

Mom studied her with a pinched expression. "All right." She pushed her walker toward the cordless telephone mounted on the kitchen wall. "I still don't understand why you're being so skeptical about Gage. He was great with Connor yesterday. If you'll let him babysit, why can't he give me a ride to the doctor?"

Skye ignored her and gingerly shifted Connor's

weight as she took a mug from the cabinet. While Mom spoke to Aunt Linda, Skye swayed back and forth and waited while the coffee brewed. How could she explain to Mom that she couldn't afford not to be skeptical? She'd been wooed one too many times by a handsome guy with a megawatt smile. A man who'd transformed into an outspoken control freak behind closed doors. This time she'd be smarter. More aware. The walls of her still-fragile heart were fortified against smooth-talking men. She wouldn't make the same mistake again.

"Take it easy. Let me help you." Gage held Mrs. Tomlinson's elbow and carefully helped her from the floor to the sofa.

She grimaced, her face pinched with concentration and perspiration dotting her forehead.

"You've got this." He held his breath until she was safely in a seated position. While she'd probably done her leg-strengthening exercises numerous times, it still made him nervous seeing her try to get up without assistance. Gage feared Skye would clobber him if anything happened to her mother on his watch.

Right on cue, his phone chimed from his back pocket. Most likely another text from Skye. She'd sent three already in the two hours she'd been at the furniture store.

Mrs. Tomlinson gave him the side-eye. "She's checking up on us again, isn't she?"

"Yes, ma'am. I believe so."

"That girl is going to wear herself out." She reached for her water bottle and twisted off the cap.

"What do you mean?" Gage pulled his phone out and sat down on the opposite end of the sofa.

"I don't make a habit of talking about my children

behind their backs, and I certainly can't blame her for getting worked up. We've got a lot going on." Mrs. Tomlinson paused and took a long sip. "On the other hand, I'd love to see her simmer down a notch, you know?"

Gage couldn't hide his smile. He hadn't expected her to speak so candidly.

"That look on your face tells me you agree."

"She does seem stressed. I'm sure she's trying to do what's best for the people she loves, though."

He glanced at his screen while Mrs. Tomlinson took another sip of water.

How is Connor doing? Does he still have a fever? Did he take a long nap? Has Mom finished her exercises? Please remind her to ice afterward.

Oh boy. He sighed and set his phone on the coffee table without responding. Maybe she did need to simmer down a notch. Connor was still napping, and Mrs. Tomlinson appeared to be doing everything she was supposed to.

"I'm sorry." Mrs. Tomlinson shot him an apologetic glance. "I shouldn't have said that. You're right, she is trying to do what's best. She's been very good about taking care of her family, especially her cousin."

The hair on Gage's arm stood on end. "How so?"

"My husband was a good man, and he thought he was doing the right thing for the family at the time, but he and his brother, McKenna's father, had a blowout over our furniture store." She pressed her lips together. "My husband was willed the store by their father, and Kenny, my brother-in-law, was much better at working with his hands. He could build a table and chairs that were absolute works of art. Most of the furniture in this house, he built. Anyway, Kenny was so upset and accused us of swindling him out of the family business. He—he took his own life a few years back, and we have always blamed ourselves."

Gage's chest tightened. "I'm sorry for your loss."

"Thank you." She patted his arm. "McKenna was always a spirited child, and her daddy's girl. She got away with a lot, growing up. Mostly silly stuff. We called her mischievous and headstrong. Never imagined it would come to this. The rift in our family and then his death wrecked her."

Her words pricked at lingering wounds. He could relate. The loss of his own parents and then Ryan's accident had done a number on him emotionally. Palming the back of his neck, Gage tried to process this new layer to an already complicated scenario. "If your family was fighting over the store, then why did she leave Connor with you and Skye? As payback?"

Mrs. Tomlinson sighed and tucked a strand of her hair behind her ear. "I don't know why exactly. I suspect she knew motherhood was not her thing, and it isn't really Skye's thing, either, but I think she knew Skye was dependable. She wouldn't turn her away."

"Did you just say motherhood isn't Skye's thing?"

"Skye has zero interest in being a mother." Mrs. Tomlinson studied him. "She has a good heart, but I know she's only here right now because she loves us and can't bear to see us struggling."

Gage could only stare at Mrs. Tomlinson. He had so many questions. The muffled sound of Connor crying broke the silence and he quickly stood.

"Gage—"

"I'd better check on him." Gage skirted the coffee table and strode toward Connor's room, his mind racing. *Skye has zero interest in being a mother.* Why did he find that so hard to believe? And what did it mean for Connor? If she didn't really want him, was she only caring for him out of guilt and obligation? What happened when she'd finally reached her limit?

He quietly pushed open the door of Connor's room and found the boy had pulled himself to a standing position inside his crib. Tears tracked down his red cheeks, and he stretched out both arms over the crib rail while repeating a string of consonants that conveyed his earnest plea for freedom.

Gage swallowed hard against the emotion clogging his throat. He couldn't let this little boy be abandoned again.

"C'mon, buddy. Let's get up." He strode to the crib and gently lifted Connor into his arms. He smelled like peach-scented soap, and damp wisps of hair were matted to his forehead. Did that mean he didn't have a fever anymore? The baby's wide blue eyes scanned Gage's face as if assessing the situation. Gage waited, holding his breath, and braced for a meltdown. Slowly, Connor's mouth morphed into a toothy smile.

Thank You. Gage offered a silent prayer of gratitude, then looked around the room. He'd managed to avoid changing Connor's diaper yesterday, but he needed to step up and make an effort today. Even though he didn't have a clue how to accomplish the task. While Connor babbled happily, Gage spotted a plastic package of diapers propped against the wall and a carton labeled Wipes with a picture of a smiling infant on the front.

He grabbed both of those and carried Connor out to the living room.

Mrs. Tomlinson glanced up from the e-reader in her hands. "There's our precious boy. Did you have a good nap?"

Connor grinned some more and clapped his hands together.

"Oh, you must be feeling better." Mrs. Tomlinson looked relieved. "Maybe his fever is gone."

"I hope so. As soon as his diaper is changed, I'll take his temperature." Gage sank awkwardly to the floor and set Connor beside him. "Would you mind giving me some tips here?"

"Excuse me?"

"The diaper. Changing it. I—I have no idea how to do that."

"Oh. Right." Mrs. Tomlinson patted the sofa cushion beside her. "If you bring him to me, I can probably take care of it."

"No, no. I need to learn." Gage felt his cheeks redden. Incompetency made him feel weak. He hated that.

"All right. Start by laying him down on his back. Maybe give him a small toy to keep him occupied."

A few minutes later, after a lot of trial and error— and very little cooperation on Connor's part—Gage managed to change the diaper. He was in the process of snapping the bazillion snaps on the legs of Connor's one-piece outfit when boots thumped up the steps outside and then the front door flew open.

Skye came in, her cheeks flushed and her eyes wide with panic. "Oh, I'm so glad you're all okay."

"Skye, you scared me to death." Mrs. Tomlinson

pressed her hand to her chest. "What are you doing home so early?"

Her icy gaze toggled from Connor to Gage. "Why didn't you answer my texts?"

Whoa. Gage sat back on his heels. Was she serious?

"Been a little busy." Gage gritted his teeth and helped Connor sit up. "Can I throw this diaper in the trash can or should I carry it outside?"

"The trash can under the kitchen sink is fine," Mrs. Tomlinson said. "Thank you."

He strode toward the kitchen, slowly counting down until Skye trotted after him. *Three, two, one.*

Sure enough, boots *tap-tap-tapped* behind him. "I need you to answer me when I text you. I was extremely worried when I didn't hear from you. My mom could've been hurt, or something might've happened to Connor. What am I supposed to think when you don't respond?"

Gage paused, one hand on the cabinet doorknob, adrenaline coursing through him. "That I'm handling it."

"It doesn't seem like you're handling things well when you can't find the time to send a brief text."

He threw the diaper in the trash, then straightened to his full height. In her navy wool peacoat belted at her slim waist, knee-high brown boots and windblown hair cascading around her shoulders, he had to admit she was stunning. Even if she was angry with him. Yet he couldn't ignore her attitude or the way her thoughtless words made him feel so unappreciated.

"You're going to have to learn to trust me, Skye."

Her face puckered, and she propped her hands on her hips.

"I understand that you have a lot on your mind. But

if I don't answer you immediately, it means I'm most likely doing what I said I would—taking care of Connor or helping your mom."

"But neither one of you answered me. My mom is recovering from surgery, and Connor had a fever last night. I assumed the worst."

"The worst about who?" He'd struck a nerve. He could tell by the way she visibly flinched. "Now that you're here, I think I'll go. I've got an exam to study for."

"I didn't mean that the way it sounded. I—"

Really? He arched an eyebrow in disbelief, then moved past her into the living room and gave Connor's head a gentle pat on his way to the door. "See you next time, little dude."

"Gage, wait." Mrs. Tomlinson rose from the sofa and reached for her walker. "Please don't leave when you're angry."

"I'm not angry." Okay, maybe he was a little angry. He calmly shrugged into his jacket, then forced a polite smile. "If you don't think this arrangement is going to work out, just let me know, but I still plan to be involved in Connor's life—one way or another."

Without another word, he stepped outside and closed the door firmly behind him. That wasn't his proudest moment—leaving with a thinly veiled threat—but she'd come at him with her frustration and her doubt in his abilities, and he'd lost his cool. Despite their fight just now, he and Skye both shared a common objective—doing what was best for Connor. But now that Mrs. Tomlinson had revealed Skye didn't want to be a mother, how would she react when she found out about Ryan's parents?

Chapter Seven

"Did you apologize to Gage yet?" her mom asked, sitting at the table and calmly sipping her morning coffee.

Skye winced. Mom's simple question only amplified her guilt. "Not yet."

"You'd better."

Skye bit her lip and tucked a plastic bag full of carrot sticks into the thermal lunch tote and zipped it shut. Connor was down for his morning nap already. If she hurried, she could still get to the furniture store in time to open by ten.

"What if he doesn't show up to help this afternoon?"

"He will." Skye turned in a slow circle, looking for her keys.

"How do you know? He seemed upset when he left yesterday."

Skye located her keys under a pile of mail on the kitchen counter and turned to face Mom. "I'll call him when I get to the store."

"Promise?" Her mother shot her a doubtful look over the rim of her coffee cup.

"I promise." Skye rounded the table and gave her

mom a quick peck on the cheek. "Aunt Linda will be here at ten fifteen to stay with you and Connor. She needs to leave after lunch."

"All the more reason for you to call and confirm that Gage is still coming." Mom flashed an innocent smile.

"You're relentless, you know that?"

"I'm only trying to help."

And maybe fix her up. Skye slid her feet into her boots. "I'll be back tonight. Call me if you need anything."

"Have a good day, sweetie," Mom called after her. "Don't forget to call Gage."

Skye chuckled as she put on her coat and grabbed her lunch bag and purse. The crisp winter air nipped at her cheeks as she stepped outside.

McKenna, where are you?

Skye had texted her a picture a few days ago of Connor smashing his fist into his birthday cake. Maybe it was a passive-aggressive move, sending her that photo, but she wanted McKenna to know what she was missing.

Still no response. Didn't McKenna care about her son? Since she'd intentionally left Connor behind and never mentioned when she'd be back, Skye was starting to question her cousin's motives. Checking in with Drew again hadn't helped, either. The missing person's report hadn't generated any leads at the sheriff's department. Was McKenna just ignoring Skye's attempts to reach out, or had something terrible happened to her?

Skye heaved a sigh and trudged through the snow to her car. McKenna's silence aside, she owed Gage an apology for the way she'd treated him. She cringed as she mentally replayed her snide words and subtle accusations, especially after he'd gone out of his way to be helpful. Why did she jump to conclusions so quickly? A small part of her—the part that hated to admit she'd been wrong—hoped he wouldn't answer when she called. Mom was right, though. If he was so angry that he didn't want to help with Connor this afternoon—or any afternoon ever again—she needed to know.

Her stomach twisted at the thought of having zero child care options. Again. Aunt Linda graciously offered to step in on an as-needed basis, and a handful of other friends had done the same, but soon she'd run out of favors to call in. She needed consistent, reliable child care—not only for her own peace of mind, but because that was what Connor needed, as well.

After putting on her gloves, she scraped the snow and ice from her windshield and gave the engine a few extra minutes to warm up. By the time she finished and slid behind the wheel, shivering, the clock on her dash indicated she only had seven minutes to get to the store. Calling Gage would have to wait.

On the drive to work, she abandoned her usual morning radio show and rehearsed a hypothetical apology. "I'm sorry I was rude."

Not sincere enough. She cleared her throat. "I'm sorry I d-doubted you."

Better. No stuttering, though. "I'm sorry I didn't tru—"

Trust you. I'm sorry I didn't trust you.

The words died on her lips. How in the world would she manage to apologize if she couldn't even verbalize it while driving alone? She sighed and shook her head. Trust. Why was it so hard for her to conquer her fears?

She tightened her grip on the steering wheel and

eased to a stop at one of the few traffic lights in Merritt's Crossing. The owner of the hardware store was neatly stacking shovels for sale in front of the entrance, while the young woman who just opened the new flower shop on the opposite corner was arranging a spring-themed display in her front window. She glanced up and waved at Skye.

Skye waved back, smiling at the stark contrast between her fellow business owners. With the whole town still looking like a winter wonderland, it was hard to imagine spring was supposedly just six weeks away. It was even harder to imagine that a flower shop might thrive in Merritt's Crossing, but the wind energy group brought new jobs and more families to town than ever before. It wasn't the sleepy little wheat-farming town just off the interstate anymore.

Could she stay here beyond Easter—manage the store and care for Connor?

A fresh wave of uncertainty washed over her. Before the idea grew legs, her phone rang. The light turned green and she cast a longing glance at her bag on the passenger seat. Not good to fumble for her phone and drive. Reluctantly, she accelerated through the intersection and down the street to the furniture store's parking lot.

By the time she found her phone in the depths of her purse, the call had gone to voice mail. She checked the ID. Her boss in Denver.

Her scalp prickled. Why was he calling? She still had six weeks of leave and one of her coworkers was covering her sales territory.

Skye tapped the screen and listened to the message.

"Hi, Skye. It's Jim. I'm sorry to bother you while

you're on leave. Just wanted to let you know there's an unexpected opening in our division. One of your colleagues resigned yesterday, and I think you'd be a great fit for the role. It would be a promotion, of course, with a larger territory. Please call me when you have a few minutes. I hope your mom's recovery is going well. Take care."

A great fit for the role. He wouldn't have called if his offer wasn't genuine. She'd worked hard to hit sales targets and even earned a bonus last year. A promotion was one of her goals. And now it seemed so close, yet life was working against her.

Jim's offer came with a downside, though. The long hours, a new territory to cover, more responsibilities—not to mention more upheaval in Connor's life. He couldn't handle that. They didn't know what was going on with McKenna, and there was no way she'd dump the responsibility of Connor's care on Mom. With each passing day, she'd grown attached to the little boy, and despite her rude behavior yesterday, her attraction to Gage had grown, as well.

She couldn't ignore Connor's obvious affection for Gage, either. When he'd intentionally reached for Gage at the birthday party, and when Mom reported that Gage and Connor had a great first afternoon together, something inside her shifted. While she valued her independence and loved her work, if McKenna didn't come back for Connor, Skye's future plans couldn't just be about what she wanted.

Connor needed a stable home, and ideally, one that included a father, too. Maybe he would be better off with someone else, someone who was already married and could provide a stable home with two parents. She closed her eyes and rested her head on the steering wheel. While full-time day care was still a viable option, how could she seriously consider going back to Denver if it meant depriving Connor of a meaningful relationship with Gage?

He couldn't put it off another day—he had to tell Skye about Gerald and Irene's email. Waiting only made it harder and introduced the possibility that she'd think he was scheming behind her back. That was the last thing he needed.

Gage turned off his truck's ignition and stared at the double doors fronting Tomlinson's Furniture. If he spoke to Skye now, he'd still have time to squeeze in some studying for his exam before he went by her mom's house to take care of Connor.

He climbed out of the truck, hunched his shoulders against the bitter wind swirling down Main Street and strode toward the store's entrance. The living room furniture staged in the front window showcased an appealing inventory. A dark leather sofa, modern lamps, paired with nice end tables, and a large vase of fresh flowers invited customers to step inside.

The aroma of leather and upholstery mixed with citrus wafted toward him when he opened the door. An impressive arrangement of chairs, sofas and timeless wood furniture filled the showroom. Brick walls and vaulted ceilings with exposed pipes hinted at the building's age, while modern accessories indicated a store owner who kept up with current trends.

"Welcome to Tomlinson's. I'll be right with you," Skye called out from across the room without making eye contact. Two young women stood beside her in front of a bedroom set.

Gage nodded and shoved his hands in his jacket pockets, nervously shifting his weight from one leg to the other. A dark mahogany desk with a matching set of shelves sat against the wall to his right. An oval container shooting mist into the air explained the fruit-infused aroma, and several framed photographs mounted on the wall nearby caught his attention.

A black-and-white photo of the building from another era was surrounded by more framed color photos of a man and woman smiling proudly under the Tomlinson's sign, flanked by two boys and a gangly preteen girl. He grinned. Skye and her family—he recognized her blue eyes.

Footsteps clicked across the hardwood behind him, and he turned around.

"Gage?" Skye approached, her smile tentative, and Gage couldn't ignore the subtle *blip-blip-blip* of his pulse accelerating. "What brings you by?"

"I—I need to talk to you."

"I'm sorry about yesterday." She glanced down and fiddled with the hem of her pink-and-navy-plaid button-down shirt. When she met his gaze again, her expression was tinged with regret. "I shouldn't have jumped to conclusions and assumed the worst. I'm sorry I didn't... trust you."

Wow. Wasn't expecting that. He opened his mouth to respond, but no words came out.

"My family and I really appreciate you stepping in and helping us with Connor."

His mouth went dry. Oh no. That sounded like the beginning of a dismissal. "I—"

She held up her palm. "Please let me finish. I hope my rude behavior didn't run you off."

"I'm not here to bail, if that's what you're thinking."

Her mouth curved into a relieved smile. "I was so afraid you'd refuse to come back after the way I treated you."

"You can't get rid of me that easy." He pulled a small plastic bag from his jacket pocket. "Your mom said Connor ran out of medicine, so I stopped at the drugstore and picked up another bottle, so you'll have some on hand for next time. I hope I bought the right thing."

"That was nice of you." She took the bag and pulled out the tiny box of fever-reducing drops. "This is perfect. Thank you."

Her genuine smile sent a jolt of electricity arcing through him. He quickly squelched those sensations with logic. Once he told her about Gerald and Irene's email, she wouldn't be happy with the news. Ryan's parents expressing an interest in Connor totally threw a wrench into her well-ordered plans.

Unless she wanted to find a more permanent home for Connor. In that case, Ryan's parents might be the solution to her long-term problems.

Her brow furrowed. "Are you all right?"

"There's something else I need to tell you," he said.

"Oh?" She glanced over her shoulder. "I guess I can talk for a couple more minutes."

"It won't take long." Her customers were out of earshot on the other side of the showroom, circling the bedroom set. He took a deep breath. "I received an email from Ryan's parents this week. They just found out about Connor and contacted me for more information."

Eyes wide, she pressed her fingertips to her lips.

"I wrote back and confirmed Connor was Ryan's son and that he's living with family. Since I'm not Connor's guardian, I didn't think it was my place to tell them exactly what was going on."

"But you're their son's best friend. They trust you, I'm sure, and deserve to know the truth." She wrapped her arms around her torso. "I can't imagine how they must be feeling."

The tension in his shoulders loosened at the realization she wasn't going to panic over this news. "I've never asked you about survivor benefits because it's none of my business, but Ryan's parents are going to want to know. Are you aware if Connor received anything from the navy after Ryan passed?"

Skye shook her head. "McKenna never mentioned a word about it."

"So it's possible she has access to the money?" Gage's stomach clenched. "That might not be a good thing."

She rubbed her forehead with her fingertips. "No, probably not a good thing, given her track record."

"Gerald and Irene seem like solid, upstanding people. I doubt they're looking for money, but they will want to know all about Connor. Maybe even be involved in his life. Are you okay with that?"

Pain flashed in her eyes. She hesitated, then lifted one shoulder in a helpless shrug. "I—I don't know. Do they live close by? Are they asking for visitation?"

Her customers strode toward them. Gage pulled his keys from his pocket. "You have customers. We can talk more later. I'll be at your house at one o'clock like we planned, all right?"

"Thank you." Sadness lingered in her expression. "For everything."

He turned to leave, rubbing his knuckles against the

hollow ache in his chest. He'd told her the truth, but it made him feel worse. Was it wrong that he wasn't okay with Gerald and Irene getting involved? Not that he didn't believe they had Connor's best interests in mind, but what if that meant Connor moved to Illinois with his grandparents? If Gage was honest, he hoped for more than just infrequent visits and the occasional photo of Connor. And he definitely wanted to spend more time with Skye, but without Connor, how was that possible?

Chapter Eight

It was standing room only around the air hockey table at Pizza Etc. on Saturday night. From her perch on a tall chair at the three-top table Skye had managed to score, she surveyed the crowded restaurant. Most of Merritt's Crossing had turned out to wish Bethany and her husband well on their new life in Arizona.

The server set a platter heaped with loaded nachos in the center of the table, along with a stack of napkins. "There you go, ladies," she said. "Can I get you anything else?"

"I think we're all set for now." Skye smiled at her. "Thank you."

"This looks amazing." Laramie reached for a napkin. "I'm not even going to think about how many calories are involved."

"Thank you for putting this party together," Bethany said. "Allen and I are really going to miss you guys."

"We're going to miss you, too." Skye patted Bethany's arm. "This is all happening so quickly."

"I know." Bethany filled her plate with some nachos.

"I can't tell you how sorry I am to leave you in a pinch with Connor. Have you found anyone else to help out?"

"Has she ever." Laramie waggled her eyebrows.

Skye rolled her eyes and reached for her diet soda. "Gage Westbrook is staying with Connor and Mom in the afternoon while I'm at the store. He's new in town and was a friend of Connor's dad. Just temporarily until I can find someone more permanent."

"It doesn't have to be temporary. I think he might be a keeper." Laramie's knowing grin made Skye chomp down on a mouthful of ice to keep from saying something snarky.

"Do you know if he's single?" Bethany asked.

"Not a clue," Skye mumbled around an ice cube. From the corner of her eye, she noted Gage lingering near the air hockey table, talking to one of Dane's friends. Again, the invisible thread tugged at her, heightening her awareness of his presence in the room.

Bethany used a napkin to mop up a glob of cheese on the table. "He might have a girlfriend we haven't met yet."

Skye's stomach lurched.

"Oh, you don't like that idea one bit, do you?" Laramie's triumphant grin made Skye wrinkle her nose in disgust. Sometimes knowing a person for more than a decade had its drawbacks. She never could hide anything from her best friend.

"If he has a girlfriend, she would not be happy to hear about you," Laramie said.

"Why not?" Skye glanced from Laramie to Bethany. How did this conversation even get started? Weren't they supposed to be talking about Bethany's new house in Arizona or something? "We're just friends."

"Right." Laramie's eyes glittered with mischief as she plucked another chip off the pile. "Friends who spend a lot of time taking care of a baby together."

"When Allen and I were first dating, he rented a garage apartment from Mrs. Gaither. Remember?" Bethany nudged Laramie's arm. "Out by the old Hartnett farm?"

"Oh yeah. Her gorgeous granddaughter moved in with her." Laramie nodded. "You were beside yourself."

"Thanks for the painful reminder." Bethany shot her a playful look. "Allen and I almost broke up over that."

"What does that have to do with Gage babysitting Connor?" Skye couldn't keep the irritation from her voice. "You guys are happily married now."

"Exactly." Laramie fired another knowing glance across their small table. "Bethany is trying to tell you that if Gage has a girlfriend, she wouldn't be happy about how much time he spends at your house, taking care of an adorable baby that isn't even his."

"Especially if she has long-term plans for the relationship," Bethany chimed in. "Just sayin'."

"Whoever this hypothetical girl is, she has nothing to worry about." Skye slid her drink aside and loaded a pile of nachos onto her own plate.

"Then why does he keep looking over here?" Laramie asked.

"What?" Skye froze, a chip coated in melted cheese and topped with black olives, jalapeños and tomatoes halfway to her mouth.

Bethany scanned the room. "He is looking over here quite a bit."

"Stop," Skye said. "Maybe he likes Laramie."

Bethany's grin stretched wide. "Then he'll have to arm wrestle your brother Jack to get to her."

Laramie's cheeks flushed, and she stared into her soda. "I don't think Jack has the nerve to speak to me."

Skye munched on her appetizer, caught in the awkward position of wanting Laramie to be happy, while acknowledging that Jack didn't seem courageous enough to offer more than polite conversation. "He did make an effort with his appearance at Connor's birthday party. Mom commented later that was the happiest she'd seen Jack since—in a long time."

She stopped short of mentioning her father's passing.

Laramie's smile wobbled. "He did look good."

Sidestepping that delicate topic, Bethany shifted the conversation back to Connor. "Connor is such a sweet little guy. I'm going to miss him, too. Will you let me know where he ends up?"

"Ends up?" Laramie's eyes widened. "What do you mean? Like foster care?"

"I'm sorry." Bethany grimaced. "Poor choice of words. Skye, you talk about Connor's situation as though it's temporary—until McKenna comes back. I assumed that was still the plan."

It was still the plan. Wasn't it? Skye wiped her greasy fingers on her napkin. "I'm still hoping she'll come back. Although we haven't heard anything from McKenna since she texted that she'd found some friends in Kansas. Gage did get an email from Connor's dad's parents, though. We're waiting to hear more about that."

"Where do they live?" Bethany asked.

"Not close by, I hope." Laramie frowned. "What if they want Connor to live with them?"

"I—I don't know what's going to happen." Skye

squirmed in her chair. Laramie's line of questioning dredged up all kinds of worries. Not to mention her boss's voice mail making her question if she could balance caring for Connor with taking on a more demanding role at work. And allowing Gage to spend time with Connor had been hard enough. The thought of letting another stranger into Connor's world felt like a punch in the gut, but she couldn't keep pretending it wasn't a real possibility. Even if Ryan's parents appeared to be the best people on the planet, Connor wouldn't—

"When do you think you'll know more details?" Laramie's question pulled her back to the conversation.

"Gage and I talked about how to respond to the email today. It's only fair that Connor's grandparents know what's going on. After all, he's their only son's child. Gage let them know that Connor is living here in Colorado with extended family, and now we're waiting to hear more from them." She braved a quick glance across the room to where he still stood. He looked her way and caught her eye, then grinned. Warmth unfurled in her abdomen and she quickly looked away.

"Just friends, huh?" Laramie lifted an eyebrow. "I don't believe you."

With a flick of his wrist, Dane sent the white plastic disk spinning past Gage's lagging defense, scoring another goal in the impromptu Saturday-night air hockey tournament. A wave of approval rippled through the crowd milling around the air hockey table at Pizza Etc.

Gage gritted his teeth. Dane was ahead 7–6. How had he allowed himself to get roped into this?

"C'mon, Westbrook. Show me watcha got," Dane

gloated, high-fiving one of his buddies standing near him at the other end of the table.

Should've stayed home and studied for his next exam.

Leaning over, Gage fished the puck out of the machine and stole a glance at the table nearby, where Skye sat with her friends. Supposedly, everyone was here to give Bethany and her husband—Dane's most recently defeated opponent—a proper send-off before they left for Arizona.

Right now, it felt more like a power move on Dane's part to maintain his title as unofficial air hockey champion. No wonder Drew had volunteered to stay with Connor and Mrs. T tonight.

"Quit stalling, man." Dane's face tightened with concentration.

"All right, all right." Gage set the puck on the smooth surface and smacked it against the left edge of the table, hoping it might ricochet into Dane's goal with sheer speed alone. Hoping that he might win the game and Skye might notice.

Dane smirked and blocked the shot effortlessly. "Why don't you challenge me a little?"

Gage bristled inside. Dane had been polite, friendly and professional during both orientation sessions. Gage had no reason to believe Dane's motivation was anything more than a drive to keep his winning streak alive. But the fierce look in his eyes, dogged determination to beat Gage as well as his appreciative comments about Skye when they were at the diner, made Gage suspect this might be something more.

He wanted to win this stupid game, too. If this was an unspoken turf war, he wasn't going down without a fight. Another volley sent the puck zinging back and forth between them, and Gage managed to defend his goal. He sneaked a glance at Skye to see if she was paying attention to this ridiculous showdown, then quickly sliced his paddle to deflect Dane's next shot.

"I see you looking at her," Dane scoffed. "How about winner asks her to dance?"

Gage's heart sped at the thought of holding Skye close. He fired another shot across the table.

"Yeah, you heard me. Winner asks her to dance."

The spectators ringing the table murmured to one another. Jack stood alone, just behind Dane, his expression unreadable. Gage hesitated. Skye wouldn't be happy if she found out about their competition.

"What's wrong?" Dane taunted. "Afraid I might win?"

He'd heard enough. There were plenty of women here they could both dance with, but if he didn't win and had to watch Dane dance with Skye—if she even said yes—he'd never hear the end of it.

"Deal." He flicked his paddle against the puck and it bounced off the right edge and sailed into Dane's goal unobstructed. Tied 7–7.

A fierce volley ensued, and the crowd around the table pressed in while the puck zipped back and forth. Gage was in the zone, blocking Dane's shots and firing back repeatedly. His arm ached from exertion, and a droplet of sweat trickled down his spine. Finally, he managed to slam one more shot across the table and it slid into Dane's goal for the win. Final score: 8–7.

"Congratulations." Dane tossed his paddle onto the table, then pushed through the crowd.

A smattering of applause broke out, but anxiety clenched Gage's stomach as he stared after him. He'd hate to do anything that might impact his local job prospects. Dane didn't have that kind of influence, though, did he? Besides, it was just a game.

"Don't worry about him." Jack clapped him on the shoulder. "He needs to lose every once in a while."

Gage offered a weak smile. "Yeah, probably."

"Here." Jack held up a quarter. "Go ask my sister to dance. I'll pick a nice slow song from the jukebox."

Gage sneaked a peek at Skye, who'd stood and put on her jacket. "It looks like she's leaving. Let me offer to walk her to her car instead."

"Good plan." Jack pocketed his quarter. "Thanks for looking after my sister."

"You're welcome." Gage grabbed his jacket from a stool nearby and worked his way toward her, trying not to shove past anyone. He didn't want to seem too aggressive, yet he didn't want her to leave before he could at least offer to walk with her.

"Skye?" He gently pressed his hand against the sleeve of her jacket.

Laramie met his gaze, then exchanged a glance with Bethany as Skye turned to face him.

"Oh, hey." Surprise flashed in her eyes and her lips curved in a friendly smile. "How's it going?"

"Not bad. Just beat Dane in a game of air hockey." He couldn't help but brag a little, although he didn't mention that was the catalyst for crossing the restaurant to speak to her.

"Good for you." Skye shouldered her purse. "We were just getting ready to go. I promised Drew I'd be home by nine thirty."

"Mind if I walk you out?"

"I rode with Laramie, so—"

"That's all right," Laramie interrupted. "You can take her home, I don't mind."

Thank you. Gage owed her one. He studied Skye's expression, half expecting her to object.

"Oh." She hesitated. "I—I guess that would be fine."

"I'm ready when you are." He put on his jacket and waited while she said goodbye to her friends.

The crowd had shifted away from the air hockey game, and Jack or someone else must've dropped a quarter in the jukebox, because a familiar country song played, drawing several couples onto the black-and-white-checked linoleum floor. Gage let Skye lead the way to the front door, resisting the urge to press his hand to the small of her back and guide her.

Outside, the neon glow from the restaurant's sign cast a purple hue onto the sidewalk at their feet.

"I'm parked down the street. Hope you don't mind the walk." Gage's hand itched to reach for hers. Instead, he balled his fists in his jacket pockets. What was he thinking? Winning that game must've given him a shot of courage.

"I don't mind. The fresh air feels good."

The streetlights did little to detract from the stars dotting the inky black sky above. A group of ladies spilled out of a tavern nearby, their laughter puncturing the night air. Snow crunched beneath their boots as Skye walked beside him toward his truck.

He reached for the passenger door and opened it.

She hesitated and gazed up at him. "Thank you for driving me home."

The subtle curve of her smile drew his gaze to her lips. His mouth felt dry. "You're welcome."

Still she didn't move past him. They were inches

apart now. His heart rate quickened as he searched her face, noticing not for the first time how her long thick eyelashes rimmed fathomless blue eyes.

Unable to resist any longer, his knuckles gently grazed her cheek as he dragged his thumb across the fullest part of her pink lower lip.

Her sharp intake of breath made him hesitate. She didn't back away, though.

"We probably shouldn't," she whispered as her hands twined around his neck.

"That doesn't feel like a no." He held back for an excruciating instant, struggling to rein in his thoughts. She had her reasons for saying they shouldn't kiss, and he'd never force her.

"Kiss me." Her breath feathered his cheek as she went up on tiptoe and leaned into his embrace.

It was bold—asking him to kiss her. Skye knew it, yet she couldn't resist. As Gage's lips brushed hers, her defenses weakened further and she let herself get lost in the moment. He deepened the kiss while cupping her face gently in his hands. His aftershave or cologne or something, woodsy and crisp, enveloped her and teased her senses.

Wait! What are you thinking?

Her cautious nature battled with her senses, and for once she tried to ignore the voice of reason and savor Gage's mouth moving against hers.

What about Connor? Your life back in Denver?

She pushed her palms against his broad chest. "Stop. We have to stop."

His fingers skimmed the length of her jacket sleeves as she stepped back. Hurt flashed in his eyes. "Skye, what's wrong? What did I do?"

"Nothing." She bit her lip and looked away.

"Please. Talk to me. What happened?"

She shook her head. No. He'd only try to convince her that she was wrong. Just like her ex-boyfriend had twisted her words and made her question her logic, all because he wanted to control her.

"We shouldn't have kissed." Her voice wobbled, and she fought to keep her composure. Lifting her chin, she narrowed her gaze and forced herself to look him in the eye. "Please take me home."

"Okay." He waited while she got in his truck, then closed the door. She pulled her phone from her purse and quickly texted Drew to let him know she was on her way.

Gage slid behind the wheel and put the key in the ignition, but didn't start the engine. The warmth of his gaze made her twist in her seat and stare out the passenger window.

"Skye, I would never do anything to hurt you. You know that, right?"

The tenderness in his words brought tears to her eyes. She dug her fingernails into her palms. "I said take me home."

Wordlessly, Gage started the truck and left the parking lot. A heavy silence filled the cab and she kept staring out into the darkness. She was an idiot. Succumbing to her selfish desires and completely losing focus on what really mattered. Connor. It might've been an amazing kiss, but it was a reckless choice, and it scared her to death. She couldn't risk being so vulnerable. Because vulnerability meant admitting she needed Gage. And the risk was too great and the pain still too raw from the last time she allowed herself to fall in love.

Chapter Nine

Why? Why had he kissed her?

Gage had asked himself that question a dozen times in the last three days and the answer hadn't changed—Skye was beautiful, they'd been alone under a star-filled sky and she'd asked him to.

Right? He'd certainly been caught up in the moment—her husky voice and slender fingers warm against the back of his neck had made him dizzy—but he hadn't imagined her request.

Connor interrupted his thoughts by handing him a blue-and-orange foam block decorated with pictures of animals and instruments, then clapped his hands awkwardly.

"Thanks, buddy. Nice clapping, by the way." Gage took the block and stacked it on top of the short tower he'd assembled in the middle of the living room floor. While the baby had napped for only an hour, Mrs. Tomlinson was still sleeping in her room after what she'd declared her toughest day at physical therapy yet. Gage didn't want to wake her. Connor squealed and kicked both feet with excitement, sending the blocks tumbling across the carpet. Instead of waiting for Gage to collect them and make a new stack, Connor got on all fours and crawled after a plastic airplane wedged under the love seat.

Gage quickly reached for his phone to record the activity. While Connor had crawled a little bit in the short time they'd spent together, Gage hadn't seen him move quite that quickly before. Skye and Mrs. Tomlinson would want to see the replay.

Skye had ignored all his efforts to interact in the three days since they'd kissed. His texts went unanswered, and she let both his calls go to voice mail. Maybe she'd respond to a cute video of Connor. While he filmed Connor in action, his thoughts cycled back to the kiss and he rehashed the whole encounter. As first kisses went, it was incredible, but he hated that he'd obviously done something to upset her.

Connor sat beside the love seat, sucking on one of the airplane's wings, so Gage stopped the video and quickly sent it to Skye, then put his phone away.

Dating hadn't been on his radar when he'd arrived in Merritt's Crossing. Finishing up his wind energy technician certification through the local community college and finding Connor were his priorities. Those objectives hadn't changed. His role in Connor's life turned into a much bigger blessing than he'd expected—and meeting Skye had made him revisit his previous failures in dating relationships. He hadn't had many healthy role models growing up. Dad left before Gage's third birthday, and when he had lived with his mom, she paraded an endless string of boyfriends in and out of their lives. His grandparents had stayed married, but Gage hadn't seen them often.

His chest tightened. Intimacy still scared him. Vulnerability seemed like a huge risk. Even with the mistakes the Tomlinson family admitted they'd made, Skye and her brothers and their mom still stuck together. He was in awe of their willingness to restructure their lives to meet Connor's needs, and still terrified about what it meant to be part of a family.

Maybe that was the problem. Skye sensed he was destined to be an outsider—a drifter—and she didn't trust him to stick around. Or maybe she thought he'd advocate for Ryan's parents to become Connor's legal guardians, which would only drive a wedge between them anyway. That certainly seemed more in line with her cautious, pragmatic nature. Whatever her reason for getting so upset, they needed to talk about it. Even if the kiss was a mistake, he couldn't leave things so unsettled. They needed to be able to work together for Connor's sake—especially when he told her about Gerald and Irene's plans.

Connor abandoned the airplane and crawled back toward Gage.

Gage had expected Skye to come home early from the store—barreling in the door and quizzing him about Connor's care. Instead, his afternoon shift had passed uneventfully, and his phone remained silent. Connor climbed into Gage's lap, then popped his thumb into his mouth. At least one person in this family trusted him.

"Want to read a book?"

Connor kicked one leg up and down repeatedly.

"I'll take that as a yes." Gage slid a stack of board books closer. "Let's see what we have here."

Resting his back against the love seat, Gage opened the book about race cars and counting to ten. As he turned the thick pages, he talked about each color and pointed out the numbers, enjoying the warmth of Connor's little body snuggled against his chest. Whatever happened in the future, he'd never forget these tender moments.

He was almost to the end of the book when a key turned in the lock and the front door opened. Skye came inside, her face drawn and smile tight.

Connor squealed and bounced up and down in Gage's lap.

"Hey, buddy." Skye's expression brightened a little, but she avoided eye contact with Gage.

His palms felt clammy and his mouth dry. "How was your day?"

"Good. Finally sold some furniture—a recliner." While she tugged off her boots and hung up her jacket, Connor chattered a string of nonsensical sounds. Gage had never been more grateful for the baby's ability to defuse the awkward tension.

"Where's Mom?" Skye padded toward them in her socks, then sank cross-legged on the floor. Connor wiggled and squirmed to get to her.

"She's taking a nap." Gage helped Connor off his lap so he could crawl to Skye.

"Look at you go." Skye held out her arms and Connor giggled as she scooped him up and pressed a juicy kiss to his cheek.

Gage looked away. Too bad she wasn't nearly as excited to see him. In her bright green sweater and dark blue jeans, gold hoop earrings and a hint of lip gloss on those kissable lips—meaningful conversation was the last thing on his mind. But her rejection stung, and he couldn't forget the look of regret he'd seen in her eyes. And they still had to talk—really talk—about their kiss and Ryan's parents' request.

"Do you have a few minutes?" He collected the blocks and put them back in the toy bin. "There's something we need to discuss."

She ran her hand along the length of her ponytail, then flipped it over her shoulder and out of Connor's reach. Her cool, determined gaze lacked the spark he'd admired when she was in his arms. "If it's about our... If it's about Saturday night, then I think we can both agree it shouldn't have happened."

Oh. He rubbed his fingers along his jaw. So she still felt the kiss was a mistake? "We got caught up in the moment."

"Right."

Wrong. He wanted to argue, to distract Connor with a toy and pull her close for another kiss.

"We both know this is a temporary arrangement." She shifted Connor to her shoulder and patted him on the back gently with her palm while he sucked noisily on his fist.

"Absolutely." He despised anything temporary. It implied chaos and a lack of uncertainty—more scenarios that he despised. Sure, he didn't have a permanent job yet, although his advisor indicated Alta Vista would probably hire him. If not for a job in Merritt's Crossing, then for their new wind farm in Wyoming. Did she care if he left town?

Connor twisted in her arms and strained for the airplane he'd left on the floor earlier. His babbling escalated until she relented and set him on the floor beside her.

"I—I think it's best for all of us if we focus on Connor and try to be just friends." Her brow furrowed as she smoothed her hand across the top of Connor's head.

Just friends. The death spiral of all romantic relationships. Gage gritted his teeth. While he'd hoped the conversation might play out differently, he wasn't going to let her see she'd crushed his hopes. "You're right."

Oh, it about killed him to agree with her.

"It was just one kiss—hardly a commitment." Her casual words felt like another knife to his heart. It wasn't *just* a kiss. It was quite possibly the best first kiss of all first kisses. How could she dismiss it so easily?

"I'm genuinely sorry if I did anything that made you feel uncomfortable." Didn't he get credit for falling on the proverbial sword?

"I didn't feel coerced." Her tight smile returned, along with her impenetrable shield. Man, keeping him at arm's length was definitely her superpower.

"Good." He linked his arms across his chest. While he'd put off telling her about Ryan's parents because he thought it might hurt her, now he didn't care. If she morphed into all-business mode, then he'd do the same. All he wanted to do now was deliver the news and get out of there as quickly as possible.

He shot a quick glance at Connor, who'd reclaimed the airplane and sat nearby, sucking on the wing. "I need to let you know that Ryan's parents responded to my message. They'd like to visit as soon as possible."

Her porcelain skin went white and her chin dropped.

So maybe he could've eased into that announcement. "They live in Illinois, and as soon as I give them the go-ahead, they'll buy plane tickets."

Skye's Adam's apple bobbed as she swallowed hard. "H-how… I mean— When do you— How soon will they be here?"

His gut twisted. This hurt her more than he expected.

"I imagine it depends on the price of tickets and if there are seats available. They have friends in Denver they can stay with, or I can offer to let them stay in my extra bedroom. You won't have to worry about hosting them or anything."

As if that somehow made the whole situation easier. The sheen of moisture in her eyes instantly made him regret he hadn't handled this differently.

"I'm not his legal guardian, so I can't stop them from seeing Connor, but… What does this mean?"

"It means they want to meet their only grandson." He palmed the back of his neck. "That's really all I know."

She glanced down and picked at her thumbnail. "Let me know when they're coming."

"Of course." His gaze traveled to Connor again, and a sickening sensation lodged in his core. What would happen when Gerald and Irene saw Connor? It wasn't like he and Skye had a future together. She'd made that abundantly clear just now. He wasn't prepared to take care of Connor by himself, not when he'd spend forty or more hours a week on a demanding, often-dangerous wind farm. Not that Skye would ever allow him to have custody anyway. So wasn't he doing the right thing by connecting Connor with his grandparents?

He had to get out of there. It hurt too much to think about where all this might lead. He pushed to his feet. "I'll keep you posted. See you tomorrow."

Cold air swirled around Skye as Gage closed the door, sending a shiver down her spine. Connor burst into tears and, honestly, she wanted to cry right along with him.

She turned around in time to see him crawl after Gage, then slap his palm against the closed door, sobbing.

Her vision blurred with fresh tears. Not only for Connor, but for the frigid conversation that created a seismic shift in her relationship with Gage. When she'd walked in a few minutes ago and saw Connor nestled in Gage's lap, reading a book, some rogue wave of domestic longing had crashed over her. With Gage in his faded jeans and gray sweatshirt that read Navy, a very attractive hint of stubble clinging to his jaw—it was a powerful image that offered a glimpse of a future she'd never imagined. Suddenly she was questioning her decision to never be a mom, and everything she'd rehearsed and planned to say about their kiss felt...wrong.

But she'd said it all anyway. Telling him the kiss was a mistake and holding fast to her boundaries didn't offer the satisfaction she'd hoped for. Instead she felt empty. Alone. This was what she wanted, right? Her independence, the career opportunities she deserved, freedom from a man who tried to diminish her dreams with his harsh words? Then why did she long to fling herself on the floor and mimic one of Connor's epic tantrums? She touched her fingers to her lips. Maybe because she couldn't forget how Gage's kiss made her feel. Safe. Cherished. Respected.

She stood and crossed to the foyer, then gently pulled Connor into her arms. "It's okay, buddy. He'll be back tomorrow."

Connor arched his back, resisting her attempts to comfort him. She carried him into the kitchen, hoping the suggestion of a snack might help, but he only wailed and pushed against her, trying to get free.

"Everything okay?"

Skye turned away from the pantry. Mom walked slowly toward them and stopped next to the dining room table, bracing her hands on the back of the chair. "He's mad because Gage left."

"I guess it's good he cries when the babysitter leaves." Mom smiled. "That's how you know you've got a good one."

Skye ignored the comment and set Connor at her feet, then pulled out the bottom cabinet drawer. "Look. Lots of containers. Want to play?"

He shook his head and screamed until his face was dark red and tears tracked down his cheeks. Oh brother. Skye dragged the cuff of her sweater across her cheeks to staunch her own tears. Anxiety and frustration churned inside as she tried to think of a way to get Connor to stop crying.

"Are you all right, sweetheart?" Mom gingerly pulled out a chair and sat down.

"Let me help him first." Skye couldn't think straight, or tell her mom what was going on, when he was so upset. She poured Cheerios into a plastic bowl with a handle and slotted lid. "Connor, look." She knelt beside him and gently shook it to get his attention. "Would you like Cheerios?"

He drew a ragged breath, then cautiously stuck his chubby hand inside the container. It took him a minute to figure it out, but he eventually managed to get some cereal into his mouth.

"Very good." Skye praised him, and his toothy grin made her heart ache. Once his grandparents saw him, they wouldn't want to let him out of their sight.

What was she going to do?

Relieved he was occupied and mostly quiet, she joined her mother at the table.

"Tell me what happened." Mom's hand clasped hers.

"Gage says Ryan's parents want to see Connor. They're making arrangements to come from Illinois."

"Oh dear."

"I—I'm afraid they'll want to take him." Skye barely choked out the words. "We aren't his legal guardians. If McKenna's not here, how will we stop them?"

"Let's not jump ahead." Mom's eyes glistened with tears. "This is all quite a shock, and I don't blame you for being upset."

Skye pulled her hand free and reached for a box of tissues. "There's more."

Mom's brow arched. "Go on."

"Gage and I, we, um, we kissed the other night. After Bethany and Allen's party."

"And that makes you cry?"

"I told him it shouldn't have happened." Shame crept over her. "I think that hurt his feelings."

Mom nodded. "I'm sure it did. Do you feel kissing him was a mistake?"

"The timing is all wrong. This—" She swept her hand in a circle. "What we're all doing for Connor feels temporary. What's going to happen when McKenna finally comes back, Gage gets a job offer and I go back to Denver?"

Her mother flinched.

Oh no. Skye's stomach plummeted. Mom thought she'd planned to stay? "Mom. You knew I was going back to Denver, right? That was our plan all along. I mean, I've already talked to my boss about this new promotion, and he says I'm one of the top candidates, so—"

"That was your plan," Mom interrupted, avoiding Skye's gaze as she picked at a loose thread in the quilted lavender place mat. "I guess I thought things were going so well you might change your mind."

"Going well?" Skye stared in disbelief. "Connor was kicked out of day care, we're relying on Aunt Linda and a stranger to help babysit, McKenna hasn't been heard from in weeks and the store—"

Whoa. Too much information. She clamped her mouth closed.

Mom's chin shot up, eyes wide. "What about the store?"

Skye's heart pounded.

"Skye." Mom's tone grew stern. "What's wrong with the store?"

Connor screeched, and Skye heard his palms slapping the linoleum as he crawled closer.

"I was going to wait until the end of the month to tell you." Skye's voice trembled.

"Tell me what?"

Connor grabbed Skye's leg and tried to stand, his little brow furrowed.

She couldn't move—paralyzed by the fear in Mom's eyes. "There isn't much money in your account, Mom. I—I don't know what Dad led you to believe, but you're not making enough to cover the utility bills."

Mom buried her face in her hands and started to sob. Connor grunted and pulled to a stand for the first time ever. Skye tried to smile at him through her blurred vision, and he began to cry, too.

They were a mess. A brokenhearted hot mess. She had no idea what to do about it, either.

Chapter Ten

Gage paced his apartment like a caged animal on Friday afternoon, anxiously awaiting Gerald and Irene's arrival. While he'd anticipated at least a week before their visit, they'd purchased tickets for the first available flight. He and Skye and her family had all of forty-eight hours to adjust to the announcement that they were coming for a weekend visit and expected to spend quality time with Connor.

Gage's stomach clenched. What if he couldn't meet their expectations? What if Connor refused to pay any attention to them? What if they announced more surprises, like further plans to be involved in Connor's life? The what-ifs were eating him alive.

It might've helped to talk with Skye about his concerns, but after his painful conversation with her about their never-should-have-happened kiss, he'd kept their interactions perfunctory. Polite. Respecting her boundaries was all he could do, because dwelling on their fleeting moment of happiness hurt too much. He wasn't the man for her, he reminded himself. It was best if he focused on keeping his word to Ryan and making sure Connor's needs were met.

He blew out a long breath and made a quick pass through the kitchen, stopping to move the vase of fresh flowers from the counter to the center of the table. Stepping back, he admired its new location. There. Irene seemed like a lady who'd appreciate a nice touch, and the woman who owned the new flower shop in town convinced him to go with the pink tulips.

Why are you trying so hard?

Regret. Fear. An intimidating mix of both. While the goal of the weekend focused on introducing them to Connor, he also anticipated a difficult conversation about Ryan's death. A shiver coursed down his spine. He didn't want to go there, either.

He continued down the hall for one last quick sweep of the guest room he'd hastily pulled together. Clearing out the last of the moving boxes, buying new sheets and a comforter, and making sure there were clean towels in the bathroom had kept him occupied the last two nights. Now the reality of hosting Ryan's parents for the weekend hit hard and part of him yearned to find an escape route. He'd mentioned a few motels and a historic bed-and-breakfast in the next town, but they'd declined. Spending time with Connor was their priority and they didn't want to waste time driving back and forth from a motel or their friends' house in Denver.

Lord, please don't let this be a huge mistake.

He breathed the earnest plea, knowing full well he'd let his guilt keep him from much more than superficial prayers lately. It was a heavy burden, yet he'd grown used to the weight of it. Would he ever break free? Was this weekend the first step toward freedom, or the makings of a more complicated scenario involving sweet, innocent Connor?

A firm knock at his door pulled him from his thoughts. With his heart kicking against his ribs, he strode across his apartment and braced for seeing Gerald and Irene again.

"Hey." He offered what he hoped was a welcoming smile as he greeted them. "Come on in."

"Thank you." Gerald Simmons extended his hand. "Nice to see you again, Gage."

"You as well, sir." Gage shook his hand, noting the older man's firm grasp and immaculate purple cashmere sweater layered over a crisp purple checked button-down and wool slacks.

"Once a navy man, always a navy man, huh?" Mr. Simmons chuckled. "No need to call me sir."

"Hello, Mrs. Simmons." Gage stepped back to allow Ryan's parents in. "How was your flight?"

"Not too bad, I suppose. We don't typically fly coach, but on short notice, we had to make do." She patted her carefully styled short blond hair, even though it didn't look like a single strand would have the audacity to rebel. Her pearl earrings and leather handbag hinted at her taste for the finer things in life.

As she followed her husband into the apartment, Gage swallowed hard and closed the door. Ryan had rarely mentioned his parents' affluence—he wasn't one to boast about stuff like that. Their backgrounds hadn't really mattered as enlisted men anyway. Now, though, standing there with Mr. and Mrs. Simmons and without Ryan serving as a buffer, their differences stretched out like a canyon between them.

"Can I get you something to drink? Coffee? Water?

Iced tea?" He smoothed his own hair self-consciously, grateful he'd taken the time to get it cut recently.

Mrs. Simmons's heels clicked on the laminate floor in the entryway, and her fingers fluttered to the buttons on her knee-length beige overcoat as her blue eyes surveyed his sparsely decorated living room. Suddenly he regretted inviting them to stay. This wasn't exactly the Ritz-Carlton. What would she think when she saw the guest room with no pictures on the walls and nothing but a single lamp on the nightstand?

"Nothing for me, thank you." Her smile was tight. "We'd prefer to see Connor as soon as possible."

Gage hesitated. Everything about her tone indicated she expected him to comply with her preferences. He glanced at the digital clock plugged in below his television.

"Connor's probably still napping, and they aren't expecting us until three thirty. Why don't I bring your bags in and give you a few minutes to get settled?"

An awkward silence filled the space between them.

"That sounds like a fantastic idea." Gerald's booming voice echoed off the walls and he clapped Gage's shoulder. "Irene, we'll be right back."

Her pencil-thin brows tented. "I suppose babies do nap, don't they? I'll wait here while you get the bags."

"We'll just be a minute." Gage stepped past her and grabbed his jacket and gloves from his closet. This weekend might be a challenge—for everyone. While he understood grief changed people, especially parents who'd lost their only child, Mrs. Simmons seemed noticeably uncomfortable and out of her element.

As he followed Gerald outside to their luxury rental car, Gage made a mental note to text Skye before he took Ryan's parents to the Tomlinsons' for the first time. If he had any hope of redeeming this situation, he had to drop a few hints. Mrs. Simmons's high expectations and abrasiveness required advance warning.

This was such a bad idea.

Skye trailed behind Connor as he crawled around the living room, casting toys aside and babbling to himself. She gathered the ones he discarded and tucked them back in the wicker basket beside the fireplace. It was a losing battle, trying to keep the house presentable for their guests. Why had she agreed to this meeting with Ryan's parents? Her empathy for their situation had morphed into dread once she found out they were coming. Gage's brief text message a few minutes ago had ratcheted her anxiety to a whole new level.

FYI… Our guests are a bit high-strung.

What did that even mean? The sound of a car pulling into the driveway sent her racing into the powder room in the hallway to check her reflection.

"Mom," she called out, "they're here."

Skye smoothed her hand down the front of her denim dress and quickly touched up her lipstick. Of all the things she'd done concerning Connor's care, she should've refused this request. McKenna wasn't even here—another major milestone and significant responsibility in the life of her son that she'd managed to avoid. It wasn't fair.

After their emergency family meeting last night, Drew had warned her this might lead to a custody battle. She didn't want to believe him but couldn't shake

the ominous feeling looming over her like a storm rolling in off the Front Range. If there was a silver lining
to these clouds, since she'd delivered the news that the
store was in danger of going under, both her brothers
had agreed to take shifts there, so she and Mom could
visit with Ryan's parents.

Mom's deliberate footsteps in the hallway indicated
she was making her way toward the living room.

"You look nice, sweetheart." Mom smiled from the
bathroom doorway. "That dress with those short boots
is so flattering."

"Thank you."

The doorbell rang, and Skye gently scooted past her
mom. "I'll get it."

Thankfully, Mom had graduated from her walker
to using a cane, and her pain had lessened. Skye was
pleased to see she'd put on a new floral blouse, khaki
pants and her nicest beige flats.

Her stomach churned as she picked Connor up and
strode quickly to the door. She hesitated and pressed a
quick kiss to his forehead. He squealed and grabbed a
fistful of her hair.

"It's going to be okay. I promise," she whispered,
more for her benefit than for his.

She opened the door and found Gage on the other
side, standing beside an impeccably dressed older couple. Something indecipherable flashed in his eyes—regret? Empathy? It was gone before she could give it a
second thought, replaced by a cautious smile.

"Hey." He reached out and gave Connor's leg a gentle
squeeze. "How's it going?"

Connor immediately flung out his arms toward Gage
and greeted him with an enthusiastic squeal.

"Hello." Skye strained to keep him from twisting out of her grasp, while forcing herself to welcome her guests. Not that it mattered, as they stood, transfixed, their eyes glued to the baby in her arms. "I'm Skye Tomlinson. You must be Mr. and Mrs. Simmons."

Mr. Simmons recovered his composure and cleared his throat. "Yes, yes. Hello, I'm Gerald. This is my wife, Irene."

Moisture glistened in Mrs. Simmons's eyes and her hand trembled as she grasped her husband's elbow.

"Please, come in." Skye moved back so they could all come inside. Connor's face puckered, and his mood threatened to shift. The longer she withheld him from Gage, the greater the risk of an epic meltdown. "Here." Panicked, she thrust him into Gage's arms. "Maybe it's better if you hold him."

"No problem." Gage grinned and gently swooped Connor into the air with a dramatic gasp. "Who wants to play airplane? This guy!"

Connor rewarded him with a belly laugh that softened the tension immediately.

Skye wanted to hug Gage but clasped her hands in front of her instead. "Mr. and Mrs. Simmons, I'd like for you to meet my mother, Rhonda Tomlinson."

Mom stepped forward and they exchanged pleasant greetings, although Mr. and Mrs. Simmons couldn't stop staring at Connor.

"He has Ryan's eyes, doesn't he?" Mrs. Simmons's smile wobbled as she glanced at her husband.

"Sure does." Mr. Simmons's voice was thick with emotion and he tracked Gage and Connor as they moved into the living room and closer to the toys.

"Please, make yourselves comfortable." Mom gestured toward the living room sofa. "Can we take your coats? Would you like some coffee or hot tea?"

"Hot tea sounds lovely." Mrs. Simmons slipped out of her wool overcoat and handed it to Skye. "Thank you."

Skye graciously took their coats and hung them up, trying not to think about how much Mrs. Simmons must've spent on her peach silk blouse and off-white linen trousers. The designer handbag she clutched probably wasn't a knockoff, either. Did McKenna know anything about Ryan's parents and their obvious wealth? Was she the one who reached out to them?

McKenna. Skye sighed. The girl had left a path of destruction wider than a tornado barreling across the High Plains. Maybe she wasn't coming back. And even if she did return, was she capable of being the mother Connor needed?

With her stomach in knots, Skye hurried into the kitchen, leaving Mom and Gage to handle the awkward small talk. Connor would undoubtedly remain the star of the show, at least until he threw a fit, giving her a few minutes to fix the tea. While she waited for the water in the electric kettle to boil, she arranged a tray of cookies Mom had somehow acquired and put cream and sugar in the china serving set reserved for special occasions.

She cringed. Why did she feel the need to impress Ryan's parents anyway? Was it her irrational compulsion to prove she was worthy of caring for Connor? That they hadn't messed him up in some way?

"Need any help?" Gage's deep voice pulled her from her thoughts.

She turned from the refrigerator to find him hovering at the end of the counter, hands tucked casually in his khaki pants pockets, while his presence seemed to fill the whole kitchen. The familiar scent of his woodsy aftershave wafted toward her, bombarding her with memories of their recent kiss. She immediately tamped those down. *Focus.*

"Where's Connor?"

His lips curved into a knowing smile, revealing a dimple she found hard to ignore. *Cue the butterflies.*

"I'm letting Irene hold him. Don't panic."

As predicted, her abdomen stirred with the unmistakable flitter she desperately longed to control. This wasn't the time to think about the mixture of warmth and amusement filling those hazel eyes of his, or the muscular curves of his upper arms, still quite evident even though he wore a moss green sweater. *Enough!*

She stubbornly tipped her chin. "I'm not panicking."

He arched a brow and held out his hands for the serving tray she'd loaded. "If you say so. Let me carry that for you."

Didn't he share her concerns about what Mr. and Mrs. Simmons might want? Or was this all part of his plan to make good on his promise to Ryan? She opened her mouth to ask him, but Connor burst into tears in the other room, and her heart rate sped as she brushed past Gage and rushed to Connor's rescue.

Gage carefully lowered the tray onto the table, then shot a quick glance over his shoulder. Mr. and Mrs. Simmons sat on the sofa, wearing stricken expressions, while Skye braced a distraught Connor against her shoulder, swaying gently to comfort him.

His breath caught as he discovered the trickle of blood oozing from Connor's mouth.

"Gage, can you get some paper towels or napkins,

please?" Mrs. Tomlinson's voice remained calm, but the look in her eyes prompted him to act quickly.

Gage grabbed a handful of napkins from the holder in the middle of the table and crossed the room to Skye and Connor in quick strides.

"I—I don't know what happened." Mrs. Simmons splayed her hand across her chest, while her frantic gaze darted around the room. "One minute I was helping him stand at the coffee table, and the next, he was—"

"He can't stand up on his own yet." Skye's voice was harsh. Unforgiving.

"Here." Gage held a napkin gently to Connor's cheek. "Let's try to stop the bleeding."

"Bleeding?" Skye's eyes widened, and she shifted Connor into her arms for a better look. He wailed louder, the tears mixing with the blood staining his cheek.

"It's not as bad as it looks." Gage fought to keep his voice calm and cupped his other hand on top of Connor's head.

"This coffee table with these sharp edges really isn't a good idea." Mrs. Simmons's brow puckered. "He—"

"My late brother-in-law built that table." Mrs. Tomlinson raised her voice to be heard above the crying. "It's never been a problem before, and I raised three children in this house."

Oh boy. Gage clamped his jaw tight. *Here we go.* This was exactly the kind of conflict he'd hoped they'd avoid. He exchanged worried glances with Skye.

"Let's make sure the baby is okay, shall we?" Mr. Simmons stood and moved closer for a more thorough inspection, his weathered brow furrowed. "I've heard mouth injuries bleed more than other types."

Gage nodded. "I've heard that, too."

Connor tried to squirm away, but Gage firmly held the napkin against his gums.

"Shh, it's all right, sweetie," Skye murmured, awkwardly shifting him in her arms. "Let us help you."

"Why don't you sit down?" Mr. Simmons suggested. "It might help him relax a little, too."

Skye hesitated, then moved to the recliner in the corner. Gage followed, kneeling on the floor at her feet. A few minutes later, the bleeding had almost stopped, and Connor had calmed down, too.

Gage handed Connor a favorite plastic ball and attempted to examine his mouth. "I don't think he's missing any baby teeth, although to tell you the truth, I'm not sure how many he had."

"Me, either." Skye rested her cheek against the top of his head. "I'm just glad he's okay."

Gage's heart turned over. For a woman who didn't want to be a mother, she'd certainly reacted the way any mother would when a child was injured. He resisted the urge to give her arm a comforting squeeze and sat back on his heels instead.

"This is exactly why Gerald and I came as quickly as we could—to make sure our grandson was receiving proper care."

Gage felt Skye stiffen and heard her sharp intake of breath. He shot her a warning glance. *Wait.*

"Irene—"

"It needs to be said, Gerald." Mrs. Simmons's ramrod-straight posture and well-manicured hands clasped in her lap made Gage's scalp prickle. "After hearing about the child's mother and her issues, we are deeply troubled about his well-being."

"Excuse me?" Mrs. Tomlinson leaned forward. "What have you heard about Connor's mother?"

Gage's heart pounded. This time he didn't hesitate and reached over and twined his fingers with Skye's. Her skin felt cool to the touch. Much to his surprise, she held on tight.

"Tell them, Gerald." Mrs. Simmons angled her head toward her husband. "Did you bring the letters and the photos?"

"What letters and photos?" Mrs. Tomlinson asked.

Mr. Simmons stood near the fireplace, hands clasped behind his back and his eyes downcast. "When we received Ryan's personal belongings from his apartment in Florida, there were a number of letters and pictures documenting his relationship with McKenna, which I did not bring along, but I'm more than willing to discuss what we've learned."

"Please do." Mrs. Tomlinson frowned, her knuckles white as she gripped her cane's handle.

"We spoke to Ryan's commanding officer once we saw the letters and pictures, and he was the one who revealed to us that Ryan had a child. That was difficult news for us to process, especially in the midst of our grief. We have a lot of questions and concerns, and in the last few months, we've pieced together a rather troubling picture of this young woman's history and...*lifestyle*." Mr. Simmons emphasized the last word, hinting at his disapproval. "While it isn't her fault Ryan never told us about her or the baby, the fact that she isn't here and has never reached out to us only confirms our deepest fears and cements our desire to make sure Connor is receiving proper care."

Gage's mind raced as he processed Mr. Simmons's

statement as well as what he hadn't said. Was he implying that Connor was being neglected, and he and his wife intended to care for Connor permanently? Without thinking, he stroked his thumb over Skye's knuckles, hoping to offer at least a little comfort. He stole a glance from the corner of his eye. Her complexion was flushed, and she glared at Gerald.

"You still haven't mentioned your specific concerns about McKenna. What issues are you referring to?" Skye asked.

Connor's babbling broke the tense silence.

"The email messages and photos she exchanged with our son indicated a lifestyle that revolved around partying, moving from place to place, an inability to hold a steady job. Nothing we've learned about her points to a woman who is able to be a mother."

"As you can imagine, it was extremely painful for us to find out about Connor this way." Mrs. Simmons's fingers glided over the strands of gold necklaces draped around her neck. "Then to learn his mother had abandoned him—I just couldn't rest until I saw for myself that he was all right."

"Despite what you might think about McKenna and my family—" Skye's voice was icy, direct "—I can assure you, we have made every effort to keep Connor safe, and to show him that he is loved."

Mrs. Simmons's thin smile was patronizing. "Have you?"

Whoa. Gage tightened his grip to keep Skye from coming unglued. If she lost her temper now, they'd have zero chance at a productive conversation. "Mrs. Simmons—"

"Perhaps we can all agree to pick this conversation

up again tomorrow," Mr. Simmons suggested. "Thank you for your hospitality. I think we'd better give you all some space."

Relieved, Gage let go of Skye's hand and stood. "Mr. and Mrs. Simmons, why don't I take you to an early dinner?"

They all managed to exchange civil goodbyes, and Gage offered Skye one more apologetic glance before he slipped out the door. The shock and anger in her and her mother's faces knifed at him. He feared she'd never forgive him for engineering this meeting with Ryan's parents and Connor—especially if the situation escalated to an intense dispute over Connor's future.

Chapter Eleven

❧

By Saturday evening, Skye was exhausted. Weary to the bone from dragging Connor all over creation, pretending to be a polite hostess for Mr. and Mrs. Simmons and still reeling from their obvious disapproval of her and her family.

Why was this happening? Hadn't she and her mother and brothers done everything in their power to make sure Connor was loved and cared for? While McKenna might not be fit for motherhood, didn't Mr. and Mrs. Simmons understand that taking him away from everything and everyone he knew was just as harmful?

In a corner booth at an upscale steak house more than an hour from home, Skye gritted her teeth and retrieved Connor's sippy cup after he'd flung it from his high chair. Mrs. Simmons insisted on one last meal together before they flew home in the morning.

"Maybe he's hungry." Mrs. Simmons glanced up from her menu, obviously quite proud of her ability to share her keen insights.

"Or tired. He's not used to skipping his nap." Skye tucked the cup in the diaper bag and handed him his pacifier instead. She wasn't in the mood for unsolicited advice, which Mrs. Simmons had doled out all day.

Satisfied, Connor sucked on it and banged his palms on the tabletop.

"Oh dear." Mrs. Simmons grimaced. "Those contraptions aren't ideal. Impacts his overbite. He should really learn to self-soothe."

"A baby who has lost both his parents should learn to self-soothe? I suppose you'd prefer he suck his thumb?" Skye forced a smile. "That contributes to a need for orthodontia later in life as well, and it's difficult to wean."

Gage nudged her leg with his own under the table. She nudged him back more forcefully. Seriously? He wanted her to behave after all they'd endured this weekend?

"What are you planning to order?" Mr. Simmons perused his menu, reading glasses perched on the end of his nose. "Skye, do you have a recommendation?"

She flipped her menu closed. "I'm having the vegetable soup and salad combo."

Gage shifted in his seat beside her. She sneaked a glance. Was he holding in a laugh? She didn't feel like steak and wasn't a fan of seafood and, frankly, didn't have much patience left. They'd insisted on the restaurant. Why did they need her input? Too bad Mom had bowed out gracefully and stayed home tonight— she'd be much better at defusing the tension blanketing their booth.

"Skye, I don't blame you for being protective, but I hope you know we want what's best for Connor, too." Mrs. Simmons's pinched expression morphed into one of sadness. "He is our only remaining connection to our son."

From the corner of her eye she saw Gage stiffen at the mention of Ryan. While she empathized with the older couple seated across from her, as well as with Gage and all they'd lost, she couldn't justify letting them have custody of a baby who'd already endured significant losses, too.

The waiter arrived to take their orders, saving her from articulating her thoughts. At least for now.

"Do you want to feed him while we wait for our meal?" Gage asked quietly. "I can go ask for some warm water to mix with the formula."

The knots in her shoulders loosened. He was trying to help make a difficult situation a tiny bit easier. "Please."

"I'll be back." Gage slid from the booth and worked his way toward the hostess at the front of the restaurant. Skye pulled out containers of prepared baby food, a bib and a plastic spoon from the diaper bag. It wasn't organic; she'd bought it at the grocery store, and Mrs. Simmons probably would have plenty to say about those choices, too.

"Have you always lived in Merritt's Crossing?" Mr. Simmons asked as she snapped the bib around Connor's neck.

"My parents have lived here their whole lives. I went to college in Fort Collins, then moved to Denver four years ago for a job in pharmaceutical sales."

"Oh, you must be eager to get back," Mrs. Simmons said.

Was she? Skye hesitated, then spooned pureed peaches into Connor's mouth. It was a slower pace here, and she had missed her friends at first. But she'd adjusted to her new routine, and Connor's sloppy kisses and contagious laughter made up for the exhaustion of meeting his needs. The notion of sticking around had crossed her mind for the first time today.

"I'm on leave until my mother fully recovers from knee surgery." Skye left her explanation at that. Honest, yet not oversharing. Who knew what sort of case they were assembling in their efforts to declare her family unfit to care for Connor.

A knot constricted her throat at the thought of him being whisked away to Chicago. They wouldn't do that, would they? Did Colorado law allow grandparents to cross state lines and demand visitation rights?

Gage returned and quickly fixed Connor's bottle.

Connor screeched as soon as he caught sight of it and pushed Skye's hand away, rejecting the rest of the baby food. The customers seated at the next booth fired disapproving glances their direction.

"How about if I give him the bottle?" Gage leaned close, his breath feathering against her cheek. She wanted to hug him but gave him a weak smile instead. How did he know she was on the verge of tears?

"Please." She maneuvered Connor out of his high chair and onto Gage's lap, then scooted over to make a little more room for the baby in their half of the booth. As Gage settled Connor in the crook of his arm and offered the bottle, another wave of longing crashed over her. Visions of dinner out with friends—instead of her new adversaries—or family meals shared with Mom and her brothers played in her head, all with Gage and Connor beside her.

"While the two of you make quite a pair, I'm sure it's no secret by now that we want custody of Connor." Mr. Simmons crossed his arms across his chest. "When we get back to Chicago, I'll have our attorney prepare the paperwork."

Like a needle to a balloon, his blunt words ruptured her domestic daydream. "Excuse me?"

"We're grateful for all you've done, taking time away from your career, but we don't expect you to rearrange your life to accommodate Connor's needs." Mrs. Simmons trotted out her patronizing smile again. "We have the resources at our fingertips to ensure he is well taken care of."

Sparks ignited in her vision. "What happens when one of you has a health crisis? Who will take care of him when you are no longer able?" Her voice rose an octave. "McKenna hasn't relinquished her parental rights. It's illegal for you to take Connor without her permission."

"Please, calm down." Mr. Simmons held up both palms. "We're not suggesting we take Connor with us now. However, your cousin might be easily persuaded to give up her rights if she knew what we were offering."

Skye wanted to throw up. "You'd bribe her? What court would allow that?"

A muscle in Mr. Simmons's jaw knotted. "No one said anything about a bribe."

"But that's what you meant, right?" Skye dug her fingernails into her palms to keep from pounding her fist on the table. "Tell me, how much would you pay her in exchange for her baby?"

"Skye." Gage's voice carried a warning, but she didn't care. Her body trembled as she leaned across the table.

"I'm sorry that you lost your son. Truly, I am, but taking Connor away from everything he's known isn't in his best interests."

"It is reasonable and prudent for us to have visitation rights," Mrs. Simmons said, her eyes flashing. "You can't keep him from us."

Skye heaved an exasperated breath. "Visitation and custody are not the same."

The waiter arrived with their meals, but Skye wasn't hungry anymore. While Gage attempted to eat, she held Connor and rocked him gently until he fell asleep with his head on her shoulder.

Mr. and Mrs. Simmons ate in silence. The hum of muffled conversation and silverware clinking against plates filtered around them, and Skye took deep breaths in an effort to calm down. She rested her cheek against Connor's head as he released a contented sigh.

They couldn't take him. Even if she exhausted all her resources, and it was an uphill battle, she'd fight to keep Connor with the only family he'd known.

Early the next morning, Gage helped Mr. Simmons load their luggage into the trunk of their rental car while Mrs. Simmons sat in the passenger seat. They'd spent the whole weekend either talking about Connor or arguing about his care, and never once mentioned Ryan. Gage's pulse sped. He was almost out of time.

"I'm sorry." He scraped his hand across his face as Mr. Simmons slammed the trunk lid closed.

"What for?"

"For everything. For not trying harder to save Ryan, for not helping you come to some sort of agreement with Skye and her family about Connor. I—"

"Listen." Mr. Simmons's blue eyes bored into Gage. "We might not agree on much, but I want you to hear me on this. You are not responsible for Ryan's death. Understand?"

"I'm afraid you're wrong, sir. If I had—"

"Son, I read the report until I had it memorized. Spoke to your former commanding officer and the senior enlisted officer numerous times. Human error, limited budget for our defense department and faulty equipment are responsible for Ryan's death. Not you."

No. Emotion clogged his throat. He should've gone back instead of thinking of himself first. If only he'd tried harder, there would've been enough time—

"I can tell you don't believe me." Mr. Simmons's breath left white puffs in the crisp morning air. "Maybe in time you'll be able to accept what I've said and finally forgive yourself. Irene and I certainly don't hold a grudge. The navy has taken appropriate disciplinary action for the men who messed up that night."

"Thank you, sir." Gage barely choked out the words.

"It's unfortunate that you're caught in the middle of this situation with our grandson." Mr. Simmons clapped Gage's shoulder one last time, then circled around to the driver's side. "I realize you don't have any skin in the game, and we appreciate you looking out for him anyway."

"I'm—"

"Thanks again. We'll be in touch." One last tight smile, an obligatory wave from Mrs. Simmons, and they drove away.

Gage stared after them in disbelief. *No skin in the game?* That wasn't true at all. He loved Connor, and he cared deeply about Skye. The realization stunned him—a one-two punch on the heels of Mr. Simmons's candid statements about Ryan's accident.

If only she cared about him. He'd managed to keep the peace at the restaurant last night, and everyone said goodbye on civil terms, but barely. Thankfully Skye and Connor had come separately, otherwise it might've been a very contentious drive to Merritt's Crossing.

He shook his head and strode back inside his apartment. She'd had trust issues before Ryan's parents visited. He could only imagine how she felt after the way they'd behaved. While he hadn't planned the visit, she no doubt blamed him for his role. Add that to the ever-growing list of reasons why she probably wasn't a fan of him.

The week ahead required more studying, completing online assignments and preparing for another climb at the wind farm on Friday. None of that held his attention, though—not with the memory of Skye's reaction at dinner last night still cycling through his brain. She was right. Bribing McKenna to give up Connor was wrong.

He went through the motions of cleaning up the breakfast dishes, his new reality weighing like an elephant on his chest. Maybe Mr. and Mrs. Simmons didn't blame him for Ryan's death, and the navy had ruled it an accident, but he kept circling back around to the fact that Connor's life was forever altered by the events of that day.

After throwing in a load of laundry, he dressed for church. On the way to Merritt's Crossing Community Church, he prayed and asked for guidance. Doubts threatened his confidence, though. The situation seemed impossible to resolve—at least the resolution he hoped for—he and Skye and Connor all together.

In the parking lot, he steered his truck into an empty space as Laramie climbed out of her car nearby and then lifted a baby from a car seat—Connor? He glanced around the parking lot. Where was Skye? He cut the engine and hurried to catch up.

"Laramie," he called after her. "Hang on."

She turned and smiled. Connor's eyes widened, and he opened and closed his fist in a clumsy wave.

Gage's steps faltered. "Nice waving, little dude."

"Hey, Gage." Laramie shifted Connor in her arms. "How's it going?"

"Not great." He palmed his neck. "Did Skye tell you about last night?"

"She did. Which is why I sent her for a short retreat."

"What do you mean? Where is she?"

"I'm taking care of Connor today, Drew is at home with Mrs. Tomlinson and we sent Skye to Denver."

"Oh." He tried not to let his disappointment show. It was great she was getting away to recharge, but he also wanted to see her. To make sure she was all right, and to talk about what might happen next.

"You didn't hear this from me, but her spa appointment is finished at three thirty." Laramie grinned. "I bet she wouldn't mind if you were waiting outside to take her to an early dinner."

He hesitated. "Are you sure she isn't sick of me?"

Connor babbled incessantly, drawing the attention of curious onlookers on their way into the church. What if Skye was angry that he surprised her? Maybe she wanted to be alone and as far away as possible from anything that reminded her of their emotionally draining weekend.

"One more teeny, tiny hint. There's a restaurant near Washington Park that she adores." Laramie fumbled for her phone. "I've made a reservation already. Give me a second, and I'll text you the addresses for the spa and the restaurant."

Gage swallowed hard. Dinner reservations. Picking her up at the spa. This had the potential to go off the rails if Skye wasn't pleased with him hijacking her plans. "If you're sure—"

"Trust me." Laramie gave him a playful shove. "Now, go."

"All right, all right." He jogged back to his truck, a smile tugging at his lips. What was the worst that could happen? Skye wasn't shy about speaking her mind. If she didn't want to go to dinner, she'd make her feelings known. More than anything, he desperately wanted to redeem this weekend and prove to her that no matter what happened with Connor, he wanted to be with her.

Chapter Twelve

"Thank you so much." Skye smiled at the attendant behind the front desk at the spa. "Everything was wonderful."

"So glad you enjoyed it." The young woman handed her a receipt. "We hope to see you again soon."

"Me, too." Skye dropped the receipt in her purse and tried not to think about how much the massage and facial cost. It was well worth it. This was the most relaxed she'd felt since, well, since she'd gone to Merritt's Crossing. Her limbs felt loose and fluid, and the muscles between her shoulder blades weren't scrunched in tense knots anymore. She'd forgotten how good it felt to be pampered, if only for a short time.

She looped her scarf around her neck, shouldered her purse, then stepped outside. While snow still edged the sidewalks, the concrete was bare and the blue sky stretched overhead with hardly a cloud in sight. The midafternoon sunshine on her face offered a hint of warmth. Maybe spring wasn't far away after all.

As she rounded the corner of the building, her steps

faltered at the sight of a familiar blue pickup parked nearby.

"Oh my." Her breath hitched. Gage leaned against the driver's side, one long denim-clad leg crossed over the other, with a bouquet of daffodils wrapped in brown paper in his arms. In his leather jacket and aviator sunglasses, his handsome features were more striking than ever.

"Hey." He straightened to his full height and removed his sunglasses. She strode closer, stopping in front of him.

"What are you doing here?"

"Can't a guy surprise a lady every once in a while?" He held out the flowers. "These are for you."

She took the bouquet, noting the way her pulse did a subtle *blip-blip-blip* as his fingers grazed hers. "Thank you. They're lovely."

"You're welcome."

"You didn't have to drive all the way to Denver to bring me flowers." She tilted her head to one side. "Didn't anyone tell you there's a new flower shop in Merritt's Crossing?"

"But you're not in Merritt's Crossing, so where's the fun in that?"

Her heart cartwheeled at his flirtatious banter.

"If you knew where to find me, were you a part of this covert operation to get me out of town?"

"I wish." He reached over and tucked a strand of hair behind her ear. "You deserve a break."

She shivered at his touch but didn't step back. His imposing presence didn't intimidate her like when they'd first met.

"If you're free, I'd love to take you to dinner. Laramie set us up with a reservation at one of your favorite places."

Skye smiled. Laramie. Her bold attempt at matchmaking was impressive. She glanced down at her yoga pants, T-shirt and ballet flats. "I'm not really dressed appropriately for dinner."

"That's debatable." He held her gaze. "I think you look wonderful."

Warmth heated her cheeks. "Thank you. I'd still rather change into something nicer than this."

"So that's a yes, then?" he asked, his expression hopeful.

"Yes."

"Good." He smiled. "I hope it's a better experience than our last visit to a nice restaurant."

Laughter bubbled up. "Me, too." She wrinkled her nose. "You don't think I was too childish?"

"Not at all." His eyes searched her face. "I thought you did a wonderful job speaking your mind. Connor's fortunate to have you in his corner."

Her heart hammered. She wanted to trust him. She really did. He hadn't given her any reason not to. He'd cared for Connor and helped Mom so selflessly. Inviting him to her apartment a few blocks away while she changed clothes was too forward, though.

"What's wrong? You look worried." He glanced down and dragged the toe of his boot against the snow-crusted parking lot. "I shouldn't have assumed you'd want to have dinner with me."

"It's—it's not that. I do want to have dinner with you." She met his cautious gaze. His expression looked guarded. Did he think she might blow him off? "I was trying to figure out the logistics, because parking can be a challenge. If I text you the address of a coffee shop in my neighborhood, will you meet me there in thirty minutes?"

"Are you sure?"

She nodded. "We can grab coffee and walk through the park before dinner."

His wide smile made warmth and excitement spread through her chest. This wasn't how she'd planned to spend the rest of her day. Did everything always have to be the way she wanted, though? Hadn't the last few months taught her there was good in embracing the unexpected? Maybe this spontaneous outing was worth the risk. Maybe *he* was worth the risk.

Gage sank into an overstuffed chair in the corner of a busy Denver coffee shop. He'd sensed Skye's discomfort at inviting him to follow her to her apartment and tried not to let it bother him. She was smart. Cautious. Accustomed to life in a midsize city. But he couldn't ignore the underlying current of uncertainty that sometimes resurfaced, flashing across her features before she quickly regained control. What had happened to her?

He dug his fingers into the armrests of his chair and tried not to think about what kind of a man might treat such a beautiful woman poorly. How could he convince her that he cared deeply and admired her strength and confidence?

The door opened, and he glanced up, hoping it was Skye. Instead, three young women strode in, all glued to their phones. A coffee grinder rumbled behind the counter, followed by the hiss of steam from the espresso machine. Gage surveyed the modern decor, people sitting at tables hunched over their laptops and the line of customers snaking from the register.

Outside, a steady stream of cars, pedestrians and even a few bike riders filled the city streets. This was quite a change from the slower pace of Merritt's Crossing. The buildings around the coffee shop looked like a mix of high-end condos and restored Victorian homes—the kind of place where young career-oriented single people might live to be close to the amenities and night-life of downtown, without giving up the vibe of a neighborhood.

Did Skye enjoy living here? She'd only committed to a short stay with her mom, and her leave from her job was probably coming to an end. What did that mean for Connor? For him? It seemed unlikely that Gerald and Irene would gain custody of Connor quickly, but if they did, might Skye resume her life here right where she'd left off?

All these questions only added to his unsettling discomfort. He shifted in his seat, bouncing his knee up and down, and stared out the window impatiently. When he caught a glimpse of Skye walking along the sidewalk in a floral-print dress, knee-high brown leather boots, with a coat draped over her arm and small purse dangling from her shoulder, his heart thrummed in his chest. Her long hair bounced across her shoulders as she walked, and he had to grit his teeth as two men passed her and offered appreciative glances.

Oblivious to them, she met Gage's eyes through the window and smiled. He stood and met her at the door.

"I'm sorry to keep you waiting," she said, joining him inside. "A friend is staying at my apartment while I'm away, and I felt rude rushing back out so quickly."

"No problem." Gage's shoulder brushed against hers as they took their places at the back of the line. "I'm a great people watcher."

"There's a lot to see compared to Merritt's Crossing."

Gage resisted the urge to ask which she preferred—Denver or Merritt's Crossing. He was afraid he might not like the answer.

A few minutes later, to-go cups in hand, they left the coffee shop.

"Feel like a walk?" Skye asked. "There's a nice trail around the lake a couple of blocks from here."

"Sounds good."

They walked in companionable silence, until his regrets from their visit with Ryan's parents threatened to steal all the joy of being alone with Skye. "I'm so sorry that our interaction with Gerald and Irene was contentious. I feel partly responsible for that."

She glanced up at him, eyes round. "Why?"

His mouth felt as dry as sandpaper as he forced the words out. "Helping Connor connect with his grandparents felt like a positive step in keeping my promise to Ryan. If I'd known what they'd propose once they got here, and what that would mean for you and your family, I—I would've given it more careful thought."

He stared at the lake coming into view and braced for Skye's reaction.

"I think you did what anyone in your situation would do—help two grieving people connect with their grandson."

The tightness in his chest loosened. "Really?"

Skye nodded. "I'm not thrilled about their strategy for being more involved in Connor's life, but I don't blame you for their actions or the things they said while they were here."

They walked in silence and then she glanced at him again. "If you don't mind my asking, why have you remained so loyal to Connor through all of this? Is it still just about keeping a promise to Ryan?"

"It's more…complicated." The anxiety of reliving those last horrifying moments sent a shiver down his spine. The darkness from the loss of power belowdecks, men scrambling to escape the damaged compartments, the acrid scent of smoke…

"The day Ryan died, we were at sea, after a long day of training exercises on our sub. I was getting ready to go to sleep, and Ryan was standing watch because we'd traded shifts. There was a horrible fire—"

His heart pounded in his chest. "I—I tried to get to Ryan's station, but the fire was spreading, and I didn't have time…" He trailed off, his throat clogged with emotion. "Ryan and five other guys didn't make it out. I've always blamed myself because I was the one who traded shifts with Ryan."

Skye gently squeezed his arm. They stopped walking, and she faced him. "I am so sorry. It must've been awful."

"Thank you." He looked away, wishing he hadn't forgotten his sunglasses in his truck. Letting her see his anguish scared him. "In the eyes of the navy and even according to Gerald and Irene, the accident was blamed on human error and equipment failure, due to budget shortfalls, but I can't help thinking that maybe if I'd tried harder, acted a split second sooner, Ryan might still be here. If I hadn't asked Ryan to trade shifts with me, Connor would have a dad."

"Look at me." Her voice was tender, and the comfort of her fingers still wrapped around his forearm drew his gaze to meet hers. "You can't keep carrying the weight of that guilt. It's going to eat you up inside. Like you said, the cause was equipment failure, so how could you have prevented that?"

He searched her face. She was right; he couldn't. Yet he didn't know how to surrender it, either. "It's not that simple."

Empathy filled her eyes. "I know," she whispered.

They stood there staring at one another, unspoken words lingering in the space between them. His arms ached to pull her against him, to ask her to share the burden she carried yet kept buried deep, as well. Instead, her hand dropped to her side, he tore his gaze away and they resumed their walk. He wouldn't force her to share, because he was afraid she'd retreat and never allow herself to be vulnerable.

Gage blamed himself. It all made sense now—his quest to find McKenna and Connor, his unwavering determination to be a part of Connor's life and his selfless care of the baby. Skye's heart swelled. She knew what it was like to carry blame like that. If she'd made better choices, maybe she wouldn't bear the emotional scars of a controlling boyfriend. If her family hadn't enabled McKenna or let the feud between Dad and Uncle Kenny fester, life might've turned out differently for her cousin. Connor, too.

"What are you thinking about?" Gage gently nudged her elbow as they left the city streets and strode down the paved path circling the lake.

The first signs of spring dotted the ground between

them and the water. New daffodils and crocuses poked up, and patches of grass had emerged in places where the sun had melted away the snow. Could these symbols of spring and renewal signal a change in her own life, too?

She sighed. "Thinking about McKenna and the past and if we will ever break free from the stuff that weighs us down. What's going to happen to Connor."

Gage chucked his coffee cup in a trash can. "If you don't mind my asking, what's weighing you down?"

She stared across the lake. A breeze rippled the blue-gray water, and a shiver raced down her spine.

Gage's arm looped around her shoulders. "Are you cold?"

The concern in his voice and the warmth of his gaze cracked something open inside, and she let herself lean into him. "Scared."

They stopped walking and he gestured to a wood-and-wrought-iron bench facing the water. "Want to sit for a few minutes?"

She nodded. Once they sat down, she set her half-finished coffee and her purse beside her, then draped her coat around her shoulders. Gage rested his arm across the back of the bench without touching her. She wanted to lean into him again but settled for her leg barely resting against his. The warmth of the sun at their backs would have to be enough.

"Is this okay?"

Her mouth was as dry as cotton and blood rushed behind her ears. Gage waited patiently, his concerned gaze trained on her. The words piled up in her head, like cars on the freeway during rush hour. Where to begin? It wasn't easy to share her story, which was probably why she hadn't told anyone other than Laramie and her therapist. "I— The guy I dated a couple years ago, he wasn't very good to me."

"What happened?"

"At first, everything seemed fine. Great, actually. He was kind and funny and very much a gentleman. There were gifts delivered to my apartment, and he took me to some of the best restaurants—" She glanced down and picked at a loose thread on the cuff of her sleeve. "I should've seen the signs. Maybe I didn't want to."

"What kind of signs?"

"He had a temper and an intense competitive streak. Most of the time it was directed at other people— sports, a competitor in a video game, a heated political debate with a friend at dinner. Occasionally, he'd say something really harsh to me, especially if I'd had a productive week at work or earned a bonus or something."

"I really don't like where this is going," Gage said.

She plowed on, staring straight ahead. "One night we went back to my apartment after dinner out with friends, and I invited him in to watch the rest of a football game. I made one comment about an assistant coach's appearance—he was very handsome—and I should've kept my opinion to myself. My boyfriend came unglued."

Gage's fingers gently cupped her shoulder and he scooted closer. "I am so sorry."

Her stomach churned, and her fingers trembled as the memories came rushing back. "He was yelling and making demeaning comments about women." Still avoiding his gaze, she smoothed her hand over her skirt. "Most of the time, I can focus on the positive and ignore the memory of the horrible things he said. But I'll never forget the way he made me feel. Like I was nothing."

"Hey." Gage touched his fingertip to her chin and tenderly angled her face toward his. "You are a beautiful, intelligent woman with a generous heart and an unwavering inner strength. Don't let anyone tell you otherwise."

Her heart soared at his kind words. "Thank you," she whispered.

"You deserve to be treated well." His eyes had darkened, and they scanned her face, before landing on her mouth.

Her breath caught, and she quickly pushed to her feet. "It's a beautiful day. Do you want to keep walking around the lake?"

Disappointment flashed in Gage's eyes before he pushed to his feet and joined her. "Sure."

She winced and turned away. Kissing Gage again now would only complicate matters. While she was determined to do what was best for Connor, she hadn't declined the promotion at work. It was still an option, as long as she found a day care with space available in Denver. If her time in Merritt's Crossing was coming to an end, she didn't want to mislead Gage. Between working full-time and caring for Connor and Gage starting his new job, they wouldn't have space in their busy lives for one another.

She stole a quick glance at him as they walked in silence. Her stomach twisted in knots. While she'd started thinking about staying in Merritt's Crossing permanently, spending the afternoon in Denver made her acutely aware of how difficult it would be to resign from her job and move back home. She'd have to tell him about her promotion. Soon.

* * *

After dinner, tucked away at a round table in an intimate corner of Skye's favorite bistro, Gage reached across the white tablecloth and took her hand. The fantastic food, including the cheesecake they'd just shared, and the flickering candlelight between them blotted out any doubts he might've had about their spontaneous outing. She smiled, and he felt his heart expand.

"I hate to ruin a perfect evening by talking about reality," he said. "But what do you think is going to happen with Connor?"

Her smile faltered. "I'm going to have to hire an attorney. I want to become Connor's permanent legal guardian."

His stomach tightened. "Have you heard from McKenna?"

"I texted her and told her Ryan's parents had come to visit and demanded to see Connor. That got her attention because she finally answered me. She said she was sorry she hadn't been in touch, but she'd checked herself into rehab in Kansas City."

Rehab. Maybe Gerald and Irene weren't so wrong about her after all.

"Do you think she'll come home when she's finished?"

Skye shrugged. "She didn't say. I tried to get her to tell me more, but she ignored the rest of my messages."

"Wouldn't the threat of losing her child motivate her?"

"Maybe in her mind, she already lost him when she left." Skye frowned. "This must seem so ridiculous. You probably had a much different upbringing with a mom, a dad and a golden retriever in your fenced yard."

Her words caught him by surprise. Had he led her to believe that was the case? He scraped some crumbs from the table with his palm and carefully measured his response before he spoke.

"Gage?" She leaned closer. "Did I say something wrong?"

"My mom was a lot like McKenna," he said softly. "That's why I care so much about what happens to Connor—I don't want him to grow up like I did."

Her eyes widened. "I—I didn't know. I'm sorry. What I said sounds so insensitive now."

"It's all right. I didn't exactly advertise my past."

"But it's the driving force behind your concern for Connor."

He nodded. "That and my promise to Ryan that I'd make sure Connor had a strong male role model in his life."

Skye leaned her elbow on the table and rested her chin on her hand. "I'd say you've honored your promise. We appreciate everything you've done, and Connor adores you."

"I think he's pretty awesome, too." Gage swallowed hard against the emotion clogging his throat at the mention of the little boy, who now took up so much space in his heart. How would he ever be able to say goodbye? What if he'd worked hard to keep his promise to Ryan but lost Connor after all?

The waiter approached to collect the check, and Gage slid his credit card into the leather folder and handed it to him.

"Thank you for dinner, and for coming to Denver to see me." Skye's eyes glistened. "It means a lot."

"You're welcome." This sounded like the beginning

of a goodbye. A rush of adrenaline pulsed through him. He didn't want it to end. Sure, they'd see each other in a couple of days when he came to the house to watch Connor, but he sensed it wouldn't be the same. "Can I walk you back to your car? We've got a two-hour drive ahead of us, right?"

"Oh." She averted her gaze and reached for her phone. "I'm actually staying the night at my apartment. I have a breakfast meeting with my boss about a promotion he'd like me to consider."

Her words landed like a gut punch. A promotion. Her boss. His mind raced, and reality closed in fast. "You're planning on moving back here soon?"

She glanced up from her phone. "Right after Easter. My leave is almost over."

Right after Easter. A month from today.

"Wait. What about Connor?" He clenched his fists in his lap. What about *him*? Had today meant nothing?

"I'm not sure McKenna will come home, or if she even wants to. When I move back, I'll have to enroll Connor in day care full-time because he can't stay with my mom or my brothers long-term. I'm assuming Ryan's parents will sue for custody or visitation, but it will be several months until there's a hearing."

The waiter returned with Gage's credit card and receipt. "Thank you, sir. Enjoy your evening."

"Yeah, thanks." Gage dismissed him, still distracted by Skye's news.

"What about the furniture store? Is your brother going to take over when you leave?" It wasn't any of his business, really, but he couldn't fathom her leaving Merritt's Crossing or the budding relationship they'd forged in recent weeks. How could she dismiss him so easily?

She slipped her arms into her coat. "I've told Mom and my brothers that the furniture store isn't viable financially. We are trying to come up with a plan to save the business, but it isn't going to be easy. Mom and Drew think we can still turn things around, especially with so many new families moving here."

He slumped back in his chair. She'd thought of everything. No mention of him, though.

"My Uber's waiting outside." Skye stood and looped her purse strap over her shoulder. "Walk out with me?"

"Yeah, sure." He stood and grabbed his jacket, trying to conceal his hurt.

Outside, a gray sedan idled at the curb.

"That's my ride." Skye turned, went up on tiptoe and pecked him on the cheek.

"Skye—" The intoxicating scent of her perfume enveloped him, and he reached for her, his hand barely skimming her jacket sleeve before she pulled away.

She bit her lip and walked backward toward the car. "Thanks again. For everything. See you Tuesday?"

He could only nod, his stomach plummeting as she climbed into the backseat and slammed the door. The driver's turn signal blinked and he waited to merge into the oncoming traffic. Gage shoved his hands in his pockets and stared after her until the car turned the corner and drove out of sight.

Why was he surprised she'd politely reconstructed her protective shield? His efforts to build a relationship with her—something more meaningful than just their mutual concern for Connor—were no match for her fierce need for independence. After spending a day in her world—the trendy shops and boutiques, fantastic restaurants, a lakefront park two blocks away—why would she choose a quiet life in Merritt's Crossing with him? But he wasn't giving up, especially now that he knew McKenna was battling an addiction. He'd fought his whole life to overcome the pain inflicted by his mom's choices, the people who enabled her and the absence of his father. Gage didn't want Connor to suffer like he had. Even if a relationship with Skye wasn't possible, Gage was more determined than ever to be a part of Connor's life.

Chapter Thirteen

"How was your date with Gage?" Laramie sat cross-legged on Mom's sofa and munched on pretzel sticks.

"It wasn't a date." Skye helped Connor into his pajamas with the fire truck pattern. As usual, he tried his best to resist her efforts.

"Um, there were flowers involved, a walk beside the lake and dinner at your favorite restaurant." Laramie ticked each off on her fingertips. "Was there any kissing involved?"

"Nope, no kisses." She helped Connor sit up. "C'mon, buddy. It's time for a bottle of milk."

Connor pressed a sloppy kiss against his chubby hand and flung it in Laramie's direction.

Skye's breath hitched. He was so precious.

"Well, aren't you the cutest thing ever." Laramie's green eyes gleamed as she blew Connor a kiss in return.

Skye picked up the bottle of milk she'd warmed before she'd changed him and sat down near Laramie in the recliner. With Connor snuggled close, she rocked softly and offered him the bottle.

"It's probably about time to wean him from this, but

I just can't." Skye smiled down at him, love and affection spreading through her. These quiet moments with him in her arms, fresh and clean from his bath, had become a part of the day she looked forward to. It was hard to imagine giving that up, especially if she didn't have many bedtimes left with him.

Meeting Mr. and Mrs. Simmons confirmed the truth she'd circled around for several days but refused to admit to anyone—she didn't want Connor to go live with his grandparents, and she didn't want McKenna to come for him. The little boy had won her over and she was terrified of losing him.

"Are you going to share any more details about your not-date with Gage, or am I going to have to fill in the gaps with my imagination?"

Skye forced herself to quit staring at Connor's cherubic face and meet Laramie's curious gaze instead. "It didn't turn out like I'd expected."

Laramie's brow furrowed. "Yeah, you don't seem like someone who had a great time. What happened?"

It was true. She wasn't acting like a woman who'd spent an amazing afternoon and evening with a gorgeous, considerate guy. Tossing and turning in her bed at her apartment last night, she'd mentally rehashed the details, trying to pinpoint when exactly her anxiety spiked. "We had a wonderful time together. The weather was nice, and we had time to process our visit with Connor's grandparents. He told me more about his backstory, and I said some things I—I don't normally share."

"It sounds pretty awesome so far." Laramie reached for her can of soda on the coffee table. "Where did it go wrong?"

"Somewhere between meeting at the coffee shop and dinner, I got really scared." Skye swallowed hard. "Once I was back in the neighborhood, saw the pace of life and stopped by my apartment, I... I don't know. Something was off."

"You started thinking about what you might be missing, didn't you?"

Skye hesitated. How to explain her feelings without sounding totally self-absorbed? "Gage is a wonderful guy, and I can feel myself falling for him. But at the same time, I don't want to lose my independence. I worked hard for my career. My boss is offering me an incredible promotion. On the other hand, McKenna texted me that she's in rehab, and I don't know if she'll ever be back. I love Connor, too. It's more than feeling obligated to do what is best—I want to find a way to be his mom."

Laramie's eyes widened, and she slowly set her drink back on the coaster. "Did you say any of this to Gage?"

Skye shook her head. "I told him about McKenna and the possibility of a promotion, and that I was leaving Merritt's Crossing right after Easter."

Laramie gasped. "But what about him? Doesn't he factor into your future plans?"

Skye sneaked a quick glance toward the hallway. Last she'd checked, Mom was in the extra bedroom working on a quilting project. Skye leaned closer to Laramie and lowered her voice. "What if I have to hire an attorney to keep Ryan's parents from gaining full custody? Who do you think is going to have to pay those fees? The furniture store is struggling. I can't quit my job now."

Laramie bit her lip. "I didn't realize Connor's grandparents wanted to be actively involved in his life."

"They know McKenna isn't in the best shape to be a full-time mother, and money doesn't seem to be an issue, so I expect we'll be in court soon. I don't mind if they want frequent visitation, but I'm afraid what they want is custody. And if McKenna isn't fit to be a mother, why wouldn't the judge rule in their favor?"

"I'm so sorry." Laramie shook her head. "What a mess."

"That's why I started to backpedal with Gage. By the end of the evening, I couldn't get into my Uber fast enough."

"What if you and Gage become a thing? Isn't that an option? Then you'd have a better chance of getting custody."

"We aren't going to 'become a thing,' not after the way I blew him off."

"I don't know," Laramie said softly. "I've seen the way Gage looks at you."

Skye shook her head. "We can't be a couple just so Connor has two parents. That's crazy."

Wasn't it?

Even if McKenna terminated her parental rights, Gerald and Irene weren't going to give up without a legal battle. What if Gage only wanted her if he could have Connor, too?

"Lots of people marry for convenience," Laramie said. "Remember all those mail-order bride novels my grandmother loves to read? It sounds romantic to me."

She glanced down at Connor, who was chugging the last of his bottle, eyelids growing heavy. He was adorable, and she'd learned to care for him and anticipate his needs, and even adapted to his squealing and affection for grabbing her hair. Her heart swelled. She really did love the little guy.

But could she be his mom? Was she ready for that kind of forever commitment?

"I'd better put him to bed." Skye pushed to her feet and set the bottle on the coffee table. "Are you going to hang out for a minute?"

"No, I have to go. I'm house-sitting for a friend, and their puppy's been in his crate for more than two hours." Laramie stood and put on her jacket. "Skye, I really do think Gage cares for you. Regardless of what happens with Connor, I hope you won't let the allure of Denver or your fears ruin a shot at a potentially wonderful relationship."

"I'm not letting fear ruin anything," Skye protested, her tone harsher than she intended.

Hurt flashed in Laramie's eyes. "Talk to you soon."

After Laramie left, pulling the door closed behind her, Skye blew out a long breath and carried Connor to his bedroom. She didn't want to be afraid—afraid of a man trying to control her again, afraid of Connor not having a stable mom or dad, afraid of hurting Gage any more than she already had. Despite all her efforts to be strong and self-sufficient, she felt just as helpless and overwhelmed as ever.

Was this what he really wanted?

Alone at the Tomlinsons' kitchen table, Gage's hand hovered over the green submit icon on his computer screen. He'd just completed his last module for his on-line training certification. One click would send his exam to the instructor and he'd move another step closer to his goal.

His professional goal anyway. On a personal note, he was pretty much a wreck.

What if becoming a wind energy technician kept him from being a part of Connor's life? If Connor moved away—especially to Chicago with the Simmonses—accepting a job in Colorado or Wyoming didn't do him any good. Did keeping his word to Ryan include leading his parents to Connor? Was that genuinely what Ryan wanted? If he did, wouldn't he have made those arrangements or at the very least, told his parents he had a child?

Gage's stomach burned at the thought of Gerald and Irene raising Connor. The little guy's belly laughs and toothy grins, even his feisty side, had worked their way into Gage's heart. Not seeing him take his first steps or hear his first words seemed unimaginable now.

On the other hand, waiting around and letting other people's actions dictate his future wasn't an option, either. McKenna, Ryan's parents and the justice system might all influence where Connor lived next and who he spent time with. Gage had zero control.

Adrenaline surged as he clicked the icon and submitted his exam.

There. At least he could control that.

He returned to a website he'd searched for earlier—the apartment listings for a community closest to the wind farm in Wyoming. It seemed like a nice small town, not too far from Cheyenne. Rent was reasonable, the building looked new and the amenities were better than what he had access to now. He'd even heard rumors that Alta Vista offered a generous signing bonus to new employees.

But it was more than four hours from Denver and

even farther from Merritt's Crossing. Half a day's drive—at least—from Skye, which meant they'd rarely see one another if he moved to Wyoming.

Another tab he'd left open on his laptop drew his gaze back to the screen and his stomach clenched. It was a website featuring the Washington Park area in Denver. For a few glorious minutes, he'd entertained the crazy idea that he and Skye might have a second and a third or even a fourth date. His imagination ran ahead, envisioning another meal at an intimate table in one of her favorite restaurants, her long hair spilling over her shoulders and those gorgeous blue eyes riveted on him, her chin resting on her hand. Later, they'd walk and talk some more, fingers entwined and—

He slammed his laptop closed and scrubbed his hand across his face.

All make-believe. He was an idiot to think he'd legitimately had a shot at a meaningful relationship with Skye. She'd made that clear when she'd rushed to her waiting Uber.

Meeting Skye was an unexpected blessing in his singular quest to find Connor. After spending months focused on his grief and guilt, she was like a burst of sunshine breaking through tumultuous storm clouds. Her obvious distrust had only made him want to prove to her that he was trustworthy. That he wouldn't hurt her.

Instead, she'd wounded him deeply by allowing him to get close, only to push him away. Determined to win her heart, he'd left himself wide-open to her brush-off.

Idiot.

He stood and moved to the sliding glass door and stared out into their backyard, willing the old familiar pain of rejection to go away. Although he'd learned to compartmentalize over the years, Ryan's passing and now his hurt and confusion over Skye dredged up the same emotions he'd tried to stuff deep down.

Rain pelted the crocuses and daffodils poking up near the concrete patio slab and he pressed his palm to the glass.

Why? Why hadn't he seen this coming?

Lord, I trust You. I believe Your ways are better than mine. This still doesn't make any sense, though. Please don't let this innocent child suffer any more than he already has.

The rain fell harder, and while Gage knew his prayers were heard, he didn't feel a sense of peace about Connor or Skye. But standing here feeling sorry for himself wouldn't change anything. Skye and Mrs. Tomlinson were both at the furniture store. They'd finally let him stay with Connor alone. How ironic. Since Connor hadn't woken from his nap yet, Gage needed to make better use of his time. The Wyoming job was only a possibility if he actually applied.

His brain stubbornly refused to fixate on anything other than Skye, though. He pivoted from the window and padded into the kitchen and poured himself another cup of coffee. While her physical beauty had certainly played a role in his initial attraction, her loyalty to her family had both terrified and wooed him.

Since he'd only known the unpredictable and often-frightening roller coaster that was his mother, the Tomlinsons' unwavering commitment to one another seemed foreign at first.

Until he caught himself wondering what it might be like if he was at the center of that devotion.

Unexpected emotion welled up and clogged his throat. He swallowed a sip of the hot liquid, nearly scorching his tongue. Good. If his brain could only process one pain impulse at a time, he'd rather focus on his mouth as opposed to his aching heart.

The fleeting glimpses of Skye's genuine faithfulness to the small number of people she allowed inside her inner circle had made him believe he had somehow earned a place in that circle, too.

And just like every other time he'd put himself out there in a romantic relationship, Skye proved to him that he couldn't have been more wrong.

"Da-da."

Gage froze, coffee mug halfway to his lips, and darted a glance toward the baby monitor on the counter.

"Da-da."

Again. Stronger this time. Connor's voice filtered through the speaker. Gage's pulse sped. That was the closest thing he'd heard to a first word in all the time they'd spent together. He left his mug on the counter and quickly strode to Connor's room.

When he pushed open the door, Connor stood in his crib, chubby hands gripping the rail.

"Da-da!" Connor pointed at Gage and offered that slobbery grin that made Gage almost melt into a puddle. Warmth flooded his chest. Even if it was a coincidence and Connor had no idea what he was saying, it was a bittersweet moment and one he'd always savor, even if he never heard it again.

"Hey, buddy." Gage crossed the bedroom and lifted Connor into his arms. "Let me tell you a story about your daddy."

Chapter Fourteen

Eight days before Easter. Skye tried not to think about her unofficial deadline as she crossed the parking lot, with Connor in her arms wearing sneakers, jeans and a navy blue sweatshirt with a hood he refused to keep on his head.

The blue sky dotted with wispy white clouds arched over the crowd gathering outside of Merritt's Crossing Community Church for the annual Easter festival. While plenty of snow remained, fresh blades of green grass tinged the wheat-colored lawn now sprinkled with hundreds of plastic eggs. Sunshine bathed the whole scene in a golden glow, yet the breeze still carried a bite. Skye was grateful she'd layered her favorite lavender sweater over a white T-shirt and paired tall brown boots with her skinny jeans.

Gage walked beside her, although he said very little. They'd reverted to their businesslike transactions with one another, and once in a while, she caught a glimpse of the hurt lingering in his eyes when he looked at her. It was better this way—pretending their kiss outside

Pizza Etc. and special evening together in Denver had never happened.

He surveyed the people milling about. "Do you know where the babies and toddlers are supposed to go?"

"Over there." Skye pointed to a sign designating age groups. "There's a separate egg hunt for kids two and under."

This felt almost like a family outing. Almost. Could she make a life here? If Gage wanted her? She chased the thought away. Even though McKenna hadn't contacted her again and the Simmonses' attorney hadn't served any papers, Skye still clung to her plans not to stay in Merritt's Crossing. Besides, he didn't say that he wanted to be with her. He'd barely said anything at all.

"Let's get in line. I don't want him to miss out." Gage pressed his hand gently against Skye's back and guided her toward the parents clustered with strollers nearby. Warmth radiated through her at his thoughtful gesture. He wasn't steering or controlling or commandeering the situation. She felt safe, cared for with Gage at her side. It had been a long time since she'd experienced that sense of security and comfort with a man. She braced for the old familiar worry to close in, but this time it didn't come. If she was honest, her feelings toward Gage were beginning to outweigh her desire for accepting the promotion. And Laramie's wise words about not letting fear get in the way of a wonderful relationship had stayed with her. Was Denver truly where she needed to be?

She was reaching into the diaper bag for her phone to take pictures when someone grabbed her arm.

"Skye, she's here." Laramie's voice was breathless.

"What?"

"McKenna. She's here. I saw her getting out of a car."

Skye's stomach plummeted. McKenna was here? With no text or phone call or warning? She looked at Gage. A muscle in his jaw twitched.

"What do you want to do?" he asked.

"Is she—" Skye shifted Connor to her shoulder, as if turning him away might shield him from whatever came next. "Is she with anyone?"

"I don't think so." Laramie glanced over her shoulder. "But she's coming this way."

Longing for reassurance, or maybe just the comfort of his presence, Skye reached over and wedged one hand in the crook of Gage's elbow. He glanced down at her, his eyes filled with uncertainty.

"We'll figure this out," he said, although his expression revealed he was wrestling with his own doubts.

Skye craned her neck to see around Laramie. Sure enough, McKenna wove her way among the people gathering on the lawn, slowing occasionally to speak to someone. All the while her eyes scanned the crowd. As she moved closer, Skye surveyed her appearance, as if some outward sign of her addiction would confirm or deny her worthiness to be a mother. It was dumb and insensitive, but Skye couldn't help it. She needed to know it was safe for Connor to see McKenna.

In jeans with a ripped knee, cowboy boots and a flowery tunic layered under a denim jacket, she looked like a typical twentysomething female at a small-town festival. When she looked up and met Skye's gaze, her steps faltered.

"Hey." McKenna's brown eyes flitted from Skye to Gage and then landed on Connor. Surprise flashed across her features, and then her mouth formed a wobbly smile. "I'm back."

"I see that." Skye choked out the words. "What are you doing here?"

"Skye." Laramie's voice was tinged with warning.

McKenna's gaze narrowed. "I came for my son."

Connor whined and twisted in Skye's arms, as if to see what the delay was all about. He regarded McKenna with a wide-eyed stare.

"Hey, cutie pie." McKenna stretched out her arms. "Come see Mama."

"Wait. Think of the baby. He hasn't seen you in months." Skye angled her body away from McKenna, desperate to reason with her. "Please, don't do this."

"He's mine. I've come all this way like you asked me to, so why won't you let me have my son?"

"Because we're not confident you can handle him," Gage said, his voice low.

McKenna stared at him. "I remember you—you're Ryan's friend." She smirked. "How nice of you to step up and play pretend baby daddy."

Skye sucked in a breath. Her legs trembled, and spots peppered her vision. Even though she'd hoped for weeks that McKenna would come back, so much had changed. She loved Connor like her own, and now she didn't want McKenna to take him.

"McKenna, please." Laramie stepped between them and placed a hand on McKenna's arm. "Why don't we take Connor to the egg hunt—all of us together—and then we can meet afterward and try to work this out?"

"Let go of me." McKenna pulled from her grasp. "I don't need your help, either. Just give me my kid."

"We only want what's best for you and Connor," Laramie said softly.

"You have no right to keep him from me."

"You're right, we don't." Hot tears pricked her eyes as Skye handed Connor to McKenna.

His face crumpled, and he began to cry.

"Do you want his car seat?" Skye swallowed hard against the lump clogging her throat and glanced down at the diaper bag. "Do you have diapers and wipes?"

"Where are you staying?" Laramie asked.

"I've got a place. You don't have to worry." She smiled at Connor and shushed him, awkwardly bouncing him up and down.

He twisted in her embrace and stretched his arms toward Skye.

Her heart cleaved in two. This couldn't be happening.

"You don't really expect us to just let you drive off with a baby, do you?" Gage's voice held a hard edge.

Skye bit her lip, desperate to hold herself together for Connor's sake. She glanced at Gage. He'd straightened to his full, very imposing height and wore a granitelike expression, while his icy gaze bored into McKenna.

McKenna shifted the very distraught Connor to her other shoulder and tipped her chin defiantly. "He's mine. You can't stop me."

"What happens when he won't stop crying? When you blow all your cash on booze and don't have any left for food? Do you even know what he eats?" Gage raised his voice, hands clenched at his sides, drawing curious glances from the onlookers forming a half circle around them in the parking lot.

"Gage." Skye touched his arm with her hand. "Settle down."

"You can't tell me what to do with my own kid." McKenna's eyes glittered. "Thanks for everything, Skye. Don't worry, I've got this."

"How about an attorney? Do you have one of those retained, too?" Gage growled.

"Stop," Skye said.

McKenna pushed through the crowd and strode toward a small economical car parked at the edge of the lot. Connor's wailing rose above the buzz of conversation.

Skye whirled and faced Gage, tears streaming from her eyes. "You shouldn't have confronted her."

"Really?" Gage stared at her in disbelief. "You're blaming me for this?"

"You're the one who yelled at her."

"Because you just stood there and let her take Connor. What else was I supposed to do? Stand back and do nothing while you tried to reason with her?"

"It's better than yelling."

"No. It's not." Anger flashed in his eyes. "You can't reason with an addict."

"She's recovered." Skye swiped at her cheeks with the cuff of her sleeve.

"How do you know?" Gage's chest heaved, his fists still clenched at his sides. "Did you even ask her if she'd completed her rehab? What if she stole that car?"

Skye wanted to throw up. She just shrugged helplessly. "Trying to talk some sense into her is better than yelling."

"Let me ask you this—all those years you and your family spent trying to talk some sense into her." He quoted the air with his fingers. "Did it work? Maybe if you-all weren't so loyal to one another, things might be different. But now she's leaving, with a baby who has no idea who she is, and we don't have a clue where she's headed."

Reeling from his harsh words, Skye stared at him, her body shaking. "Wh-what did you say?"

Gage huffed out a breath and shook his head. "I can't stand here and watch you fall apart." He turned and jogged toward his truck. "I'm going to follow her," he called over his shoulder.

Skye leaned into Laramie's embrace, sobbing. Why did he flip out and blame this on her?

Skye was out of her mind.

Gage clenched his jaw until it hurt. Her ability to enable McKenna had sunk to a new low today.

How could she tell him he shouldn't have *yelled*? Somebody needed to get through to McKenna, and it sure wasn't going to be Skye—not when she handed the baby over like a sack of groceries. Gage gripped his steering wheel tighter and forced himself to concentrate as he trailed McKenna's small white car to a new neighborhood on the edge of town—the one where a lot of the new Alta Vista Energy employees had bought homes.

Where was she getting the money to cover a mortgage or a month's rent? Had she hooked up with some new guy already? The thought of yet another stranger spending time with Connor spiked fear in his gut.

It was all he could do not to jump out of his truck and confront her again.

Instead, he kept a safe distance and left the engine running while he tracked her every move through his windshield. She parked and got out, then carefully lifted Connor into her arms and carried him, along with the diaper bag Skye gave her, toward the front of the house. His view was obstructed by shrubs and the corner of the two-car garage, so he couldn't see who answered the door or if she had a key of her own.

A few minutes later, he slowly drove by the house and snapped a quick picture of her license plate and made a note of the street address. He'd already called Drew, who'd confirmed that while he wasn't thrilled with his cousin's actions, no laws were violated. McKenna had every right to take her child, whether they thought she was capable of being a mother or not. Unless she endangered her child or committed a crime, there was nothing they could do.

Nothing they could do.

He scraped his hand across his face and slowly accelerated, while a hollow ache settled in his chest. Although he couldn't hang around and spy on McKenna, it physically hurt to drive away knowing Connor was inside with her. Was he still crying? Did he have any idea who she was? Who else was in the house with them?

The same unanswered questions spun through his mind—even if she was his mother, what if she didn't know how to take care of a one-year-old? She hadn't smelled like alcohol when they saw her at the festival, and she'd appeared sober and lucid. Still—he couldn't believe this was happening. So what if she was his mother? They shouldn't have allowed Connor to go with her.

Back at his own apartment, he reached for his phone to call Skye and tell her what he'd observed, and then he hesitated. She was angry. Distraught. The hurt and disbelief in her eyes when he'd told her what he really thought was an image he wouldn't soon forget. He put his phone away and started pacing. He was angry, too. If it weren't for the way her family had handled this whole situation, Connor might still be—

A knock sounded at his door. His boots clomped across the floor as he crossed his apartment in quick strides. A peek out the peephole revealed Drew waiting on the other side. In jeans, a hooded sweatshirt and a ball cap, he didn't look like he was on official business from the sheriff's department. So why was he here?

"Hey," Gage greeted him, his heart kicking against his rib cage. He knew it. McKenna had blown it already, just like he feared. "What happened?"

Drew's brows arched. "Take it easy. I'm just stopping by to check on you."

Oh. Gage crossed his arms over his chest. "So no updates, then."

"Not that I know of. Mind if I come in?"

Gage stepped back without saying anything. Drew walked inside and glanced around. Gage closed the door behind him. An awkward silence filled the air as they stood in the entryway, staring each other down. It wasn't like Gage planned to offer him a soda or anything. This was hardly the time to kick back and watch a ball game together.

Drew cleared his throat. "I ran the plates on McKenna's car. She didn't steal it. My aunt Willa is the owner."

Of course she is. Gage swallowed back the snarky reply. That wasn't fair. He didn't know McKenna or her mother, but he couldn't help chalking it up to one more way the family had enabled McKenna to get whatever she wanted.

"How about the place where she's staying—whose house is that?" Gage asked.

"No clue." Drew removed his ball cap and swiped his palm across his face. "I know this has been a tough day—for everybody—and I wanted to make sure you were all right."

What? How could he possibly be all right? Gage narrowed his gaze. "It's hard to imagine how anyone could hand over an innocent child—a baby—to the same woman who abandoned him."

Drew sighed and tugged his cap back into place, ignoring Gage's barb at his family. "Like I said, she didn't break any laws. We can't keep her from her own kid."

"What if she leaves again? Or—or worse, leaves Connor with a total stranger?" Blood whooshed in Gage's ears. How did Drew stay so calm—so matter-of-fact—about all this? They didn't know who McKenna was with or how she was planning to provide for herself and a helpless child.

"We are going to hope and pray that this time she's got her act together and she'll do what's best for herself and for Connor."

Gage scoffed. "I gotta be honest, I'm not real optimistic."

Drew pursed his lips. "Look, you're fired up about this, and your feelings are justified, but I—"

"If you know I'm right, then why not do something about it?" Gage's voice rose an octave, but he didn't care.

"I told you, there's nothing I can do."

"What about Skye? She hasn't asked you to intervene, either?"

Empathy filled Drew's eyes. He paused and then shook his head. "She didn't ask me to come here, if that's what you're asking."

Ouch. While he suspected that was the case, it didn't hurt any less to hear Drew confirm it. Probably shouldn't have asked if he didn't want to hear the answer. Gage brushed past him and opened the door. If Drew wasn't here to help, then there wasn't much left to say. "Let me know if you hear anything."

"Gage—"

"Thanks for stopping by."

Drew jammed his hands in the front pocket of his hoodie and left without another word. Gage stood there, staring at the closed door, a sickening sensation in his gut. Connor was going to spend the night in an unfamiliar place with a woman who was his mother, but basically a stranger, and there wasn't one thing Gage could do about it.

"I'm sorry, little buddy," he whispered, his voice breaking. "This wasn't supposed to happen. I'm going to fix it, I promise."

Tears stung the backs of his eyes and he wedged the heels of his palms against them to staunch the flow. He feared his words, like so many times before, were empty promises he couldn't deliver. He'd failed Connor just like he'd failed Ryan.

The house was way too quiet.

Skye sat on the sofa next to Mom and dabbed at her eyes with a tissue. How could the absence of one little boy make her cry so much?

"I'm proud of you, sweetie. You did the best you could." Mom patted her leg. "This is all in the Lord's hands now."

Was it? She hadn't relied on the Lord much lately. Sure, she believed all those things she'd learned in Sunday school growing up and felt gratitude for her many blessings, but that was the extent of her relationship with Him. If He loved them, why had Connor—all of them, really—lost so much?

"I can't believe Gage." Skye huffed out a breath. "First of all, he yelled at me, which was completely out of character, and then, as if that wasn't enough, he blamed you and me and—and our whole family for McKenna's behavior."

The ticking of the mantel clock filled the silence.

"Mmm."

Her mother's empathetic murmur got under Skye's skin. "Don't tell me you agree with him."

"I do."

"What?" Skye stared at her. "How?"

"The feud between Uncle Kenny and your father impacted all of us, including McKenna," Mom said. "Your aunt Willa did the best she could, but Kenny's rage was all consuming. He truly believed your dad had deprived him of a fortune."

Skye scoffed. "I don't know about a fortune, but Dad sure made some lousy choices about money."

"True. I wish I'd known sooner." Mom smoothed her hand over Skye's hair. "I'm not much different than your aunt Willa after all. Maybe I didn't want to see the truth about your dad, either. By the time she realized McKenna's wild ways, it was too late."

Skye twisted her crumpled tissue between her fingers. "It's not our fault she ran off and got pregnant, though."

"No, it isn't. She bears some responsibility in bringing Connor into this world." Mom sighed. "Now that I've lost your dad and we've learned he harbored secrets of his own, I have more empathy and grace for people and their struggles."

Skye winced. Too bad she couldn't embrace Mom's perspective. It just hurt too much.

"What happened to you?" Mom reached for Skye's hand. "Somebody must've done or said something terrible. You seem...closed off. Do you want to talk about it?"

Skye pressed her lips together and a fresh wave of shame washed over her.

"You can tell me anything. You know that, right?"

Skye drew a ragged breath. "A guy I dated for a while, he—he was very cruel."

Mom stiffened. "Oh, Skye."

"With his words, not with his fists." She forced herself to look at her mom. "But I don't ever want to feel that intimidated or belittled again."

"Sweetheart, I am so sorry." Tears glistened in Mom's eyes. "Why didn't you tell me?"

She ducked her head. "At first, I was embarrassed because I should've known better than to date someone who didn't treat me well. Then ashamed and afraid of what people might say or think."

"Your brothers and I, we wouldn't shame you. We love you and we are so proud of you. There's nothing you could tell us that changes how we feel."

"I—I know." Skye rested her head against her mother's and more tears tracked down her cheeks.

"Have you spoken to anyone else about this—your pastor or a counselor?"

"I saw a therapist in Denver." Skye sniffed. "That helped a lot. She told me I didn't need to see her while I was staying here."

Silence filled the air. Skye's pulse sped. Did Mom

disapprove of her decision to get professional help? Tentatively, her gaze swung toward her mother.

Tenderness filled her eyes. "Have you felt comfortable dating anyone else?"

"Mom." Skye didn't bother to keep the irritation from her voice. She looked away. What happened to empathy and compassion for people and their struggles? She knew exactly where this discussion was going.

"Gage is a wonderful man, and he's a natural with Connor."

"I can't be with someone who loses their temper in a crisis."

Mom shifted to face Skye. "Perhaps his anger wasn't directed at you but more at the circumstances. He—"

Skye shot her a warning look. "He yelled at me. In front of everyone. And he said it was our fault for being too loyal."

Mom's lips formed an O. "We all say things we don't mean sometimes in the heat of the moment."

Skye bit back a snide remark. It wasn't that simple.

"I suppose this means you'll be going back to Denver after Easter," Mom said quietly.

Skye's stomach knotted tight. "I think that would be best. My boss isn't obligated to hold my job open, and I don't see how I can turn things around at the furniture store."

"No one expects you to rescue the store all by yourself."

Skye studied her. "Are you sure?"

"Positive." Mom's smile was sad. "The store had a good, long run. Times are changing here. My hope is that business will improve, or somehow we'll transform that building into a space that benefits the community."

"Even if the store does close, part of me feels like I should stick around because I'm not sure McKenna will be able to handle full-time motherhood." Skye tipped her head back and stared at the ceiling. "But I can't keep her from her son."

"You need to follow your heart," Mom said. "My knee is much better, and I'll be able to drive again starting Monday. I want you to be free to make the decision that's best for you."

A fresh wave of tears threatened to fall, and Skye's vision blurred as she offered Mom a smile. "Then I'll leave for Denver after our Easter brunch."

With Mom's blessing, she'd return to work, get settled in her Denver apartment and reconnect with her friends. After the way Gage had treated her at the festival, she didn't want to speak to him or even see him again. Now that Connor and McKenna had reunited, there was no reason to extend her stay in Merritt's Crossing.

Chapter Fifteen

Gage tugged at his starched collar and gravel crunched under his black wing tips as he strode across the parking lot at Alta Vista Energy Group on Thursday afternoon. Man, he couldn't wait to get to his truck and loosen his tie. The sun slanted through the trees, which displayed tiny green buds, hinting that spring might've finally arrived. Birds chirped, and he didn't need a winter jacket for the first time in months.

Newly certified as a wind energy technician, his first job interview had gone well. The hiring manager said he'd get back to him soon. While he had a lot to be thankful for, regret and sadness over the absence of Connor and Skye weighed him down.

"There he is." Max's voice derailed the beginning of Gage's pity party.

Max climbed out of his truck nearby and waved. "Congratulations, by the way. I hear you had an interview."

"Thanks." Gage darted a glance to the back of the truck, where Dane was unloading equipment. They hadn't seen much of each other since their contentious air hockey duel. It was probably for the best. If they ended up being coworkers or even partners, he'd have to have a conversation about that night. Dane tipped his chin with the obligatory nod, then disappeared into the garage.

"Has anyone else offered you a job?" Max asked.

"Not yet. This is my first interview," Gage said. "I applied for an opening in Wyoming, too."

"Well that's a no-brainer." Max chuckled. "Merritt's Crossing is much better than the middle of nowhere in Wyoming."

Gage didn't answer.

"Unless you like the middle of nowhere." Max scrambled to recover. "Some folks do, I suppose."

Thoughts of Skye and Connor flitted through his head. "I've got some time to think about it—weigh the pros and cons."

Max nodded. "Anyone would be fortunate to have you on their team."

"Thanks, Max." Gage smiled. "I appreciate that."

Max glanced at his watch. "The grandkids are driving down from Boulder today, so I'd better get home. Any Easter plans?"

"Not really."

None, actually. Gage looked away. Spending the holiday alone wasn't his idea of fun, but he didn't need Max feeling sorry for him, too.

"Why don't you come over to our place? Lots of kids, tons of food—my wife's been cooking all week. We'd love to have you."

Gage hesitated. "I don't want to impose."

"No imposition. Come to think of it, why don't you come by at nine and go to church with us? We belong to a little country church near Limon. Great people."

"All right. I'll be there."

"Good. I'll let my wife know." Max clapped him on the shoulder, his eyes twinkling. "See you then."

"Thanks, Max. I really appreciate it."

"Not a problem."

They said goodbye and Gage strode toward his truck parked on the other side of the lot. Easter was only three days away. Hard to believe less than a week had passed since McKenna had taken Connor. His heart felt hollow. He missed the little guy. Skye, too. He hadn't seen or heard from any of the Tomlinsons since Drew's visit to his apartment. While he'd driven by the house where McKenna was supposedly staying more than once, he'd intentionally avoided Skye.

It hurt too much.

Gage shed his suit coat and loosened his tie before getting behind the wheel of his truck. While he turned the key in the ignition, his gaze swung to Ryan's photo on the dash.

"Sorry, man," Gage whispered. "I messed this all up."

He'd said those words a lot lately. The end result was still the same: Ryan was gone and Connor didn't have a dad. Gritting his teeth, Gage drove away, his promise to Ryan playing on endless repeat in his head. How could he keep his word if McKenna didn't let him be involved in Connor's life?

As he passed the grocery store, his foot pressed harder on the accelerator, his mind rehashing last night's conversation when he'd bumped into Laramie in the dairy aisle. She'd mentioned that Skye planned to go back to work next week in Denver. The news struck like a fist to his gut. He hadn't been able to stop thinking about her, or the harsh words he'd spewed at the festival.

Max was wrong.

He deserved the middle of nowhere. Alone. Because he totally blew it with Skye. He shouldn't have accused her of being too loyal. If it weren't for Skye's willingness to help her cousin, McKenna might've left Connor with a stranger. Skye's love and faithfulness to her family despite their grief and broken relationships is what kept Connor safe and well cared for.

He'd failed on so many levels.

And now the realization of how much both Connor and Skye meant to him was unbearable. He loved her. Connor, too. Even if he couldn't be a part of Connor's life anymore, he wanted Skye.

Not that she'd ever speak to him again after the horrible things he'd said.

But leaving town without telling her how he felt or at the very least saying goodbye made him feel like a coward.

And he didn't need any more reasons to feel like a coward. He'd already spent weeks—no, make that months—fixating on his guilt and regret over not being able to say goodbye to Ryan or rescue him during the submarine fire. While those feelings had lessened slightly, it was still something he'd carry with him for the rest of his life.

He released a heavy sigh as he slowed to make a turn. What good did it do to stay in Merritt's Crossing now? McKenna seemed determined to care for Connor on her own anyway. The thought of Connor growing up without a positive male influence in his life planted an icy ball of dread in Gage's stomach. Ryan's parents hadn't filed for permanent custody—at least not that he knew of.

If he had a job offer in Merritt's Crossing and stayed, but McKenna took Connor and moved away again, then he was stuck working in this place surrounded by painful reminders of all he'd lost—Skye, Connor and a chance to have a family of his own.

Maybe Wyoming was the better option. His only option now.

Standing under the gazebo in the community park, Skye bowed her head as the pastor prayed the benediction and the Easter sunrise service ended. A breeze blew off the pond, and she shoved her hands deeper in the pockets of her peacoat. If only she could shove aside the lonely ache taking up residence in her heart.

This was her last morning in Merritt's Crossing. The car was packed. After church and brunch with her family, she'd be on her way back to Denver.

Leaving was the right decision, wasn't it?

She turned her face upward to admire the pinks and oranges streaking overhead and savored the hum of quiet conversation buzzing around her as folks greeted each other. Uncle Milt's familiar chuckle wafted through the small crowd and Skye felt a smile tug at her lips. For all the struggles and challenges of small-town life, this would always be home.

"Happy Easter." Laramie walked up beside her, wearing a denim jacket over a yellow dress and a patterned scarf layered around her neck. "Is your family here?"

Skye shook her head. "I came alone. Mom was worried about standing too long, so she's going to the ten fifteen service." She gave her best friend a long look. "Jack didn't come, either, in case you're wondering."

Laramie looked away, two splotches of color darkening her cheeks. "I wasn't wondering."

"Not even a little bit?"

She sighed, then lifted her chin, a hint of mischief glinting in her eyes. "Okay, maybe a little. I do have a thing for that particular handsome, brooding brother of yours."

Skye flung her arm around Laramie's shoulders. "Don't give up. One of these days, he'll come to his senses and see how amazing you are."

"Doubtful but thank you. Too much history there," Laramie said. "Speaking of coming to our senses, have you spoken to Gage lately?"

"No." Her pulse ratcheted at the mention of his name. She'd thought about calling him. The days since the Easter festival crawled by, and every time a car drove past the house, she'd hoped it was Gage. Maybe he was fine with the way things ended. Maybe he'd made peace with the fact that McKenna and Connor were reunited.

Maybe he didn't want her in his life.

That last part was the hardest for her to accept.

"C'mon, let's talk." Laramie's gaze darted around the crowd. "Privately."

Arms linked, they walked slowly across the lawn toward their respective cars. The pastor's message about God being a good Father, one who loved unconditionally and didn't hold her shortcomings against her, still resonated in Skye's mind. Only this time, she let the familiar words blossom and flourish, instead of strangling the life out of them and pretending they didn't apply to her. The realization that she'd allowed so much guilt and resentment to build up, keeping her from fully living—and loving—nearly stole her breath.

"Good message this morning," Laramie said, picking her way through the grass in her peep-toe wedges.

"Uh-huh."

Laramie stopped walking and faced Skye. "I'll spare you the lecture, but I just want to say one more thing before you pack up and go."

"Don't use what happened with Connor as an excuse to push Gage away?"

Laramie's eyes lit up. "Exactly."

The breeze blew a strand of hair across Skye's cheek and she carefully extracted it from her lipstick and tucked it behind her ear. "I messed up, Lare. I've let my fear hold me back, and now I'm afraid I missed out on a wonderful relationship."

Laramie's expression morphed into one of empathy. "I'm sorry that some of the men in your life have let you down. Everybody is going to mess up and disappoint us. That's part of being human. Gage doesn't seem like he has anything but your best interests in mind."

"I know that now. Now that it's too late." She swallowed back the lump burning in her throat and dipped her chin. "I—I was afraid of losing my independence, and I didn't want to be a victim, too weak to speak my mind or defend myself."

"He might've been angry about McKenna taking Connor and said some things that were hard to hear, but he wasn't demeaning."

"And he was right about our family. We have enabled McKenna in so many ways for such a long time." She cringed, thinking about how their efforts to help had often caused more hurt and dysfunction instead.

"On the upside, what if your independence and fierce

love for your family is one of the things he really admires?"

"I'm not sure there's anything he loves about me right now. I was an idiot."

"But you don't have to stay an idiot."

Skye shot her a look. "Aren't you clever."

Laramie grinned. "That's why I'm your best friend." She gently steered Skye toward her car. "Why don't you go tell Gage everything you just told me?"

Skye's breath caught. "Now?"

"Yes, now." Laramie's tone was firm. Resolute. "Rumor has it he has a job interview in Wyoming this week."

Adrenaline surged as she thought about showing up at Gage's apartment, only to have the door slammed firmly in her face.

"I know what you're thinking," Laramie said, hands planted firmly at her waist and the skirt of her dress swirling around her legs. "But isn't the risk of rejection worth the effort?"

Skye hesitated, then nodded slowly.

"That's my girl." Laramie swept her into an enthusiastic hug. "I'm praying for you."

"Thank you. For everything." Skye pulled away, more tears threatening to fall. "What am I going to do in Denver without you?"

Laramie shook her head and held up her palm. "We aren't going there right now. You're on a new mission, remember?"

"Right."

Her heart in her throat, Skye climbed into her car and drove to Gage's apartment. As she strode across the parking lot, she scanned the space for a glimpse of his truck. Nothing. She hadn't called or texted first because she didn't want him to have the opportunity to avoid her. Buoyed by Laramie's pep talk, she hadn't stopped to consider that he might not be home at eight thirty on Easter morning. Had he been at the sunrise service and she'd missed him? That couldn't be. Laramie and her eagle eyes would've noticed.

She knocked on his door and waited. *Please, please, please be here.* Now that she realized how wrong she'd been, she didn't want to wait another minute to apologize and tell him she cared deeply. That somewhere between the babysitting and their evening in Denver, she'd fallen in love with him.

When she knocked again, only silence greeted her.

With a heavy heart, she dug through her purse for a pen and something to write. A text hardly seemed adequate at this point. All she found was a pen and a receipt from the coffee shop in Denver—the one they'd visited before their walk around the lake. She smiled at the bittersweet memory, scrawled a note asking Gage to call her, then tucked it into the door frame.

She sighed and returned to her car. Maybe this was a lesson learned—her fear had kept her from living openhandedly and receiving the blessing she'd been too guarded and resistant to accept—the love of a strong, devoted, wonderful man. And now it was too late.

Gage set a container full of leftovers from Max's wife on the passenger seat of his truck, then slid behind the wheel and slammed the door. Spending Easter with Max's family was a lot of fun, but he hated that he hadn't spoken to Skye. Now it was too late. She was probably in Denver by now, getting ready for her first day back at work.

And he was alone.

Even the prospect of a road trip to Wyoming and a job interview first thing Monday morning didn't brighten his mood. He huffed out a long breath and angled his truck out of Max's long driveway. Their farmhouse—situated in the middle of several acres about forty-five minutes from town—was stunning, and Gage had enjoyed spending the day with Max and his family.

But it wasn't the same as being with Skye and Connor.

Why hadn't he made the effort to track her down and speak with her? To admit he'd said all the wrong things at the Easter festival, and that he wanted to be a part of her life—with or without Connor? While he'd convinced himself that letting her go was best for both of them, the loneliness and regret were eating him up inside.

The late-afternoon sunshine bathed the cab of his truck in a soft glow, and he reached for his sunglasses. As he merged onto the highway, his thoughts alternated between Skye and Connor. Occasionally, an image of the three of them together again materialized, but he didn't allow himself to dwell there for long. What was the use? She was gone, and he'd been too stubborn to ask her to stay.

Lord, I need help. I don't want to live like this—trapped in my own insecurity.

Up ahead, a vehicle on the side of the road caught his attention, and he merged to the right and slowed down. The small white car sat on the shoulder, its front end angled toward the wire fence dividing the pasture from the highway. As he eased in behind it and surveyed the scene, his heart lurched.

McKenna's car. He'd memorized the license plate number.

"Please, please let them be okay." Gage flung up the prayer, then jumped out of his truck and jogged toward the driver's side. Through the closed windows he could hear Connor crying.

"McKenna!" Gage rapped his knuckles on her window. "Open up."

She glanced up, eyes wide and tears evident on her splotchy cheeks.

Connor caught sight of him and screamed louder.

Adrenaline pulsed through Gage's veins as he grabbed the door handle and tried to open it.

Locked.

McKenna looked down and a second later he heard the automatic locks release. The door sprang open.

"Are you all right?" he asked, scanning her face again for any sign of injury.

"I—I don't— I don't think so." She shook her head and looked around.

Was she in shock?

"What happened?"

Her fingers trembled as she reached up and rubbed her forehead, a gesture that vaguely reminded him of Skye. "I must've fallen asleep for a second."

"I need to get Connor out of his car seat and make sure he's okay." Gage kept his voice calm but firm. Did she really fall asleep? Should he call 911?

She glanced up at him again, her teeth chattering. "Th-th-that would be good."

He hesitated. Were her pupils dilated? He couldn't tell for sure. There wasn't time to interrogate her anyway, not with Connor still screaming from the backseat. He had to make sure the baby was all right.

Gage lunged for the back door and yanked it open, his heart in his throat. Connor's face was red, and tears clung to his lashes. He stretched his arms toward Gage.

"Aw, buddy. It's okay." Gage worked quickly to unfasten the car seat harness. He recognized the fear in Connor's cry and the realization that he'd learned to differentiate made a lump form in Gage's throat. Pulling the little guy into his arms, Gage pressed a kiss to Connor's cheek and then nestled him close to his chest. Breathing in the scent of baby shampoo, Gage swayed gently, blinking back tears of his own.

"Is he okay?" McKenna asked, swiping at her nose with the back of her hand.

Connor's cries quieted, and he drew several hiccupy breaths, while his fist clung to the lapel of Gage's fleece pullover.

Gage cleared his throat. "I think so." He carefully examined Connor's face and hands. No scrapes, cuts or bruises. He shifted his gaze to check inside the car. When he saw the brown paper bag on the floor, his stomach plummeted.

"McKenna." He could barely choke out her name. Worry shifted to alarm. "What's in the bag?"

She didn't answer.

"McKenna, have you been drinking and driving?"

She shook her head quickly. "I haven't. I promise. You can look, the bottles haven't been opened."

"You shouldn't have alcohol in your car." Gage fought to keep his tone even. He didn't want to lose his temper this time, but he couldn't believe she'd started drinking again. Not when she was solely responsible for Connor.

"I wasn't drinking. Not yet anyway." She pressed her lips together. "On Saturday I—I tried to get my old job back waitressing at the diner in Limon, but they said I had to prove I had reliable child care first."

Connor started to fuss again, and Gage shifted him in his arms and kept swaying gently, hoping to soothe him.

McKenna glanced up at him, squinting in the sunlight. "He isn't very easy for me to take care of, and he isn't sleeping well at night. I—I don't know who to ask to babysit him that I can trust, either."

"That still doesn't explain why you have alcohol in your car."

"I'm getting to that part. After I left the diner, I was upset that they'd told me no. Connor fell asleep in his car seat, so I went into the liquor store and...stocked up." She ducked her head. "But I didn't open them. You have to believe me."

The hum of another vehicle approaching kept Gage from answering. He circled around the front of McKenna's car to find a safer place to stand. The truck slowed, but Gage gave the driver a thumbs-up, and the truck kept moving.

McKenna got out of the car and faced him. She wrapped her arms around her torso. When her gaze met his, he saw only defeat and sorrow etched in her features.

"Will you please drive us to my aunt's house? I think I need her and Skye to take Connor for me."

"Skye's gone."

Surprise popped in McKenna's eyes. "Denver?"

He gritted his teeth and nodded slowly.

McKenna shivered and stared off in the distance. "Can you take me to my aunt's house anyway? I need to find someone to take Connor. Permanently."

Gage's breath caught. "Are you sure?"

She glanced at him again, tears clinging to her eyelashes. "I can't be his mother. At least not the mother he needs and deserves."

"If you'll hold Connor, I'll transfer his car seat to my truck."

"All right."

While Gage got Connor and McKenna situated in his truck and made arrangements to have her car towed, his mind raced ahead to possible scenarios. Skye had said she didn't want to be a mother. Was that still true? Would she change her mind if she knew McKenna was ready to relinquish her rights? Ryan's parents and their attorney would certainly be thrilled to hear the news.

His gut tightened at the thought of Connor moving to Illinois permanently. While he'd promised Ryan he'd look out for Connor, deep down, he didn't believe Gerald and Irene were the best long-term caregivers. As he drove back to Merritt's Crossing, McKenna and Connor both fell asleep, and he relished the peace and quiet, seizing the opportunity to pour out his heart's desire to the Lord. He wanted to be more than a male role model or a family friend. He longed to be Connor's father, and he'd give anything to make that a reality.

Chapter Sixteen

⁀◠

Exhausted, Skye carried the last box of her belongings from the elevator to the door of her apartment in Denver. What a marathon, trying to unpack the car by herself. She fumbled in her handbag for her keys. Her back ached from heaving her overstuffed suitcases in and out of the trunk, and her head felt like it was caught in a vise grip. Even though she didn't start back at work until tomorrow, her stomach twisted as she thought about the impossible-to-meet sales goals, the benefits of a new anti-inflammatory medication she was supposed to start promoting to physicians right away, plus her new territory, which was much larger than her manager had initially indicated.

Suddenly, returning to work didn't seem as exciting as she'd hoped. Right now, she'd give anything for another afternoon at the furniture store and a simple spreadsheet of last year's earnings and expenses. Or another day with Gage and an opportunity to tell him how she truly felt about him. Why had she given up so easily?

Her phone buzzed again, and she groaned. That was probably her manager or her sales team asking her to meet for dinner tomorrow night. *No, thank you.* She'd let the call go to voice mail. Just like the six other calls that came in while she was driving back from Merritt's Crossing today. Her phone had fallen from the center console and slid under the passenger seat about forty minutes into her trip and she'd ignored it the rest of the way to Denver. All she wanted was to get settled and take a luxurious bubble bath.

Four more familiar chimes came in quick succession, indicating a flurry of text messages. Probably not Bethany, her former babysitter. A pang of regret thrummed at the unexpected reminder of Connor and her time in Merritt's Crossing. Although she tried not to think about him, the sweet little fella had stolen a piece of her heart and was never far from her thoughts. Was he taking his first steps yet? Did McKenna have a good job? Was he safe?

She dug her phone from her bag and glanced at the screen. Ten missed calls and multiple text messages waited. What in the world?

The first text from Mom made her pulse race.

Connor is here. McKenna wants us to take him. Permanently. Is there any way you could come home??

The next messages from Laramie, Jack and Drew were all variations on the same piece of shocking news. The last message from Gage made tears well.

Skye, I found McKenna and Connor on the side of the highway. If you don't want to text me, I understand, but please contact your mom ASAP. It's important. Connor needs you.

"The side of the *highway*?" She quickly scrolled through the messages for more details. What had happened to McKenna? Was she hurt? Was Connor hurt? There were far more questions than answers.

Her hands shook as she attempted to text them all at once. Leaving Denver now.

She quickly shoved the box inside her apartment, grabbed one of the suitcases she'd recently unloaded, locked the door and rushed back to her car. While she navigated the Sunday-evening and holiday traffic, one important question surfaced above all the others. What about Gage? Did he need her? Or was he merely the messenger, dutifully informing her of what he'd observed as a first responder?

As the city lights faded behind her in the rearview mirror and darkness closed in, sheer adrenaline kept her barreling down the interstate toward Merritt's Crossing. It was after nine when she pulled into her mom's driveway, and her headlights bounced across a familiar pickup truck. Gage.

Her pulse skittered as Mom's front door opened and his broad, muscular frame was silhouetted by the light spilling out from the living room. The visual image of him waiting for her—welcoming her home—propelled her out of the car. She left the engine running and raced up the driveway, then flung herself into his open arms.

"I'm so sorry." Her voice broke and she clung to him, her arms roped around his neck and her cheek pressed against his chest.

Gage's strong arms encircled her waist and he held her close, enveloping her, like a shelter in the middle of a brutal storm. Even if McKenna hadn't changed her mind about Connor, Skye would've come back. In her heart, she knew Denver and her career didn't offer happiness and contentment. Gage did. She belonged with him.

This—this felt like home. *He* was her home.

She closed her eyes, the realization prompting a wave of fresh tears, and she earnestly hoped that he felt the same way.

Slowly, she pulled back and searched his face. "Say something. Please."

A half smile formed, and he tenderly wiped away her tears with the pad of his thumb, sending a warm, tingly sensation straight through her.

"I'm glad you're here," he said, his voice husky. "I've missed you so much."

"Will you please forgive me?" She kept her gaze riveted on his. "I was such an idiot, letting my fear stand between us."

"*Idiot* is not a word I would ever use to describe you." The golden glow of the lamplight emphasized the broad planes of his face and he cupped her cheek with his palm. "You are beautiful and intelligent, and your fierce loyalty to the people you love is a force to be reckoned with."

"It's also the thing that gets me in the most trouble, especially when it blinds me to what's right in front of me." She swallowed hard. "I'm so sorry for the things I said at the festival. You were right. We've enabled McKenna for a long time and it wreaked havoc in our lives. And even if she hadn't changed her mind, I'm here because I want to be with you."

"I'm sorry, too. I said things about you and your family that I'd take back in a heartbeat if I could. My mother's addiction issues were fueled by people enabling her—people I trusted to keep me safe—which meant I had to go into the foster care system. When McKenna showed up and took Connor, it brought back so many painful memories, and that's why I was so angry." Gage caressed her arms with his hands. "But Connor's asleep inside, and he and McKenna are both safe, and you're back. That's all that matters."

"You're being very gracious." She clasped her hands behind his neck. "Are you sure that's all you want to say?"

His smooth brow furrowed. "There is one more thing."

She knew it. Her stomach lurched. Was he going to extract himself from her embrace and tell her they didn't have a future together?

His gaze flitted to her lips for an instant. When his eyes met hers again, only approval and affection filled those gorgeous green-gold pools. "I need you, Skye. No matter what the future holds for Connor, I don't want to be apart from you anymore. I love you."

"I love you, too."

Then her eyelids fluttered, and he claimed her mouth with his. As Mr. Handsome-Hazel-Eyes deepened the kiss, she tunneled her fingers through the hair at the nape of his neck. The warmth of his touch and the comfort and safety she found in his embrace confirmed what she'd secretly known from the beginning—Gage wasn't a man who led with harsh words and intimidation. Quite the opposite. All along, he'd only used his strength to protect.

Gage sat on the Tomlinsons' couch, his arm wrapped around Skye's shoulders, and his other hand entwined with hers. He hadn't stopped holding on to her since she'd raced up the driveway and back into his life over an hour ago, and until Mrs. Tomlinson sent him home, he had no plans to let go. McKenna and Mrs. Tomlinson sat across from them, staring at him expectantly.

"Gage?" Skye squeezed his hand. "Did you hear McKenna?"

"I—I'm sorry, I didn't." He grinned at her. "Got distracted."

Her mouth curved into a knowing smile, drawing his gaze to the fullness of her lower lip. His arms ached to pull her into another embrace and re-create their reunion on the front porch, but not with her mother and cousin as an audience. He tore his gaze away and forced himself to focus on McKenna.

"I said I want you and Skye to be Connor's legal guardians."

"What?"

"Since you're together—I'm assuming that's the case, since you can't stop staring or touching each other." McKenna's eyes gleamed with tears as she offered a wobbly smile. "I want you to be his permanent guardians."

His pulse spiked. Was she serious? And how was that even possible? He and Skye weren't married or even engaged. Not that he hadn't thought about both those events happening in the very near future. He opened his mouth to respond, but the words wouldn't come. "What about Gerald and Irene?"

"I've been in touch with an attorney," Mrs. Tomlinson said. "He's preparing a response in case they sue for custody."

"Not that I have any right to be critical, but Irene

was not very hands-on as a mother. Ryan told me once that she was way more interested in her hobbies than him." McKenna twisted a tissue around her fingers. "I should have told you sooner because he said that whatever happened between us, he didn't want his parents raising Connor."

The hair on the back of Gage's neck stood up. That explained why Ryan hadn't spent a lot of time talking about his parents. "When did he say that?"

"He wrote it in an email. I still have it." McKenna glanced at Mrs. Tomlinson. "At least I did one thing right."

"Don't be too hard on yourself," Mrs. Tomlinson said. "You're being very brave."

Gage's mind raced, eager to map out the facts.

"After I told him I was pregnant, he asked me to move to Florida. I said I was too afraid to move that far, especially when he spent so much time at sea, and I didn't have any support. That's when he said he could borrow money from his parents to help me move, but if they found out about the baby, he warned me they'd... be a challenge to deal with."

McKenna dabbed at her tears with the tissue. "Ryan wanted Connor to have a different childhood than he did."

Gage released a heavy sigh. Skye's thumb slid gently across the back of his hand, offering comfort.

"I know this is a big decision, but I'm not capable of taking care of Connor on my own. I—I'm scared I'll just keep hurting him."

"Oh, sweetheart." Mrs. Tomlinson pulled McKenna close. "We are going to figure this out. Together. It's getting late. Why don't you try to get some sleep?"

McKenna nodded and pushed to her feet. Her teary-eyed gaze lingered on Skye and Gage. "Please think about what I said."

"We will." Skye's eyes flitted to his, and the tenderness there filled him with love. She'd make such an amazing mother, to Connor and to any future children they had together. Warmth crawled up his neck at the image of a house full of kids. For the second time in only a few minutes, he forced himself to rein in his thoughts.

"Looks like you two have a lot to talk about. I'll help McKenna get settled in the guest room." Mrs. Tomlinson stood and followed McKenna down the hall. "Don't stay up too late."

When they were alone, Gage dipped his head and brushed his lips against Skye's. "I've been waiting almost an hour to do that."

Her soft laughter made his heart beat double time. "I thought they'd never go to bed."

While he wanted to kiss her senseless, Mrs. Tomlinson had gently hinted that he ought to go soon, and they still had so much to talk about. He straightened and put a fraction of an inch between them, just so he could think straight. And ask her the question that had been top of mind since she'd come back to Merritt's Crossing.

"Are you still going back to Denver?"

"Nope. I'll call my boss first thing tomorrow and resign."

He felt the tiniest embers of hope ignite.

"What about you? Still heading for Wyoming in the morning?"

He studied her. "Who told you?"

Eyes gleaming, she shook her head in mock disbelief.

"If you're going to live in Merritt's Crossing, you'll have to accept what I'm about to tell you as absolute fact."

"Oh? What's that?"

"We all make it our business to know everyone else's business."

He nodded. "Good to know. Sounds like my kind of place."

Her eyes grew wide. "Does that mean you'll stay?"

"Only if you will."

She grinned. "I hear there's a furniture store that still has hope of surviving and a little boy who needs a mom and a dad."

"I thought motherhood wasn't part of your long game. What changed your mind?"

Reaching up to cup his cheek with her palm, she stared deeply into his eyes. "Connor. And you."

Goose bumps raced across his skin. "What do you think about McKenna's request?"

She stared at him for what seemed like an eternity. "I plan to say yes, but I need to know if you're willing to take on a family? Because Connor and I are a package deal."

Tears pricked his eyelids, but he battled them back. Reaching for her hand, he pressed a kiss to the inside of her wrist. "Nothing in the world would make me happier than to build a life with you and be Connor's dad." His voice cracked. "Marry me?"

"Yes." Her heavy-lidded gaze made warmth flare. "Now, kiss me again."

He moved within inches of her mouth, drinking her in, memorizing every curve of her face before he complied with her request.

The realization that they were planning a life together seeped into him, chasing away the guilt and regret that had plagued him for far too long. While he'd valued his time in the navy and the structure offered by the military lifestyle, it had enabled him to avoid any serious romantic relationships. While he'd once equated family and intimacy with pain and rejection, Skye gave him the courage to risk his heart again. Finding Connor and meeting the Tomlinsons taught him what a real family looked like, not only the faults but the unconditional love, too. He'd kept his word to Ryan and gained more than he ever dreamed possible.

Epilogue

One year later

Skye was glad she'd said yes.

Yes to McKenna's request to become Connor's guardian, yes to staying in Merritt's Crossing and, most of all, yes to Gage's marriage proposal.

"You look stunning." Laramie caught her gaze in the mirror hanging in the church's Sunday school classroom that they'd transformed into a makeshift dressing area as she adjusted the gauzy veil pinned carefully around Skye's elegant French twist.

"Thank you." Skye admired the long-sleeved gown with a fitted lace bodice that tapered down to her waist and then billowed out into a full satin skirt with flowers embroidered along the hemline.

She smiled at her reflection, then turned and hugged her best friend and maid of honor. "We couldn't have pulled this wedding off without your help."

"Nonsense," Laramie said. "You did most of the planning."

"I want today to be amazing. For me and for Gage."

Waiting a whole year to become Mrs. Gage West-brook had been challenging, and more than once they'd seriously considered eloping at the county courthouse. But since they were about to become a family of three in a most nontraditional way, having an intimate traditional ceremony and reception with their closest friends and family was important. Connor meant the world to both of them, but they'd dedicated so much time and energy to his needs.

Since the adoption was finalized and they were officially Connor's mother and father now, today was meant to be a celebration of their love as they became husband and wife.

Skye's legs trembled, and goose bumps raced down her spine. She wasn't apprehensive—just overwhelmed with joy. For a long time, she'd written off the possibility of ever wearing a gown like this. Scarcely allowed herself to dream of one day walking down the aisle toward a man like Gage.

But God, in His infinite love and grace, had healed the broken places and orchestrated something beautiful where once she'd only seen chaos and heartache.

"I've loved every minute of this hectic whirlwind that's become your life, by the way." Laramie popped open a compact and quickly powdered Skye's nose one more time. "It's been quite a year, hasn't it?"

"It has," she agreed. "Today couldn't get here soon enough."

Between Gage's long hours at Alta Vista's wind farm and her efforts to turn the furniture store into a successful business, they'd needed a year to plan the wedding and jump through all the hoops to win the custody battle waged by Ryan's parents. Thankfully, the judge had officially declared Skye and Gage Connor's parents and granted Gerald and Irene weekend visitation once every other month. They were required to come to Colorado to spend time with Connor.

Laramie checked her own reflection in the mirror one last time, smoothed her hands over the simple navy satin bridesmaid's dress with the floral lace overlay, then stepped into her sling-back heels.

A knock sounded at the door and her mother and Bethany came in, wearing dresses similar to Laramie's.

"Oh, look at you." Mom splayed her hand across her chest, eyes glistening with tears.

"No crying." Bethany fanned Mom's face with her hand. "If you start, we won't be able to stop."

"I'm so happy for you, sweetheart." Her mom gently pulled Skye into an embrace and then tenderly kissed her cheek. "You are going to make Gage very happy, and you are already an incredible mother to Connor."

"Thank you," Skye whispered, determined not to melt into a puddle of tears before she and Gage saw each other.

They picked up their bouquets, and the photographer slipped in and took more pictures. When she was finished, Laramie circled around behind Skye and lifted the train of her gown. "C'mon, you've kept your groom waiting long enough."

They moved slowly toward the door. Skye heard Connor's contagious laugh echoing out in the hallway, and she smiled. Drew said something, his voice muffled, and Connor giggled again. He'd been the star of the show last night at the rehearsal dinner. Hopefully between Drew and Jack, they'd steer him down the aisle as the ring bearer and keep him occupied during the ceremony. It was a lot to ask of a two-year-old, but she couldn't imagine not including him.

Mom was babysitting Connor for the next five days, but once she and Gage came home from their honeymoon in Estes Park, near Rocky Mountain National Park, they'd finally be a family of three.

As the bridal party moved toward the closed double doors at the back of the sanctuary, the violinist's prelude filtered through the air.

Connor caught sight of Skye, toddled over to her in his miniature gray suit and reached for her hand. He tipped his head up and offered a smile. "Mama."

How could two little syllables make her heart soar? "Hey, pumpkin. You look handsome."

The doors opened, and Drew seated Mom in the front row. Connor wiggled uncontrollably, his chubby hand still clasping hers. While she waited for Drew to return so he and Jack could both walk her down the aisle and into her future with the man she loved, she stared at Connor in amazement.

It was incredible how one little guy had burst into her life, brought Gage to Merritt's Crossing and forged an unbreakable bond.

* * * * *

Lois Richer loves traveling, swimming and quilting, but mostly she loves writing stories that show God's boundless love for His precious children. As she says, "His love never changes or gives up. It's always waiting for me. My stories feature imperfect characters learning that love doesn't mean attaining perfection. Love is about keeping on keeping on." You can contact Lois via email, loisricher@gmail.com, or on Facebook (loisricherauthor).

Books by Lois Richer

Love Inspired

The Calhoun Cowboys

Hoping for a Father
Home to Heal
Christmas in a Snowstorm
A Plan for Her Future

Rocky Mountain Haven

Meant-to-Be Baby
Mistletoe Twins
Rocky Mountain Daddy
Rocky Mountain Memories

Visit the Author Profile page at LoveInspired.com for more titles.

A BABY BY EASTER

Lois Richer

It's in Christ that we find out who we are and what we are living for. Long before we first heard of Christ and got our hopes up, he had his eye on us for glorious living, part of the overall purpose he is working out in everything and everyone.
—*Ephesians* 1:11, 12

This story is for those generous souls
who open homes and hearts to kids of all ages
who crave love and affection. Your dedication
will be revealed in tomorrow's generation.

Chapter One

Evenings in Tucson were a lot cooler than the Los Angeles' dusk Susannah Wells was used to.

Remember, Suze, we foster kids never know about tomorrow. Save whatever you can so you'll be prepared.

Susannah squeezed her hand in her pocket, fingering the last bits of change leftover from her meager savings. Connie's advice about money had been right on, like so much other guidance she'd given in those long-ago days when they'd shared a room in their North Dakota foster home.

What advice would Connie have for her this time—or would she even want to be bothered with her former foster sister?

Susannah hugged her thinly clad arms around her waist and breathed in the heady scent of hot pink oleanders. Deliberately she forced one foot in front of the other. Moving quickly wasn't an option when the world occasionally tilted too far to the right. Beads of moisture on her forehead chilled her hot skin, making her shiver.

The bus driver had said two blocks—surely she'd come at least that far?

Suddenly off balance, Susannah stopped to steady herself. She focused her blurry eyes on the paper in her hand, peering to confirm that the numbers on the page were the same as those on the house. Her sluggish brain responded as if obscured by fog. She squinted for a second look.

This was it.

Susannah's heart sank a little lower. Such a grand home. How could she possibly walk into that perfectly manicured courtyard, knock on that elegant glass and wrought-iron door and ask Connie for help?

You're not worth helping, but you don't have a choice.

Nothing harder to stomach than the truth. Susannah knew that too well. She gritted her teeth, pushed open the gate and moved forward. Droplets of perspiration ran into her eyes, blurring her vision. She swiped them away with a quick brush of her hand, afraid to release the branches of the hedge for more than a second, lest she flop to the ground. She was cold, and yet she was so hot.

What was wrong with her?

Finally she stood at the entrance. Music floated out from the brightly lit house. Or maybe the melody was just stuck in her head.

Susannah lifted a hand and tapped gingerly, inhaling as the world spun faster.

The door opened, light and laughter flooding out.

"Yes?" A man's voice, rich and smooth, like butterscotch candy, flowed over her. It was hard to see his face, but light brown eyes gleamed through the dusk. "Can I help you?"

"Connie," Susannah whispered.

Then everything went black.

* * *

David Foster stared at the unconscious woman lying on his best friend Wade's doorstep. Wade's wife, Connie, always had someone stopping by, friends from the foster home where she'd once lived, acquaintances she'd met and offered to help, even total strangers who'd heard about her charities. This frail woman must fit into one of those categories.

But Connie and Wade were celebrating their return from Brazil with a houseful of guests. He didn't want to disturb them. As Wade's lawyer, David was accustomed to handling things for his friend. He decided he'd handle this guest, for now.

He bent and scooped the young woman into his arms.

"Who's that?" Darla asked. His little sister had a habit of soundlessly appearing at his elbow.

"I don't know," he murmured, leading the way to the study. "One of Connie's friends, I guess. She fainted. I think she's sick."

"Oh." Darla watched as he laid the young woman on the sofa. "Can I help, Davy?"

David smiled, brushed his hand over her shiny brown hair in a fond caress. Darla loved to help. Though nineteen, a skiing accident had left Darla with a brain injury that cut her mental age in half. David's goal in life was to make his sister's life as rich and happy as possible. It was becoming a challenge.

"Sure you can help, sweetie. Why don't you go in the bathroom over there and get a wet cloth?" he suggested. "You can wipe her forehead. She seems to have a fever."

"Okay."

Darla hurried to do as asked, her mood bright because of Connie's party. "Like this?" she asked him, dabbing the cloth on the woman's face.

"Very gently. That's good." He watched for a few moments. "She had a bag," he mused. "It must have dropped. Can you take care of her while I go look for it?"

"Yes." Darla hummed quietly as she gently removed the traces of dust and grime from the visitor's pale skin. Not that it mattered—their guest was gorgeous.

"I'll be right back." David hurried toward the front door, his mind filled with questions.

She was tiny, light as a feather. Her delicate features made him think of fashion magazine covers—thin, high cheekbones, full lips and wide-set eyes. She'd pulled her golden blond hair back and plaited it so it fell down her back, but little wisps had worked free to frame her face in delicate curls. He caught himself speculating what the color of her eyes would turn out to be when those incredible lashes lifted.

She's obviously needy, and your docket is full.

Boy, did he know that.

A denim backpack lay outside on the step. David bent to pick it up. Well used, even ragged. Like her clothes.

He carried the bag inside, quickening his step. Darla couldn't be left alone for long. He stepped into the room.

"You're Sleeping Beauty, aren't you?" his sister whispered as she slid her cloth over the girl's thin, ringless fingers. "You need Prince Charming to wake you up."

David knew what was coming. He tried to stall by taking the woman's pulse.

"She'll wake up in a few minutes, sis."

"No," Darla said, eyes darkening as her temper

flared. "She needs you to kiss her, Davy. That's how Sleeping Beauty wakes up."

David sighed. Apparently he'd read her that particular fairy tale one too many times.

"It would be wrong of me to kiss her, Darla," he said firmly, ignoring the allure of full pink lips. "I don't know her. She wouldn't want a strange man to kiss her. Women don't like that."

"It's the only way to get her to wake up." Darla was growing agitated.

David closed the study door and prayed their visitor would soon rouse. He didn't want a scene at his friends' party. And Darla would make one. She'd grown used to getting her own way, and when she didn't, she tantrumed. That was the main reason she'd gone through so many caregivers in the past six months. None of the helpers he'd hired had been strong enough to stand up to Darla's iron will.

Like he was?

"Kiss her." Darla scowled at him, her mouth tight.

"No." David kept his voice firm. "It's no good getting angry, Darla. I'm not going to kiss her. This isn't a fairy tale, and she's not Sleeping Beauty. She's real and she might be quite ill. Look how she's shivering." He lifted a coverlet from the sofa and laid it over the small form.

"You have to kiss her." Darla stamped her foot. "I want you to." She swung out her hand. It connected with a lamp, which shattered against a table.

"Darla! Now you've broken Connie's lamp. Stop this immediately." David reached for her arm to keep her from wrecking anything else, but Darla was quick. She sidestepped him.

"Kiss her," she ordered, her face stormy as any thundercloud.

"Nobody's going to kiss me," a soft voice murmured. "And I wish you'd stop yelling. You sound like a spoiled brat."

Darla glowered at their visitor. Then she grinned. "Sometimes I am," she admitted shamelessly.

"Why? It's not very nice to live with people who are spoiled." The woman shifted the cover over her shoulders then swung her feet to the floor as she sat up. Her face paled a little and her fingers tightened on a sofa cushion.

"Easy," David murmured. "Not too fast. You fainted. Remember?"

"Unfortunately I do remember. What an entrance." She tilted her head back to rest it as she studied him.

Her eyes were a deep, vivid green. Their shadowed intensity reminded David of the Amazon forest—he'd once taken a trip there with Wade and their friend Jared. Before his world had become consumed by responsibility.

"My name is David Foster," he said. "This is my sister, Darla."

"I'm Susannah Wells. So this isn't Connie Ladden's home?" She looked defeated.

"Oh, yes. Connie and Wade *Abbot* live here," he assured her.

"They're having a party," Darla butted in. She frowned. "Did you come for the party? You don't have a party dress on. You're not supposed to come to a party if you don't dress nice," she chided.

"Darla." David frowned at her.

"She's only saying the truth. You're not supposed to

show up at a party dressed as I am." Susannah smiled at him tentatively then turned to Darla. "But I didn't know it was a party, you see. Anyway, I don't have party dresses."

"Not even one?" Clearly this mystified Darla. "I have lots."

"Lucky you." Susannah frowned. "Maybe I should leave and come back tomorrow."

"You can't." Darla flopped down beside her.

Susannah blinked. "Why can't I?"

"'Cause you don't have any place to go. Do you?" Darla asked.

David tried to intervene but Susannah merely waved her hand at him to wait.

"How do you know that, Darla?" she asked, brows lowering.

"I'm a detective today."

"Oh." The visitor glanced at him, her confusion evident.

David shrugged but didn't speak.

"I'm Detective Darla Foster. You don't have any suitcases. All you have is a backpack." Darla trailed one finger over the frayed embroidery work on the bag. "If you had a hotel, you would go there and wash first. But you came here dirty. I washed your face." She lifted the wet washcloth off the floor and held it out to show the grime. "See?"

A ruby flush moved from the V of Susannah's neck up to her chin and over her thin cheeks.

"There was a wind," she muttered, avoiding David's gaze. "It was so dusty."

"It's none of our business," he assured her hastily,

giving Darla a warning look. "Except that I don't think you're well. Should I call a doctor?"

"You actually know doctors who make house calls?" Her big eyes expressed incredulity.

"Dr. Boo came to my house. She asks too many questions." Darla's bottom lip jutted out. "Detectives don't like Dr. Boo."

"Dr. Boone," David clarified, interpreting Susannah's stare as a query. "Actually she's here. Shall I call her?"

"No." The word came out fast. Susannah donned a quick smile to cover. "I'm not very good with doctors. I'll be fine. I think I caught a little cold, that's all. But they never hang around for long."

"You're shivering." David didn't miss the way she hugged the coverlet around her shoulders as if craving warmth, or the way her stomach issued a noisy rumble. "And hungry, by the sounds of it. Shall I go get Connie?"

"Oh, please, I don't want to disturb her party." Susannah shook her head. "Can't I just stay here quietly until everyone's gone?"

"You don't want to go to the party?" Darla frowned, then grinned. "Me, neither," she declared. She patted Susannah's arm. "Let's have our own party. Davy, you get Silver," she ordered.

"Silver?" Susannah looked horrified. "I don't want money!'

"Silver is Wade's daughter." Darla giggled. "She's nice."

"I think Connie took Silver up to bed a while ago." David held his breath, wondering if that would engender another explosion.

And that was exactly his problem. He worried too much about Darla's temper and not enough about insisting she modify her behavior. But it was so hard to be firm with her. She was his baby sister. She'd lost so much since the accident. All he wanted was to make her world easier, to see her happy.

Still, it was his job to take care of her, no matter what. Which meant that tomorrow David would start scouting the agencies—again—to find someone to be with his sister when he couldn't be.

Lowered voices drew him back to the present. Two heads, one dark, one blond, bent together as his sister laid out her plans for their impromptu party.

"Darla?" David waited until she lifted her head and smiled her dazzling smile at him. "I'm going to find something for Susannah to eat. Will you stay *here*?" He emphasized the word so she'd understand she wasn't to leave the study.

"Okay." Darla tore a piece of paper off the pad by the telephone and began scribbling. "Here's our order, Davy. Crackers and cheese and soup. Chicken soup. Eighty-six percent of doctors say chicken soup is an effective aid in treating cold and flu."

Darla had a knack for reciting television commercials verbatim.

"Cold and flu—is that what I have?" Susannah asked, tongue in cheek. "How do you know?"

"I'm a nurse. We just know." Darla pulled the cover tighter around her patient's shoulders.

David hid his smile at Susannah's surprise.

"I thought you were a detective," he said.

"Not anymore." Darla glared at him. "Food, Davy.

This child is starving," she said in her bossy grandmother voice.

"Yes, ma'am." He choked back his laughter. Darla
had always been able to make him laugh. He headed
for the door. "I'll be right back." He thought he heard a
giggle from the blond woman before he closed the door,
but it was quickly smothered.

David went searching for Connie and caught her between guests.

"There's a woman in the study, a Susannah Wells,"
he began, but got no further.

"Really? Suze? How wonderful." Connie beamed
with happiness. It faded a little as she glanced around
the room. "We're about to eat dinner. I can't leave right
now." She thought a moment. "Bring her to the table,
will you, David? I'll get another place set."

Before Connie could continue, David stopped her.

"I don't think that's a good idea," he said softly. "I
don't think she's well. She fainted when I opened the
door and she's been shivering ever since."

"Oh, dear." Connie looked distracted. "Cora just
gave me the nod. I need to get everyone seated."

"Then go ahead. Darla and I will keep Ms. Susannah entertained until you're free." David smiled at her.
"Don't worry. Darla has everything under control. She's
a nurse."

"Ah." Connie grinned in understanding and stood
on her tiptoes to kiss his cheek. "What would we do
without Darla, David?"

"I don't know," he answered her, perfectly serious.
"Go enjoy dinner and don't worry about your friend.
I'll look after her."

"You always look after everyone." Connie touched

his cheek. "Thank you for all you do for us. You're a dear."

David watched her hurry away. He couldn't help but envy Connie. She and Wade shared the kind of home he'd always wanted—one filled with love and joy, hope and the laughter of friends and family. But he shook himself out of it. Having a family was a dream he'd given up.

For Darla.

He escaped to the kitchen. A whisper of concern that Darla might cause problems lingered at the back of his mind as he hurriedly filled a tray and carried it to the study. He hadn't gotten what she'd asked for, but she would have to manage. He pushed open the study door—and froze.

"You could marry Davy. He would look after you. He looks after me." Darla's bright voice dropped. "He had a girlfriend. They were going to get married, but she didn't want me. She wanted Davy to send me away."

David almost groaned. How had she found out? He'd been so careful—

"I'm sure your brother is very nice, Darla. And I'm glad he's taking care of you. But I don't want to marry him. I don't want to marry anyone," Susannah said. "I only came to Connie's to see if I could stay here for a while."

"But Davy needs someone to love him. Somebody else but me." Darla's face crumpled, the way it always did before she lost her temper. David was about to step forward when Susannah reached out and hugged his sister.

"Thank you for offering, Darla. You're very generous. I think your brother is lucky to have you love him."

Susannah brushed the bangs from Darla's sad face. "If I end up staying with Connie, I promise I'll see you lots. We could go to that playground you talked about—" Susannah suddenly lurched up from the sofa and stumbled toward the bathroom. The door slammed closed.

"What's wrong?" Darla jumped to her feet. She saw him and rushed over. "What's wrong with her, Davy? Did I do something?"

"No, sweetie. You didn't do anything." He set the tray on a nearby table, then hugged Darla close. "I told you. She's sick."

"But I don't want Susannah to be sick. I want us to be friends and do things together." Tears welled in Darla's brown eyes. "Susannah doesn't think I'm dumb. She talks to me like you do, Davy."

David could hardly stand the plaintive tone in his sister's voice. But he dared not promise Darla anything. Not until he'd learned a lot more about Susannah Wells.

As he hugged Darla, the sounds of retching penetrated the silence. Susannah sounded really ill. Maybe he should have ignored her wishes and called the doctor in anyway.

"Davy?" Darla peered up at him, her eyes glossy from tears. "Do you think she's going to die like Mama and Papa?"

"No, honey. Susannah's just sick. But she'll get better." He squeezed her shoulders, wishing he could make everything right with Darla's world.

A moment later the bathroom door opened and Susannah emerged, paler than before, if that was even possible. She sat on the sofa gingerly, as if afraid she'd jar something loose.

"I'm sorry," she whispered. "I shouldn't have come."

"Of course you should have come." Connie breezed into the room and wrapped Susannah in her arms. "I'm so glad to see you, Suze. But you're ill." She leaned back to study the circles of red now dotting Susannah's cheeks. "I'll call the doctor."

"No."

David noted Susannah's quick intake of breath, the way she vehemently shook her head as her fingers clenched the sofa cushion. He wondered again why she was so nervous.

"But honey, you're obviously unwell. Maybe you have a virus."

Susannah began to laugh, but tears soon fell and the laughter turned to sobs. "I don't have a virus, Connie." She risked a quick look at David.

He understood immediately. He grasped Darla's hand.

"We'll leave you two alone."

"No!" Darla jerked away from him and sat down beside Susannah. "I want to help my friend. Can I help you?" she asked quietly, sliding her fingers into Susannah's.

David had never seen his sister bond with anyone like this. He prayed Susannah wouldn't reject her offer of friendship.

"You already have helped me, Darla." Susannah smiled. "You looked after me and helped me the way a very good friend would, even though I hardly know you."

"I know you," Darla insisted. "You're Sleeping Beauty."

"I'm not really." Susannah caressed Darla's cheek. She glanced at him, then Connie. "I'm just an idiot who's made another huge mistake."

"Davy says everybody makes mistakes. He said that's how we learn." Darla faced Connie. "I made a mistake and broke your lamp. I'm sorry."

"That's okay, honey. You and I will go shopping for a new one." Connie smiled her forgiveness, then turned back to Susannah. "Can you tell me what's wrong, Suze? Because you're very pale and I still think you need to see a doctor."

"I've already seen one." The blond head dipped. "I know what's wrong with me."

"Tell me and we'll do whatever it takes to get you well," Connie promised.

"If only it were that easy," Susannah whispered.

"There's me and Davy and Connie and Wade and Silver. That's lots of people to help." Darla twisted, trying to peer into Susannah's face. "We can all help you. That's what friends do."

David had to smile at the certainty in his sister's voice. But his smile quickly died.

"I'm pregnant." The words burst out of Susannah in a rush. Then she lifted her head and looked him straight in the eye, as if awaiting his condemnation.

But it wasn't condemnation David felt. It was hurt. He'd prayed so long, so hard, for a family, a wife, a child. And he'd lost all chance of that—not once, but twice.

How could God deny him the longing of his heart, yet give this homeless, ill woman a child she was in no way prepared to care for?

"Come on, Darla," he said. "We're going home now. Connie and Susannah need to talk. Alone."

Darla must have heard intransigence in his voice because she didn't argue. She leaned over and kissed both women on the cheek, whispered something to Susannah, then placidly followed him from the room. She walked home beside him in silence, peeking at him from time to time. It was only when they'd stepped through the front door that Darla finally spoke.

"I know what it means, Davy. Susannah's going to have a baby."

"Yes." He felt horrible about his attitude, but he just didn't want to get involved with Connie's friend. He had enough responsibility with Darla. He couldn't—wouldn't—take on any more.

"Is it hard to have a baby?" she asked.

"Yes. I guess so."

"Then we have to help Susannah, don't we? That's what the Bible says." Darla took his hand and held it between hers. "She's my friend, and I want to help her."

"I don't think there's much that we can do, sis." Brain injury or not, Darla had always tried to fix the world. David loved that. Loved her. "It's not our problem."

"Yes, it is our problem. We have to show love." Darla let go of his hand and stepped back. Her face was set in stern lines, her dark eyes glowing with the unyielding resolve he'd run into before. "I'm going to help Susannah. I'm going to ask God to show me how."

Then she turned and walked to her room, determination in every step.

David went into his study but he didn't turn on the lights. Instead he stood in the dark, thinking. Finally he could contain his hurt no longer.

"I don't want to take on anyone else's problems, God," he whispered. "I was Silver's guardian for four years while Wade worked in South America. When Dad died, I took over his law firm, and then managed Mom's care until she passed away. Then Darla had her accident and it was up to me again. I can't take on any more."

"I'll be good, Davy," Darla whispered.

He whirled around, saw her standing in the doorway with tears coursing down her cheeks and cursed his stupidity.

"Oh, Darla, honey, I didn't mean—"

"I promise I won't be bad anymore. I won't yell or break things or be nasty, if we could have Susannah look after me. Please?" She stood in her white cotton nightgown, a penitent child where a woman should have been. She'd lost so much.

His heart ached to make her world better. But not this way.

"Sweetie, I don't think Susannah is going to be able to work. I think she'll have to rest and get well."

"For a little while, till she's not sick. But then Susannah will want to work. She told me she came to see if Connie could help her get a job." Darla dragged on his arm. "Ms. Evans said she isn't ever coming back here to stay with me again, so we have a job, Davy. Please, could we get Susannah?"

David had never been able to deny his sister her heart's desire. Not since the day she'd been born. Certainly not since her accident. But David couldn't promise this. Darla took every spare moment he had and then some. He had to be her buffer, protect her and make sure her world was safe and secure. He couldn't take on the responsibility for a pregnant woman, too. He just couldn't take on another obligation for anything or anyone else.

Can't or won't? his conscience probed.

"Please, Davy?"

"I'm not saying yes," he warned. "I'm saying I'll think about it. But don't get your hopes up, Darla, because I don't believe Susannah will want to do it."

And I don't want her here. I don't want to be responsible if she works too hard or you cause her problems and that child is jeopardized. I don't want more responsibility.

"Thank you, Davy." Darla flung her arms around him and hugged him as hard as she could.

"I haven't said Susannah can come, remember."

"I know." She tipped her head back and grinned like the old Darla would have. "But I'm going to pray God will change your mind." She kissed him, then raced toward the kitchen. "I didn't have dinner. I'm hungry."

Darla's faith.

David wished his own was as strong.

Chapter Two

"So you thought you were married to this man?" Connie said.

"Nick. Yes." Susannah nodded.

"But—"

"I know it sounds stupid and gullible," Susannah muttered and hung her head. "He said he didn't want a fuss, that he wanted our wedding to be just us, private and intimate."

"But to lie about marriage—I am so sorry." Connie touched her hand in wordless sympathy.

"So am I—sorry that I was so dumb. Nick arranged everything that I asked for—the minister, the church, everything. But it wasn't real. None of it was." Susannah pushed away the rest of the soup David had brought. She shook her head. "I thought Nick loved me. I guess I should have known better."

"Why? When you're in love, you do trust the one you love." Connie's fingers smoothed hers. "That's natural, exactly how God meant love to be."

"Only God didn't mean love for me." Guilt settled

on Susannah for ruining her friend's party. "Shouldn't you go back to your guests?"

"I told them an emergency had arisen."

"I'm an emergency? Yuk." Susannah made a face.

"Just like the old days, huh?" Connie teased. She shook her head. "Don't worry. They're friends and well used to my 'emergencies.' Wade will take care of them."

"Is he nice?" Susannah asked softly, studying her friend's glowing face with a twinge of envy.

"Wade is—wonderful." Connie's face radiated happiness.

"How did you meet?"

"Silver is Wade's daughter. Wade had to leave her here while he worked in South America. David was her guardian. He hired me to be Silver's nanny."

"How romantic. Like Cinderella." Susannah thought Darla would have loved that.

"Not at first. When Wade came home he was nothing like I expected. But God knew what he was doing when he put us together. We were married a year ago." Connie held out her hand. "My engagement ring was Wade's mother's."

"It's beautiful." Susannah thought of the cheap gold circlet she'd tucked into her bag. Nick had promised he'd get something nicer later on. Another lie. "Nick died and I didn't have anywhere else to go."

"Oh, Suze, I'm so glad you came here. You were only seventeen when you ran away from our foster home. What have you been doing?" Connie asked, her voice grave. "I called home several times, but Mom said she didn't know where you'd gone."

"I got in with the wrong group and went to Los Angeles. It took me a while to get my head on straight, but eventually I got a job in a nursing home. That's where I met Nick." She inhaled to ease the constriction in her throat. No more tears.

Connie squeezed her fingers. "How did you find me?"

"I finally phoned Mom day before yesterday."

"She misses you." Connie's eyes blazed with sympathy.

"I miss her, too." Susannah sniffed. "I was stupid to run away. So stupid."

"Everybody makes mistakes."

"Even you?" Susannah asked, glancing around.

"Especially me." Connie laughed. "I'll tell you later about my mistakes." Her voice grew serious. "But what about the baby, Suze? When are you due?"

"April. Around Easter."

"An Easter baby."

Susannah gulped. "I'm on my own and I have about two nickels to rub together. I guess, first of all, I need to find a job. Do you know of any?"

"First of all you need to get better," Connie said in her familiar "mother" tone. "Do you want to keep your baby?"

"I don't think any child would want a mother like me." She deliberately didn't look at Connie.

"But you'd make a wonderful mother!" her friend protested.

"Hardly," Susannah scoffed. "Look how I messed up my own family. I'm so not the poster woman for motherhood."

"You were nine the day they brought you to our foster home. I told you then and I'll tell you again, *you* did not break up your family, Suze. Nothing you did caused your father to leave you, or your mother to start drinking. And you did not start that fire." Connie tucked a finger under her chin and forced her to look up.

Susannah couldn't stop the tears. "Why did God let this happen to me, Connie?"

"Oh, sweetheart." Connie wrapped comforting arms around her shoulders and hugged her close, rocking back and forth as she had when Susannah was younger.

"I feel like He hates me," Susannah sobbed.

"God? No way." Connie let go and leaned back. "Listen to me, kiddo, and hear me well. God does not hate you. He loves you more than you could ever imagine."

"But I've messed up—"

"There are no 'buts' where God is concerned. He loves you. Period." Connie pressed the tendrils away from Susannah's face, then cupped her cheeks and peered straight into her eyes. "God has a plan. He's going to work all of this out for your benefit."

"You sound so sure."

"I am sure. Positive." Connie smiled. "But until He shows us the next step, I have the perfect guest room upstairs. You'll stay as long as you need to. Now finish that soup and try to swallow a few of the crackers," she insisted. "You're thinner now than you were when you first came to North Dakota, and you were a stick then. Eat."

"Still as bossy," Susannah teased, her heart swelling at the relief of being able to count on a friend.

"Still needing bossing," Connie shot back, laughing. "You need taking care of, and I'm just the person to do it." She watched while Susannah ate. "What was Darla saying about Sleeping Beauty?"

Susannah shrugged but couldn't stop her blush. "I

passed out on the doorstep. Her brother carried me in here. When I came to, she was demanding he kiss me, like Sleeping Beauty." Susannah crunched another cracker, enjoying the feeling of having enough to satisfy her hunger. It had been ages since she'd been able to eat her fill.

"She loves that story." Connie smiled fondly.

"Darla is a bit old for fairy tales," Susannah mused. "Something's wrong with her, right?"

"She had a skiing accident." Connie's voice filled with sadness. "It happened a few months after her mother died. Their father was already gone so David had to handle everything. He's been looking after her the best he can, but it's been a challenge for him."

"What do you mean?" Susannah struggled to decipher the cautious tone in Connie's voice.

"Well, David was engaged. Twice."

"Oh." Not much wonder, Susannah thought. He was very good-looking.

"Each time his fiancées backed out because of Darla."

"They wanted him to dump her into some home?" Indignation filled Susannah. "Typical."

"Why do you say that, Suze?"

"It was like that where I worked," Susannah fumed. "So often the seniors were seen as burdens because they took a little extra time and attention, or couldn't remember as well."

"Well, in Darla's case, David's fiancées might have had a point," Connie said, her voice quiet.

"Oh?" Susannah frowned. "Why?"

"Darla has had—" Connie paused "—difficulty adjusting to her world since the accident."

"But surely she goes to a program of some sort?" Susannah asked.

"She does. The problem is Darla. She has trouble working with anyone. Her temper gets very bad. I'm sure that's what happened with my lamp." Connie inclined her head toward the shattered glass.

"When I came to, she was yelling." Susannah frowned. "But she didn't act up when I was speaking with her. She was sweet and quite charming."

"That's the way she is, until someone doesn't do as she wants. Then she balks and makes a scene. It's part of her brain injury. She's had a number of workers try to teach her stronger self-control." Connie made a face. "With little success, so far. They keep quitting."

"Well, maybe David hasn't found the right people to work with her," Susannah said. "He seemed kind of frustrated by her."

"Maybe he is," Connie agreed, "but he devotes himself to his sister."

"To the exclusion of everything else?" Was that why he looked so tired?

"Yes, sometimes. David is convinced it's his duty to his parents to ensure Darla's happiness, even if he has to sacrifice his own." Connie pulled a vacuum hose from a cupboard and cleaned up the shards of glass before tucking the lampshade into a closet.

"Aren't you mad about the lamp?" Susannah asked curiously.

"It was just a thing." Connie loaded the used dishes onto the tray. "People are more important than things. Come."

Connie opened a door that led to a staircase. Susannah followed her, curious to see the rest of this lovely house.

"We'll sneak up to your room this way." Connie shot her a conspiratorial grin.

Their footsteps were muffled by thickly carpeted stairs. Connie grasped her hand and led her to a beautiful room tucked under the eaves.

"This used to be my room," she said. Her face reflected a flurry of emotions as she sank onto the window seat. "I spent a lot of time right here, praying."

"Are you happy, Connie?" Susannah asked, sitting beside her. "Truly?"

"Happier than I ever imagined I'd be." Connie hugged her. "You will be, too, Suze. But you have to give God time to work things out for you. You have to have faith that He has great things in store for your future."

"That's hard, given my past," Susannah muttered.

"That's when it's most important to read your Bible and pray," Connie murmured. "You have a lot of decisions to make. But you don't have to rush. You can stay right here, get well and figure things out in your own time."

"Is it hard—being a mother?" The question slipped out in spite of her determination not to ask.

But the prospect of motherhood scared her silly.

"You're worried about the baby, aren't you, Suze. Why?" Connie moved to sit on the bed, patting the space beside her. When Susannah sat down, she hugged her close. "What's really bothering you?"

"My role model for motherhood wasn't exactly nurturing. Nothing mattered to my mother more than her next drink." She heard the resentment in her own voice but couldn't control it. "Nothing."

"Suze, honey, you can't hold on to the bitterness."

"Can't I?" Susannah opened her bag and pulled out her wallet. She flipped it to two pictures nestled inside. "They're dead, Connie. Because of me."

"No."

"Yes." Susannah nodded. "I should have been there."

"Then you would have died, too." Connie gripped her hand.

"But if only I hadn't chosen—"

"The fire wasn't your fault, Susannah." Connie's soft voice hardened. "No matter what your mother said when you were a kid."

Susannah had gone round and round this argument in her head for years. But nothing erased the little voice of blame in the back of her brain. Her hand rested for an instant on her stomach.

"A new life," Connie murmured. "Hard to wrap your mind around it?"

"Very," Susannah agreed with a grimace. "Even harder to imagine coping."

"You'll do fine," Connie assured her.

"It's easy for you to say that. You spent all those years in our foster home caring for everybody else. I don't know anything about caring for a baby, except that you need to feed it and change it." Just saying that made Susannah feel helpless. "What if it gets sick?"

"Then you'll get help." Connie patted her shoulder. "One thing I've learned with Silver is that there are no easy answers, no recipe you can follow. You do your best, pray really hard and have faith that God will answer. And He does. David told me that when he first hired me."

"Really?" So David Foster was a man of faith, too.

"David is one of the good guys. My husband is another. So is their friend Jared." Connie smiled with pride. "They're the kind of men who do the right thing, no matter what. Integrity. They have it in spades."

Susannah couldn't dislodge the image of the tall dark-haired man with the slow spreading grin that started with a slight lift at the corners of his mouth, followed by a gradual widening until it reached his toffee eyes. David Foster had the kind of smile that took forever to get where it was going, but once it got there, it took your breath.

"A lawyer with integrity," she mused. "How novel."

Connie drew back the quilt and patted a pillow. "Come on, into bed. Your eyelids are drooping. Rest. We'll talk again whenever you're ready."

"Did I say thank you?" Tears swelled Susannah's throat.

"What are sisters for?" Connie hugged her. "Don't worry about anything, Suze. You're here now. Relax. In due time you can start planning for the future. Just remember—you're not alone."

A moment later she was gone, the door whispering closed behind her. Susannah stood up, tiredness washing over her. Then she spied the bathroom door.

Five minutes later she was up to her neck in bubbles in a huge tub, enjoying the relaxing lavender fragrance as jets pulsed water over her weary flesh.

Are You really watching out for me, God?

She thought over the past months and the tumble from joy to despair that she'd experienced. Unbidden, thoughts of David's troubles rose. How difficult to lose both your parents, and then the sister you'd known and loved. They had that in common—loss.

Susannah hadn't said anything to Darla or Connie, but when David had carried her into the house, she had come to, for a second. And in that moment, she *had* felt like Sleeping Beauty. Awakening to a whole new perspective on life.

Which was really stupid. She didn't want anything to do with love. Certainly not the romantic fairy-tale kind—that only led to disappointment and pain.

Susannah Wells had never had a fairy-tale life and she doubted it was about to start now, just because a nice man and his sister had cared for her. She didn't deserve a picture-perfect life.

And you won't have one. You're pregnant, Susannah. David Foster won't give you a second look.

Not that she wanted him to. Depend on yourself. She'd learned that lesson very well a long time ago.

Wearied by all the questions that had no answers, Susannah rose, drained the tub and prepared for bed. But when she finally climbed in between the sheets, she felt wide awake. She pulled open the drawer of the nightstand to search for something to read. A Bible lay there.

She picked it up with no idea of where to start reading. She let it fall open on the bed. Isaiah 43.

I, I am the One who forgives all your sins, for My sake, I will not remember your sins.

God forgave her? That's what Connie had said. But maybe it was only an accident that she was reading these words. Susannah closed the Bible, let it fall open again.

2 Corinthians.

God is the Father who is full of mercy and all comfort. He comforts us every time we have trouble, so when others have trouble, we can comfort them with the same comfort God gives us.

So many times she'd asked herself, where is God? According to this, He was right here, comforting her with Connie's house. He was the father who didn't walk out when life got rough.

A flicker of hope burst into flame inside Susannah's heart.

Maybe God could forgive the stupid choices she'd made. Maybe...but she doubted it. She wasn't like Connie—good and smart and worth saving.

God had let her get duped by Nick. Why?

Because she wasn't worth loving. Her whole life was proof of that.

Susannah let her tears flow far into the night.

Chapter Three

David screeched to a halt in front of his home and jumped out of the car.

"I'm sorry, Mr. Foster. I only went to get Darla a drink because she said she was thirsty. When I came back, she was gone." The caregiver wrung her hands. "I've looked everywhere. She's not in the house or the yard."

"Okay. Okay." He forced his brain to focus. "Show me what she was doing."

"Here."

He studied the reams of pictures Darla had drawn. Nothing made sense to him.

"What were you talking about?" he asked.

"Actually I was reading."

"Reading what?" Suspicions rose.

"*Sleeping Beauty.* From that big book she likes so much." The woman pointed. "I tried to read something else, but she wouldn't listen.

Two weeks of Darla nagging him to visit Connie's.

Suddenly it all made sense to David.

"Wait here a moment, would you please?" He picked up the phone and dialed, chagrined when Susannah

Wells answered. "This is David Foster. By chance, did Darla walk over there?"

"Connie is just now calling your office," Susannah explained. "We were having lunch by the pool when Darla showed up. She was quite upset. Connie didn't want to make it worse so she included her in our lunch. Not that you need to worry," she added.

"Why's that?"

"Darla calmed down immediately once we got her busy. Connie has tons of puzzles. Darla seems fascinated by them, too."

Puzzles? Since when?

"I'll be over in a few minutes to pick her up," he said. "I'm sorry she bothered you."

"Darla's no bother at all," Susannah said. She paused, then spoke slowly, thoughtfully. "It would be nice if she could stay for a while, though, if that won't upset your plans."

Ha! David's plans had gone on hold the moment he'd received the call.

"I'm afraid I've been at loose ends, taking up too much of Connie's time," Susannah explained. "Having Darla here would free Connie to attend to her own issues. She wouldn't have to keep babysitting me."

"You're feeling better?" Not that he wanted to know. He'd spent hours shoving the memory of Susannah's face out of his brain.

"Oh, yes. Much recovered." She chuckled. "Especially with Darla here. She's got a wicked sense of humor."

"Mmm." What was he supposed to say to that? "Well, I'll come and get her out of your hair."

"Really, it's not— Oh, here's Connie."

"David?" Connie sounded breathless.

"Sorry for the invasion," he apologized.

"Invasion? Darla's like a refreshing breeze off the mountains. Which, given today's heat, I could use. This is not autumn in Tucson as I've known it." She chuckled.

"Hang around, you'll get used to it." He swallowed. "Connie—"

She cut him off.

"David, I was thinking—" He could almost hear the wheels grinding in Connie's head. "Couldn't Darla stay? Susannah and I are enjoying the visit as much as she. In fact, I've just had the most wonderful idea."

"Oh?" He glanced at his watch, not really listening to Connie's plan. Ten minutes before his next client arrived in his office. Could he get back in ten minutes?

"…Susannah would be great at it. They really connect."

"I'm sorry, Connie," he interrupted. "What did you say?"

"I said, why don't you ask Susannah about caring for Darla after school? She has her certification as a special care aide. And she's very level-headed. They get along so well. I'm sure Darla would love it."

"I don't think a pregnant woman—"

"Don't be silly. This is October and Susannah's not due until Easter. I think it would be perfect," Connie enthused. She lowered her voice. "Susannah really needs a job, David. Working with Darla is taxing but it would only be for a few hours a day and it would keep her mind occupied. The hours Darla spends at her school would also give Susannah some time on her own."

David hated the whole idea. He didn't want a pregnant woman in his employ, someone else to be responsible for. Especially someone he was faintly attracted to.

Faintly?

David shut off the mocking laughter in his head and refocused. His sister had to have someone, and clearly the woman the agency had sent over wasn't going to work out. Again.

"Will you consider it?" Connie asked. "Please?"

"I can't decide this right now. I left the office in a rush and I've got an urgent appointment in a few minutes." David thought for a moment. "Could Darla stay there for the afternoon, just till I get home? Then I'm going to have to talk to her. This can't happen again."

"I'll make sure she stays. You go do your work. We'll be fine," Connie insisted. "But promise me you'll think about my suggestion. It would be so perfect."

"Connie, Darla is bigger than Susannah. And stronger, judging by what I saw. She could hurt your friend. Not intentionally, but she does lash out."

"But that's the funny thing. She hasn't with Susannah. Maybe because of the baby, I don't know." Connie sighed. "I know how you like to dot all the *i*'s, David. Go back to your office. Think on it. We'll be here."

"Thanks. You're a good friend, Connie." David hung up and wasted a few minutes musing on the idea.

"Am I fired?"

He blinked and saw the helper he'd hired staring at him.

"Because if I'm not, I quit. I can't do this. She's—violent."

"She just gets a little frustrated. I'm sorry if Darla scared you. Here." He handed her a wad of money. "That should cover your expenses. Thanks a lot."

By the time David returned to his office, his father's former client was antsy and David had his work cut out assuring the high-profile man that his case wouldn't suffer just because his father wasn't handling it. David worked steadily until he suddenly noticed the office was quiet and the clock said ten to six.

He was so far behind he could have used another three hours to catch up. But no way was he going to add to Connie's responsibilities by shirking his. Traffic was backed up and by the time he arrived on their street the sun had long since dipped below the craggy red Rincon Mountain tips.

"I'm so sorry," he began as the door opened. He stopped. Susannah. "Hello." She looked infinitely better than she had last time. In fact, she glowed.

"Hello, yourself." She didn't smile. "We're about to sit down to dinner."

"Then I won't bother you." He could feel the ice in her voice. "If you'll call Darla?"

"No, I won't." She stepped forward and pulled the door closed behind her, forcing him to take a step back. "You can't make her leave now."

"Why not?" The peremptory tone of her voice confused him.

"Darla's spent a huge amount of time helping prepare this meal," Susannah informed him. "It's only fair she should get to enjoy it."

"I'm not sure this is about fairness. But—"
She cut him off.

"Look, I get that you don't like me, that you think I'm some kind of a tramp. It was evident in the way you looked at me when I told Connie I was pregnant." Her face flushed red but she didn't stop glaring at him. "Fine. No problem. But this isn't about me."

If that's what she thought, her perceptions were way

off. David had lost valuable billing time in the past two weeks thinking about Susannah Wells, and not one thought had been negative.

"Did you hear me?" she asked, frowning.

"This isn't about you," he repeated, noting the way the porch light reflected the emerald sparks in her eyes. The deep hollows under her cheeks had filled out a little and that pallid, sickly look was completely gone. Her blond hair shone like a swath of hammered gold as it tumbled down her back.

"It isn't about you, either. It's about Darla. She's tried very hard to make up for worrying you by leaving your house without telling anyone. Helping with dinner is her way of making up." Susannah lowered her voice as the door creaked open. "Can't you let her have that much?"

She made it sound like he was some kind of an ogre. David fumed. But he kept his lips buttoned because Darla's dark head appeared in the doorway.

"Can we stay for dinner, Davy? Connie invited, I didn't ask." His sister stood in front of him, hands clasped at her waist as she waited. She looked different and it took David a minute to figure out why. Her hair. It had been styled in a way that showed off her pretty eyes.

"Do you deserve to stay?" he asked, waiting for her to blow up.

But Darla simply shook her head.

"No, I don't," she murmured. "I promised not to leave the house without asking, and I broke my promise. I'm sorry, Davy."

"Are you really?" he asked, suspicious of the meek tone in her voice. He glanced at Susannah but she was watching Darla, her face an expressionless mask.

"I really am." Darla peeked at Susannah who gave

a slight nod. "I got mad because Ms. Matchett said my fairy-tale book was silly. We argued, and she said I was a dummy." Her bottom lip trembled, but after a moment she collected herself. "I didn't like her calling me that so I left. But I shouldn't have. I'm sorry, Davy."

His hands tightened into balls of anger. Dummy. The one put-down Darla hated most of all. No wonder she'd run.

"I was really scared, Darla," he said quietly. "I didn't know if you'd been hurt or got lost or what had happened. I was ready to call the police."

"The police?" Her eyes grew huge, then flared. "But I didn't do anything wrong!" She stamped her foot.

Susannah cleared her throat. Darla's entire demeanor altered.

"I'm sorry, Davy," she said. "I did do something wrong. I know it. And I won't do that ever again. I promise. Okay?"

Those big brown eyes—they always got to him. Peering up at him so adoringly from the first day he'd seen her in her bassinet. The innocence was still there.

"Okay. I forgive you."

She threw her arms around him in an exuberant hug and nearly squeezed the breath out of him. Behind her, Susannah hid her grin behind her hand.

"Thank you, Davy." Darla was all smiles now. "So can we stay for dinner? I helped," she said proudly.

"If Connie says it's okay," he muttered, knowing he'd been bested.

"She will."

He watched his sister and Susannah share a grin before Darla hurried into the house.

"She was very hurt by that Matchett person's comment," Susannah murmured.

He nodded.

"She hates to be called dumb." He studied her. "What did you say to her?"

"What makes you think I said anything?" She preceded him into the house.

"Connie seems to think the two of you have developed some kind of rapport." He couldn't help but notice the way Susannah's face tightened.

"You don't like that, do you?" she challenged. "You don't think someone like me should be anywhere around Darla."

"I don't think that at all," he argued.

"Darla is a lot smarter than you give her credit for, Mr. Foster."

"My name is David."

Susannah paused in the foyer, her face serious. "Your sister is very smart, David. She craves your attention. She feels alone and she desperately wants to please you." She tilted her head to one side, watching him. "I'm no psychiatrist, but I think Darla wants to prove to you that she's good at something. Hence the reciting of commercials and such."

"That's—interesting," he said.

"She could do so many things." Susannah's voice grew intense. "But she says you won't let her try. You're afraid she'll hurt herself. That's hard on her."

"Uh—"

"You don't think I know what I'm talking about. I get that. I guess I wouldn't listen to me, either. I don't have any credentials and I'm not exactly a walking advertisement for responsibility. But please, don't write off Darla's ideas too quickly. That's worse to her than being called dumb."

She'd put her hand on his arm as she spoke, imploring him to listen. David glanced at it. Susannah only then seemed aware of what she'd done and hurriedly jerked her hand away.

"Never mind," she whispered and hurried toward the others.

All through dinner David kept watch over his sister and the woman she seemed to adore. Darla told Susannah all about the pottery she'd made in her therapy classes, but it was the first time David had heard that she missed working with clay.

Or that she didn't like the outfit she wore. His choice.

Susannah Wells had been busy.

"Aren't they great together?" Connie sat by him in the family room, watching Susannah and Darla with Silver outside in the courtyard. "Darla has a way with flowers, David. She repotted several cacti with Hornby this afternoon and you know he never lets anyone help him do that."

Just yesterday David had refused to let Darla weed the flower garden, afraid she'd hurt herself on the prickly thorns of the cholla.

Was Susannah right? Was he holding her back?

No. Susannah was full of advice, but she wasn't the one who had to rescue Darla when something bad happened, or calm her when life didn't go her way.

"She's been asking Susannah questions about the baby all day." Connie chuckled. "She's very excited."

"Connie." David frowned as he struggled to find the right words. "I'm sure Susannah is a nice person. And I'm guessing something bad landed her here, but—"

"Something bad? You could say that," Connie said, her voice harsh. "She married a guy she thought loved her. When he found out she was pregnant, he told her they weren't actually married at all and he kicked her out." She smiled grimly. "Susannah has a long history of those she trusts letting her down, so much so that she doesn't believe she's worthy of love."

"I'm sorry." He didn't know what else to say.

"Give her a chance, David," Connie pleaded. "Susannah's smart, she's funny, but most of all, she is good for Darla. Isn't that the kind of caregiver you want?"

What he wanted was a stranger, someone with no ties to him, who would come in, do her job and leave without affecting him. Susannah was beautiful, he'd already noticed that. And she was pregnant.

There would be complications if he hired her. Lots of them.

I don't have to get personally involved, other than making sure she's medically fit for work and that she can handle Darla. There's no need for me to treat Susannah Wells as anything more than an employee.

Somewhere in the recesses of his brain David heard mocking laughter.

Like he hadn't already noticed her intense eyes, fine-limbed figure or model-perfect face.

"David?" Connie's voice prodded him back to reality.

Laughter, sweet and carefree, floated into the family room from the courtyard. Susannah. She stood in a patch of light, gilded by the silvery beams, her delicate features faintly pink from the exertion of tossing a ball. She looked the same age as Darla.

"How old is she?" he asked.

"Twenty-two. Just." Connie frowned. "Does her age matter?"

Three years older than Darla. And about to be a mother.

"Come on, Darla," Susannah cheered. "You can throw it all the way from there. I know you can."

And Darla did.

"I'll give her a trial period of two weeks," David told Connie. "If she finds the work too hard or Darla too difficult, she can back out. I just hope Darla doesn't change her mind and blow up."

"I don't think that's going to happen, David." Connie laughed. "Just look at the two of them."

Susannah and Darla stood together, arms around each other's waists as they watched Silver dive into the pool. Susannah said something to Darla, who was now clad in a swimsuit. When had that happened?

David jumped to his feet. Darla was scared of water. She panicked when it closed over her head and after being rescued, always took hours of calming. And then came the nightmares.

"No!" he yelled.

But he was too late. Darla jumped into the pool. The water closed over her body. David rushed outside, furious that he hadn't been paying enough attention. He saw her black swimsuit sink to the bottom and yanked off his shirt.

"Wait." Susannah pulled on his arm. "Give her a chance."

"She hates it," he hissed. "She freezes underwater."

But after what seemed an eternity, Darla resurfaced and began to move, pushing herself across the pool until she reached the other side. She grabbed the side, gasping for air but grinning.

"I did it." She pumped her fist in the air. "Did you see, Susannah? I did it."

"I knew you would." Susannah smiled at her, watching as Darla darted through the shallow water to chase Silver. "You have to believe in her, David," she murmured. "Otherwise, how will she believe in herself?"

Then Susannah turned away, found a lounger and sank into it, her attention wholly focused on the pair in the pool.

She was right.

That was the thing that shocked David the most. This girl, seven years his junior with no training, not only saw Darla's potential but helped his sister find it.

He walked toward her.

"I'd like to offer you a job," he said. "But only if you are checked out by a doctor and he okays you to work with Darla. It would be only a few hours a day with perhaps some time on Saturdays." He told her how much he was willing to pay.

"There's a catch, isn't there?" Susannah said after a long silence, during which she studied him with those intense green eyes. "What is it?"

David didn't hesitate.

"Every activity you plan has to be approved by me," he told her.

"Every one?" She smiled. "Wow, you are a control freak, aren't you?"

"I insist on keeping my sister safe," he said firmly. "That's my condition."

"I see." Susannah's scrutiny didn't diminish. After a long silence she frowned. "Did you ever consider that you might be keeping her too safe?"

"No." He wasn't going to start out with her questioning his rules. "I'd like to start with a trial period of two weeks. Do you want the job or not?"

She kept him waiting, a blond beauty whose pink cheeks had been freshly kissed by the sun. Finally she nodded once. "Yes."

"Good. As soon as you get the doctor's approval, you can start." He turned to leave.

"I have a condition of my own."

He wheeled around, frustrated by the way she challenged him. "Which is?"

"When you disagree with my suggestions, and you will disagree," Susannah said, her smile kicking up the corners of her pretty lips, "will you at least try to understand that I'm making them for Darla's benefit?"

What did she think—that he was some bitter, angry, power monger who had to lord it over everyone to feel complete?

"I'll listen," David agreed, staring at her midriff. "As long as you promise you won't take any undue chances."

"With the baby?" Her face tightened. "No," she said firmly. "I want my baby to be healthy. I won't risk anything for that. That's one thing I don't intend to mess up."

"Then we have a deal."

David turned and walked away.

That's one thing I don't intend to mess up.

For the rest of the day, David couldn't stop speculating on Susannah's comment. What—or who—had let Susannah down, making her believe she had to earn love?

He found no satisfactory answers to stop his thoughts about Darla's newest caregiver—at least, that's how he *should* be thinking of the beautiful Susannah Wells.

Chapter Four

Two weeks later Susannah stirred under the November sun, stretched and blinked. The scene in front of her brought her wide awake.

"Do you like it?" Darla preened, scissors dangling from one finger.

"Um, it's different." Susannah slid her legs to one side and slowly rose. Thankfully her recent light-headedness seemed to have abated. She lifted the scissors from Darla's hands and put them on the patio table. "Let's put these away."

She'd slept a full eight hours last night. It wasn't as if she was tired. And yet, one minute of sun and she went out like a light. Sleeping on the job. David would be furious.

"Why did you cut off the bottom of your dress, sweetie?" Susannah asked.

"I don't like this dress," Darla grumbled. She flopped down into a chair. "Davy says it's nice but I think it's ugly."

"Because it's black?" Susannah asked. "But you look good in black. You have the right coloring."

Darla didn't look at her. Instead she drew her knees to her chin and peered into space.

"Why so serious?" Susannah laid a hand on the shiny dark head. "What are you thinking about, honey?"

"When my mom died, it was like today," Darla whispered. "There were leaves falling off the trees."

And you wore a black dress.

"Black isn't only for funerals, you know, Darla," she soothed. "Evening wear is often black because it looks so dressy. And a lot of women wear black to look slimmer."

"Am I fat?" Darla asked, eyes widening.

"No! Of course you're not. I didn't mean that." Susannah couldn't tell what was going on in the girl's mind, so she waited.

"Black clothes don't show marks when you spill stuff," the whisper came a minute later.

"Oh?" Something told Susannah to proceed very carefully.

"Davy and me went out for pizza last night. It was good, but I spilled."

"I'm sure the pizza people didn't care. Restaurants are used to spills," Susannah encouraged. "Besides, everyone gets messy eating pizza."

"Davy didn't. He had on a white shirt." Darla wouldn't look at her. "I wore my soccer shirt. It got stains. I looked like a baby."

Darla was worried about her appearance?

"Davy was embarr—" She frowned, unable to find the word.

"Embarrassed? I don't think David gets embarrassed." Susannah wasn't sure she completely understood what was behind these comments. But it was time to find out why her clothes bothered Darla. She held out a hand. "Come on."

"Where are we going?" Darla asked, taking Susannah's hand to help her rise.

"To look at your closet."

"Okay." Darla picked up the scissors.

"Without those," she added hastily.

"Oh." Darla put them back, then led the way to her room.

As they poked through the contents of the closet for the rest of the afternoon, Susannah watched Darla's reaction to each item. Mostly negative. Susannah had no idea how much time had passed when a sardonic voice in the doorway asked, "Did you lose something?"

"Oh. Hi." Darla had a point, Susannah decided. David looked as neat and pristine as he'd probably looked when he left the house this morning. She felt rumpled and dingy even being in the same room. "We're taking inventory."

"Ah." He blinked. "I'm going to change. You won't— er, leave the room like that, will you?"

"I think so." Susannah winked at Darla. "Has a certain carefree look, don't you think?"

But Darla didn't laugh. Instead she rose and began scooping up handfuls of hangers and placing them on the rod in her closet.

"I'll make it good, Davy," she said as she scurried back and forth.

"What happened to your dress?" he asked, staring at the ragged, sawed-off hem.

"Oh, that," Susannah said, noting Darla's flush of embarrassment. "I'm afraid that's a fashion plan gone wrong."

"You did it deliberately?" Pure shock robbed all expression from his face.

"It was unplanned," she hedged. "But the dress didn't work in its original state anyway."

"It worked for—never mind." His mouth drooped before he quickly closed it. He turned to leave, then stopped and turned back, dark eyes suspicious. "Did anything else happen today?"

"We did a little work in the back flower bed. Darla's really good at planting and we both like mums, so we planted a few pots."

"Then I owe you some money." He nodded. "If you'll meet me downstairs in a few minutes, I'll pay you."

"Good idea. I want to talk to you anyway." Susannah frowned. Was that fear flickering through his tawny eyes? Of her? "Five minutes?"

He nodded and left.

"Davy paid for my clothes. He likes them. So do I," Darla insisted loudly. She hurried to get the clothes hung, and in her haste the hangers dangled helter-skelter.

"Hey, slow down," Susannah chuckled. "I helped create this mess. I'm going to help you clean it up." By showing Darla how to group clothes, they reorganized the closet and rearranged the drawers. She paused when she pulled out an old pair of almost-white jeans tucked at the back of the closet. "How come you never wear these, Darla?"

"Davy doesn't like them. And I'm too big." Darla took them from her and relegated them to their hiding place. She took off the dress she'd cut and drew on another exactly the same except it was navy instead of black.

Clearly Darla didn't want to irritate the brother who had done so much for her. A lump of pity swelled in Susannah's throat. Darla was willing to be unhappy rather than tell her brother she hated her clothes.

They walked downstairs together. Mrs. Peters, David's housekeeper, asked Darla to set the table just as he came loping down the stairs.

"Now how much do I owe you for the flowers?"

Susannah glanced down the hall, grabbed his elbow and drew him into his study. She closed the door.

"We have to make this quick before she finishes the table."

"Make what quick?" he asked, one eyebrow elegantly arched.

"Listen, I want to take Darla shopping," she explained.

"Shopping?" He nodded. "More flowers?"

"New clothes." She held up a hand. "You're going to say her clothes are almost new. I'm sure someone at the goodwill center will appreciate that."

"You cut her dress because you don't like her clothes," he guessed, a frown line marring the smooth perfection of his forehead. "Um—"

"Darla cut it. Because she hates it. And the rest of her clothes." Susannah flopped onto a couch and crossed her feet under her. "I can't say I blame her."

His chest puffed out. His face got that indignant look and his caramel eyes turned brittle. Susannah gulped. Okay, that could have been worded differently.

"What I mean is—"

"You mean her clothes aren't trendy. No holes in her jeans, no skintight shirts," he snapped. "Ms. Wells, my sister's clothes are from an expensive store. They are the best—"

"—money can buy," she finished. "I'm sure they are." She sat back and waited for him to cool down.

David continued to glare at her. Eventually he sat down and sighed. "Explain, please."

"Did you choose Darla's clothes? No, let me guess. You told a sales associate what you wanted and she picked them out." Susannah chuckled at the evidence radiating across his face. "I thought so. Probably a commissioned sales woman."

"What difference would that make?" he demanded. "I got the best for my sister. Darla doesn't need to alter her own clothes."

"She might be happier if she could tear them all apart," she mused.

"What? Where is this going?" He looked defensive and frustrated. That was not her goal. Susannah straightened, leaned forward.

"After she cut her dress, Darla told me she wore black the day of her mother's funeral. Then she talked a lot about spilling and messes." She inhaled a deep breath for courage. "Did you notice when you were in her room how many of her clothes are black, brown or gray?"

"Good serviceable colors," David said.

"For men s suits!" Susannah blew the straggling wisps of hair off her forehead and tried again. "Your sister is, what, three years younger than me? Can you imagine me in any of her clothes?"

"No."

Susannah surveyed her jeans. "I don't have good clothes, David. I bought most of mine at a thrift store.

But you're right," she said flatly, "I wouldn't wear Darla's clothes if you gave them to me."

David glared at her. "Why don't you just come right out and say what you mean?"

"Did Darla choose any of those clothes?"

"I don't recall." He frowned, his gaze on some past memory. "Her arm was still bothering her and she had some bandages yet to be removed when we shopped. We went for snaps and zips she could manage." Then he refocused. "Does it matter?"

"Yes!"

"Because?" He waited, shuffling one foot in front of the other.

"Because she should be young and carefree. Instead she wears the clothes of a forty-year-old," Susannah snapped, unable to hold in her irritation. "Because she needs to dress in something that lets her personality shine through. Because Darla is smothering under this blanket you keep putting over her."

"Well. Don't hold back." David stiffened, his face frozen.

"I wouldn't even if I could," she assured him. "I'm here to help Darla. That's what I'm trying to do."

"I'm not sure you fully understand Darla's situation," David said crisply. "Until about eight months ago, she could barely walk. She'd been wearing jogging suits while she did rehab. By the time she finished that, she'd outgrown everything she owned."

He'd done his best. That was the thing that kept Susannah from screaming at him to lighten up. No matter what, David Foster had done the very best he could for his sister. Because he loved her. Connie was right. He did have integrity. How could you fault that?

But Darla was her concern, not sparing David's feelings. Susannah leaned forward, intent on making him understand what she'd only begun to decipher.

"Darla is smart and funny. She's got a sweet heart and she loves people. But she doesn't have any confidence in herself." Susannah touched his arm. "She gets frustrated because she wants so badly to be what you want, and yet somehow, she just can't get there."

"I don't want her to be anything," he protested.

"You want her to be neat and tidy." Susannah pressed on, determined to make him see what she saw.

"That's wrong?" David asked.

"How many teens do you know who fit that designation? By nature teens are exploring, innovating, trying to figure out their world. Darla is no different." Susannah said. "Except that she thinks you're embarrassed when she spills something."

"I'm not embarrassed about anything to do with my sister." She saw the truth in his frank stare. "I thought…"

The complete uncertainty washing over his face gripped a soft spot in her heart.

"David, listen to me and, just for a moment, pretend that I know what I'm talking about." She drew in a breath of courage. "Most teen girls love fashion, they love color. They experiment with style, trying to achieve the looks they see in magazines. It's part of figuring out who they are. I'll bet Darla used to do that, didn't she?"

"She always liked red," he said slowly.

"I didn't see anything red in her closet."

"No." His solemn voice said he'd absorbed what she'd hinted at. "Go on."

"With her current wardrobe, Darla couldn't experiment if she wanted to," Susannah told him. "Her clothes are like a mute button on a TV. They squash everything unique and wonderful about her."

"But—" David stopped, closed his mouth and stared at her.

His silence encouraged Susannah to continue, though she softened her tone.

"I think her accident left her trying to figure out how she fits into her new world. She's struggling to make what she is inside match with those boring clothes."

"So how should she dress?" he asked, his eyes on her worn jeans.

"I want her to express herself. If she's in a happy mood, I want her to be able to pull on something bright and cheerful. If she's feeling down, I want her to express that, instead of becoming so frustrated she blows out of control and tantrums."

A timid knock interrupted.

"Are you mad at me for cutting my dress, Davy?" Darla peeked around the door, her big brown eyes soulful as a puppy's. "I'm sorry."

"It's okay, Dar. It was just a dress." David patted the seat beside him. "Come here for a minute, will you?"

Susannah wanted to cry as the tall, beautiful girl shuffled across the room, shoulders down, misery written all over her demeanor when she flopped down beside her brother.

"Ms. Wells has been telling me she thinks you need some new clothes."

"Really?" Darla jerked upright, her face brightening.

"Would you like to go shopping?" he asked.

For a moment hope glittered in Darla's dark eyes but it fizzled out when she shook her head.

"No. I have lots of clothes. I hung them all up, Davy."

"I know you did, honey. That's great." He smoothed her hair back. "You know, Dar, when we got those clothes you were still getting better from your accident and you had trouble with zippers and buttons." He laid an arm around her shoulders and hugged her. "But you're much better now. I think we should get you some new things, especially with Thanksgiving and Christmas coming. What do you think?"

"Connie's going to have a party. I could get a new dress for that." Darla's face cleared and she grinned. "Okay, Davy."

Susannah wanted to cheer. He'd phrased it just right. Everyone got new clothes for the holidays. It was a natural decision, revealing no reflection on the ugly things now in Darla's wardrobe. Little by little they could be shifted out.

"Can Susannah get a party dress, too?"

Susannah blinked, then shook her head. "Oh, no, I don't—"

"Why not?" David smiled at Darla.

"I don't want a new dress," Susannah protested. "With the baby, that is—" She blushed and avoided his stare. "I won't fit in anything for very long and—"

"There are such things as maternity dresses," he said mildly. "Besides, you'll need something for Connie's Christmas party. It's quite a fancy affair. Tomorrow's Saturday. That's a good day for shopping. I'll pay you overtime."

"No, you won't." Distressed by the way this had turned on her, Susannah rose. "I'm sure the two of you will manage very well tomorrow."

"Oh, no. You're not sticking me with a shopping trip

on my own. We'll pick you up at ten. Right, Darla?" He grinned at his sister, who grinned right back.

"Right. I'm going to tell Mrs. Peters." She rushed away, all arms and legs and excitement, exactly as a teenage girl would.

Susannah stared after her, amazed by the change. When she felt David watching her, she looked away from the intensity of his gaze and walked toward the front door.

"We could start at Bayley's Store for Women," he said, following her.

Her hand on the doorknob, Susannah froze. She turned and looked at him.

"For more of the same?" she asked.

"Point made." He sighed. "Okay, you can pick the stores. But nothing too…"

Susannah couldn't help but roll her eyes. "David, could you just lighten up? Try to remember what it was like when you were her age. It wasn't that long ago," she teased gently.

She thought she saw humor in those toffee-toned eyes, but before she could be sure, David blinked.

"Ten o'clock, remember. How much did you spend on the flowers?" He pulled out his wallet and handed her some money. "Will this cover it?"

"It's too much." Susannah held out her hand, offering it back. But David shook his head.

"No, it isn't. I'm pretty sure you stopped somewhere along the way for a drink, didn't you? And something to eat?"

"How do you know that?" she asked. He grinned, his smile dazzling her. She was momentarily stunned by how great he looked when he smiled.

"Because I'm getting to know you." He reached out and touched the corner of her mouth. "And because you have a little smear of chocolate right here."

"Oh." Her stomach shivered and it had nothing to do with the baby or morning sickness. "Right. Well, I guess I'll see you tomorrow," she said. "Bye."

Susannah turned and literally fled from the man whose touch had just sent warmth flooding through her. Her skin burned where he'd brushed his fingers.

She'd thought David stern and taciturn, but he'd surprised her. Maybe under all that lawyerly reserve and rule making, David Foster wasn't quite the ogre she'd thought.

David shifted uncomfortably on the dinky little chair someone had thought to provide for men stuck waiting while women tried on clothes. He'd like to leave, but he wanted to vet every outfit his sister tried on. So far, his decisions had not been popular with Susannah, who, by the way, seemed perfectly at home on her little perch.

"Uh, I don't think so," he said, when Darla emerged in a swirling lime-green tank top and matching pants.

"Oh, why not?" Susannah asked. "Too much color?"

"No. The pants don't fit her properly. They're too short." He didn't understand the droll look Darla and Susannah exchanged.

"It's a capri pant," Susannah explained. "They're supposed to be that length. It's the fashion."

"Oh." Fashion. He felt like he was drowning.

"So?" Susannah nudged him with her elbow.

"Do you like it?" he asked his sister, studying her face.

"Yes." At least she was definite. "Emmaline wears clothes like this at my school. She's pretty."

"You look pretty, too," he told her. And she did.

Contrary to David's expectations, Susannah's choices for his sister were not outlandish or edgy. Nor were they as expensive as the clothes he'd chosen. He was amazed at Susannah's patience as she taught Darla to choose the things that brought out her natural beauty. With each outfit, as Darla caught a glimpse of herself in the mirror, she grew more graceful. More and more she was becoming the sister he remembered, leaving behind the mulish child he'd battled with for the last eight months.

It wouldn't last, of course. Darla had a long way to go. But she was learning, and Susannah had lasted much longer than any of Darla's other caregivers.

"You should be proud. She's a very beautiful woman," Susannah murmured.

Woman? His sister?

David did a double take at the girl in the red dress now preening in the mirror. But Susannah was right. Darla looked more like a young woman than a girl. She was growing up and he'd have to face all that implied.

"I want Susannah to try on this dress." Darla held out a garment of swirling patterns in deep, rich green. "It has room for the baby," she said.

"It's very beautiful, Darla, and I appreciate you thinking of me," Susannah said quietly. "But I can't try it on. It's too expensive."

"I want you to. It's a present." Darla the woman disappeared, and the petulant girl returned, face turning red when Susannah continued to shake her head. "Davy, buy it," she insisted, thrusting the hanger at her brother.

"Darla, I can't accept it." Susannah was firm but insistent. "Please put it back on the rack."

"No. It's your dress." Darla was working herself up into a snit.

David rose, preparing to leave.

"Sit down please, David. We're not finished yet." Susannah never even looked at him, but her firm tone and calm manner left him in no doubt as to who was in charge.

David sat.

"Put the dress back, please, Darla. Then we need to look at shoes." Susannah blandly continued to survey the list in her hand.

Darla was still angry but now she looked confused.

"I want you to have a new dress, too," she said, her voice quieter as she stood in front of Susannah.

"I know you do, sweetie. And it's very kind of you, but this shopping day is for you. When I decide to get a new dress, I promise you and I will go shopping for it. But not today." She paused, studied the girl. "Okay?"

Darla's internal battle was written all over her face. But Susannah's calm tone and manner won. Darla returned the dress to the rack, changed back into her own clothes and calmly waited while the sales clerk totaled her purchases.

David handed over his credit card in total bemusement. How did Susannah do it?

"Can we have lunch before we start shoe shopping?" he asked as they stored the many packages in his vehicle. "I'm starving."

"That's because you didn't eat a good breakfast. Breakfast is the most important meal of the day. More than half of North Americans skip breakfast." Darla told him, stuffing her last package into the trunk.

"Half?" Susannah sputtered.

David looked at her. She was trying to hide her laughter.

"Yes, half," Darla insisted.

"Then I guess I'm one of those statistics," Susannah told her. "I'm starving, too. And your stomach is growling." She giggled out loud and soon Darla was giggling with her.

Shaking his head, David led them to a restaurant and left Susannah to deal with Darla's insistence on chocolate cake while he scoured the menu for himself. He'd forgotten how nice it was to relax over a meal.

Susannah didn't insist Darla choose anything, he discovered. She commented on the results of certain choices, and then left the decision totally up to Darla, who glanced at him for approval.

"You decide," David said quietly.

And she did, visibly gaining confidence as she discarded the chocolate cake in favor of another choice.

"I don't like soup," she told the server. "It's messy. Can I have something else?"

They settled on a salad to go with her cheeseburger and fries. Usually David ordered something she could munch on right away, but Darla seemed perfectly content to talk as they waited for their food. After a moment she excused herself and went to wash her hands.

"How do you do it?" David asked Susannah the moment his sister was out of hearing range. "She hasn't tantrumed with you once, though I thought we'd have one in the store."

"I did, too," Susannah confessed with a grin. "And if she had, I would have sat there and waited it out."

"Really?" He couldn't imagine sitting through one of Darla's tantrums.

"It's a behavior she's learned, David. She needs time to unlearn it." She shrugged. "If we make her responsible for her actions, she'll soon realize that the results she gets are determined by her. I want her to learn independence."

"We had a big argument about her bedtime last night," he admitted. "She thinks she should stay up longer. Maybe she should," he admitted. "I guess I still think of her as a little kid."

"She is in some ways." Susannah sipped her lemonade. "Why don't you let her choose a time on the condition that she has to get up in the morning when her alarm clock rings without your help? Make her responsible."

"Good idea." He sipped his coffee. "I can't believe you learned all this caring for the elderly."

"Some of it," she admitted. "But most of what I know about behavior, I learned in our foster home. And I took some university classes for a semester. They helped. I'm going to take some more. I want to get a degree in psychology."

He was intrigued by her. More than a boss should be.

"The bathroom is really pretty," Darla told them as she slipped back into her seat. "Lots of red."

Their food arrived and conversation became sporadic. David dug into his steak, then paused to notice that Susannah picked certain items off her plate and set them aside but eagerly bit into a sour pickle.

"So it's true what they say about pregnancies and pickles," he teased.

She flushed a rich ruby flood of color that tinted her skin from the V neckline of her sweater to the roots of her hair. Finally she nodded.

"It's true. For me anyway."

"I don't like pickles," Darla said. "You can have mine, Susannah."

"Thank you." Susannah laid the pickles on one slice of toast, then spread peanut butter on the other. She put them together, cut the whole thing in half and then took a bite.

"That's lunch?"

She blushed again when she caught him staring at her. "It's very good. You should try it."

"I'll take your word for it." Then it dawned on him. "Some foods bother you."

"Mostly the smell of some foods," she murmured, eyeing his steak with her nose turned up. She returned to munching contentedly on her sandwich.

"Connie said you'd seen the doctor I researched. She says everything is okay." It sounded like he was prying, he realized—which he was.

"I'm fine," she said. She set down her sandwich and stared at him. "The baby is fine. I'm very healthy. There's nothing to worry about."

"There's always something to worry about," he muttered, pushing away his plate.

"Why?" Susannah dabbed absently at a dribble of pickle juice and waited for an answer. "I thought Connie told me you believe in God."

"I do."

"People who believe in God usually talk about the faith they have in Him to lead them," she mused, perking up when a dessert cart arrived at the table next to theirs. "What are you worried about?"

"A new study says ninety percent of the things people worry about will never happen," Darla chimed in.

Susannah tucked her chin against her neck but not fast enough to hide her grin. David was beginning to wish he'd never said a word about worry, so he grabbed at their server's suggestions for dessert and bought everyone a huge piece of key lime pie. With the meal finished, he begged off shoe shopping and agreed to meet the two women in a little courtyard area outside. Better to trust Susannah than sit through another round of fashion do's and don'ts.

He was enjoying a well-creamed cup of coffee and working out a schedule of Darla's activities on his smartphone when Susannah arrived lugging several bags, visibly weary. He took them from her and insisted she sit down.

"Where's Darla?" he asked, searching the area behind her.

"She's coming. She met a friend and they're buying an ice cream cone. Her friend's mother will meet us here shortly." Susannah chose a seat in a shady spot where she could study the dangling seed pods of a desert willow. "You were working," she said. "Don't let me bother you."

"No bother." He stuffed the device in his pocket. "I just got an email about Darla's after-school soccer group. I guess I forgot to reregister her."

"Does she have to go?" Susannah asked.

"She loves soccer." He frowned. "Doesn't she?"

"Yes." Susannah didn't meet his stare. "But there are so many more things she wants to try."

"Such as?" He could feel the tension crawling across his shoulders. What was wrong with the status quo? Why did she have to change everything?

"Did you know she wants to do pottery again?"

"I know she liked it before. But it's not very active and Darla needs to keep her muscles toned. Soccer is good for that," he explained.

"Swimming is better."

David tensed. Why was she always so eager to push him?

"I'm not comfortable with her swimming. At least not without me present," he said, waving when Darla emerged from the store. "For now I think we'll stick to the activities she knows."

"The ones you've decided are safe for her, right?" Susannah smiled at Darla but her tone was troubled. "I hope you don't regret it," she said quietly.

David was going to ask what she meant but Darla snagged his attention, showing him the massive cone she was trying to eat before it melted. She giggled and laughed, teased Susannah about the pickle juice that had spattered her shirt and insisted David taste her triple-fudge-and-marshmallow ice cream.

David discarded Susannah's comment. Darla was happy, like a big kid enjoying the pleasures of life. That was exactly what he wanted for her.

Wasn't it?

Unbidden, the image of Darla twirling in front of the store's floor-length mirror in her red dress fluttered through his mind. Not a kid, a woman. He felt the intensity of a stare and caught Susannah looking at him.

She was good for his sister. He didn't deny that. But there were things in Darla's life that *were* working, things that didn't need changing. One of those was soccer.

He urged them back to the car and drove Susannah to Connie's, anxious to escape her probing questions and retreat to the normalcy of his home.

But that night, when the house had quieted and there was no one to disturb his thoughts, David couldn't dislodge Susannah's warning from his brain.

I hope you don't regret it.

"Maybe I'm not supposed to worry about things, Lord," he whispered as he sat in the dark, watching stars diamond-stud the black velvet of the night sky. "But I am worried. She's changing everything. What if Susannah's wrong about Darla?"

But what if she was right?

Chapter Five

This is wrong.

It wasn't the first time Susannah had thought those words as she stood in the church basement and watched Darla try to interact with the young girls in the club.

It wasn't that they were mean or did anything to Darla. In fact, they were most impressed with Darla's new outfit and offered many compliments.

The problem was Darla didn't fit here and she knew it. The other girls were younger, faster and more nimble with their handicrafts. Darla tried, but only halfheartedly, and when her kite didn't work out, she crushed it and threw it into the trash in a fit of anger.

Susannah saw the glint in her eye and the set of her jaw and knew the girl was not happy. The ride home was tense. On an impulse she pulled into a park.

"Let's go for a walk," she said.

After they'd gone a short way, Darla stopped.

"I hate girls' club. I can't do it." She stamped her foot, caught Susannah's eye and sighed. "I'm sorry," she said, flopping onto the grass.

"Actually, I think you did very well at girls' club,

but maybe you've been there long enough," Susannah mused, sitting beside her. Maybe here Darla would open up and speak of things she did want to do.

"Davy likes girls' club. He says it's safe."

"I suppose it is safe," Susannah said, striving to sound noncommittal.

"It's for little kids. I'm not little." After a few minutes Darla began talking about the bed of flowers nearby. She described each one.

"You know a lot about flowers." Susannah's mind had begun to whirl with ideas but she gave nothing away. She'd have to talk to David first, get his permission. And that would probably not be easy.

"I like them. Flowers don't make me feel stupid," Darla muttered. Then her face brightened. "There's the ice cream man. I love ice cream. Maybe they have pistachio. Can I get one, Susannah?" Darla begged.

"I don't know if I have enough cash. Maybe you should find out how much a cone costs first?" Susannah stayed where she was, swamped by a rush of tiredness as Darla raced across the grass.

In a few minutes Darla came rushing back. Susannah held out her wallet and Darla counted out what she needed. It seemed a lot to Susannah. She'd been trying to save every cent she could for the baby but these little side trips were digging into that meager account.

Still, it was worth it to see Darla's proud face as she returned with two fudge bars.

"One for you and one for me."

"Thank you." Susannah took the bar, impressed again by Darla's kind heart. "That's very kind of you to share. Didn't they have pistachio?"

"I'd rather have a fudge one with you," Darla said.

She'd given up her first choice to share. Susannah felt proud as any new mom.

While they ate their cones, Darla talked about her brother.

"Davy's an awfully good brother," she said, her eyes soft with love. "He was on a vacation when my dad died. Davy had to come home and take over his work. When my mom got sick, Davy looked after her, too." Her smile dimmed. "And he always looks after me."

"He loves you a lot."

"I love him, too," Darla said. "I wish he would have gotten married. But Erin didn't want me around." Darla peeked sideways at Susannah, her guilt obvious.

"What happened?" She kept her voice even.

"I wasn't nice. I spilled ketchup on her shirt. Her favorite shirt." A glower replaced Darla's sunny smile. "She told Davy I was a baby, too young to make pots."

"Pots? Oh, you mean pottery?" She shrugged. "Maybe you were too young, honey. I'm afraid I don't know anything about it."

"I do. A man came to my school and showed us how to make pots. He said mine was the best," she said proudly. "Davy put it in the garden."

"You mean the blue one?" Susannah asked, surprised by the information.

"Uh-huh. It was going to be a fountain but it dried too hard and I couldn't put a hole in it." She sighed. "The teacher told me I should try again."

"Maybe you should."

"You mean it, Susannah? You'll let me do pottery?" Darla leaned over and hugged her tightly. "Oh, thank you."

Susannah ignored the blob of chocolate on her shirt-front and hugged back. "It isn't up to me, so don't get in a rush. I have to ask your brother. He's the boss and if he says no—"

She left it hanging. Finished with the ice cream, they rinsed off under a tap and then drove home. Darla immediately stormed David with a demand to make pottery.

As Susannah watched them, she grew very conscious of the way he surveyed her, his gaze resting on the twin ice cream stains the two of them wore. Well, so what? They'd had fun.

His mouth pursed in that thin line that meant he was going to deny Darla's request out of hand. Susannah had to do something.

"Darla, would you show me the pot you made? I'd really like to see it again." She followed the young woman to the back garden to admire the shiny blue pot that held a barrel cactus. "It would have made a lovely fountain," she agreed.

After much discussion about pottery, Mrs. Peters came to ask Darla's help. Darla left, and David turned to her. Susannah stiffened, knowing what was coming.

"Why this sudden need for pottery?" David asked. He pointed to a chair. "Please sit down. You look worn out."

Just what every woman wanted to hear.

"It's not *my* need, it's Darla's," she said, folding into the comfortable garden chair with relief. "She didn't have the best time at the girls' club—again."

"What happened," he demanded. "What did she do?"

"Darla didn't *do* anything," Susannah told him. "But she's too big for that club and she knows it. It doesn't interest her." She straightened and told him in a rush, "I don't think she should go anymore."

"What?" He glared at her. "Why not?"

"David, Darla can do so much more than play with little girls. She's lost some faculties, but she still has lots of skills and interests. Plants, for instance," she said, cutting off the question she knew was coming.

"I suppose I could clear out some of the things my mother planted," he said, studying the lovely garden.

"You could, but she needs more than that." Susannah struggled to explain what she'd begun to understand about Darla. "What would you do if you didn't have your work, David?" she asked.

"Me?" He shrugged. "I always wanted to fly. I have my private license. Why?"

"You have options. Darla is trying to figure out what hers are," Susannah told him. "She wants to do something that makes her feel good about herself, something that shows for her efforts and maybe something that helps others. She needs to feel confident about herself first, though."

"I don't think pottery is an option right now," he mused. "I don't think there are any classes going that she could attend. What else do you have in mind to help her learn this confidence?"

"Swimming." She shook her head at him. "I know *you're* afraid for her, but I think she's ready to challenge herself. She's ashamed that she can't go with her class when they go for swimming lessons. She knows she's missing out, David. Think how much self-esteem she'd have if she went with the class and had no problem in the water."

She knew he understood. He was clever and thoughtful and he wanted Darla to be happy. But something was holding him back.

"What if she panics?" he demanded in a tense voice.

"What if she does? They have trained staff who deal with that all the time. Darla isn't the first one to be afraid of water." Susannah touched his hand. "I know you want to keep her safe. And she will be. But she needs personal and physical challenges to grow and develop."

"But swimming?" He drew back from her touch, his face shadowed by the awning above.

A thought crossed Susannah's mind. "Do you swim, David?"

"Why do you ask?" He looked at her then, straight and head on.

"I ask because it seems like you're projecting your fears onto Darla. And I know that isn't what you want to do." She waited a few moments, watching the truth fill his face. "What happened?" she murmured.

"Are you psychoanalyzing me, Ms. Wells?"

"Do you have something to hide, Mr. Foster?"

It took several moments before he let out a deep breath.

"I was twenty-five. Old enough I suppose, but I never expected—" He shook his head. "My mother was a swimmer. We used to have a pool back here. She loved that pool, did laps every day. I came home one afternoon and found her floating on the water. She'd had a stroke."

"I'm so sorry." He was in his own world now, tied up in a knot of guilt. Susannah tried to nudge him out. "Did she recover?"

"Not really. She was paralyzed till she died. She never swam again."

"But that wasn't your fault." Something in his face didn't compute. "David?"

"I was so scared," he blurted. "I did all the wrong things. It took forever to get her out of the water because

I was afraid of hurting her. I should have done more resuscitation but when she didn't come to, I panicked." He stared at her. "If it hadn't been for my friend Jared showing up, she would have died."

"So you had the pool filled in and you've been blaming yourself and trying desperately to stop anything like that from happening to Darla." Susannah smiled sadly. "But you're drowning her with your rules and regulations, David."

He held her gaze, not looking away even when Darla returned.

"It's late. I'd better go." Susannah rose slowly, forcing herself not to give away the fact that the yard was spinning.

"Can Susannah stay for dinner, Davy?" Darla asked.

"Not tonight, thanks," Susannah said before he could refuse. "I think I'm going to go home and lie down."

"Shall I drive you?" David's face was drawn and serious.

"Don't be silly. It's just a couple of blocks." She headed for the front door.

"All the same, you look pale. I think you should ride." He told Darla to stay with Mrs. Peters, then took Susannah's elbow and escorted her to his car.

"This is silly. I'm fine," she protested, but he ignored her.

"You're overdoing it. That was not my intent when you took this job. Maybe you should cut back. I can find someone else to work with Darla." He backed out of his driveway and pulled onto the street.

"Look, the doctor assures me that part of pregnancy is the occasional tiredness. I'm really fine." She saw him glance at her stomach and pulled down her shirt defensively. "I'm not some delicate flower. I'm tough, resilient." She breathed a mocking laugh. "I survived Nick. I can handle having a baby."

"Nick's the guy who left you?" he asked as he pulled up in front of Connie's house.

"He was the man I thought I married." Shame washed over her. "I stupidly thought he loved me."

"Why stupidly?" David turned in his seat to face her. "Why wouldn't he love you?"

"Because I'm a total failure," she told him, trying to suppress the tears. "People like me aren't the type who get happily ever after. I'm not like Connie. She took her life and made something of it. I messed up."

Susannah was too ashamed to sit there and let him see her give way to tears so she hastily exited the car.

"Thanks for the ride. Good night."

She hurried away, listening for the sound of the car leaving. But in her room, when she glanced out of the window, she saw him still sitting there, a puzzled look on his face.

A long time passed before he finally left.

"And now it's finally clear to him what a twit I am." Susannah sighed and started a bath. Some days were better forgotten. This was definitely one of them.

She caught a glimpse of herself in the mirror just before she stepped into the tub.

"Your mother is an idiot," she whispered, allowing the tears to fall unheeded. "Not the kind of mommy you deserve at all."

"Darla, did Susannah seem okay today?" David pretended nonchalance as he waited for his sister's response later that evening.

"I dunno." Darla looked up. "She gets tired sometimes. I pretend I am, too, so she can rest."

"That's nice of you. What did you do today?" He listened as Darla recited their activities. "That doesn't seem too bad."

"No. But I don't think Susannah has much money. When we were in the park, I wanted an ice cream cone, but when she opened her wallet, I saw that she only had enough money for me to have a cone. So I got two little bars instead. One for each of us."

"I'm proud of you for thinking of that." David's chest swelled.

"Yeah." She grinned at him.

"Maybe she doesn't carry much money with her," he mused.

"She always puts some of her money in a little can at Connie's. It's her baby can. She's saving." Darla grabbed the remote. "Can I watch my TV program now?"

"Sure."

Susannah didn't have much money. Well, of course she didn't. He'd forgotten to give her money for gas. Darla's old hot rod would bankrupt Midas.

Come to think of it, Susannah wouldn't have an easy time with those bucket seats a few months down the road, either. Maybe it was time to trade it in. The car had been secondhand when he'd got it for Darla, just before her skiing accident. It still ran, but he didn't like the idea of Susannah possibly getting stopped somewhere.

You're worried about her safety now? The chiding voice in the back of his head mocked.

David returned to the television room, oblivious to Darla's program. He wanted to shut that voice down, but the memory of Susannah's face when he'd driven

her home, the pain in her voice as she'd spoken about
the louse who dumped her, the thought of her innocent
child caught in the midst of it all—well, David couldn't
get rid of those thoughts.

"Davy?" Darla shut off the television. "Can I talk
to you?"

"Of course. You can always talk to me." He patted the sofa and waited for her to curl up beside him.
"What's up?"

"I was wondering who will be the daddy for Susannah's baby."

"Umm, what makes you ask, honey?" he side-stepped.

"Well, today I saw her watching a little boy when
we were in the park. What if her baby is a boy? Boys
need daddies to play with them and teach them stuff
that mommies can't." Darla's nose scrunched up as she
mulled over the problem.

"Well, maybe the father will come when the baby's
born."

But Darla shook her head.

"Nope. His name was Nick and he died. I heard Aunt
Connie telling Uncle Wade. He was a scoun—" She
squeezed her eyes closed, trying to recall the word, but
finally gave up. "I can't remember," she finally admitted.

The baby's father was dead—meaning there was no
chance for Susannah to get support from him, financially or otherwise. And he *was* a scoundrel, David
thought as his back teeth clenched.

*You're not getting involved. You don't need any more
responsibilities.*

"*Scoundrel.* I think he was a bad man," Darla continued. "Don't you?"

"I don't know." He shouldn't even be listening to this,

but David was curious. More curious than he should have been.

"I don't think a nice man would tell Susannah to get out. That's mean." Darla snuggled up to him. "She let me touch her tummy where the baby is growing."

"Oh." David smoothed her hair. Was it wrong to talk about this? He found himself eager to hear every detail about the beautiful blonde and her child. Maybe because he felt he'd never have his own child.

"Susannah said she doesn't know anything about how to be a mommy," Darla said. "But I think she'll be a good mother. She's really nice to me, even when I'm not nice."

"I think Susannah's nice, too, Dar." Wasn't that an understatement.

He kissed the top of her head, surprised when she jumped up. "Hey, where are you going?"

"To make some popcorn. I'm hungry." She scurried away in her jeans and bright red shirt, her bare feet slapping against the hardwood.

David could count on one hand the evenings they'd shared like this before Susannah. Evenings were usually a battle zone, but since Connie's friend had shown up Darla was more like her old self. Susannah was doing amazing work.

His mind suddenly replayed what Darla had told him.

So this Nick had told Susannah to get out? Knowing she was pregnant?

No wonder she sometimes seemed like a glass ornament, brittle and ready to shatter. Her tough veneer was just a facade, perhaps to shield herself from being hurt again. Connie had hinted at something in her past. Something ugly.

But David wasn't going to get involved.

Keep telling yourself that.

He had to. Though David felt a rush of relief that no bitter, angry boyfriend or husband was likely to come after Susannah, though he was glad that she and Darla would be safe from that, and though he was also grateful for the progress she was making with his sister—well, the rest of it was her life.

And none of his business.

"What are you thinking about, Davy?" Darla flopped at his feet, her cheeks bulging with popcorn.

He snatched one of the fluffy white bits and popped it into his mouth.

"I'm thinking about buying a different car for you and Susannah to use."

"Good. Susannah will be glad, too," Darla told him. "She says the seat hurts her back. And she has to sit on a cushion to see."

The things you could learn if you only paid attention.

"Davy?"

"Yeah?"

"Could you think about something else now?" Darla said, her brown eyes on him, sizing him up.

"What's that?" He was half-afraid to ask.

"I don't want to go to girls' club anymore. I'm too big." She thrust her feet in front of her and stared at her poppy-red toenails.

"Okay. I'll tell them you won't be coming." He waited, knowing Darla was forming another thought.

"Do you think I'm too dumb to swim, Davy?"

He might have known.

"What do you think?"

"I don't know. At first I was scared to try, but Susannah says new things often scare us but that doesn't mean we shouldn't try them." Darla stared at him quizzically. "Do you think I can learn to not be afraid in the water, Davy?" The yearning in her voice was his undoing.

"I think you're very smart. I think that if you try hard, listen to the teacher and don't get frustrated, you can do a whole lot of things you never thought you could do," he said with certainty.

"I think maybe I can, too," she whispered. And then she grinned at him and held up her hand for a high five.

"I'll check on lessons tomorrow," he promised.

"Good. Because I don't like watching when my class goes swimming." Suddenly her eyes danced with excitement. "I'm going to surprise them when I swim right to the other end of the big pool!"

David could hardly believe the transformation in his sister.

What a difference Susannah Wells had made in their lives.

David wasn't going to get involved in her life, but that didn't have to stop him from praying that God would help her.

Her and her baby.

The beginning of a family.

He shut down that thought. A family was the one thing he couldn't have. He knew that wasn't God's plan for his life and had accepted it.

No point in dwelling on the impossible.

Chapter Six

"There are tons of flowers," Darla burbled, her voice rising. "And you know what else they had at the botanical garden?"

"No. What?"

On Friday afternoon Susannah drove the almost-new station wagon away from the school with a light heart. It was so much easier to handle than David's other car. She had no idea what had prompted him to change vehicles, but she was glad of it.

"There's a butterfly room. It's a special glass room with plants and fish and stuff, and butterflies live there. They came and sat on me!" Darla rushed on, enthusiastic about her latest school trip.

Susannah let her talk as they drove home, knowing that she needed to spill all the things that were tumbling around in her head. They were still bubbling over when David arrived.

"Can we go back tomorrow, Davy? I want to show you the butterflies."

"I'm sorry, Dar, I can't. Tomorrow's my day for my boys." He turned to Susannah. "Actually I was going to ask you if you could come tomorrow. I'm big brother to three boys and we do something special once a month. Tomorrow it's a hockey game in Phoenix. I just got the tickets."

Big brother? David? Surprise kept her silent.

"Darla doesn't like hockey so she doesn't want to come. Do you have other plans, Susannah?" he asked.

He was always so polite, yet somehow distant. As if he didn't want to get too involved in her world. Not that Susannah blamed him. Her world was messed up.

"Susannah?" Darla poked her in the arm. "Are you sick?"

"No." She smiled to ease Darla's worried expression. "I was just thinking that I'd like to see your botanical gardens tomorrow. I should see some of the sights while I'm here."

"Are you thinking of leaving Tucson?" David suddenly seemed to stumble over his words. "Not that you owe me any answers. But I would like a bit of notice to find someone else to stay with Darla."

"I don't want you to go away, Susannah." Darla's face darkened. Her hands fisted at her sides and her body stiffened. "You can't go."

"I never said I was going anywhere right now," Susannah reminded quietly. "But if I had to leave, I hope you would wish me the best."

Darla thought about it for several moments. Finally the anger drained away and her sunny smile flashed again.

"I would," she agreed, winding her arm around Susannah's waist. She leaned her head on her shoulder. "You're my best friend, and I like doing things with you. Please stay." She glanced over one shoulder at David before she leaned near to whisper, "I want to see your baby when it's born."

Susannah flushed. David would not want to hear that. He might be glad she was here to watch Darla, but Susannah didn't need him to say out loud how much he disapproved of her. It was evident in the distant way he acted.

"The baby won't be here for a long time," Susannah murmured, with a quick peek at his face. It was hard to read anything in those inscrutable eyes. "So how about I go with you tomorrow and see those butterflies? They sound fun."

"They are." Darla once more launched into a description that lasted until Mrs. Peters came to say good-night and reminded them of the potluck supper at church.

"I forgot all about that supper. Go change, Dar." David waited until she ran up the stairs, then beckoned to Susannah to follow him to the kitchen. "I've wanted to hear tonight's speaker for a long time. He worked on a mission in the Amazon."

"You know the Amazon?"

"I took a trip there with Wade and Jared just after we all finished college." He smiled. A certain wistfulness tinged his voice. "It was amazing. Unfortunately we had to leave early."

Was that when his father had died? She hated to ask and bring up painful memories.

"You never went back?" she asked.

"Haven't had time so far." He pulled an envelope out of a drawer and handed it to her. "This is yours."

"What's this?" she asked, confused when she saw the money tucked inside. "You already paid me for the last two weeks."

"Wages, yes. That's for incidentals. Like gas for the car, the botanical garden tomorrow and the numerous ice creams and other treats my sister seems to inhale. I never expected you to pay for them, Susannah. I just didn't think about it until Darla reminded me." He glanced once at her midsection. "I'm sure you're trying to save—for the baby, I mean."

"I am, but it doesn't seem right to take this." Susannah set the envelope on the table. "You already pay me very well for doing almost nothing."

"Nothing?" He said with incredulity. "It's a lot more than nothing to me. It's been ages since I've been so caught up at work."

"Oh, good." She blushed under his praise.

"It means a great deal to me to know Darla's safe and happy under your care, Susannah. And she's learning, too. Take it. Please." He handed her the envelope again. "You'll get the same every week. And if you need more for some activity, please tell me."

"Well—thank you." She tucked it into her bag while mentally calculating how much more she'd need to save before she could get the sonogram the doctor had recommended.

An awkward silence yawned.

"Are you feeling all right? She's not too much for you?" David asked in a careful voice.

"I'm fine. Darla's wonderful. She goes out of her way to watch out for me," Susannah told him. "She's always bringing me a cushion or a glass of water. She fusses too much. She shouldn't waste her attention on me."

He'd been packing items into a cooler, but he stopped and turned to study her, his brow furrowed.

"Waste?" He shook his head. "Darla loves you."

"She shouldn't."

"Why?" His eyes were wide with surprise.

"You wouldn't understand," she murmured, trying to think up some way to get out of this conversation.

"Because you think I've had the perfect life?" His dark eyes flashed with intensity. "I'm a spoiled rich kid because I never went through foster care like you and Connie?"

"No." She did meet his stare. "I don't believe anyone has a perfect life. No one I know anyway."

"Then?" He stood where he was, waiting, palms up, for some answer.

"Look, you had your life mapped out in front of you and you followed that map." It frustrated her to have to put into words what hurt so deeply. "You weren't like me. You didn't mess up over and over. Your choices were smart. Mine weren't."

"But you were a kid and that was ages ago," he said. "You've changed."

"Have I? I hope so. But the results of my stupid decisions live on," she said, laying a hand over her stomach as if she could protect her baby. "They're certainly not the decisions a mother wants to tell her child."

"Susannah, that's ridiculous. Everyone makes mistakes—"

"You didn't," she said, daring him to contradict.

"I'm ready." Darla stood in the doorway, her smile fading. "Are you arguing?" she asked, her voice worried.

"No. Just discussing." David touched her nose. "You look very pretty," he complimented.

"It's the same color as Susannah's shirt," she said proudly. "We both like pink."

Susannah's heart lifted, as it always did in the presence of this lovely girl. "Connie made this shirt. She's decided she is going to sew me a whole new wardrobe and she won't take no for an answer."

"Connie's like Davy." Darla peeked through her lashes at her big brother. "He doesn't take no, either."

"Hey! No dissing me." He smiled at Susannah. "You look very nice."

"Thank you." She fought to keep from blushing again, but that didn't stop her heart from bouncing with pleasure at the compliment. How stupid was that—to be glad a man who looked down on you thought you looked nice? Pregnancy was fooling with her brain.

"Darla, why don't you go put on your coat?" David said. When she'd left, he turned to Susannah. "Would you like to come to the potluck with us?" he asked as he closed the lid on the cooler. "I'm sure the presentation will be worth seeing."

"Go with you?" Susannah didn't understand for a moment. "Oh, you mean to watch her? Sure, I—"

"No, that's okay—Darla will be fine. I meant would you like to come to the potluck supper and presentation with Darla and me." He leaned back against the granite counter and waited, lips tilted up in a quirky smile.

Susannah debated. It might be okay for tonight, but later, when the baby was showing more, everyone would wonder. Maybe the speculation would ruin his business and then she'd be responsible...but she was tired of hiding out at Connie's or the mall.

"I didn't realize it was such a major decision," he chuckled.

"I would like to go," she said so fast her tongue couldn't rescind it. "Thank you very much."

"You're welcome." Just for a second, he gazed at her in a way that made her face feel warm. Then his attention moved to his sister as she came back into the room. "Ready?" he asked.

"Yes. I put the soda in the trunk," Darla told him. She giggled as she told Susannah, "Davy bought root beer for his boys to have when they visit, but they don't like it. Neither do I," she said, her nose wrinkling. "We're taking it to the potluck."

"And if they don't like it, they can pass it on," David said, urging them toward the car. "I'm sick of looking at those cases taking up room in the garage." He stowed the cooler, then held the car doors while Darla and Susannah climbed inside. Once seated, he grinned at her. "Just one of the bad choices *I've* made," he said as they pulled out of the driveway and headed toward the church.

"What about that man you hired to put the carpet in your office?" Darla asked.

David winced. "Okay, two bad choices," he admitted. "He was the worst carpet layer I've ever seen. Can we let it go?"

But Darla was beginning to enjoy herself and Susannah was, too.

"Mrs. Peter's Christmas sweater?" Darla giggled.

"I didn't know she was allergic to cashmere!" he protested.

"Asking Mr. Hornby to fix the mess you made in the garden?" Darla laughed out loud at the chagrin on his face.

"He wasn't supposed to do it all at once." David's pained look spoke volumes. "I wasn't trying to kill him." Darla laughed until they pulled into the church parking lot.

"What about the cat?" she asked, ignoring his groan.

When David refused to answer, Susannah asked Darla, "What about a cat?"

"He got me a gift. A sweet cat, all white. I called her Snow White 'cause she loved to sleep." Darla's face softened, her dark eyes began to glow. "Davy *said* she was a special cat, that she'd be my best friend. That was when I was really sick. I had to stay home and I hurt a lot. Holding Snow White made me feel better."

They'd arrived at the church. David climbed out of the car, but after one look at Darla's face, he shook his head and left them to carry the cooler into the church. Susannah nudged the girl's arm.

"What happened?" This she had to hear.

"Well, Snow White ran away a whole bunch of times. If Mrs. Peter's opened the door, that cat would race outside and she didn't come back." Darla frowned. "I didn't hurt her or anything."

"I know you wouldn't do that," Susannah assured her.

"No, I wouldn't," Darla huffed. "Well, every time Snow White would run away, Davy would go and look for her. Sometimes it took a long time and I could hear him calling and calling. But he always brought her home. Except one night."

Surely the poor thing hadn't been hurt? Susannah bit her lip. She had a special affection for cats, honed by years of sitting in the barn on her foster family's farm, crying over her mother's refusal to answer her letters.

"It's okay, Susannah, you don't have to be sad." Darla

bent her head trying to see into Susannah's eyes. "It's not bad," she rushed to reassure.

"You'd better explain, Dar. I can see she already thinks the worst." David leaned against the car while Darla explained.

"Well, Snow White had babies. She didn't want to stay with me. She just wanted to come to my house and eat so she could feed her babies," Darla explained. "Mrs. Murphy was away and the boy she hired didn't take care of Snow White very well so Snow White had to take care of her family herself."

"By mooching off of us," David grumbled.

"When Mrs. Murphy came home and saw Davy picking up Snow White and carrying her away, she got really mad at him. It was her cat, you see. She called the police and she followed him home. She was yelling and her face was all red."

"How was I supposed to know it was her cat? I didn't even know the woman, let alone that she had a cat." Obviously disgruntled, David picked a fuzz ball off his sweater. "It was wandering around, yowling all the time. I thought we could give it a home. I paid over a hundred dollars for shots for that animal."

"That's okay, Davy. Snow White was grateful." Darla patted his arm.

"Well, Mrs. Murphy wasn't." His averted his face. "Calling the police on me was a bit extreme."

"Yes, that must have been—er—challenging." Susannah struggled to suppress her mirth.

"Snow White scratched Davy and tore his pants. Then Mrs. Murphy hit him with a broom." Darla reached out and touched him. "I'm sorry, Davy."

"So am I," David said in an aggrieved tone. "I fed

that great hulking thing fresh fish for two weeks and neither that cat nor her mistress said thank you even once."

"Snow White still comes over for a visit sometimes," Darla interjected. "But not if Davy's home."

"And don't think I'm unhappy about that." He gave a snort of derision.

Susannah couldn't help it, she burst out laughing. The thought of this big, accomplished, well-respected man avoiding a little white cat made her giggle. She could not imagine him prowling the streets, calling the cat and enduring all manner of indignities from Mrs. Murphy.

"Now that you know my mistakes, let's go inside. I'd like to eat some of that food before it's gone," David said with a hint of a grin in his eyes.

He walked around the car to open Susannah's door and help her out. She was very conscious of David's helping hand under her elbow.

She walked up the sidewalk with David and Darla, mentally steeling herself for what was to come. This was one reason why she'd refused to go to church with Connie; she feared people would start asking questions that she didn't want to answer.

But no one asked her a thing. David introduced her by name as their friend, and that seemed to be enough for people. Everyone she spoke to welcomed her and invited her to enjoy herself. And she did.

It was only later, when Susannah was seated in a pew beside David that she began to feel self-conscious as the speaker, Rick Green, talked about God's love.

"It was my privilege to teach these people that nothing they've done could erase the love of God," he said confidently. "Nothing."

He spoke at length about conditions along the river and the many trials he endured in his work. His pictures were a graphic testimony to his endurance. But Susannah kept hearing her mother's voice screaming condemnation.

It's your fault. It's your fault.

As always, a punch of pain accompanied the words and she squeezed her eyes closed to brace against it.

The social worker had insisted the deaths of her sisters, Cara and Misty, weren't her fault. But even after all these years, in the recesses of her heart, Susannah couldn't rid herself of the guilt that dogged her.

It *was* her fault. She *should* have been there.

She was a failure.

A hand pressed against hers, warm, comforting.

She opened her eyes and found David staring at her, concern in his gaze.

"Are you all right?" he whispered.

She dredged up a smile and nodded as she eased her fingers from his, forcing herself to pretend a calm she didn't feel. Why did his touch affect her so deeply?

After several moments of scrutiny he finally returned his attention to the speaker, but he kept giving her little sideways looks, as if he thought she might faint or do something equally inappropriate.

"Hear me tonight," Rick Green said softly. "There is nothing God wouldn't do for you. In fact, He's already done it by sending His son to die for you. All you have to do is accept His love."

By the time the meeting broke up, Susannah had regained her equilibrium. She was able to tease Darla and smile at David who still looked concerned. Connie and Wade joined them.

"You must have loved your trip down to the Amazon, judging by those amazing pictures," Susannah said to Wade.

"We did," Wade agreed. "Especially the piranhas." He held up a threatening hand and began tickling the back of Darla's neck. In a fit of giggles, she wiggled away.

"You know, we never did get to finish that trip because of Dad's heart attack," David mused. "We should go back sometime."

"I second that." A tall, lean man with sandy blond hair exchanged a complicated handshake with the other two men, hugged Connie and Darla and then held out a hand to Susannah. "I'm Jared Hornby," he said.

"Oh. I've heard a lot about you." Susannah shook his hand. She could see the easy camaraderie between the three men. "Darla shared some information, too," she added.

"Aw, kiddo! Can't you ever keep a secret," Jared asked Darla and grinned when she said, "No."

"I'm not putting money in that basket. I just don't agree with raising money to feed kids who live in this country." A shrill voice broke through their conversation, carrying from the foyer into the sanctuary. "Did you see the pictures of those children in the Amazon, how poor they are? It seems criminal to me that in this country of plenty, we give our hard-earned money to people who have social assistance and all kinds of government handouts. If they won't look after their own children, then the government can take over. Not a dime should go to that Mary's Kids Foundation."

"Uh-oh," Connie murmured. Mary's Kids was one of the charities she'd recently set up with a friend to help kids on the streets of Tucson. "I'll go—"

"I'm afraid I have to disagree with you there, Mrs. Beesom." David's voice carried clearly, his tone calm. "Needy kids are needy wherever they are, whether in Tucson or the Amazon. We should be ashamed that we've let American children get to the point where they are so desperate to eat that they have to rob and steal. It's disgraceful that in America a child isn't cared for by the whole community."

Susannah moved with the rest toward the foyer. She couldn't help admiring David's casual stance. There was no hint of anger in his voice or manner, though she saw a flicker of golden fire in the depths of his eyes.

"Disgraceful? Well, that's just silly. They have mothers and fathers," Mrs. Beesom blustered.

"That isn't the point," he said quietly. "The point is that there are children hurting around the world. It's our God-given responsibility to do whatever we can to alleviate the hurt of children whenever we can, no matter where they live."

"But—"

David wasn't finished.

"Thank God Connie Abbot has taken it upon herself to show God's love to the children of Tucson, just as this gentleman has been showing love to those he meets in the Amazon. We should all be doing more to support both of them."

After a couple of coughs and a few murmured amens, the foyer quickly cleared, but not before people dropped donations into both baskets.

Susannah followed Connie and Wade outside. The group paused in the parking lot.

"Look guys, I'm so sorry," Connie murmured, her embarrassment obvious. "I had no idea that would happen. I should have removed everything about Mary's Kids from the bulletin board."

"Don't be silly, Connie," David said. "She should have thought first."

"I'm sure David saw it as an opportunity to try and educate narrow-minded people rather than let their bigotry go unchallenged, didn't you, old man?" Jared slapped him on the back. "You always were a defender of the weak."

"I'm not a saint." David brushed away the praise. "What say we go out for coffee? I'm buying."

"But I don't drink coffee, Davy," Darla complained.

Everyone burst out laughing. David assured his sister they'd find her something to drink. As they drove to the coffee house, Susannah couldn't help but replay the scene in her mind.

She'd always seen David as cool and distant. But his defense of Connie's charity tonight showed her a new side. She assumed he thought her stupid, beneath him. But the truth was, he had never verbally condemned or judged her. Maybe she was misreading him, and shutting him out without giving him a chance to show who he really was.

David was great with Darla—understanding and gentle. He went out of his way to empathize with his sister's issues. He was exactly the kind of man who could listen and then help you figure out the next step. Connie was a great friend, but Susannah was sure that if she told her the plans she had to adopt her baby, Connie would try to change her mind. Susannah needed another confidant, someone who could advise her about adoption. Someone who wouldn't try to sway her, who would listen and even help

Tonight, David had shown he could empathize.

Tomorrow, Susannah would find out if he would help her.

Chapter Seven

"Surprise!"

On Saturday evening, David stared at the array of food on his kitchen counter and was dumbfounded.

He'd never expected this when he'd called to ask Susannah if she and Darla wanted to join him and the boys for dinner.

"I thought a barbecue might be more fun for your little brothers than being stuck in a stuffy restaurant." Susannah's cheeks burned a hot pink. But whether from effort or something else, he couldn't tell.

"We made a dinner," Darla told him, beaming with pride.

"You certainly did." He glanced at his three little brothers who were eyeing the fixings for a wonderful grilled meal with huge eyes. "But I'm sure they'd rather go out, wouldn't you, guys?" he teased.

"No way." Their team had won the hockey game and they were high on excitement. "Can we have both a burger and a hot dog?" the eldest asked in awe. "And some of the other stuff?"

"If you can find room after all that junk food you ate." He told them to wash up, then went out to the patio.

David couldn't remember the last time he'd worked so hard over a grill—nor the last time he'd heard so much laughter in his backyard.

Nor had he ever seen Susannah so happy. She insisted on dashing around, making sure everyone had enough to eat until David finally ordered her to sit down and enjoy her own meal.

She had a way with the boys. She didn't duck their questions about her baby, or try to change the subject. She answered honestly and they seemed to appreciate that. In fact, David was gratified to see them ask her to remain at the table while they cleared the dishes. He stacked the dishwasher himself, so he could listen in on their conversation.

"Boy, David, Susannah's sure pretty. What happened to her husband?" Caden, the eldest, asked.

"He died, I think." David wasn't sure he wanted to reveal more about Susannah without her permission. "Thanks for pitching in, guys."

"It was nothing." Charles, the youngest, peered out the window where Darla and Susannah sat together on the deck swing. "Does she live here?"

"No. She comes over to watch Darla when I can't be here," he explained.

"Darla's different than the last time we saw her," Cory said. "She doesn't look so sad. And she didn't yell even once."

"Yeah. She's fun," Caden agreed. "And she's pretty now."

Like she wasn't before? David choked back his brotherly ire and picked up the platter of cookies Susannah had left on the top of the fridge.

"We've barely got enough time to eat these before I have to get you home," he said as he shepherded them outside. "Your mom said no later than eight, remember?"

They grumbled but devoured the cookies as they asked Darla about the butterfly exhibit. To David's surprise, his sister knew a lot about it and was able to clearly explain what she and Susannah had seen.

"I won't be more than half an hour," he told Susannah before leaving. "The boys' place isn't too far away."

"We'll be here," Susannah promised. She hugged each of the boys, then handed Caden a bag. "Extra cookies in case you want a snack tomorrow. And there might be some fudge brownies in there, too," she added with a wink.

"Really?" Caden's eyes widened. "Thanks a lot."

David shooed them out to the car, but stopped when Susannah's hand pressed his arm.

"They're not allergic or anything, are they?" she asked.

"To chocolate?" He grinned. "More like addicted. Thanks for doing that. It was very thoughtful. They don't get treats like that very often."

"It was mostly Darla," she said. "I just helped."

He thought about that as he took the boys home. It seemed Susannah "just helped" everyone. He knew from Wade that Susannah took over meals when their housekeeper had the day off. Which was a good thing because Connie, for all her achievements, was no cook.

Susannah "just helped" Darla take swimming lessons, with the result that Darla had zipped through the first four levels and was almost done with the fifth. She'd "just helped" his little brothers enjoy a wonderful barbecue in a homey atmosphere, gently urging them out of their shells, until all three boys had lost their shyness.

Susannah Wells was quite a woman.

David pulled into the garage and waited for the door to close.

He liked her. He really liked her. Susannah didn't pretend to be someone else. She didn't seem to bear a grudge, though she had plenty of reason to. She was honest with Darla, yet wonderfully calm and soothing.

Like a sister.

Only David didn't think of Susannah as a sister.

Careful.

He found her inside, staring into space.

"Oh, you're back," she said, startled, as if she'd been deep in thought. "Darla's upstairs having a bath."

"Good. She was pretty sticky from all the cookies." Something was going on. He could see it in her eyes. "Do you—"

"Could I talk to you?" she blurted. "Confidentially, as a lawyer?"

"Okay," he said cautiously.

"I'll pay you and everything," she promised, "but I don't want what I say to leave this room." A desperate look washed over her delicate features, as if she'd been brooding over something and finally felt driven to bring it to light.

"As your lawyer, I'm forbidden to release anything you tell me to anyone else," he assured her. "Would you like some tea while we talk?" He had to do something to try to ease her discomfort. The uncertainty in her voice touched him. He wanted to help her, to ease the strain in her lovely eyes. He wanted to give her some of the joy she so freely encouraged in others.

"Yes. Please." Susannah waited until he'd made the tea and set everything on the table in front of them.

"Talk to me, Susannah. Please? I promise I'll try to help," he said when silence continued to reign.

"I need to know how to give up my baby for adoption."

The question hit him squarely in the gut.

Give away her child?

David forced his face to remain neutral, but inside his brain churned with questions.

"I can't keep it, that's for sure." She twisted her fingers together, staring at them as if she hoped to find answers there.

"Do you have someone in mind? Connie and Wade?" he guessed.

"No!" Susannah stared at him. "You can't tell them about this. Not a word."

"I'm not going to say anything to anyone, Susannah. I promise. Relax." He laid his hands over hers to help her calm down. "It's just—this is a bit of a surprise. I don't understand. Maybe you could explain some more?"

"No." She yanked her hands away and jumped to her feet. "I shouldn't have bothered you. I'll figure things out. But please, don't tell Connie."

"Susannah." David saw a myriad of conflicting emotions on her face. He could tell she was really struggling with her decision, with her feelings. "As your lawyer, I *can't* talk to Connie or anyone else. That's the law." He rose, touched her shoulder. "I really want to help you.

But in order to give you the best advice I can, I need to know more about what's driving your decision."

She frowned, her uncertainty obvious. His heart gave a lurch as he watched her struggle to find some trust.

"Let's just talk. No decisions, no judging—just talking," he coaxed quietly. "You don't have to decide anything right now. But I'd like to know what you're thinking and feeling. This is a big decision."

He found himself holding his breath. Would she trust him?

"I know exactly how big it is," she said. Finally she sat down. "I've been fighting it for a while. But I think the best thing for my baby would be for me to find a good family to raise it."

So now he was going to arrange an adoption?

So much for not getting involved, buddy.

With grim determination, David shut down the voice in his head. The truth was he was already involved in Susannah's life way more than he'd ever imagined he'd be. Over the past few weeks he'd caught himself watching to be sure she drank the freshly squeezed juice with which he'd insisted Mrs. Peters stock the fridge, and that she'd sampled the variety of organic fruit he kept buying at the health food store. He'd even checked the house for repairs that needed doing so she wouldn't trip on something, or hurt herself.

If he had to, David could recite every detail Darla had ever mentioned about Susannah's baby. Yeah, he wasn't getting involved.

"I would prefer if the adopters didn't know about my mistakes." The words emerged in a quiet, painful whisper.

"Okay." He nodded. "Now tell me why."

"Why?" She gave a half laugh, chewed on her bottom lip then looked directly at him. "Because my past is not the kind of fairy-tale reading a child needs."

"I meant why do you want to have someone adopt your baby?" he clarified.

"Isn't it obvious?" She frowned at him. "I can't be the kind of mother this baby needs."

"Why not?" he asked, pouring tea for both of them.

"I shouldn't even be a mother," she whispered.

"And yet you will be."

"I know." She nodded soberly. "But I can't provide the best environment for a child." Her eyes brimmed with shame.

"You're not a criminal. You haven't hurt anyone. You like kids and you're good with people." He shook his head. "I don't understand what possibly disqualifies you as a mother."

"Look around, David," she said, a tinge of bitterness edging her voice. "Look at what your parents provided for you and Darla. I'll bet your mother stayed home to care for you, didn't she?"

"Actually she was a partner in my father's firm." David smiled at the cascade of memories. "Best litigator I've ever known. But she would not do wills or family law. Absolutely refused."

"Oh." Susannah swallowed. "Well, anyway, I meant your parents provided a home and income for their children. They had a reputation that covered you."

"You have a bad reputation?" he asked, half in jest.

Susannah's eyes, dark and swirling with secrets, met his. After a moment she nodded. "Did Connie ever tell you about our foster home?" She glanced away, focusing on something outside the window.

"A little. How much she was loved, cared for. How much she appreciated what they did for her. That kind of thing. Why?" He didn't understand where this was going.

"I was sent to that foster home after a house fire—which was my fault." Susannah straightened. Her shoulders went back. Her jaw tightened. "Do you know where I was when the fire started?"

David gave a grim shake of his head.

"I snuck into a theater," she said, her voice brimming with unshed tears. "I ran away. My—mother was at home. She got badly burned in that fire, because of me."

Years of past misery now darkened her gorgeous eyes to green-black shadows. Pain oozed from her. David wanted to help but he didn't know the words to dissolve this kind of agony. It had festered too long.

"Susannah—"

"There's another reason I can't keep my baby." Susannah dragged her hand away from his and tucked it under her.

"What is that?" David asked, longing to hold her, to ease her obvious distress.

"My mother was not a good mother. I might be like her."

David wanted to laugh at the utter ridiculousness of it. But Susannah's face made it clear how serious she was.

"You are not like her, Susannah," he said, certain of that truth.

"I don't drink, but maybe—"

He shook his head and continued shaking it as she listed other faults she thought she might have inherited.

"No way."

"How can you say that?" A hint of defiance colored her voice. "You barely know me."

"I actually know you quite well, Susannah Wells." He smiled at her blink of surprise. "You are sweet and gentle with Darla when she's acting her worst. You go out of your way to make three boys you don't even know the most fantastic barbecue. You listen when I whine and complain and you never stop looking for opportunities to help anyone who needs a hand." He touched her cheek. "You'll make a wonderful mother."

She was silent a long time, head bent as she thought about it. But when she lifted her golden head and looked at him, David knew she hadn't heard him, not in her heart where the insecurities had taken root.

"You don't know what kind of mother I'll be, and neither do I. And I'm not going to risk the life of my baby. My track record isn't good. I'm not worthy of motherhood and I won't risk my baby." She gathered her jacket. "So are you going to help me figure out how to do an adoption, or should I find someone else?"

David rose, determined to make her see herself the way others saw her.

"In the past you made some bad choices, Susannah," he said seriously. "Maybe partly because of what you were told and partly because you were afraid to expect better of yourself."

"So?" Her long hair twisted up on the top of her head lent her a quiet dignity, its sheen a golden crown under the kitchen lights.

"I wish you could believe that your past doesn't determine your future. I wish you could let go of all those feelings of unworthiness," he told her, letting his soul speak. "You have so much inside you to give. You just need to trust God to help you and give yourself another chance."

"God isn't going to be bothered with me."

"God is bothered with everyone," he assured her quietly.

"And what if I blow that chance? I've done it a hundred times before. What happens to my baby then?" she challenged him. Then she cleared her voice. "Are you going to help me with this adoption or not?"

"Of course I'll help you. After all you've done for us, I would feel ashamed not to. You're the best thing I could ever have wished for Darla." He bent and brushed his lips against her silky cheek, surprised by the rush of longing he felt to make her world better. "Thank you."

She lifted a hand and touched her cheek where he'd kissed her.

"You're welcome," she whispered.

Then she was gone.

David stood in the kitchen and let his spirit talk to God because he couldn't find the words to convey all that was in his heart.

Sometime later he became aware he was not alone.

"Davy?"

"Yes, sweetie?"

Darla stood behind him, her face very sad.

"What's wrong?"

"Why does Susannah want to give away her baby, Davy?"

"That's a secret, sis. You can't ever talk about it. Not to anyone."

"Okay. But I love Susannah's baby."

"I know." He gathered her in his arms and let her cry on his shoulder, his sweet baby sister who was alive and getting better every day thanks to a small woman who oozed love.

Oh, Susannah, his heart wept.

"I'll only talk about it to God," Darla promised, sniffing. "He'll help. Let's ask Him."

So right then and there they prayed for Susannah and the child she was afraid to love.

But even that didn't ease David's concern over the heart-wrenching choices Susannah was determined to make.

"There's got to be something I can do," he prayed after Darla had gone to bed. "Show me some way to help her avoid making this tragic mistake."

Being Susannah's friend/lawyer hardly seemed enough.

Chapter Eight

"I can't believe you actually brought my sister to this place."

All signs of last week's gentle, understanding man whom Susannah had trusted with her deepest secrets was gone. She'd felt so close to him, even more so after that kiss. Her brain said it was all part of his thank-you, but her heart had sensed the tenderness in him, felt the gentleness of his eyes when his lips touched her. What a difference a week made.

Susannah tried to explain.

"They have a wonderful program with pottery here. Darla can finally dig her fingers into the clay and create as she wants to. She's ecstatic."

"Do you see who these people are? Drunks. Addicts. Criminals. Pottery is fine, but here?" He cast a disparaging glance at the disheveled young man working beside Darla's table. "He looks like he's been living on the street."

"He has. Burt's had some bad luck." Susannah hated the way David looked at the man—because Burt could have been her not so long ago.

"I'm sure he has." David took her arm and steered her to a corner. "This could be dangerous, Susannah. I don't like Darla in a place like this. You know she's had a couple of tantrums this past week."

"She's not going to be perfect all the time," she replied. "No one is."

"I didn't say *perfect*." He tightened his lips as a woman walked past, talking to herself in a high, screechy voice. "What if Darla gets upset and acts up? One of them could take exception and attack her. There is mental illness here."

"You're being ridiculous," she snapped, irritated by his attitude. "Connie's come here to New Horizons many times. No one's ever bothered her."

"Connie isn't a nineteen-year-old girl who—"

"Hi, Davy." Darla wound her arm through his, her face beaming with happiness. "This is my friend, Oliver. He likes to make pottery, too, but Oliver is way better at it than I am."

"Hey." Oliver gave David the once-over, then shook his head. "He's mad," he said to Darla. "I told you he was."

"Davy?" Darla shifted so she could stare into his eyes. "Are you mad?"

"He is," Oliver asserted. "His face is tight and his eyes are all crinkled and mad-looking. I'm leaving." He trotted to the far side of the room where he sat down in a chair and watched them.

"Why are you mad, Davy? Oliver is my friend. I thought you'd be nice to him." Storm clouds rolled across Darla's face.

"We *were* nice, Darla," Susannah intervened before David could give voice to his thoughts about this place.

"I'm sure Oliver is fine. Can we show David what you made this afternoon? I think it's going to be beautiful."

After a sidelong look at her friend, Darla proudly led the way to the massive vase she'd begun creating from coils of clay.

"Oliver showed me how to put them together. Oliver knows a lot about clay." Darla glanced around the room, but Oliver had disappeared.

"He was a sculptor," Susannah murmured for David's ears only. "His fiancée died in a car crash. He's had a hard time since then."

"It's very nice, Dar." David walked around the piece. "How big is it going to be?"

"Big. That's why Oliver has to help," Darla said, her forehead pleated in a frown.

"Why? You're the one creating it." David didn't have to say he disapproved of Oliver. It was there in his tone.

And Darla picked up on it.

"You don't know about Oliver, Davy. You think 'cause he's different than other people that he isn't smart. But he's really smart about pottery." Darla pointed. "That's his work."

Susannah felt a ping of satisfaction at the surprise filling David's eyes as he studied the massive sculpture.

"Very nice."

"I told you, Oliver is good." Darla touched her work with pride. "I'm going to be good, too."

"You already are," Susannah said.

"You have to put pots in the kiln. But this pot will be too high," Darla explained. "Oliver is going to show me how to make it so I can fire it and put it together after. No one will even know it was two pieces."

"I see. Well, I guess you would have to know kilns

to know how to do that," he admitted. "Are you finished for today?"

"Not quite," Susannah intervened. "We need to pay the course fee today. This week was just a trial period. That's why I asked you to meet us here. I thought you'd like to see what Darla would be doing."

"Fine," he said in an inflexible voice. "But I don't think we'll pay the fee today. We should talk about it first."

"But, Davy, I can't come and work here if we don't pay." Darla's voice rose with each word.

Susannah knew David expected her to do something to help Darla regain control, but the truth was, she was angry, too. She'd spent weeks searching for some way Susannah could make pottery with the guidance of someone who knew about clay and could help her realize her dreams.

Now that they'd found it, David objected because it wasn't up to his social standards?

"Come on," he said, reaching for her arm. "Let's go home and discuss it."

"No." Darla glared at him and yanked her arm away. "I want you to give the money for classes so I can come back here." Her voice had risen but she was not yet in the full throes of a tantrum.

"Excuse me?"

They turned as one to stare at the small, wizened gentleman who stood behind David.

"Are you having a problem here, Susannah?" He grinned at her, his almost toothless smile lighting up his wrinkled and worn face. "Can't have that baby of yours upset, now can we?"

"I think we're okay, Robert." She smiled, loving the

way he'd rushed to her defense. Nobody but Connie had done that before.

"Well, you tell me if there's a problem, because we don't want arguing and fighting here." He waved a hand encompassing the room. "People come here to feel safe. If this man is bothering you—"

"This is Darla's brother, David Foster. David, this is Robert. He's a friend of mine."

"Robert. What line of work are you in?" David's tone offended Susannah, but she kept silent.

"Oh, I retired years ago. I just come here for a cup of coffee and a chat. Susannah will tell you I like to chat. And do woodworking." He winked at Susannah. "One of these days I'm going to get this little mama working on the lathe."

"It's nice of you to offer, Robert," Susannah said, patting his hand. "But I think I should learn something about pottery first. Darla's so good at it."

"Excuse us. We have to go." David waited until the old man wished them a good day, then turned to Darla. "You can make a scene if you want to, but I am leaving. This is not a place where you should be. I want you to go home. Now." He glared at Susannah, then turned and walked out of the room.

"Davy!" Darla wailed.

"We'll talk to him at home," Susannah whispered to Darla, concerned by the girl's white face. "You can tell him all about the center and explain it."

"Davy doesn't want me to explain," Darla said, tears edging her voice. She walked out of the room biting her lip to keep control. "Davy's already decided that I can't come here. He's embarrassed of me."

It was pointless to argue with her—especially since

Susannah wasn't sure she was wrong. So she said nothing. She drove the girl home and helped her carry in her clay tools before hugging her goodbye.

"I have to go now, but it will be all right, Darla," she whispered, hoping she was right.

"I'm going to pray and ask God to help," Darla said before she fled upstairs.

Susannah bit her lip and turned to leave.

"Don't leave yet. I want to talk to you." David motioned to his study.

"Fine." Susannah followed him, tired and wishing she could crawl into a hot bath instead.

She smoothed a hand over her hair as she sank into the nearest chair. She noticed the clay stuck to her shoe, the streak of brown on her sleeve.

David sat down behind his desk, elegant, completely unmussed. That irritated her even more.

"Well? What do you need to say?" She crossed her feet. "It's been a long day. I'm tired. I'd like to go home."

"I want to know what on earth possessed you to take my sister to that place," he demanded, his voice icy.

"Pottery. Pottery possessed me," she shot back. "That and your sister's love of it. Which is something you seem to have difficulty grasping. If you'd only seen her face while she was working," she mourned.

"She can do pottery somewhere else." There was no give in his tone.

"That's the thing, David." Susannah was tired of his attitude. "She can't. Other programs have already begun. They won't allow her to join late."

"So she waits."

"And does what? Goes to more girls' clubs where she

is miserable?" Susannah rose. "I suggest you think long and hard about denying her this opportunity."

"Did you even look at Oliver? Didn't you recognize him?" David's scathing tone left her in no doubt that he had recognized the sculptor.

"I told you he was well-known for his work with clay." Susannah fiddled with the strap on her purse, wishing she'd hadn't already eaten the apple she'd put in her bag earlier.

"Oh, Oliver is famous for more than pottery." A smug look washed over David's face. "He has some actions pending for damaging a building downtown. That's what I mean about being unsuitable."

"You don't even know the circumstances and yet you've already passed sentence on him." Susannah shook her head. "I wonder how judgmental you'd be if it was Darla who'd damaged something and was being charged. I wonder if you wouldn't make sure she got all the chances you could give her or if you'd just toss her away the way you seem to be willing to cross Oliver off your 'worthwhile human being' list." Another thought intruded, making her even angrier. "Or is it me you're really afraid of, of my being among like kind like that? Maybe I'll revert to my old habits."

"In my opinion," he said, his voice harsh and un-yielding, "it is a bad decision on your part to make friends there and associate with those kinds of people."

"Those kind of people." She smiled. "I *am* those kind of people, David. Worthless, useless—society's write-offs."

"I didn't mean—"

"Yes, you did, David." Susannah had to get out of there before she said something horrible, something that she couldn't retract. Most of all, she had to forget the man who had so tenderly kissed her cheek.

She held his gaze for a moment more, then left, closing the door silently behind her. She walked home slowly, allowing the tears to fall without even trying to stop them.

So now she knew what he really thought. She'd suspected it all along—so why did it hurt so much that this man she admired more than any she'd ever known could write her off as worthless so easily?

David couldn't sleep.

Over and over he kept hearing her.

I am that kind of people. Worthless. Useless. Society's write-offs.

He'd argued when Susannah claimed herself unworthy to be a mother—but he'd just confirmed her judgment.

Irritated with himself and the persistent squawk of his brain telling him not to get involved, David went downstairs, brewed some tea and carried it to the family room. To his surprise, Darla was there.

"What are you doing up?" he asked.

She didn't answer. Her deep brown eyes studied him for a long time, long enough to make him shift uncomfortable.

"I don't like you today," she said finally. "You were mean to Susannah. She tried really hard to help me, and you were rude."

"I wasn't trying to be rude," he began, but Darla wouldn't let him get away with that.

"Yes, you were. You wanted to make yourself better than all the other people at the center. That was rude."

When had his sister acquired such understanding?

"I was afraid for you," he admitted simply.

"Don't you know Susannah? Don't you know she would never let anything happen to me? Even if it was going to, which it wasn't. The center is a good place."

Her voice touched a chord deep inside David and reverberated through his mind. For the first time since the accident, Darla was confronting him with her anger instead of throwing a tantrum.

"Susannah is the best friend I ever had and you're going to make her go away."

"I hope not." That was the last thing he wanted.

"You made her feel like I feel when people call me a dummy," Darla said bluntly.

"I never said—"

"And you made our friends at the center feel like that, too. They're not dummies, Davy," she said, her face earnest. "And it doesn't matter if you say it or not. When you talk the way you did, they know what you mean."

How could he argue with that? He'd been a jerk.

"Susannah knows that. She talks to Oliver and Burt and the others like she talks to me, like she talks to you." Darla bowed her head. "When she talks to us, she makes us feel strong. She makes us feel like we can do things. Lots of things."

Meaning he didn't do that for her?

"You're my brother and I love you lots, but sometimes you say things that hurt people," Darla said, her voice grave. "Today you made Susannah feel bad and I don't like that. You should apologize."

"But—"

"My Sunday school teacher said God wants people to help one another."

"Darla, it's not that simple."

"Everybody at the center likes Susannah because she knows that sometimes you just need help." She narrowed her gaze. "I don't think they like you, Davy."

"Sweetie," he said, "it's not that I didn't like them."

"Then why do you think they'll do bad things? When I make mistakes, do you think I'll do bad things?"

"No, but—"

"Susannah says everybody makes mistakes." *Even you*, Darla's eyes seemed to say. "But people can change. That's what Susannah says."

Susannah. She had pitted his own sister against him now.

Susannah didn't do that. I did.

"The Bible says you're supposed to love everybody, no matter what. Doesn't it, Davy?" she challenged.

"Yes, but—"

"Then you should have love in your heart for Oliver and Burt and Susannah and everyone. You should expect them to do good things, not bad things." She crossed her arms over her chest, her face set.

Darla had just summed up the Christian life in action.

Shamed by his words and his attitude, and the fact that God had used his little sister to show him his own arrogance, David rose and moved to sit beside Darla.

"You know what?" he said as he took her hand.

"What?" she demanded.

"I think you're the smartest woman I know."

"Really?" A beatific smile lit up her face.

He kissed her cheek and hugged her as he praised God for Darla. "I'll apologize to Susannah tomorrow."

"Good. And Davy?" She pulled back, her face worried.

"Yes, sweetie?" He tucked a strand of her glossy hair behind one ear. "What is it?"

"It's her birthday tomorrow. Connie told me she's having a surprise party for Susannah tomorrow night and we're invited." Darla beamed with the excitement of keeping a secret. "I wasn't going to tell you if you were mean, but if you apologize, that's okay. Can we get Susannah a gift?"

"We'll go in the morning," he promised. "Now, let's get some sleep."

"I already know what I want to give Susannah," Darla said. "A dress for Thanksgiving. That green one we saw."

"That will be nice."

"Uh-huh." She flung her arms around him and hugged him so tightly David almost lost his balance. "Good night, Davy," she called.

He spent a long time thinking about the nurturer that was Susannah Wells, and about how he'd treated her. And about that kiss he had planted on her cheek…

She was amazing. Nothing seemed to faze the woman. She thrived on helping anyone who needed her.

How could such a nurturing woman ever give up her child?

She couldn't. It would haunt her for the rest of her life.

David knew then that he couldn't help her find adoptive parents for her baby. He wanted Susannah to keep the child, to make a new life for both of them, a life of second chances.

He'd talk to her about that tomorrow. Right after he apologized.

Chapter Nine

"Connie, you shouldn't have done this!" Susannah said, looking at the gifts piled in the living room. The dining table was set with fancy dishes.

"It's your birthday and we're having a party. Get over it." Connie grinned.

"But you're having your Thanksgiving party tomorrow night." Susannah wished she hadn't spent the afternoon sleeping—perhaps she could have put a stop to all this fuss. "This is a lot of extra work."

"It's not work. It's fun." Connie grabbed Susannah's hands and whirled her around. She stopped abruptly. "Oops, sorry. I keep forgetting this little one makes you dizzy." Tenderly she set her hand over Susannah's ever-increasing baby bump. "What a miracle."

Her baby was a miracle? But weren't miracles for those God thought special? Susannah found herself blown away by the thought that God had singled her out, specially gifted her with this child.

Could God have trusted *her* with such a gift?

An instant later the wonder dissolved as reality hit. This baby might be a gift, but it was a gift she couldn't keep.

Guilt assailed Susannah.

"Suze? You feeling okay?"

"Yes, thanks."

"Sure?" Connie's fingertips brushed her forehead before smoothing back her hair. "You don't feel warm."

"I'm absolutely fine." She pulled back. "Don't fuss."

"I have to take care of my best friend, don't I?"

The doorbell rang and a moment later Darla's excited voice, followed by David's lower rumble echoed through the house. Her stomach clenched just as the baby kicked her in the ribs.

"Surprise!" Obviously delighted with her secret, Connie beamed. "I take it Darla didn't squeal on me when she called this morning?"

"Not a word." Susannah hadn't told Connie about her argument with David because she didn't want her friend fighting her battles. She schooled her expression into a placid mask and followed Connie from the room to welcome her guests.

David's gaze caught hers. He smiled at her, eyes melting to butterscotch. There was nothing in his manner to suggest the least problem between them. In fact, he looked happy to see her. Susannah's heart jumped when he continued to stare at her. She swallowed hard and felt a little sick. Not a pregnancy sickness—more a kind of this-can't-be-happening, heart-dropping sickness.

How could he look at her like that, as if he thought she was something special, when she knew he thought she was nothing, nobody? And why did one man get the full package—height, good looks—along with a strong sense of who he was, a sense that would never make him feel unworthy of anything?

"Happy birthday," he said in that low growl she'd become accustomed to. He handed her a small silver box. An envelope was attached. "For you."

His fingers brushed hers. Susannah pulled away, burning at the contact. "Thank you," she whispered.

"I hope you have a great year."

What did that mean? Was that sweet grin a prelude to firing her?

"This is from me." Darla edged in front of him and held out a beautifully wrapped flat box. "Can we open the gifts now?" she asked Connie, impatience showing in her dancing feet.

"Yeah, can we?" Silver echoed, just as excited.

"Why not?" Connie led the way to the family room.

"Open Davy's first," Darla directed.

Embarrassed at being on display, Susannah lifted the lid of the box and found a lovely glass bottle of expensive perfume tucked inside, the kind she sometimes dabbed on at the cosmetics counter but could never afford to buy.

"Thank you," she said, avoiding his gaze.

"You're welcome," David said.

Susannah found nothing in those calm, smooth tones to give away his thoughts. Didn't he feel anything after their argument?

"Now open mine." Darla thrust the box into her hands and flopped down beside her. "I picked it out myself. And I paid for it."

"You shouldn't have spent your money on—oh, my." Susannah lifted out the dress she'd refused to try on in the store the day they'd chosen Darla's new clothes. The green-into-turquoise swirls were just as gorgeous as they had been that day, the fabric just as luxurious. "It's beautiful, Darla. Thank you."

Never had she been more conscious of the shabbiness of her clothes. Connie had tried to help out, but she hadn't had time to sew more than a pair of pants and two simple cotton shirts.

"Put it on," Darla ordered. She pushed the box off Susannah's lap and grabbed her hand. "I want you to put it on."

"But Connie has dinner—" Susannah looked at her friend.

"We can wait," Connie assured her. "It's lovely. Go try it on."

"C'mon, Silver," Darla said, grabbing Connie's stepdaughter's hand.

So up the stairs the three of them went. Susannah was glad to escape. She could feel David's stare boring into her back.

"I might not fit it, Darla," she warned as she peeled off her clothes. "With the baby, I'm—"

"It will fit," Darla assured her. "You'll see."

And in fact, Susannah thought it fit very well, skimming over her body in a swish of fabric. She twirled back and forth in front of the mirror, unable to believe her reflection.

"Put your hair up," Darla ordered.

She clipped her mass of curls to the top of her head with a huge bronze barrette. Then she slipped her feet into a pair of low sandals. They were old, but they suited the dress.

"You look so pretty, Susannah. Let's go show the others," Darla implored. She and Silver raced back downstairs.

Susannah followed more slowly, oddly proud. She knew that for the first time in a very long time, she looked good.

"You're lovely, Susannah." David's low, intimate voice brought a flush to her cheeks.

"It's the dress." Susannah couldn't look at him.

"No." Darla shook her head. "My mom used to say you had to be beautiful inside to be truly beautiful outside." With a quick press, she hugged her then drew away.

Connie coaxed Susannah to sit down and open the rest of her gifts. There was a lovely bracelet from Silver, matching earrings from Connie and Wade, and two new maternity pantsuits, which Connie had sewn.

"It's so much. Thank you, everyone. I think this is the best birthday I've ever had," she said, looking at David as she spritzed a little of the perfume on her wrists.

David's dark-honey gaze locked with hers. Susannah gulped, but she couldn't look away. She felt as if he could see right to the pain she'd tucked deep inside her soul, pain that still stung because her mother couldn't forgive enough to send her only living daughter a birthday greeting. Susannah had tried so hard to gain her forgiveness, to be a good daughter. But it always went back to the fire. Her fault.

And just like that, the guilt returned, clawing its way up her spine and around her throat, like ivy on steroids, choking the breath out of her.

You don't deserve a birthday party. Or anything else.

"Okay, now it's time for dinner." Connie swatted at Wade's shoulder. "Don't you make that face at me. I didn't cook it."

"Well, now I know what to give thanks for tomorrow." He smirked and ushered them into the dining room.

The meal was a delight. Connie wouldn't allow Susannah to move. Wade and Silver helped her carry in the many dishes of Chinese food and insisted everyone sample some of each.

"How did you know I was craving chicken balls?" Susannah asked, savoring the tangy sweet-and-sour sauce. "You'll have to roll me out of here."

"Not just yet." Connie beckoned to Darla and Silver who scurried into the kitchen with Wade behind.

"I wonder if I could talk to you later, Susannah," David murmured.

He was going to fire her. She knew it. He was so disgusted with her choice of the center for Darla, he was probably going to find someone else to do her job. Fierce, deep pain ripped through her.

Fool, he's not your friend. He's just a man who tolerated you because Darla liked you. You should have expected this. It's what you deserve.

"Fine. Later," she answered. There was no time to say anything else because an enormous cake appeared in the doorway, candles glowing merrily. Four voices broke out in song. "Thank you," she said when they were finished. "Thank you very much." And she meant it.

"Cut it, Susannah. I want to taste it." Darla wiggled on her chair. "I love cake!"

"Me, too," she said.

Who threw Darla's birthday party? David? The errant thought made Susannah pause before she slid the knife into the cake as she tried to picture what kind of party he would give her, what sort of cake they'd get her…

And then she remembered it was none of her business anymore.

David sat in the corner, sipped his coffee and paid little attention to the game he was supposed to be playing. All he could think about was how beautiful Susannah was, how she glowed in the soft lamplight of the family room.

She kept twiddling with her hair, trying to decide her next move. As a result, more and more tendrils had tumbled free and now curled around her long, slim neck. Her skin gleamed with the same porcelain translucence as the old master's paintings he'd seen in museums. Every so often she laid a delicate palm over her stomach and a funny, tender smile caressed her lips.

Once she'd caught him staring and turned an intense peach shade, the color of an Easter sunrise. David quickly looked away, pretending to concentrate on the task at hand.

Pointless. The mental image would not leave him.

"You won, Susannah!"

"I did?" She stared at Connie as if she couldn't imagine winning anything.

And once more David was reminded of her words, of her inability to grasp her own worth.

"Let's play charades now," Darla crowed.

David rose and left her to explain her favorite game. He wandered out to the back patio, studied the gleam of the water in the moon's bright light and tried to think about something other than Susannah Wells.

"You wanted to talk to me?" She stood behind him, her small body tense, her face a mask of no emotion.

"Will you sit down?"

"I'd rather walk a bit, if you don't mind?" She tried to smile and failed.

"Sure." David waited while she lifted the latch on the back gate. He held it open for her, breathing in her scent as she walked past.

"I eat so much and I don't get enough exercise. I'm going to have to go on a serious diet after the ba—" She cut herself off and said no more.

"I think you look beautiful."

"You do?" She'd been walking fast, trying to put some distance between them. But suddenly she stopped, turned and stared at him. "Me?"

"Pregnancy only enhances your beauty." He was surprised by how much he wanted her to believe him.

"Oh. Well, thank you." She stood there, a tiny furrow marring the perfection of her forehead. Then she shivered.

He slid off his jacket and laid it over her shoulders, watching her snuggle into the warmth as they walked down the street. "We won't stay out long. I'll just say my piece and go."

Susannah didn't say anything. But her wide green eyes darkened to the murky tones of the deep forest at dusk.

"I would like to apologize, Susannah."

"What?" She stared at him, shock swelling her pupils.

"I should never have said what I did at the center. I was way out of line." Shame filled David all over again. "Here I am, telling some woman in church to have a little Christian charity for Connie's work and I don't walk my talk. I've been worse than anyone for judging people and I'm sorry you had to hear that." He handed her an envelope. "This contains Darla's fee, and yours, for the pottery class."

"But—" Susannah's fine golden eyebrows rose. "I don't know how to do pottery."

He shrugged. "Use the money for whatever you feel is right. But please accept my apology for what I said."

"It doesn't matter." She turned and began walking toward Connie's home.

"Yes, Susannah, it does. It matters a lot that I hurt you." He caught her arm and coaxed her to stop so he could look into her eyes. "I know you're doing your best for Darla, and I appreciate it. There is no one else I'd feel as comfortable having with her as you, and I will never, ever question your judgment again. I promise."

She stared at him for a long time. Finally a tiny grin appeared.

"Ever? We'll see," she teased. Then her green eyes tipped down to his hand. Somehow he'd slid it down her arm until his fingers meshed with hers.

As if they were...good friends.

"They're not bad, you know." She whispered her plea for him to understand. "People won't give them a chance because they made some mistakes, but they're trying. Oliver hasn't had an easy life, but he's working it through."

"I know." He nodded. "And you're helping. I admire that."

"You do?" Susannah looked dumbfounded at first. Then she looked embarrassed. "I don't do anything."

"Give yourself some credit, will you?" he said. "Because of you, their paths, like Darla's, are a little easier. You take the time to find out what's bothering them, and then you put it right. That matters."

She didn't argue. She simply stood in place and studied him as if he were some foreign substance newly arrived on planet earth.

"I envy you, Susannah. Do you know that?" It cost a lot to admit it, but then David owed her a lot. He took her chin and tilted her face up so he could look into those amazing eyes. "You seem to intrinsically know what to do to soothe people. That's a gift from God, a serious gift. There aren't a lot of people who leave you feeling better about yourself than when they arrived. But you do."

She lowered her eyelids, hiding her expression. But her smooth cheeks turned a pearly pink in the shadows of a streetlight and she drew her hand away from his.

"I think you would make an awesome mother to your baby. I don't think there would be a child on earth that could have a woman more determined to give her baby all the love it needs to make it through this world." He took both her forearms then and tugged so she would look at him. "Won't you reconsider this adoption thing, Susannah? Please?"

He held his breath, hoping. Praying.

"I can't." She drew away. "And I don't want to talk about this anymore. Connie might overhear." She frowned at him. "You promised."

"I won't break my word." He waited while she lifted the hook on the gate, and then followed her through. "But I wish you'd reconsider."

Susannah closed the gate. She slid his jacket off her

shoulders and handed it to him. Her small pointed chin lifted in determination.

"It would never work." Her face closed up tight, the radiance that had lit her from the inside dimmed, quashed by some fear he couldn't see.

"Susannah—"

She shook her head.

"I'm not who you think I am, David."

"I don't think you are who you think you are, either," he replied. "Nor do I think you have any idea of what you could become."

She gazed at him for a moment longer, then walked into the house.

His heart pinched at the sadness of it. Susannah wouldn't let herself consider keeping her child. Wouldn't believe in herself that much. And he wasn't exactly sure why, except that the problem was rooted in her past—rooted firmly.

But what could he do?

Instead of returning inside he sat down beside the pool to think. As usual, images of Susannah filled his mind. He saw again that tender, bemused smile flickering over her face, the bewildered yet amazed way she touched her midsection.

A baby, a tiny, innocent child. A son. Or a daughter to whom she would give life and upon whom she could pour out the love she gave so freely to others.

Darla had told him Susannah had begun to talk about her child, and had mentioned how Susannah often offered to hold other women's children at the center.

To give up her child would leave a scar. One that would wound far deeper than the pain sweet Susannah now carried from her past.

And that was something David could not even con-
template, let alone allow. To see this beautiful woman
retreat back to the scared, sad person who'd arrived here
only a few months ago tore at his heart.

Don't get involved, his head reminded.

Only David knew it wasn't a matter of involvement
now. Susannah had breached his defenses, pushed her
way past all his intentions to remain aloof, and availed
herself into his world through Darla. Susannah had become part of his days, sneaked into his dreams and
made his heart wish for things he couldn't have.

It was silly, impossible to think of a future with her.
His brain had long since accepted that God's choice for
his life's path didn't lie that way. He had responsibilities. Love wasn't for him. Hadn't he learned that lesson twice? If only that lesson would sink into the secret
parts of him that longed to experience being a husband
and a father.

But that silly longing for something he couldn't have
didn't mean he should give up trying to persuade Susannah that adoption was not the way to go.

All David had to figure out was how to do that.

He'd start with money. A little nest egg for her baby.
Maybe if she felt she had something to fall back on, that
she wasn't teetering on the brink—maybe then Susannah wouldn't feel so compelled to give up her child for
adoption.

Maybe.

Chapter Ten

Susannah felt only relief when Thanksgiving and Christmas slid past in a rush that left her little time to think.

Pregnancy was a confusing business and no one was more confused than she. Especially with the increased fluttering her baby now made.

Her baby.

She had to stop thinking of it that way. It could never be hers.

On New Year's, Susannah decided to make plans for her future and wrote lists of actions she needed to take. But in the days following, she rewrote them over and over, depending on where her moods took her.

Those moods took her a lot of places. Into the pool late at night when she couldn't sleep. To the ice cream shop to taste weird flavors. To a crochet class at the center where she struggled to make a baby blanket the instructor insisted was "simple."

When no answer from her mother arrived to respond to the plea for forgiveness she'd sent earlier, Susannah found herself weepy and tearful, unable to accept Connie's assurance that God loved her. How could God love someone who'd made the mistakes she had? Her mother sure didn't love her. Susannah couldn't even love herself.

But she loved her baby. She loved that life inside her with every ounce of passion in her body. She would do anything, anything to protect it, including finding new parents for her baby—if only she could.

But that wasn't her only problem. Susannah was growing fearful of her burgeoning feelings for David Foster. Especially since he'd become so thoughtful, so—nice. But though she enjoyed being around him, enjoyed the way he made her feel part of his and Darla's world—Susannah would not let those feelings grow. She couldn't. She couldn't afford a repeat mistake— not with this baby's future at stake.

So Susannah was confused, wary and seven months pregnant when she arrived at David's office late one January morning. Thus far they'd always talked when he came home at the end of the day. But today he'd asked her to come to his office.

As she entered the exquisitely appointed building, she was enthralled by a granite wall down which water trickled. In contrast to the Tucson desert, lush plants thrived all around it with light from the massive windows. The office felt grand—and she felt totally out of place.

"Hello, Susannah. Welcome." David escorted her to his office, his hand firm but gentle against her back.

"It's beautiful in here," she whispered.

"Thank you." He seated her in a cranberry velvet chair that folded around her weary body, and then asked his secretary to bring them tea.

The girl flirted with David, batting her long lashes, making sure to bend over in front of him when she set down the tea and sumptuous-looking lemon and poppy seed muffins. Susannah disliked the secretary immediately and she refused both tea and muffins, though her stomach grumbled a complaint.

"I'd rather have coffee," she said when David held out a steaming white china cup that probably cost the earth.

"You're supposed to cut down on coffee, aren't you?" He set the cup in front of her, undaunted by her glower.

"Who told you that?" she demanded, then sighed. "Darla."

"She loves to talk about you and your baby. And I like to hear," he added.

"You do?" That shocked her. "Why?"

"Who doesn't like to hear about a new life preparing to join our world?" One brown eyebrow lifted. "It's generous of you to share the details of your pregnancy with her." He leaned back in his chair as he sipped his tea. "I imagine it's quite amazing to have a life growing inside you."

"It is," she admitted. Susannah tilted her head down to hide her smile of pure delight. It was astonishing, in fact. But she felt embarrassed to tell him that. Especially here, where she was so out of place.

She hoped the coffee table hid her feet as she slipped off her shoes. Even they didn't seem to fit anymore.

"You're probably wondering why I asked you here." His voice changed from gentle concern to businesslike.

"Yes." In fact, curiosity was eating her up.

"I've done quite a bit of research into adoptions." He caught her surprise. "I had to," he explained. "It's not exactly my field."

"Oh." So she'd put him to a lot of trouble. How much would all that cost? He kept telling her not to worry about the cost, but she did worry.

"The thing is, Susannah, I need some direction. There are so many kinds of adoptions. I'm not sure which you prefer." He handed her a file filled with papers. "These describe open and closed adoptions and what choices, responsibilities and rights the mother had in specific cases."

"Okay." She set the sheaf down on the glass table. She'd think about it later. She picked up her teacup. Suddenly she was very thirsty.

"There are many variations," he continued. "For instance, do you want contact with your baby after you give it away?"

He made her baby sound like a used toy she was getting rid of.

"I don't know," Susannah murmured.

"Do you want to be involved in raising your child or are you intending to hand over all rights to the child's future and give the adoptive parents total freedom?" David leaned back in his chair and studied her.

"I don't—"

"Will you want the adoptive parents to tell the child about you or do you prefer your baby never know its real mother?"

"Uh—" Susannah frowned.

Never know anything about her? Never know that she loved her child desperately, that she yearned to keep it for her very own, to shower on it all the love she kept hidden inside? An arrow of pain pierced her heart. She laid a protective hand on her stomach.

"I—I'm not sure about that yet," she whispered.

"Will you release medical records?" he asked.

"I don't know." So many questions. She was growing more confused.

"Grandparents?"

"No!" At least she knew the answer to that question. Her hand squeezed tight against her purse where the condemning letter lay. "Never."

"You don't want the child to be able to trace his family roots someday?" David asked, his face puzzled.

"My father left when I was four. I doubt even I could trace his whereabouts," she told him, her body clenching with tension.

"What about your mother? Wouldn't she—"

"She's in prison." She watched his eyes, steeling herself to see disgust. But David never flinched.

"Do you ever see her?" he asked.

"She doesn't want to see me." Susannah's cheeks burned. She picked up her cup again and sipped just to have something to do with her hands. "She hates me."

"I see." Those dark eyes pinned her down, as if she was a witness on the stand. "So no family history. That's what you want for your child?"

Susannah almost gagged.

"It will be better that way," she blurted. "It's what I have to do."

"Actually you don't. That's what I'm trying to clarify," he said, leaning forward so his elbows were on his knees. "You have choices, Susannah. Lots of them. Your child is yours. You make the decisions. I'll do whatever you want."

"Okay." She nodded.

"But I have to be certain you understand what you're

doing," he said, his voice solemn. "I would be failing you as your lawyer if later you regretted your decision."

"Let's not go over that again," she said, rising. She stepped away from the coffee table, searching with her feet for her shoes. But as she tried to slip her foot into one, she lost her balance and reached out to grab something to steady herself.

That something was him.

"Easy." His arm slid around her waist. "Sit down and I'll put them on for you."

"I can manage." She drew back and wished she hadn't. Her head whirled. Being this near to him made her want all kinds of things—like someone to care about her, someone to love her.

Stupid. David Foster wasn't interested in her. He was just being nice.

"Do you ever let someone help you without an argument?" His mouth tipped in a crooked grin. With gentleness and great care, he helped her sit. Then he knelt down in front of her to slide on her sandals. "You should put your feet up," he murmured, brushing his fingers against her calf. "Your ankles are swollen."

"All of me is swollen. I look like a truck."

David chuckled. Susannah burst into tears.

"Stop laughing at me!"

"I'm not laughing at you." Somehow he was there beside her, holding her close, allowing her to weep all over his expensive suit jacket. "I'm laughing at the way you mistake things. You are beautiful, Susannah, one of the most beautiful women I've ever known. Motherhood has only made you more beautiful."

"I can never be a mother." Grief swamped her.

"Talk to me, Susannah." David cupped her face in

his hand. "Tell me what this is really about," he said in a soft, tender voice. "Tell me the whole story."

The burden was so heavy. And Susannah was so tired.

The words emerged of their own volition. She stared into his concerned face and let it pour out of her.

"I was the oldest. I promised my sisters I'd always be there for them. They were only four and seven. Little girls who needed someone to watch out for them. But I didn't do that. I ran away." Loathing scathed her voice. "They died because of me."

"No." He seemed dazed, incredulous.

She smiled bitterly. "Believe it. They're dead."

"You said there was a fire," he said. "How could that be your fault?"

"Easy." She pulled out of his hold and gathered her courage. When he knew, he would send her away. Might as well just get it over with. "I wanted to get away from the chaos. I was so tired of having to figure out what was for dinner, what we were supposed to wear to school, how we were going to pay the electric bill. Scared of being scared all the time."

She'd never told anyone that, not even Connie.

"Those are things your mother should have handled."

"She couldn't, so I did." Tears glossed her eyes, but she refused to shed them. She forced herself to continue. "My sisters died because of me, David. It was my fault. I killed them."

Give me words, Lord, because I don't have any, David prayed silently. His heart ached to ease the inner torment her eyes revealed.

"Susannah—"

"Now do you understand why I cannot—I will not—raise this child?"

David studied the weeping woman in front of him. He doubted Susannah even realized that she was cradling her baby as she spoke. He couldn't begin to imagine how one small woman could bear so much pain.

"Why don't you say anything? Are you disgusted? Revolted?" she asked, anger sparking her eyes. "Well, so am I. And I will never let a child of mine feel that way."

Help her!

"Susannah, how old were you when they died?"

"Nine. I was their big sister. S'ana they used to call me when they hugged me at night." A flicker of a smile appeared and vanished. "I tried so hard to keep them safe."

"Of course you did," he whispered, smoothing damp curls from her brow. "You protected them and loved them as much or more than your mom did, didn't you? You would have done anything for them."

She stared at him, nodding in a dazed manner as if she'd never thought of it in those terms.

"You were a great big sister, Susannah. But doesn't it seem to you, now that you're older and can look back, that nine was far too young to be responsible for two other children?" David held his breath as she frowned, tilted her head to one side.

"I was responsible," she repeated, confusion evident.

"You weren't, sweetheart. You were not their mother."

She simply looked at him.

"Your mother was there, right?" He waited for her nod. "She was in the house when you left?"

"Yes."

"Doing what?" He had to get to the bottom of it, had to make her see.

Susannah was quiet for a long time. Finally she lifted her eyes and looked at him. "She was drunk. She was often drunk."

He touched her cheek. "But that didn't make it your job to do any of those things you said, Susannah. It was only your job to love your sisters, and it sounds to me like you did. Very much. Enough to take care of them the very best you could. All by yourself."

"You make me sound like some kind of hero," she protested. "I wasn't. I left them. I ran away."

"What nine-year-old doesn't run away from home at least once? I did." He took her hand in his, marveling at the coldness of it. Such a small, frail hand, a frail body to house such a big heart. "Maybe you shouldn't have sneaked out, but that does not make you responsible for their deaths."

"Legally, you mean." Was that hope dawning?

"I mean you were not responsible in any way, shape or form. Not legally and not morally," David insisted. "You were a child, as your sisters were. The guilty person was your mother, Susannah."

"No." She shook her head with determination. "She couldn't help it. When my dad walked out she was so hurt. She was always crying."

"So she got drunk to dull the pain?"

"I guess so." Susannah blinked away the tears. "She fell asleep that day and...it wasn't her fault. I should have been there." She shrugged dully. "It doesn't matter anymore."

"Yes, it does." David had to make her see it. "It matters a lot. You cut your mother plenty of slack, but you can't do that for yourself?"

"I don't deserve it."

"Why don't you? You were a child." He swallowed hard, then spoke the words he knew in his heart were true. "She told you it was your fault, didn't she? Your mom blamed you?"

"Yes," Susannah whispered. "But she was right—"

"She was wrong," he said, his anger burning white-hot. "So wrong."

"No." Susannah shook her head. "She was in pain. She didn't know, didn't realize that I wasn't there—"

"But she should have, don't you see? She was the one who was responsible for taking care of the three of you and she dumped that duty on you, a young child." He could hardly speak, so infuriated was he at this woman who had so wounded her own grieving child.

"She must have thought I was home to watch them," she murmured.

"You told her you were leaving?"

"Yes, but I didn't make sure she heard. I wanted to escape." Susannah lifted her head and stared at him through her tears. "Why did God let my sisters die? Why didn't He let me die instead?"

"Oh, Susannah." He gathered her into his arms and held her tightly, trying to ease the burden of her loss. "God doesn't want you to die. He wants you to live and make something wonderful out of your life. And you're doing it."

"I am?" She lifted her head, her face inches from his, hope flickering.

It was all David could do not to kiss her. But he held back because he understood that now more than ever,

Susannah needed to know about the kind of love that would always be there for her.

"Of course you are." He smoothed the tendrils off her face. "God has given you this opportunity and you're doing your best to make good."

"How?" she asked, forehead furrowed.

"You're making sure your baby has a good start, for one thing. You're eating right and exercising. You're seeing your doctor regularly, right?" He didn't like the way her gaze skewed away from his. "Aren't you?"

"I will go again, as soon as I can pay," she whispered.

"What? No, Susannah." David shook his head. He tilted her chin so she had to look at him. "You don't have to pay. Didn't the doctor's office tell you that?"

"No." She leaned back to look at him, her face troubled. "Why wouldn't I pay?"

"Because you have insurance. I bought it for you." He liked the way she fit in his arms—liked it a lot. "All of my employees have health insurance."

"Oh." A soft glow flickered through her eyes. "Does it cover sonograms?"

"It covers whatever you need," David said. He wanted to keep holding her, keep reassuring her. He wanted more. He wanted…everything.

The realization shocked him.

And terrified him.

He couldn't have love, or marriage and a family. The things other men took for granted—a wife, family— God had not chosen for him. He knew that.

So why this irrational need to protect Susannah, to make sure she was cared for, that her child was not given away to strangers?

"I had a sonogram a while ago," she was saying. "I

was supposed to have another one, but I didn't have quite enough money saved." She explained that she'd paid for the first one.

David needed distance between them to calm his racing heart. He eased her out of his arms as he made a mental note to claim Susannah's money back.

"Make the appointment and have the test done immediately," he insisted. "If you need another doctor, special treatment, anything—I'll make sure it's covered. We want this baby healthy. Don't we?"

"Yes." She struggled to rise.

He rushed to help her, realizing anew how difficult her pregnancy was making things.

"Susannah, I want you to know something."

"What?" She peered at him warily.

"I've put away some money for you. In case you change your mind about the baby." He put one finger on her lips to stop her protest. "I don't want you to feel that adoption is your only option. If you want to keep your baby, you can do it." He slid the bankbook from his pocket and into her hand.

"You shouldn't have done this, David." She opened it and blanched at the amount, going even whiter than she was before. "This is wrong."

"I pay into a pension plan for my staff," he said quietly. "Think of that as your pension plan." When she still frowned, he folded her fingers around it. "I won't take it back. It's yours, to help however you want."

"It's unbelievable." Susannah was silent for several moments. Then she looked at him, her eyes glossy with unshed tears, and nodded. "I don't know how to thank you."

"You don't have to." He frowned at her pallor. "Are

you certain you're all right to look after Darla? You're not overdoing it?"

"I'm fine. I shouldn't say this but it's a really easy job." She smiled. "Darla has changed a lot, hasn't she?"

"Thanks to you." He smiled at her, loving the way she glowed with pride whenever she spoke about his sister. "You've done a great job."

She lowered her gaze, shy as always when compliments came her way. His anger flared again at the mother who'd treated her so shabbily.

"I better go." She walked toward the door and paused. "Oh, one other thing." She fiddled with the strap on her handbag. "Darla wants to work as a junior assistant at the butterfly exhibit at the botanical garden. We've visited frequently and the director thinks she has a knack for speaking to the kids who visit."

"When? Her schedule already seems pretty full," David mused.

"It is," Susannah agreed. "But I think she can do this. I think she needs to do it, David. She needs the confidence this public responsibility will give her. Isn't that what we've been trying to achieve?"

He liked the "we" part of what Susannah said. But Darla on show in a public place? It was something he'd secretly avoided ever since her accident.

"She isn't the same girl, David. She's learned how to manage her feelings. This can only help her gain further control." Susannah's quiet plea reached into his heart and touched a chord there. "Darla needs to feel needed. This is her chance to prove to herself that she has a place in the world."

David hesitated. He didn't like it, would never have

countenanced it if Susannah hadn't pushed. But so far she had been right about his sister.

"Are you going to be there?" How had he and Darla managed before Susannah's arrival?

"Of course. For the first time or two, anyway. Just in case she needs me." Susannah smiled at him. "She can do it?"

"Okay."

"Great!" She raced across the floor and threw her arms around him in a burst of exuberance. "Thank you," she said, hugging him. Then she stepped back, cheeks hot pink as her arms dropped to her side. "Sorry."

"No problem." David grinned. She was truly the most beautiful woman—inside and out—that he'd ever known. "I enjoyed it."

That made her cheeks even pinker. David enjoyed seeing her so flustered.

"When is her first day?" he asked. "I'd like to visit."

"Probably Saturday." She checked her watch. "I have to go. Thank you, David, for everything." She started for the door.

"Susannah?"

"Yes?" She stopped and turned.

"Take these and read them." He picked up the sheaf of papers from the table and offered them to her. "Will you please think about what I said, about keeping your baby?"

She took the papers but shook her head.

"Why not?"

"It's better if my baby has a new mother." Then she hurried away.

It wasn't better at all, David fumed. It was wrong. Totally wrong that Susannah of the loving heart should give up her child. What kind of a mother had she lived with to skew her thinking so much?

He decided to find out. He sat down at his desk, picked up the phone and asked his research assistant to dig up everything on Susannah's mother.

"There has to be a way, Lord. You surely couldn't want Susannah to give up this gift You've given her."

Why do I care?

Because I love her.

The admittance knocked him sideways. It shouldn't have—he quickly realized that he'd been carrying strong feelings for Susannah for a long time.

She was gentle, loving and tender. She'd made a ton of mistakes and she knew it. Which meant she carried a boatload of guilt from her past.

None of which mattered one iota to him.

Susannah loved Darla. She'd gone beyond what any caregiver could be expected to do to help his sister figure out her world. David would have loved her for that alone. But he loved her for so much more.

He loved her because she didn't let him get away with anything, because she listened—really listened—to him, because she never once, in all these months, had asked for anything for herself. Yet he wanted to give her everything.

And because of that, David wanted—no, needed—to make it possible for Susannah to keep her baby.

He picked up the phone.

"Wade? Can you and Jared meet me tomorrow for lunch? I really need to talk to you guys. Thanks."

They were his best friends, they knew his history and most important of all, they shared his faith. David had no clear-cut answer from God on what to do with his feelings but they could help him figure out his next step.

Love was something that wasn't for him. He knew that.

Yet love was exactly what he felt for Susannah Wells. So what was he supposed to do?

Chapter Eleven

"So you've fallen in love with Susannah," Wade said and clapped him on the shoulder. "Congratulations."

"It's not that simple," David said.

"Why?" Jared demanded. "What's wrong with love?"

"It's not for me, that's what. It's not part of God's plan for me." David rose and paced around Wade's patio. But that silence got to him. He looked up and caught the puzzled look his buddies were sharing. "I've been engaged before," he reminded them.

"So?" Jared shrugged. "They weren't the right ones. Susannah is."

"But how can I be sure of that?"

"Dave, sit down and let's work this through. You care about Susannah, right?" Wade asked after he'd flopped onto one of the chairs beside the pool.

"Yes."

"Okay." Wade nodded. "And you want her and her baby in your life permanently?"

"Yes," he repeated with certainty.

"But you think that's somehow wrong?" Jared frowned. "Why?"

"Because I'm not good husband material. I have Darla to care for, I work long hours." He glared at them. "Two other women walked away from me."

"Yes, we know. And if they'd been God's choice, don't you think He would have sent one of them back?" Jared rested his elbows on his knees. "I'm no expert on love, but I've read the Bible and I can't find a place where it says you have no right to love. In fact, God is love. He patterns love for us. He doesn't place love in your heart and then demand that you ignore it. Where does it say that in the Bible, David?"

"I agree. If that's your thinking, you ought to be able to line it up against His word. Chapter and verse, buddy." Wade leaned back, waiting.

"Of course there's no verse," David said, irritated that they kept pushing. "It's just something I know."

"How do you know it?" Jared demanded. "Because you were thrown over twice? That's not proof that you can't have love in your life, that you can't love someone."

"There's one thing I've learned about love this past year, David." Wade's voice dropped but remained intense. "God gives us love to enrich our lives, so we can share with someone who will be there for us, help us through the good stuff and the bad stuff. It seems to me that's what you have going with Susannah. And I think it's wonderful. What I don't get is why you can't accept a gift like that from your heavenly Father."

"It's just—I don't believe He meant that kind of relationship for me." David didn't know how else to express it.

"Exactly. *You* don't believe. You." Jared glanced at Wade who nodded and began speaking again.

"Listen, buddy. Jared and I think that this so-called truth of yours, that God doesn't want you to love, is something you've convinced yourself of. I know being dumped the second time, especially when she blamed Darla for your failing relationship, had to be hard on your ego." Wade winced. "When my first wife took off with some other guy, I felt gutted. I couldn't even imagine I'd be able to care for another woman, let alone love one again. I made up my mind that I would never get involved again. But God brought Connie into my life."

"And now look at him," Jared teased. "Seriously, though, just because Wade thought and felt like that didn't make it God's plan for him, Dave. It's the same with you. You wanted to avoid the hurt and embarrassment those fiancées brought you. That's understandable. But you don't care for either of them now, do you?"

"No." David was emphatic on that. The only woman in his heart now was Susannah.

"Because you love Susannah," Wade said.

"Yes." It felt so good to admit that aloud.

"There's nothing wrong with that," Jared insisted. "Love is God-given. You might also tell Susannah how you feel. Maybe she feels the same?"

How David wished that were true.

"But if you're still doubting," Jared said, "why don't you pray about it and ask God to work it out for you? If she's the one, don't you think God had a hand in bringing you two together? Don't you think He has a plan to make it all work out?"

"Is it God you don't trust, David?" Wade asked. "Or is it yourself?"

"Hello, baby."

Susannah blinked through her tears at the shadowy image of her child on the sonogram picture the technician had given her. With her fingertip she traced the tiny head, the neck, two perfect arms and legs—her baby. The wonder of this life growing inside her blindsided her to everything else.

So tiny. So precious.

How could she let this child go?

How could I not?

Her baby would soon be born and she'd have to hand him or her over to strangers. Forever.

Susannah's heartache intensified as the desolating loss swamped her. Though she tried to suppress them, tears flowed in a steady stream down her cheeks.

If only David was right, if only she could keep her child. What a sweet and generous gesture to give her the money. Susannah's Baby, he'd written on the bankbook. Once again she marveled at his generosity and the way he saw beyond what everyone else did, probing to the heart of things. He figured out she didn't have anything and went the extra mile to ensure she could make her choice with no regret.

But it wasn't about the money, never had been. It was about her inability to handle such a massive responsibility without messing up. And so she decided that when she left Tucson she'd make sure he got his money back.

Susannah stared down at the picture again and new tears flowed. She was glad Darla was outside playing with Silver. She didn't want anyone to witness her weakness. Because it was weak to want what you couldn't have, what you knew you'd ruin.

"Susannah?" David stood before her. "What's wrong?"

He crouched down to study the paper in her hand. She watched him examine the image, a huge smile spreading across his face from one side to the other.

Delight lit his eyes as he examined the picture in minute detail. Finally he lifted his gaze to meet hers.

"Your baby," he whispered. "It's perfect, Susannah. Is it a boy or a girl?"

"I didn't ask." She dashed the tears away. "I only asked if it was healthy," she said. The words dissolved into a blubber as her emotions seesawed again.

"And?" he asked, sitting beside her. Somehow she was in his arms again, and she didn't mind one bit.

"It is." She sighed as he gathered her close and let her rest against him. She was so tired. "The doctor says everything is great."

"Good. Then we should celebrate this gift of life God's given you. Not cry about it." His hand smoothed over her back in a soothing caress that made her feel loved, cherished, cared for.

"Celebrate?" She leaned back. "How?"

David chuckled as he brushed her cheek with his knuckles, drying her tears. He gently released her before smoothing the long strands of hair she'd left free. Susannah felt the faintest caress of his lips against her forehead before he rose.

"I'm not sure how," he said, staring at her. "But this healthy baby definitely deserves a pre-birthday celebration."

"Can we have a party, Davy?" Darla said from the doorway. "Silver is staying for dinner."

"I hope you have a lovely time," Susannah murmured, too tired to get up. Everything seemed to suck her energy these days. "I think I'll go home."

"Connie and Wade went out for dinner, didn't they? So you haven't eaten. I could order in a pizza," David offered.

"No." Darla shook her head at him. "No pizza."

"I thought you liked pizza," he said, obviously bewildered.

"I do. But Susannah's baby doesn't like it." Darla moved to sit beside Susannah. She put her hand on her stomach and gently stroked. "It kicks her and upsets her stomach when she eats pizza. Then she can't sleep, and Susannah needs to sleep lots." She frowned at her big brother. "We have to have something else."

What a girl. Susannah smiled at her protector, glad she wouldn't be forced to eat the spicy Italian food she usually loved.

"Okay. What would you prefer, Susannah? I'm guessing sushi is out?"

She made a face.

"That's what I thought." He grinned. "Is that because you can't put peanut butter on sushi?"

"Ew, gross." Darla made a gagging motion.

"You don't have to order anything for me, but I'm sure the girls would love cheeseburgers," Susannah said, trying to get the focus off of herself.

"Too greasy. I think stir-fried vegetables would be good." Darla glanced at her friend. "We like Chinese food, don't we, Silver?"

"We like it lots," Silver agreed, grinning. "Especially me."

"Good. Chinese it is. How about if you two come with me to pick it up. Then Susannah can have a rest." David bent over Susannah, his nose a centimeter from hers. "And I do mean rest. Put your feet up and have a nap. No setting the table or anything else."

"It sounds lovely," she agreed, enjoying the way he slipped off her shoes and playfully placed them across the room. "Thank you."

"You're welcome." His toffee-toned eyes held hers for a moment.

It had been a very warm day, but Darla insisted on covering her with an afghan before they left. She tucked it around Susannah's feet, her face brimming with concern.

"You won't get up?" she asked anxiously.

"I promise." Susannah waved as they left. She'd intended to watch a documentary about childbirth, but somehow her brain began replaying that moment when David had kissed her forehead. She fell to dreaming about what it would be like to be cared for, loved, by a man like him, a man who wouldn't dump you the moment life took a wrong turn.

A man who would cherish you and protect you and make life fun again.

A man who would love a baby that wasn't even his.

"Davy, can you help me?"

"Sure, sis. With what?"

"Susannah." Darla frowned. "Me and Silver are worried about her."

"You are? Why?" He'd been a little worried himself when he'd found her weeping like that. "I think she was crying because she was so happy to see that picture of her baby," he said.

"I don't mean that." Darla shook her head. "Susannah gets really tired. Silver heard her tell Connie that the baby is moving around a lot and she can't sleep. One night Silver saw her swimming and it was really late."

"I think that's the way it is with babies," he said, wondering where she was going with this. "I think Susannah is okay though, Darla."

"But Connie said the doctor told Susannah to slow down, to stop trying to do so much, and she doesn't. Susannah thinks she has to do everything with me. It's my fault she gets so tired." She glanced at Silver who was playing at the juke box, then leaned closer. "Maybe if she didn't get so tired all the time, Susannah wouldn't want to give away her baby," she whispered.

"Sweetie, she doesn't want to give it away, exactly. She's just afraid she won't be able to look after it," he explained.

"She won't if she's too tired," Darla said. "We could adopt it. I would help."

"I know you would, sweetie," David said. He touched her hand. "But I don't think Susannah wants that."

"I guess not. We're not a family and Susannah wants a family." Darla sighed.

"Listen kid, you and I are a family. Always have been, always will be. Got it?" He bussed her cheek with his fist.

"Yeah, but we're not the kind of family that can take care of a baby, are we, Davy?"

He shook his head, unsure of how to deny that. So far he'd been focused on the two of them, not on including anyone else, though he'd wanted exactly that for years.

"Could you come with us to the botanical garden tomorrow?" Darla said. "Susannah says she has to be there, but it's hot in the butterfly exhibit and she might get too tired. She could go and rest if you were there."

"I have an appointment tomorrow afternoon. I was going to come after that," he told her.

"Could you put it off? Or send somebody else?" Darla asked anxiously. "We have to help Susannah now. 'Cause we love her."

Yes, we do, he thought.

"Okay, I'll do my best," he promised.

"And can we get a chair and an umbrella for soccer?" she asked. "There are only hard benches there and there's no shade."

"I'll figure something out, sweetie." He hugged her, touched by her compassion. "You just tell me when you see something we can do to help, and I'll do it."

"Well, we were talking about that," she said, waving at Silver to come over. "Tell him," she ordered.

"Susannah likes flowers." Having abandoned the juke box, Silver flopped down on a stool. "She told me nobody ever gave her flowers before. My dad gives Connie flowers lots of times."

"Hmm. How about if we pick up some flowers on the way home." David made a mental note to make sure Susannah got lots of flowers. Such a small thing. How sad that no one had been there to do that for her. He intended to change that.

Their food arrived and David carried it out to the car. On the way home he pulled into a flower shop and let the girls choose a bouquet for Susannah—a bright spring one. He also spotted a portable chair with a little umbrella attached.

"Perfect," Darla told him with a grin.

Satisfied, David drove home—and found Susannah sleeping on the sofa.

"She really is Sleeping Beauty," Darla whispered.

"No, I'm not. I'm a troll who needs her dinner. Grr," Susannah said, eyes closed. She grinned at them as she eased upright.

David extended a hand to help her to her feet, marveling at the difference a little sleep made. Her green eyes shone with life, her skin luminous.

"Feeling better?" he asked as they laid the table.

"Much." She blushed when he held out her chair for her and quickly sat. "Thanks."

"You're welcome." He couldn't resist touching the swath of golden curls that cascaded down her back.

"These are for you, from us." Darla held out the bouquet with pride.

"Oh. Thank you." Susannah glanced at him, startled. Then she accepted the flowers and buried her nose in the fragrant petals. "They're beautiful."

David could have sworn he saw tears in her eyes, but when she looked at the girls, she'd blinked them away and was smiling. He got a vase, filled it with water and set it in the middle of the table so she could enjoy her bouquet.

"Only two months till Easter," he said, holding up his water glass to toast her. "Not long to go now."

"That's easy for you to say. I have a quite different perspective." She peeked through her eyelashes, grinning.

And David lost his breath. She actually sounded happy about the future.

"I'm starving," Darla said.

"Me, two," Susannah agreed and winked at Silver.

"Me, three." Silver giggled.

They all looked at him with expectant eyes.

"Me, four?" Susannah burst into laughter.

"Say grace, Davy."

David offered a quick prayer of thanks then served everyone, enjoying the pleasure of making sure each had enough to eat. It had been a long time since a meal around this kitchen table had been so happy and he knew it had everything to do with Susannah's presence. He couldn't stop staring at her.

David felt compelled to study Susannah's radiant face as the girls teased her about her appetite. This afternoon Wade and Jared had helped David realize that he wanted this woman and her child in his life permanently. His friends had insisted there was no reason why David couldn't care for Susannah, that cutting love out of his life had never been something God had told him. Repeatedly they'd asked him to show a Biblical foundation for his belief that love was wrong for him. Wade had even said he thought David had made himself believe that after being thrown over twice.

But were they right?

And how risky was it to love her?

Susannah wasn't like David's former fiancées. He didn't have to wonder if she'd walk out because he worked too long, or because of something Darla did. Susannah knew what his life was like, knew he was committed to his sister. She was committed, too.

But could she love him?

"You're not eating," she said, frowning at him. "Is something wrong?"

"No." He felt the worries, the cares, the heavy thoughts go as he returned her smile. "Nothing is wrong at all."

Life seemed so simple, so enjoyable when Susannah was there.

"I'll help clean up," she offered when the food had disappeared.

"There isn't much to clean up." David chuckled at the one lonely chicken ball rolling in sauce. "I can load everything into the dishwasher. You go and rest."

"I did rest," she told him, a glimmer of spirit flickering in her gorgeous eyes. "And I'm fine. Perfectly able to clean up a few dishes. So don't argue," she added when he opened his mouth.

"Okay. You can help a little," he agreed, pretending he'd made the decision.

David enjoyed the camaraderie of working beside Susannah. He made a big fuss about giving her plenty of room for the sheer pleasure of watching her blush.

He drove back to Connie and Wade's enjoying the sound of laughter and happy voices. Darla raced out of the car and up the walk with Silver, leaving him and Susannah alone in the car.

"It was nice to have someone to share our table with," he said. "I'd forgotten how long it's been since Darla and I entertained."

"I hope you don't feel you have to entertain me," Susannah said, frowning at him. "I'm just the help."

"Susannah, you must know you mean a lot more than that to us," he said meaningfully. He held her gaze until she looked away.

"Thank you for these," she said, burying her nose in her flowers. "I've never had—well, thank you."

"You're welcome." David climbed out and went to open her car door. "What time will Darla be working at the butterfly exhibit tomorrow?"

"You're going to come?" She didn't look exactly thrilled at the prospect.

"I'll try to get there," he said. "I want to see how she does. Is that a problem?"

Susannah drew in a breath and stared past his shoulder. She wore a pained look that made him wonder if he'd said something wrong.

"Susannah? Are you all right?"

Finally she exhaled and nodded. "Yes."

"Did something just happen?" he asked as a wave of concern rushed over him. He grasped her elbow in case she felt faint or something. "You don't look pale."

She slid her arm out of his touch and smiled. "I can't get used to the soccer game going on inside me, that's all."

She let him escort her to the door before she hugged Darla and waved at him. "See you tomorrow." She inclined her head at Darla. "She'll be helping after school till five o'clock."

"Oh. Yes. Okay." David scanned her face once more. "You're sure you're all right?"

"I'm fine. Good night." She stood in the doorway, waiting for them to leave.

"Good night." He helped Darla into the car, and they drove away. Susannah remained in the doorway, her focus on the picture she clutched in her hands, the picture of her baby.

A wash of yearning swamped him. All down the block families were heading inside their homes, gathering their loved ones around them. David wanted to be able to do the same thing with Susannah. To protect her, to share her life, to have the right to help her with her child, and not just be an outsider.

He wanted to be able to kiss her good-night and wake up to her smiling face, to share his hopes and dreams with her, to discuss Darla and seek her opinion. He wanted Susannah to help him build a family.

God, please give me the sense to wait for the right time and find the words to tell her how much she means to me.

"I love Susannah, Davy," Darla said, yawning as she

followed him inside their dark and silent home. "She makes everything happy."

"She sure does."

Darla stopped at the bottom of the stairs and frowned at him.

"What's wrong?" he asked.

"Susannah might come and stay with us forever if you kissed her like Prince Charming kissed Sleeping Beauty," she said. "Couldn't you kiss her, Davy?"

"We'll see," he said as he struggled to keep a straight face. "Have a good sleep, sweetie."

"Yeah." She hugged him, started up the stairs, then paused. "Davy?"

"Yes?" He waited, knowing something important was coming.

"Are you sure we couldn't adopt Susannah's baby?" Sadness drained the joy from her face. "I don't want that baby or Susannah to go away. I love them both."

"I know." David embraced her and tried to soothe her, but he couldn't tell her everything would be okay. Because he wasn't sure it would be—not for Susannah once she let her child go, and not for him if he let Susannah go.

"What can we do, Davy?"

"Pray," was the only answer he could think of.

Darla was doing an amazing job explaining the butterfly exhibit to the group of day-care children who were visiting the botanical garden. Susannah smiled encouragement when two older boys wandered in and began to ask Darla a hundred questions. Susannah listened but her mind was on finding somewhere to sit. She was so tired and the little butterfly gazebo was so hot.

Loud voices drew her attention.

Darla was supposed to inspect and brush off each person to ensure no butterflies hid in their clothes and escaped the enclosure. But the boys would not let her do it. In fact, they taunted her. Susannah stepped forward to intervene, but at that moment one of the boys jerked back and knocked her off balance. She reached out, desperate to grab on to a metal fountain to stop her fall.

Next thing she was lying on the ground, winded and dazed, and Darla stood over her, berating the boys.

"You hurt Susannah," she bellowed, her anger flaring. "Get out." She pointed to the door. As soon as they'd pushed their way through the hanging plastic panels in the exhibit, she knelt beside Susannah and searched her face. "You have a cut," she whispered fearfully, pointing to a mark on Susannah's arm.

"I'm okay, I think. Can you help me up?"

"Yes." Darla almost lifted her to her feet. Thankfully the enclosure was empty.

Susannah felt woozy and worried. Darla insisted she leave the exhibit and sit down on a bench outside. Once Susannah was seated she took her phone and dialed.

"Darla, no," Susannah protested, but it was too late.

"You said you'd come, Davy. Where are you?" Darla was angry, her brown eyes intense. "Some boys pushed Susannah and she fell down. She has a cut."

Susannah heard David's low voice assuring her he was on his way. She'd fallen so awkwardly—was the baby okay? It wasn't moving. She laid one hand over her stomach protectively and tried to form a prayer for help.

"We're really sorry." The boys had returned to apologize. "We didn't mean to bump into you."

Susannah opened her mouth but Darla spoke first.

"You should be more careful," Darla lectured. "A butterfly exhibit isn't a good place to fool around. And you shouldn't make fun of people, either," she added, her face very severe.

"Yeah, we know," the bigger one said with a sheepish grin. "You were just doing your job. Sorry, miss."

As they left, Susannah shifted, feeling bruised and uncomfortable.

"You shouldn't have phoned him, Darla. I'll be fine. It was just a little fall."

"At your stage, there are no little falls," David said, striding up to them. He knelt, touching the mark on her arm before his fingers slid down to thread with hers. He squeezed them and closed his eyes. "Woman, you scared the daylights out of me."

To her shock he gathered her in his arms and held her close.

"I'm sorry." Susannah marveled at how right it felt to be held like this. But then she noticed how pale he was, and that his hand trembled as it smoothed back her hair. "I'm fine, David."

"We're going to make sure of that," he said grimly. "You have a bruise on your chin." His jaw clenched.

"It's nothing." She wouldn't tell him how off balance she felt.

"Shall I carry you?" David held her as if he'd never let her go.

"Of course not. I can still walk." She touched his face, smoothed away the lines on his forehead, completely overwhelmed by his concern. "I'm really all right, David," she whispered.

"I'd prefer to hear that from a doctor," he growled. "Darla, tell the lady you have to leave now."

"Okay." She hurried away but was back in a flash. "Ready."

"All right, you walk on one side of Susannah. I'll walk on the other," David directed. "We'll go slowly. Okay?"

At least he waited for her nod of approval, Susannah mused. But truthfully, she was very glad of his support. A hint of fear that she'd messed up again would not leave her.

Please don't take my baby, she silently prayed. *Please?*

Deep in her heart Susannah repeated the words Connie had been telling her ever since she'd arrived in Tucson. *God is the God of love.*

Chapter Twelve

God? Are you listening?

David waited outside the examining room, his heart in his throat.

She's so small, so delicate. That baby is all she has. Please, please don't let—

He couldn't bear to even let the thought develop as fear like he'd known only twice before burgeoned and clutched at his heart. The only time it had loosened its hold in the past half hour was when he'd had Susannah in his arms.

Where she belonged.

In that instant David made up his mind. He was going to tell Susannah that he loved her, just as Wade and Jared had advised. More than that, he was going to ask her to marry him.

"David?" Connie rushed up, laid a hand on his arm, her face worried. "Have you heard anything?"

"Not yet—" The words died on his lips as Susannah's doctor emerged from the room they'd taken her into. "Doctor?"

"You're David?" Dr. Grace Karrang smiled at him. "Susannah said you'd be hovering out here, waiting."

So she knew he wouldn't just leave her. Good.

"How is she?" Connie asked.

"Everything seems okay. I'll keep her overnight, just to make sure. But as far as I can tell now, Susannah and her baby are fine."

"Can I see her?" he asked.

"Yes. They'll move her to a room shortly, but you can all talk to her for a while. One at a time, though."

"You go first, Davy." Darla slid her hand into Connie's. "We'll wait."

"Thanks, sis. I'll hurry," he promised.

"It's okay, Davy." She touched his cheek, her eyes clear. "I prayed. Susannah and her baby are going to be all right."

"Yes." He kissed her forehead.

Susannah looked so petite on the bed, her skin ashen against the pristine sheet. Her hair had been pushed back off her face. Her eyes were closed.

David picked up her hand and threaded his fingers in hers.

"Susannah?"

She blinked a couple of times before those incredible lashes lifted and she smiled. His Sleeping Beauty.

"Hello, David. I guess I drifted off." Her soft, sweet voice sounded like music to him. "You're pale. Are you all right?"

"Me? I'm fine. It's you I'm worried about." He couldn't stop brushing his thumb against her skin, reassuring himself that she was alive and well. "How are you?"

"A little tired. The doctor said I have to stay here

overnight." She frowned. "That's going to be expensive."

"It's taken care of. Don't worry." When she licked her lips, David poured a little water from the carafe and held it to her mouth. "Sip slowly."

"Thank you." She leaned back, smoothed the cover over her stomach. "I'm sorry if I worried you."

"Of course I was worried."

"Because I let this happen." She squeezed her eyes closed. "You think I'll let something happen with Darla, too. You want me to quit." She stared at him. "Is that it?"

"No!" He frowned. "I care about what happens to you, Susannah. I care a lot."

"You do?" She stared at him in disbelief, emerald eyes wide in her pale face.

"Susannah, I'm in love with you. I have been for some time." David waited to see how she'd react.

"In love—with me?" She peeked at him through her lashes, then hid her eyes.

What if she still loved the baby's father? The idea hadn't occurred to him before. He couldn't think about that now—he just needed to show her.

"I've known how I felt for a while." He loved the way she let him finish his stumbling admission. "I just wasn't sure what to do about it. Until today."

"W-what have you decided?" she whispered, worry filling her face.

"Why do you always expect the worst?" he asked with tender mirth.

"I don't. Not always," she argued, her feistiness back.

"Susannah." He smiled, cupping her face in his palms. "I want to marry you, Susannah. I want you to stay with Darla and me forever. I want a future with you."

"And the baby?" she asked, fear in the shadows of her eyes. "What about my baby?"

"You'll have to learn to share because it will be our baby. Every bit as much mine and Darla's as yours," he said firmly, holding her gaze. "We'll raise him or her together. With love and laughter and faith in God."

"My faith in God isn't very strong right now," she whispered, tears welling in her eyes.

"It'll grow. We'll both work on trusting God."

Susannah studied him without speaking. David could see she was thinking deep and hard and he could only pray that she would at least think about his proposal.

"Susannah, you're not the only one who has made mistakes," he admitted, loving the feel of her skin as he caressed her face. "I let failed relationships from the past influence me into thinking God didn't want me to love again. I knew I was beginning to care for you, but I assumed I was supposed to remain single, for Darla."

"David, I—" she started, then faltered.

"You've shown me that Darla and I both need you in our lives." He slid his arms around her, drawing her close. Then he leaned forward and touched her lips with his. To his surprise, she returned his kiss with a sweetness he'd only dared dream about.

David felt relief wash over him. Maybe, just maybe, somewhere deep inside, she had at least some feelings for him. He felt joy welling up inside him.

"I love you, Susannah. And so does Darla. She would love to have a sister."

"She was like a mother bear today, protecting her cub." She smiled reflectively and reached up to smooth his hair. "Darla is amazing. You're pretty amazing, too," Susannah whispered shyly, brushing her fingers against his cheek. "Thank you for getting me here so quickly."

"I love you. How could I do anything else?" he asked, content to savor the pure bliss of holding her in his arms. "Anyway, I was scared stupid. You were so pale. Still are."

David waited but Susannah didn't respond with the words he wanted to hear. He told himself to be patient. She needed time, he reasoned. He'd sprung it on her. He kissed her quickly, then rose.

"Darla's champing at the bit to get in here. And Connie. I'll give them a turn."

"Okay." She let him go, her arms dropping to the bed.

"Susannah?"

"Yes?"

"Will you think about my proposal?" he asked, his heart jammed into his throat.

"I have to think it over. Marriage isn't something to be rushed into." Her green eyes held shadows. "I did that before and I made some huge mistakes. I'm not going to make them again."

She hadn't said yes.

But neither had she said no.

"Take all the time you need," he said as a giant geyser of hope flowed inside his heart. "I'll be waiting."

"Thank you." He turned to leave but she stopped him by catching his hand. "David?"

"Yes?"

"Will you do me a favor?" Her eyes grew huge in her small face.

He wanted to say yes, but he had a hunch he wasn't

going to like it. So he quirked an eyebrow upward and waited.

"Can we not tell the others?" Her eyes were turbulent like the sea during a tempestuous storm. "Not yet anyway."

The geyser of hope inside sputtered. "Because?"

"Because I need this to be between us for now," she whispered. "There's another life at stake. I have to make the right decision."

He wasted several moments studying her then nodded, squeezed her hand and left. "Your turn," he said to an eager Darla.

Wade stood in the hallway.

"Connie went to get some coffee," he explained. "So?"

"I asked her to marry me. She wants to think about it." David studied his friend. "She also wants to keep my proposal quiet. For now."

"So we'll pray. Hard."

"Thanks." David had laid his heart out there. What more could he do but trust that God would see him through?

While he walked on tenterhooks.

David loved her?

Susannah couldn't quite assimilate that knowledge and there wasn't time anyway. Darla burst through the doorway and came bounding over to the bed.

"Is the baby all right?" she whispered. "Are you?"

"We're both just fine. Thanks to you." Susannah hugged her. "I don't know what I would have done without you there, Darla."

"But I wasn't good," Darla countered, her face glum. "I got mad and yelled at those guys."

"You know, sometimes anger is a good thing," Susannah told her, patting the side of her bed so Darla would sit near. "Sometimes we have to get angry against injustice or when somebody does something wrong so that the wrong gets corrected. You did very well and I'm proud of you."

"Really?" Darla's huge smile lit up the room.

"Really. Thank you for protecting me. It's just the kind of thing one sister would do for another," she said quietly. "That's how I think of you, you know. As my little sister."

"I love you, Susannah." Darla hugged her enthusiastically. "And I love the baby, too." She patted her rounded stomach. "Hello, Baby."

Susannah listened to her talking to the child in her body and marveled at the love she felt for this wonderful girl. How was it possible to feel such a bond with Darla? What strange coincidence was it that Darla had slipped into her heart and nestled right next to her unborn child?

She said as much to Connie after Darla left. Her old friend simply smiled.

"It's not coincidence, Susannah," Connie assured her. "It's God."

Susannah wasn't sure about that. God didn't seem quite so personal to her, though she'd been trying to breach the gap between them by reading the Bible Connie had left in her room and taking time each night to pray.

"See, that's the thing about God," Connie said. "His love doesn't hiccup when we make mistakes or turn away from Him. His love isn't like human love, Susannah. And He never, ever turns us away."

Rick Green had said the same thing, Susannah remembered.

"God's love never changes, no matter what." Connie shook her head. "There's a verse in the Bible that says nothing can separate us from the love of God. The verse goes on to list a whole bunch of things and then repeats that none of them, nothing can come between us and the love God has for His precious children."

"I hear that" she admitted, "but then it sounds like there's a *but*."

"The *but* is us, Suze." Connie shook her head. "We forget how great the love of God is, or we think we're too bad, or that we've done something too terrible." A serious note lowered her voice. "But the Bible says nothing can stop God's love."

It sounded nice, Susannah thought. Comforting, if only she could believe it. But Connie had no idea about her past, about the things she'd done since she'd left the foster home. And Susannah had no intention of telling her.

"We need to move Ms. Wells to a room now. You can see her later."

Susannah was glad for the nurse's intrusion. She wished her friend goodbye.

As they moved her to her room, she couldn't shut out that inner voice that kept offering hope. Connie's words made her wish for the impossible. But in her heart of hearts Susannah couldn't quite believe that God's love extended to her.

David claimed to love her, too. His words pinged into her brain. Was it real love he felt? How could he love someone like her?

You're pregnant with another man's child. You are

so dependent on Connie and Wade you don't even have your own place. What is there to love?

But David *had* said he loved her.

And she loved him. Why deny it any longer? He'd snuck into her heart, a bit each day. She'd simply refused to let herself believe that such love could ever be returned.

For a moment, Susannah let herself bask in the knowledge of what David's love could mean. Happiness. Peace at last. Contentment. A home for her and her baby, a husband who cared about her, loved her and would help her make the right decisions for the future. A sister to share with—something Susannah had missed for so long. She wouldn't have to be alone.

But what if she failed him? What if she did something stupid, something that embarrassed him? What if he became ashamed of her? The thought made her physically sick. She admired David so much, but could she live up to what he'd expect? Did she dare risk loving again?

The pros and cons circled her brain as Susannah struggled to envision exactly how her life would change if she said yes to David. The images were dazzling, alluring and so far beyond anything Susannah knew that she could hardly believe in a life like that. He would come this evening, however. And by then she had to have her answer ready.

Connie had said God loved her. Susannah wasn't sure that was possible. But surely He could help her.

God? Don't let me make another mistake. Please?

Susannah curled up in the armchair behind the curtain and inhaled the heady fragrance from the lush bouquet of crimson roses David had sent. Her fingers trailed over the words on the enclosed note. *For Susannah. With love, David.*

To be loved just for yourself—how wonderful that would be. As she fingered the velvet petals, for a moment she let herself dream that she could actually live the happily-ever-after of Darla's beloved fairy tales.

Dare she dream?

"What does that hunky lawyer see in our white-trash girl?"

Susannah froze at the voices coming from the other bed in her room. She huddled tighter into the curtain and prayed they wouldn't see her.

"Watch it." A nurse's aide checked Susannah's bed. "She's not there. Be careful what you say, will you? She might overhear us."

"She's having a shower. Primping, no doubt," the other nurse's scathing voice condemned. "A man like him, from a wealthy family—he could have his pick of women. Why send *her* roses? She's nothing. Nobody. What's she got to offer him—an illegitimate kid?"

They left moments later but the damage was done. Even Susannah's gorgeous roses couldn't erase those harsh words from her brain. Over and over they replayed, driving the shaft of pain deeper into her heart.

Why did they have to ruin it?

Because they were right. Susannah Wells wasn't worthy of David Foster's love.

The harsh truth smacked her with reality. It was an illusion, a fantasy to think she could marry him. And she couldn't afford to deal in daydreams when her baby's future depended on her making rational, sensible choices.

Susannah shook off the fairy tale, rose from her dream world and prepared for her meeting with David. Her heart cried out to God, begging Him to help her say the hardest thing she'd ever had to say.

"You're a wonderful man, David." Susannah's voice was quiet yet he heard every word. "You're gentle, caring, kind. You'd make a wonderful husband."

"But not for you." He sat down, amazed by the decimation that rushed to swamp him. Was it possible for love to root so deeply in such a short time? *Yes*, his heart thumped. "Is it because you think I won't love your baby?"

"No."

He felt relief that she knew him that well, at least.

Susannah shook her golden head, her green eyes darkening. "That's the last thing I'd worry about. You would be the best father any child could have."

"You don't love me?" He noted the way her glance veered from his.

"I'm sorry, David. I can't accept your proposal."

"Why?" he demanded, ashamed of his desperate need to know.

"I can't use you like that," she whispered, her face sad.

"Use me?" He didn't get it.

"David, I'd ruin your life—embarrass you and Darla. Eventually you'd be ashamed when you realized I'm not someone worthy of being your wife." She put her hand over her mouth and looked down.

"Ashamed of you?" he scoffed. "That's ridiculous. I've always been very proud of you."

"Thank you for saying that." Susannah hesitated,

then shook her head. "But I can't marry you, David. I'm sorry. I think the best thing is for me to give my baby a chance with someone who won't mess up as I have, someone who will make sure he or she grows up happy. That way I won't risk making another mistake."

"Won't you?" He studied her. "Or will you be making the biggest mistake of all?"

She met his gaze but said nothing.

So that was it? He'd gambled, taken a chance on telling her his true feelings, and lost. Now he was supposed to just give up?

"You haven't said anything about love, Susannah."

"I—uh—"

David tilted her chin so she had to look at him. "Do you love me?"

She didn't speak but her green eyes flashed a warning not to push.

"So you won't risk even saying the words, let alone allow yourself to feel love." He shook his head. "How sad that is—because I know you care for me. I think you love me almost as much as I love you."

"David—"

"Don't you see, Susannah? Your fear has taken over." He had to make her understand. "It controls you so much you won't let yourself believe that you can be more than the past. You won't stretch your mind and imagine yourself living with love, being the mother your child needs, being the wife I believe you can be."

"Don't waste your feelings on me—"

"Waste?" he scoffed. "It's not a waste for me to love you, Susannah. It's a joy and a privilege. You enrich my life, you make it worth living. I finish work as fast as

I can so I can come home and see you, talk to you and listen to your laugh."

She looked at him, eyes welling with tears. "I'm not worth loving."

"Then you don't know Susannah as I do because I find you eminently lovable," he insisted. "I can hardly wait to hear how you're feeling and learn what you did each day. I ache to be included in your life, to be part of it all, to help you plan for that child."

She was shaking her head but David couldn't stop. He was desperate to make her understand the place she'd carved out for herself in his heart.

"Do you want to know how much I care about you, Susannah?" He should have felt embarrassed to be so needy, but he didn't. He was fighting for his future and that demanded honesty. "I question Darla every night to make sure nothing's wrong, that you didn't get too tired, that you weren't bored. I make her repeat conversations just so I can be part of your world. I can't get enough of you."

"David—"

"I love you and your child, Susannah. So don't pretend it's to spare my feelings that you're turning me down."

"I am trying to spare you," she insisted. "My past isn't—"

"Your past is not you," he said fiercely. "Not who you are today, or who you could be tomorrow. You are not that little Susannah your mother blamed."

"Yes, I am."

"No. What you are is an amazing woman who doesn't spare herself for others. You've made an endless number of good choices since you came here. But all you can do is look backward and focus on the past." Frustration surged inside him. "Why won't you risk being more than the old Susannah? Why aren't you willing to stretch yourself to be the mother your child needs?"

"People don't change, David," she whispered. "Not that much."

"You have."

"I fell for a man who lied to me, and I believed his lies." She sniffed, head bent, refusing to look at him.

His heart ached for her but he resolved to keep fighting.

"Okay, so you fell for the wrong man. Did you ever ask yourself why?" David grabbed her hands and hung on. "Because you didn't trust your inner warnings. That was a mistake people make every day."

"A bad one." Despair edged her voice.

"So?" He had to help her understand what she was throwing away. "You aren't that person anymore. You've grown, matured and taken responsibility for a baby. You've changed my life and certainly Darla's. You have a lot to give, Susannah. And by refusing to accept love, you're cheating all of us."

"I'm not cheating anyone." She yanked her hands from his. Bright spots of pink dotted her cheeks as she glared at him. "Don't you dare say that!"

Good, he wanted her to get worked up about her future and stop passively accepting what her mother had told her.

"You're cheating all of us, including yourself. But mostly you're cheating God." David hunkered down to see into her eyes. "He's given you a chance to change the course of your life, Susannah. He's given me a deep, strong love for you that can withstand your past. And

I believe you share that love. Are you going to accept His gift, or throw it away?"

He held his breath, waiting, praying, hoping.

An announcement came on asking visitors to leave the hospital. David ignored it. A nurse ducked her head in and told him visiting hours were over. He ignored that, too. And waited.

Finally Susannah inhaled. Then she straightened, met his gaze directly and shook her head.

"I'm sorry, David. Thank you for your proposal, but I have to refuse." No quaver in her voice, no hesitancy—nothing that exposed what she was feeling inside. "You don't know how I wish that I could be the person you think I am. But I'm not."

"That's it? You're just going to walk away from everything—me, your child, Darla, your future? God?"

"No, I'm planning my future the best way I know how." Her voice was firm. "And I've made a decision."

David knew he wasn't going to like the next part.

"I'm resigning, David." Her big green eyes emptied of all emotion. "I promised Darla I'd take her to the pre-Easter presentation at the desert museum. That's in two weeks. It should be enough time for you to find someone else to work with Darla."

"And the baby?" he managed to choke out.

"I want to thank you for all your help, David, but I think it's better if I find someone to adopt my child on my own," she murmured. "But I will pay you what I owe you."

"Money? Will that make you feel better, Susannah?" he asked as bitterness welled.

"Yes." She lifted her chin. "Being able to pay what

I owe is something I haven't always been able to do. That's just one of the things you don't know about me."

David couldn't think of a response that wouldn't dump all his anger and hurt and frustration on her, and Susannah, with her pale cheeks and hurting eyes, didn't need the extra grief.

So he did the only thing he could.

He leaned forward and kissed her, pouring all the love he felt into that kiss. To his joy, she responded. When he finally drew back, they were both breathless.

"I love you, Susannah. That isn't going to change, no matter what you do or where you go. And because I love you, I will support whatever decision you make." He smiled, touched her cheek. "You see, I have no worry about you. I know your heart. Maybe better than you do."

He walked out of the room without looking back.

But his soul wept for all he'd lost.

Chapter Thirteen

Tucson's warm desert wind stole moisture the way it stole energy. Susannah was drained.

She'd expected her last two weeks with Darla to be problematic, and they were. But not for the reasons she expected.

For one thing, Darla kept asking her about the baby and Susannah had no definitive answer.

Then there was David. He didn't press her to change her mind about marriage, didn't ask her why and didn't insist she rethink her decision. In fact, Susannah scarcely saw him, though each day there was some small reminder that he'd said he loved her.

A jar of the gourmet pickles she loved, a little book about the hilarious woes of pregnancy, a pretty bouquet in pinks or blues or both, a box of luscious chocolates, trinkets that were original and thoughtfully chosen, never duplicated.

Each one would appear with Susannah's name carefully printed on the tag in his precise writing with "Love, David" etched beneath. His manners were faultless when he arrived at home in the evening, and his demeanor as considerate as anyone could ask for. He was everything a good friend would be—kind, considerate and very gentle.

Except Susannah wanted more.

Which was totally unreasonable, and she knew it. She'd refused his proposal. She couldn't expect him to hold her when she felt ugly and horrible, or understand that she ached to hear a word of encouragement. She waited, but he never inquired about her most recent doctor's visit or commented on the fact that her feet had become all but invisible.

But she wanted that. She wanted all of it. Badly.

Each day when she left his house in the evening, he said the same thing.

"I love you, Susannah." Then he kissed her.

And each night she sat awake with her child doing acrobatics inside her, and wished the fairy tale she dreamed about could come true.

Susannah's days were full as she escorted Darla to her programs, watching the girl blossom with confidence in every activity. One evening she sat Darla down and told her she would be leaving shortly. Darla didn't argue, as she'd expected. Instead she accepted Susannah's words, hugged her tightly and told her she loved her. Then she'd disappeared to her room. Later Susannah heard her weeping.

Susannah found herself in tears often. It was so hard to think of never watching her child grow, take her first step, stumble and know she wouldn't be there to see that baby walk. Her heart squeezed tight whenever she realized she would never hear her child say "Mommy." She felt a special bond with her baby now, a secret flush of wonder each time a tiny leg stretched or a hand reached up. The wonder of this life had turned her prayers to God into pleas for help to do the hardest thing she'd ever contemplated.

But God didn't seem to be listening, because the ache intensified right along with her feelings of worthlessness. That, more than anything, reinforced her belief that she couldn't be a mom.

The warm spring air added a precious clarity to Susannah's days as the desert began to bloom and come alive in ways she'd never imagined. One afternoon Connie drove her out to the desert museum so she could get her bearings for her trip with Darla the following week, and to witness the first burst of cactus flowers.

"I never imagined there were so many cacti," Susannah said when they'd wandered the paths for a while.

"Those are hedgehog, those are fishhook and those are saguaro cacti," Connie pointed out. "Don't walk there," she warned, grabbing Susannah's arm and drawing her back. "That's a Jumping Cholla and its spines are nasty."

So many dangerous things in this world. Would her child's adoptive mother be sure to protect her baby from all of them?

"This will all be decorated for Easter. It's unbelievable. We came last year and Silver was tongue-tied for at least ten minutes." Connie chuckled and waved a hand. "There will be specially trained museum volunteers all over the place. They'll be wearing white shirts. They can answer questions about the plants and animals in the Sonoran Desert—pretty well any that Darla can think up, I'm sure."

"She wants to know everything." Susannah smiled

as pride swelled inside. "I think she wants to be a docent. Someday."

"It would be perfect for her." Connie took her arm to steer her away from the cactus garden. "You look tired, Suze. There's a café. Let's stop and relax. We can get some coffee. Or tea."

"And maybe some sorbet?"

"Sure." Connie giggled. "You and Darla seem to share a fondness for that treat."

"Yeah. Only she prefers pistachio and I love key lime." Susannah laughed and pretended everything was fine, but inside she wept. She and Darla had grown so close. Who would love and care for this sister of her heart?

David. At least she knew Darla would be safe with him.

It was a relief to sit in the shade of the cottonwood trees and sip their hot drinks in between spoonfuls of frosty sorbet. Nearby a rock-surrounded garden burgeoned with the buzz of bees from the pollination gardens and cut the stillness of the warm afternoon.

"How are you feeling?" Connie asked.

"Big. Ugly. Tired." Susannah forced a smile. "I don't seem to be able to sleep much at night anymore." She touched her stomach. "She's always dancing."

"Or maybe *he's* playing football," Connie teased. "Are you sure you'll be well enough to trail around here with Darla? You're getting awfully close to your due date, aren't you?"

"Not that close. The doctor says I probably have at least two more weeks, and I will most likely go overdue." Susannah made a face. "How much bigger can I get?"

"You're so small, it just shows a lot. You look beautiful," Connie reassured. She was silent for several minutes before asking, "How are things with David?"

Tired of being alone and struggling to sort out her confusing feelings, Susannah had confided in Connie after David's hospital visit. Connie hadn't been surprised to hear of David's proposal. Susannah had a hunch her friend had long since guessed at her feelings, too.

"He's fine, I guess. Very busy at work, I think, but he always takes time to compliment me about something each evening." She didn't tell her friend about the good-night I love you's that kept her awake. "He keeps leaving me little gifts." Susannah tipped back her head and let the breeze cool her neck. "I feel guilty but he won't stop no matter what I say."

"Don't you like his gifts?" Connie asked, frowning.

"Oh, yes. I like being surprised by them." Susannah called herself a fool to be so transparent. "Yesterday he left the catalogue from the college. He's gathered a lot of information on the courses I will need to take to get my degree. I didn't think he'd even heard me talk about it."

"Good thing you'll have the summer to get used to the baby's schedule." Connie smiled. "You can start your program in the fall and then add as you feel able."

"I probably should have told you this before," Susannah murmured, knowing it was way past time to tell her friend. "But I'm going to give the baby up for adoption."

"Oh, Suze." Connie's eyes brimmed with tears.

"I can't keep this baby," she said firmly. "I'm a horrible role model."

"That's not true." Connie reached out and squeezed her hands, her face serious. "Listen, Susannah, I know you've been working hard to rebuild a relationship with

God. Well, part of that needs to include letting the past go. It says in the Bible that God remembers our sins no more. If He can forget, why can't you?"

"David said the same thing. I haven't thought much about it," she said.

"Well, think about it now," Connie insisted.

"Why?" Susannah asked. "What difference will it make?"

"It will help you understand why you shouldn't keep hanging on to guilt from the past," Connie said, her voice stern. "When God forgives, it's gone. He doesn't keep going back and harping on it over and over. What good does His forgiveness do if we keep bashing ourselves over the heads with our mistakes?"

"But you don't know—" Susannah gulped.

"No, I don't. But the thing is, God knows, Suze. And He's forgiven it all."

Susannah sipped her tea and wondered how it felt to be clean, forgiven, made all right.

"Suze, there's always been part of your story that you held back. All that time at the farm—I've always known you never told me everything that happened with that fire." Connie squeezed her fingers.

A shadow fell over them. They glanced up. David stood staring at Susannah. It was clear he'd overheard Connie's last remarks.

"David?" Connie blinked.

"Wade sent me. Silver fell off her bike. He wants you to meet them at the hospital." He shook his head when she rushed to her feet. "She's fine, just needs a stitch. Darla's with her but she's calling for you."

"I'll go with you." Susannah pushed away her glass.

"No, stay. David can bring you back." Connie glanced at him, waiting for his nod.

"Yes, I can. No problem. In fact, I could use a drink myself. It's hot this afternoon. Drive carefully," he said to Connie.

"I will. See you later, Suze?" It was a question.

Susannah knew Connie was asking if she'd be all right with David. "Go, Connie. And kiss Silver for me."

David hailed a passing vendor and purchased a drink. Then he sat down across from her, his stare intense.

"What?" she said, feeling as if she was under a microscope.

"I overheard Connie. And I agree with her. I think you have held back something that happened at that fire." He leaned forward, touched her cheek with a forefinger. "I think you need to say it, to get it out so you can forget it."

"I'll never forget," Susannah said bleakly.

"Why?"

"Because I was the cause of that fire." She couldn't look at David, couldn't bear to see the condemnation in his eyes. "I am the reason my sisters died."

"I don't believe it." He shook her head, as if that put an end to it.

"Believe it. I left a pan on the stove. It used to get so dry in our house in Illinois in the winter. I got nosebleeds sometimes. My mother told me that if I kept a pan of water on the stove, the moisture would help. So that's what I did." She gulped as the memories flooded back, then turned to look at David. "I didn't turn it off before I left. It must have burned dry, got too hot and caught on a dishtowel or something. I was mad, you see. I wanted to get away and I never checked…"

The tears would not be stopped, grief for years of trying to erase the images of her little sisters alone, crying for help.

"Oh, Susannah." David shifted his chair nearer and wrapped a loving arm around her shoulder. "Sweetheart, you were too young to be responsible for any of that— even if it did happen that way, and I'm not sure it did."

"It did." She scrubbed her cheeks, irritated by her emotions. Good thing she had said no to David. This was just something else he'd be ashamed of.

"It doesn't matter what happened. Don't you understand? God doesn't say that one mistake is worse than another, that He'll forgive some things but not all." David smoothed her hair, his voice brimming with love that soothed. "He says 'I forgive' and He means everything. Whatever it is. And He wants you to forgive yourself, too. He wants you to enjoy a full life, to experience love and joy. He planned that especially for you, Susannah."

"I've done a lot of things I'm ashamed of."

David only smiled.

"Doesn't matter," he said. "You asked for forgiveness and God gave it. He doesn't hold it against you. He knows you, Susannah. He knows you were young and mixed up and hanging with the wrong group. He knows who you are, everything that you've done, and He loves you anyway."

"I don't understand how that could be." Susannah listened as David explained more about forgiveness on the way home. And she promised him she'd try and forgive herself for her past.

But late that night, as she sat on the window seat watching the moon slide in and out behind clouds, Susannah knew that while forgiveness might be possible, forgetting was not. She would carry those scars of guilt for the rest of her life.

And she couldn't bear it if her child found out. Adoption was the only way.

"So you're saying Susannah Wells's mother is still in jail?" David scribbled the information on a pad to study later.

"Not still—again. And not exactly jail," the social worker said. "It's a facility to help Mrs. Wells deal with her personal issues. But yes, she has been committed to staying there until the doctors feel she can handle life on the outside. Given her refusal to accept any responsibility for her recent actions, my understanding is that she will not be leaving soon." The social worker listed the most recent charges that had been added to Mrs. Wells's latest sentence.

She wouldn't give him specific details, of course. And David hadn't expected any.

"The lady has a problem with responsibility," she finished.

"Me, too," David muttered after he'd hung up.

But his problem was of another kind. He'd been so preoccupied with being overwhelmed with responsibility, he now realized he'd missed out on a lot of what life offered. Now he desperately craved the opportunity to be responsible for Susannah and the life she carried. But she would have none of it.

And he didn't know what to do about that.

For years after his father's death, David had believed he had to be in control of everything in his world. But when Susannah came along, she'd inadvertently forced him to realize that he needed to surrender the controls of his life. Recently Wade and Jared, too, had helped him realize he needed to completely surrender his past, present and future to God.

"Jared Hornby is on line two." His secretary cut into his thoughts.

David picked up the phone.

"You called?"

"Yeah." David proposed lunch with his old friend. "I need to pick your brain again," he explained.

"Oh, so then you'd be buying," Jared said. "Great. I'm not far away. Fifteen minutes at Scarfies? We haven't been there in ages."

"Okay." David left the office immediately. He needed to get outside, breathe the fresh spring air and think as he walked the few blocks to their favorite lunch place. But when he arrived, his brain was more knotted than ever.

Jared sat waiting, his iced tea half gone.

"Hi." David hurriedly ordered the special. When Jared had placed his order and their server had left, he cleared his throat. "I feel like I'm drowning," he said.

"Susannah," Jared guessed.

"I believe she is God's choice for me, Jared. She's the only woman I want in my life."

"And her past?" His old friend hunched forward to study him.

David crossed his arms over his chest. "I couldn't care less about her past, except that whatever happened, it made her into the woman I love."

"You can't write it off that easily, pal." Jared shook his head. "Susannah has had some bad things happen to her. It's got to impact her."

"Where are you going with this?" David frowned.

"Wade and I advised you to tell Susannah how you felt." Jared shrugged. "Okay, you did that. And she didn't respond the way you wanted. I think you have to accept her response, buddy. I think that you have to leave the future with God." Jared sipped his iced tea.

"Just give up. That's what you mean?" Even the idea left a bad taste in David's mouth.

"Give it up to God," Jared corrected. "If she's His choice for you, let God work it out."

David shook his head. "I don't think God expects me to sit back and do nothing here, Jared. I can't do that. What if she gives her child away?"

"David, she *is* going to give her baby away," Jared said.

"Her past and her mistakes are exactly why she has to keep that baby," he insisted. "If she doesn't, that will only be one more thing Susannah will regret."

Jared thought about it a moment. "You said her mother's blame is at the root of all her feelings of unworthiness?"

"I'm no psychologist," David said, "but I think her mother's accusation that Susannah caused her sisters' deaths left a pretty big wound, yeah."

"Maybe you should go see her mother, try and get her to show some compassion for the only daughter she has left?" Jared quirked one eyebrow.

"It's worth a try, I suppose." David hated the thought of it. Intruding into someone else's past, reopening old wounds—everything in him protested at the depth of involvement. Susannah would be furious. But if it would help her…

"I'll pray. So will Wade." Jared leaned back as their food was delivered. "We'll keep a steady line going to heaven while you talk to this woman. There's just one thing."

"Yeah?" Personally David thought there was a lot more than *one* thing, but he waited for his friend to finish.

"What if none of it makes any difference to Susannah?" he asked.

David stalled, taking a bite of his burger and chewing it thoroughly. Finally he met Jared's gaze.

"I don't know," he admitted. "I can't think that far ahead."

"I don't know you." The woman flopped herself into the easy chair, her silver-blond hair tumbling to her shoulders. A more mature Susannah. "Do I?"

"No. David Foster. I'm a friend of Susannah's."

A spark of interest lit the green eyes before she covered with a lackluster shrug. He held out a hand, which she declined to shake.

"Your daughter Susannah," he said as anger surged up.

"I haven't seen her in years." Sara Wells looked at him balefully.

"Since the fire." He nodded. "I know. Why is that?"

"Look," she bristled, "I don't know who you think you are or why you're poking your nose into something that isn't any of your business, but—"

"It is my business." David leaned back and chose another tack. "Do you know you're going to be a grandmother?"

She leaned forward, intrigued in spite of herself.

"Congratulations." Her lips curled.

"It's not my child. But I would like it to be," he said. He felt a rush of love as the words resounded to his soul.

"I love Susannah. I want to marry her. She's a wonderful woman—loving, caring, gentle and courageous."

"Everything I'm not, is that what you mean?" Her eyes darkened.

"This isn't about you," David assured her. "You cut your own daughter out of your life."

"I have my reasons."

"I know all about your reasons. To make yourself look innocent. To ease your own pain. You blamed Susannah for her sisters' deaths. That was a lie, wasn't it?"

Sara Wells remained silent.

"She was a child, a little girl with far too much responsibility."

"Do you think I don't know that?" Sara's face tightened.

"Then why?" he asked quietly. "You weren't the only one who lost. She lost her sisters. And she's spent all these years believing the lie you told her."

Tears flowed down her cheeks unchecked, but she stayed silent.

"Everything Susannah does is colored by her guilt, her belief that she was responsible," he said, but he moderated his voice because her tears touched his heart. This woman had lost her children. There was enough pain to go around.

Sara still said nothing. David knew he had to jar her out of her silence.

"This is a picture of her." He slid his favorite photo of Susannah across the table. She was daydreaming about something, staring into the lens, a small smile lifting her lips. "She's beautiful inside and out. She'd be a wonderful mother."

One hand reached out to trace the features on Susannah's lovely face. The tears did not stop. A flicker

of empathy rose inside David's heart for this woman—
she'd never known the wonderful beauty of what her
child had become in spite of her.

"She's going to give away her baby to someone else,
to adopt, because she thinks she's unworthy and because
she's afraid she won't be the kind of mother she wants
to be," David explained.

"She thinks she'll be like me. A drunk?" Finally Sara
looked at him. Her excruciating pain engulfed him like
a tidal wave and sucked all his anger away.

"She needs your forgiveness," David told her. "She
needs to hear you say that her sisters' deaths were not
her fault. This pain, this hurt—hasn't it gone on long
enough, Sara? Your daughter needs you. Susannah needs
the mother who abandoned her all those years ago."

"I'm sorry but your time is up." A guard waited at
his elbow.

David rose, but he left the picture on the table.

"Susannah's baby is due very soon," he said, keeping his voice soft. "If you're going to help her, it must
be quickly, before the baby's born. Otherwise it will be
too late to repair the past."

Sara simply sat there, staring at her daughter. He laid
a hand on her shoulder.

"I'll pray for you, Sara. I'll ask God to heal your heart
and soul and show you that He has plans for your future, something beautiful that you can't even imagine."

As he drove home, he prayed harder than he had in
his entire life.

For all of them.

Susannah was miserable.

"I'm tired all the time," she told her doctor. "I can't

see my toes anymore, let alone polish them. I feel like a limp rag even first thing in the morning."

"It's spring and this is the desert. It's only going to get warmer. Rest," the doctor advised.

"That's what everyone says," Susannah complained. "I do almost nothing but rest, and I'm still tired."

"Then rest some more. You're carrying a baby, Susannah. That's hard work. Probably the hardest job you'll ever have. You have to save your strength. Did you go to those Lamaze classes?"

"Yes." She'd gone with Connie and Darla. Precious, poignant, bittersweet evenings, full of laughter and tears.

"So you're ready," the doctor said. "Now you're just going to have to wait patiently until this baby decides its arrival date. Relax."

Connie also kept telling her to slow down but Susannah was frantic to find a family for her baby, and without David's help she floundered. How could you know about anyone's real intent through an internet profile?

As she made her way to pick up Darla, Susannah realized anew how difficult she was finding it, keeping up with Darla's activities, though her charge was always solicitous about Susannah's health. Darla fussed about the baby constantly, monitoring what Susannah ate and when. She insisted Susannah take frequent rests and offered water so often Susannah worried she'd float away during soccer practice or while waiting for Darla at the botanical garden. She made her way into David's house with Darla dancing attendance.

"Sixty-seven percent of pregnant women do not drink enough water," Darla declared. She was quoting statistics less often now, but the odd one still popped out whenever she wanted to defend her actions.

"I'm fine, Darla. Oh." The Braxton-Hicks contraction grabbed and held on, forcing Susannah to sit down on David's sofa and wait it out. "We'll make cookies in a little while," she promised with a gasp.

"Okay." Darla flopped down at the coffee table. "I'm going to draw some of the butterflies from the botanical garden so I can show the people at the center what I do." She plugged in her headphones and began humming to the music as her fingers flew across the page.

Once the tension in her stomach relaxed, Susannah closed her eyes. Just for a minute. Then she'd get up and make the cookies Darla wanted to take to school tomorrow. As she lay there, the scent from roses David had cut from the garden filled her senses. How wonderful to have your own rose bushes.

It was just one of the things Susannah was going to miss about this job. Each day had proven harder than the one before as she realized exactly what she was giving up by refusing David's proposal. Once she took Darla to the desert museum, her lovely life here would be over and all she'd have left were memories.

"I'm only asking You for one thing, God," she whispered. "Just please make sure my baby is healthy."

The house was quiet when he arrived home. Too quiet.

David tucked the packet of key lime-flavored mints under Susannah's purse. She'd mentioned she liked them last week, so today, on the way home, he'd made a special trip to the candy store to get them for her.

Not that she'd said it specifically to him. She hadn't.

Susannah barely said two words to him anymore, and if she did, she made sure to keep her gaze averted. Ever since he'd proposed she'd been shy around him—hesitant, quiet.

But that didn't stop David from noting her likes and dislikes—Susannah liked lime-flavored anything, and it gave him great pleasure to seek out little gifts and leave them for her enjoyment. He'd wait like a kid and watch for her to discover his surprise, and then treasure that moment when she closed her eyes and hugged the treat to her heart.

Those few seconds made the bereft moments in his life bearable. That and the way she leaned into his nightly embrace before she remembered and pulled away...

David was going to call out, but then he stepped into the family room and saw Darla flopped on the floor, her headphones in her ears, her eyes closed. Her chest moved up and down in a soft, rhythmic snore. He found Susannah lying on the sofa with her eyes closed and a faint smile on her lips as she dozed.

Darla's Sleeping Beauty.

One hand lay on top of her stomach, as if to protect the precious life within. Mother and child. Was there anything more beautiful?

He wondered again about Susannah's mother. Would she do the right thing? Or would she stay in her self-imposed prison? Once more he prayed for the troubled Sara and asked God to release her heart so that she could reach out to the daughter who needed peace so badly.

David spent some time just watching Susannah, treasuring the moment because he didn't know when it might happen again. One more day, that's all she had left to work for him. Then—who knew?

"Oh, I didn't realize it was so late." She blinked at him, then struggled to sit up, grasping David's hand when he held it out, easing herself off the sofa. "Thank you. I feel like an elephant."

"You look beautiful," he murmured. He touched her cheek with his fingers and pressed a kiss against her forehead. "Very beautiful."

She gave him a look that said she thought he was fibbing.

"I mean it. Your skin has this amazing luminosity— it's very attractive," he said, finishing hurriedly, amazed at his newfound ability to be so poetic.

"Well." Susannah stepped around him. "I shouldn't be sleepng. Darla needs to take some cookies to school tomorrow and we haven't baked them yet."

"Let's have dinner, and then we'll make them together. I think Mrs. Peters left everything in the slow cooker."

"I don't need to stay for dinner," Susannah said. "I can come back later."

"Susannah, please. Just stay for dinner. It's not a big deal, okay?" He woke Darla, then followed them both into the kitchen.

Darla made short work of setting the table. She put the kettle on to boil for tea, lifted a salad from the fridge and a freshly made loaf of bread from the cupboard. "Everything's ready, Davy."

They sat, and as he held out his hand for Darla's to say grace, David also reached out for Susannah's.

Please let her stay permanently, he prayed silently. *She's a part of our family.*

Susannah bowed her head for the grace. The moment it was over she took her hand from his. She said little during the meal. She picked at her food, eating only a small fraction of what she was served.

"Are you all right?" he asked when Darla went to answer the phone.

"Fine. Just a little uncomfortable." She smiled rue-fully. "I'll get in the pool tonight and stretch everything out. That should help."

"I'm sorry it's so hard on you," he said, touching her shoulder. "I'd do it for you, if I could."

She smiled faintly, her gaze finally meeting his. "Thank you," she whispered.

While David cleared the table, Susannah helped Darla assemble the ingredients for cookies. But when he thought it might be best to leave the two alone with their baking, Darla suddenly said she had to finish her homework. David waved her off, then noticed how Susannah flagged, leaning against the counter.

"Sit down," he ordered, easing her into a chair. "There's no need to bake cookies tonight. I can stop by a bakery tomorrow."

"Darla said everyone is bringing some from home. She wanted to do the same." She began pulling out ingredients.

"You are so stubborn." He rolled up his sleeves. "Okay, tell me what to do."

She would have argued but he guessed from the lines of weariness around her eyes that she was too tired. So he listened carefully and followed each step she gave until the batter was mixed.

"Darla and I will bake them later." David was inor-dinately pleased with his accomplishment.

"You don't know how to bake," she said with a frown.

"Three hundred fifty degrees for about eight minutes," he repeated, and then added before she could interrupt, "and watch they don't burn."

"But—"

"But now it's time for you to go home." He held up a hand so she wouldn't argue. "You need to take care of yourself, Susannah. And that baby."

"But this is my job," she protested, though it sounded weak.

"You have done an amazing job. Darla and I both know that. You've gone way beyond anything I ever expected." He drew her into the circle of his arms and pressed his lips against the top of her head. To his joy she rested against him and relaxed, letting him hold her. "I don't want you to overdo. Not now. So go home. Take the car. Please?" he asked, tilting her head back so he could look into her eyes.

"You're a very nice man, David," she whispered against his chest. "I wish…"

So did he. Unfortunately wishing didn't make your heart's desire come true. And he couldn't badger her about it now. So David kissed her tenderly, then set her away from him.

"Go home and rest," he ordered.

He waited while she gathered up her handbag. Her hand paused on the mints. She lifted her head to stare at him, green eyes shiny with tears.

"Thank you," she whispered.

"It's my pleasure." And it was. Whatever he could do for her was so little and he only wanted to do more. "I love you."

She searched his eyes, touched his cheek with her small delicate fingers then reached for the door.

"Good night," she whispered.

He watched her get in the car, pull out and drive away as his sister emerged.

"Tomorrow is Susannah's last day, Davy. Then what will we do?" Darla's hand curved into his. Her troubled eyes searched his for reassurance.

"I don't know, Darla. Keep loving her, I guess."

"And pray."

Yeah. Pray.

Lord?

But the only answer David heard was "trust."

Chapter Fourteen

"I've got to get back to the office," David said Saturday morning.

"Today? Tomorrow is Easter Sunday." Susannah had been hoping he'd volunteer to take Darla to the museum, or at least accompany them.

Truth to tell, she hadn't felt well since she'd risen. Still wasn't. She had thought about backing out of this trip, but had been unable to deny Darla when she learned David would be working. Also, Susannah had greedily wanted a few more moments together before she was permanently out of their lives.

Like so many other things, that wasn't to be.

"I wish I could go with you, but I've got a big court case next week. It's my last chance to interview some people I intend to call as witnesses." He held out an envelope. "But I wanted to personally make sure you got this."

"What is it?" She stared at the plain white envelope curiously.

"A letter. Someone asked that I give it to you." He

tucked it into her purse. "Don't forget to read it, please. It might change your life."

Susannah puzzled over that and over the kiss David gave her. It was deep and rich and satisfying, but there was also a longing to it. She kissed him back in spite of herself. When he finally drew back, he kept hold of her and stared deep into her eyes.

"I love you, Susannah. I wish you could accept that, because it's not going to change." David laid a fingertip over her lips. "Don't say anything. Just know that if you ever need me, for anything, promise you'll call me. I'll come, no matter what. No matter what, Susannah."

She nodded, but she knew she would not be calling him. This was goodbye.

"The same thing is true of God," David murmured. "He's there waiting to hear from you. If you could only accept that God is about forgiveness, not condemnation. He loves you. He loves you so much He gave His only son for you. Because He thinks you are worth it." He cupped her cheek, brushed his hand over her hair and cupped the back of her neck in his palm. "All you have to do is believe it."

One last kiss, then he was gone.

"Did you see that?" Darla asked, hours later.

"Uh-huh." Susannah smiled but continued her search for a chair.

"I got that little girl to move back from the edge so she wouldn't get hurt and I didn't yell at all." Darla preened, her chest thrust out.

"I'm very proud of you." No longer appreciative of the vista in front of her, Susannah shifted from one foot to the other, trying to ease the ache in her lower back. She wanted—no needed—to sit down after tramping around the desert museum for the better part of two hours.

"I got those kids to be quiet in the underground exhibits, too," Darla reminded. "They wouldn't listen at first, but then I explained how the animals like to sleep in the day and work at night, and the kids stopped making so much noise."

"You did a fantastic job." Susannah smoothed her hair and smiled at the triumph on Darla's pretty face. "Should we go have lunch?"

"Not yet. The docent—" Darla paused, serious. "That's what they're called, docents," she explained.

"Uh-huh." Susannah forced herself not to smile.

"Well, the docents said there is going to be a demonstration of the raptor free flights." She checked her watch. "That's in ten minutes."

Susannah wanted to groan. The raptor area was way at the back. She knew she could not walk that far right now.

"Listen sweetie, can you go with the docents and stay right beside them?" Guilt overwhelmed her at letting Darla go alone, but she'd waited so long to see the birds and the raptor flights were a seasonal thing. "I'll stay here."

"Are you sick, Susannah?" Darla tilted her head to one side and studied her with those wise-owl brown eyes. "I don't have to see the raptors," she decided.

"Yes, you do. And I'm fine. Just really tired and hot. I'm going to sit down right over there—" she pointed to the nearby coffee bar "—and wait for you. Okay?"

"Are you sure you're not sick?" Darla frowned.

"I'm not. I'm fine. I'm only tired," Susannah reassured her.

"Because of the baby," Darla said. "Pretty soon I'll see it, won't I?"

"I think so. Pretty soon." She rubbed her side as a funny little cramp uncoiled.

"I asked God to make your baby strong, Susannah. I pray for it and you every night." Darla trailed along beside her until they found a chair where Susannah could sit, still visible, but out of the hot sun.

"Thank you, sweetie. I appreciate your prayers." Susannah saw one of the many volunteers nearby. She handed Darla some money and asked her to buy two cold drinks from the vendor inside. Left alone, she waved over the docent and explained her situation.

"It's not a problem, ma'am. I'll be happy to take her to the raptors, and I'll bring her back when it's over," the girl said.

"Thank you very much." Susannah shifted, trying to find a more comfortable position.

"Are you okay? Can I get someone to help you?"

"That's very kind of you, but I just need to sit awhile. I'll be fine." When Darla returned, Susannah thanked her for the drink and introduced the girl. "You go with her and come back with her," she said firmly. "Don't wander away."

"I won't." Darla hugged her tightly. "You rest. I'll be back."

"Have fun." Susannah waited until they'd disappeared, then closed her eyes and sipped her drink. Five minutes later she felt much better.

Then she remembered the envelope in her bag.

Now Susannah lifted the envelope free and opened the flap. A single sheet of paper was inside, plain white with writing scrawled across it.

Dear Susannah:
I write that because you are dear to me. So pre-
cious. You are the best thing to come out of my
stupid, wasted life. I know that now. A daughter
who took over when I wouldn't. How can I ever
thank you? I can't. And I owe you so much. Most
of all, I owe you an apology.

Susannah's breath jammed in her throat as she read
on.

Susannah, I want you to hear me on this. And
hear me well. You did not cause your sisters'
deaths. I did. That night I was in a drunken stu-
por. Some ash from my cigarette fell on me and
burned my leg and I realized the sofa was on fire,
so was the carpet. I ran to the kitchen to get some
water. I thought I could put it out. But it was in the
drapes then and flaring. The smoke was so thick. I
tried, but I couldn't reach Misty and Cara. They'd
fallen asleep, waiting for me to tell them a story.
A fireman told me later that they never woke up.

Every breath was agony as Susannah remembered
their happy, smiling faces. How could God let two
small lives be taken like that? The familiar tidal wave
of loss filled her with pain that reached into her soul
and squeezed.

Susannah wanted to stop reading. She wanted to fold
up the letter and hide it away and never look at it again.
But she couldn't. The past had dogged her for so long.
The desperate yearning to hear from her mother, long
buried deep within, now would not be silenced.

The truth.

She needed to hear the whole truth about that terrible night.

Sniffing back her tears, she refocused on the scribbled words.

I wanted to die with them, Susannah. I wanted to go with Misty and Cara and be rid of my awful life. But you came and found me in the kitchen and pulled me out. I hated you for keeping me alive. I wanted to die and you wouldn't let me and the pain was excruciating. So I lashed out and said it was your fault they died—because I needed to get rid of my own guilt.

Oh, Susannah, until your boyfriend came to see me, I never realized that no one had ever told you the real truth of that awful night—that you were not to blame. All these years I've kept away from you, distanced myself because the guilt and the shame were so great when I looked at you that I knew I could never be the parent you needed, that I could never be worthy of being entrusted with another child. So I pushed you away and made sure you didn't come back. But I've missed you.

David? David had gone to see her mother? But then, it fit with what she knew of him. David Foster had shown time and again that he loved her. No wonder Darla liked fairy tales. Her brother was hero stuff through and through.

Susannah, you are not like me. You never were. You are strong and courageous and the best

mother to your sisters that they could have had.
They loved you so much. And you loved them. It
was not your fault they died. You did your best,
even tried to get to them. No sister could have
done more.

Susannah blinked through the tears as the devastating scene from that night replayed through her mind again. But this time it had a new part, a part she'd never recalled until now. A part where she remembered pushing open the back door, seeing her mother on the floor and dragging her outside. As if in a trance, Susannah felt the heat stinging her hands as she knocked away a burning chair and slapped at her mother's dress to put out the flames. And now she also remembered lying on the lawn, gasping for air, struggling to inhale enough oxygen to go inside and find her sisters.

She'd made it to the door before the firefighters had stopped her. They'd put a mask over her mouth and something cool on her hands. The next thing Susannah recalled was awakening in the hospital with bandages on her hands and face and a terrible sadness in her heart for the sisters she knew were gone.

For so long she'd forgotten those details. That's why her mother's screams of blame had stuck. That's why she'd never questioned that it was her fault that Cara and Misty had died. That's why she'd always felt so guilty.

Because she'd forgotten the truth. The truth.

Bemused by this new insight, she glanced down.

Your young man loves you, Susannah. Don't
throw it away because of my mistakes. Love
doesn't come so often that we can waste it. Your

sisters would want you to be happy, to enjoy your life. I don't know much about God, but your boyfriend has made me think that He might someday forgive me.

You are more than I will ever be, Susannah. I know that no child of yours would ever be without your love. And love, more than anything, is what we need to survive. You were always fearless as a child, Susannah. Be fearless now and embrace your life.
Your mother.

She wasn't guilty. She hadn't caused their deaths. It wasn't her fault.

The words kept racing around and around her brain, rejuvenating her soul with relief and joy. After reading the precious words once more, Susannah refolded the letter and tucked it back into its envelope. A tiny slip of paper lay there. She pulled it out and read it.

It's in Christ that we find out who we are and what we are living for. Long before we first heard of Christ and got our hopes up, He had His eye on us, had designs on us for glorious living, part of the overall purpose He is working out in everything and everyone.
Ephesians 1:11-12 from The Message.

David. Dear darling David, who had gone to see her mother, dug until he found the truth and made sure Susannah knew it. David who'd said he loved her so many times and refused to give up on her. David—a man who practiced love.

Carefully, Susannah placed her precious papers in her purse. How could she ever thank him? As she sat waiting for Darla, she tried to think of ways to tell him what his actions meant to her. And yet, she couldn't do that. It would be too painful and he might think that she'd changed her mind about marrying him. Which she hadn't. Not because she didn't love him, but because she did.

Her thoughts got sideswiped by a rip of pain through her midsection. It dulled to a steady ache that would not go away even after Darla returned and they went for lunch. Susannah ate a little to keep her strength up, but as the day went on, she felt progressively worse.

"Susannah, we should go home." Darla frowned when Susannah declined to enter the aviary but insisted Darla go without her. "You're too tired."

"I just need to walk a bit more. When I walk I feel better. Go ahead. I'll be out here." But eventually even walking didn't help and when the museum announced they would be closing in five minutes, Susannah was forced to agree that they should leave. But she asked Darla to buy her some bottled water first. "I'm really thirsty," she said.

"Because it's too hot for you," Darla said. She trotted off to get the water but quickly returned, her face showing her concern. "I wish I could drive."

"I'll be fine once I'm in the air-conditioning."

Only Susannah wasn't fine. She'd no sooner sat down in the driver's seat when her water broke. She turned on the radio.

"I need a minute to hear the news," she said, desperate to keep Darla from knowing how scared she was.

The baby was coming. Susannah had read enough to know that. It was simply a matter of how long she had before it arrived. She shifted into gear and began the drive home.

She'd gone only a few miles when a fierce contraction grabbed her. Susannah pulled into a vista point along the way and told Darla to go ahead and look. As soon as Darla left the car, Susannah began breathing the way she'd learned in Lamaze class. She puffed through the contractions before Darla returned.

It was well past six now. The road from the museum was almost deserted. Easter weekend. People were home with their families. Susannah bit her lip as another contraction hit. She tried to keep her concentration on the road but they were too strong and too fast and there was so little time to regroup in between. She veered sideways and felt the car lurch to a halt as the front wheel struck a huge stone at the side of the road. The grinding sound of metal made her cringe.

"Darla, are you okay?" she asked, fighting to breathe through the ferocity of this contraction.

"Yes. I'm fine." Darla touched her hand. "Susannah, what's wrong?" She had to wait while Susannah worked her way through the pain before she could explain what was happening.

"I'm so sorry, Darla. I should never have brought you out here today." She slid her seat all the way back and caressed her fingers over her stomach, breathing more normally as the skin grew less taut. "The baby's coming."

"Now?" Darla's brown eyes widened.

"Pretty soon, I think." Again she had to stop and work her way through another contraction. They were much closer together now. And getting stronger.

"We have to pray, Susannah," Darla insisted. "We'll ask God to help us and help the baby. He loves us, Susannah. He knows about your baby and that we need help."

"Just another thing I've messed up," she muttered.

"God doesn't care about that. He always forgives, if we ask." Darla closed her eyes and began to speak to her heavenly father, asking His help. Then she opened her eyes and smiled. "God loves children," she said with supreme confidence. "In the Bible Jesus told His disciples they had to let the kids come to Him. He won't let anything happen to your baby."

Susannah wished she was as sure.

"I should never have waited so long," she said, tears slipping down her cheeks as the pain began with renewed force. "How could I make such a stupid mistake?"

"I'm going to call for help." Darla took Susannah's phone and dialed 911 and in a clear, precise voice told the operator what was happening. "I can't stay on the phone," she said. "I have to call my brother, Davy."

Susannah didn't hear the rest of her conversation—she was too busy managing her breathing. When finally she was through the contraction, she heard Darla say, "Susannah is having her baby, Davy. We need help. Hurry, okay? Susannah's really scared. But I'm not. I prayed. Davy?" She frowned, shook the phone then held it out. "Something's wrong with it."

"The battery is dead," she explained after glancing at it. Terror clawed at Susannah's throat. What if something went wrong with the baby?

"Darla, I'm so sorry. I should have left earlier," Susannah searched the girl's eyes, wondering if she would panic.

"It doesn't matter, Susannah. Davy will find us."

Darla used her scarf to dab some of the water from her bottle on her forehead.

"I hope somebody does. It will be dark in less than an hour. Ooh," Susannah groaned, losing a bit of her focus as the pain grew.

Darla waited until the spasm was gone.

"I don't think you can have the baby sitting there, Susannah. I think you should get into the backseat." She scooted out and around the car and in between huffing and puffing right along with Susannah, managed to get her lying in the rear seat. "Put your feet in my lap," she ordered after she'd closed and locked the doors.

Susannah got caught up in another contraction but Darla was right there with her, encouraging her to follow her breathing pattern as they'd done so often in Lamaze.

"You're doing very well, Susannah," she encouraged, smoothing back her hair as she spoke. "Don't be afraid. I remember all the steps they said you have to go through before the baby comes. I'll help you."

"I know you will, sweetie. You're a great help."

She had Darla—and God. Trusting was so hard.

After several fierce contractions, Susannah was convinced her baby's birth was imminent. She had to count on Darla's help and she had to prepare her before things progressed any further.

"Listen to me, honey."

"I'm listening." Darla remained silent and attentive as Susannah explained what she'd need.

"Do you think you can do all that?" Susannah asked.

"Yes." She nodded confidently and calmly. "I can do it. And I won't get scared, Susannah. I'll keep praying." With that simple assurance, she began assessing their resources. "There's a blanket here. Mrs. Peters put it in last week. She thought it would be good for a picnic. And we have the water. Everything is going to be okay, Susannah."

There was no other choice, Susannah realized. She had to trust that God loved her. In that moment she realized the truth of that Scripture verse David had written. God was working out a glorious purpose in her life. He'd helped her during the fire; He'd sent her to a good home to grow up in; He'd led her to David and Darla.

"Susannah?" Darla touched her hand, her wise eyes soft. "Are you okay?"

"I'm scared, Darla. What if something goes wrong? What if the baby needs help?" She wanted to trust, but she hurt so much and now the fears and worries she'd kept tamped down for so long rose in a tumult of terror. "What if I did something to hurt my baby? What if God is going to punish it because of me?"

"No, Susannah." Darla shook her head firmly. "God isn't like that. He loves us. That's all. Love." She spread her hands.

And finally the truth penetrated to Susannah's heart. God was about forgiveness, not punishment. The guilt she felt, the condemnation she'd lived with for years—that didn't come from God. That was something she put on herself. She'd wanted her baby to be adopted because she was scared—scared to risk moving past the fear, scared to risk being hurt by loving David, scared to accept that she could be more than she'd allowed herself to dream of.

Susannah grabbed her purse and pulled out the note David had written.

It's in Christ that we find out who we are and what we are living for.

Doing things her way had resulted in nothing but trouble. Was she going to stay alone and afraid, and keep getting the same results? Or was she going to get some backbone, accept the love God offered and live her life in a newer, better way?

When she considered what was at stake, there was no contest.

"Please help me, God. Please help my baby. Please help Darla," she whispered.

A wonderful sensation of warmth suffused her, as if someone had drawn her into warm sheltering arms.

"Oh!" Susannah groaned. "Darla, I think the baby is coming. I have to push."

"That's okay," Darla said with a grin. "I'm ready. I remember everything the lady said. Seventy-two percent of births have no complications. And besides, we have God helping."

"Yes, we do," Susannah cried. And then she pushed.

Chapter Fifteen

"Oh, Lord, be with them both."

David wove in and out of traffic until he was free of the city. Then he barreled through the desert like a madman, desperate to get to Darla and Susannah. He'd wasted minutes trying to remember where they were going today, only recalling the desert museum when a frantic call to Connie had reminded him.

He still felt the shock of Darla's message. Why hadn't he answered the stupid phone, instead of letting the call go to messages? Was work so much more important than the two women in his life? Why hadn't he gone with them today?

A big lump of fear stuck in his throat as he tried again to reach their cell phone. There was still no answer. He'd contacted Susannah's doctor and received some assurance that labor in a first birth usually took its time. He could only pray that was true because he was afraid to envision anything else.

Darla had gone to the Lamaze classes. She'd regaled him with all the knowledge she'd learned. But she couldn't handle a birth. Not alone. And Susannah—

this was her first child. She'd be alone, afraid and worrying she'd made another bad decision.

If only he'd—no. David wasn't going to doubt. Susannah, her baby and Darla were all in God's hands. He
had Wade, Jared and Connie praying. He had to trust
that God would show him how to help the woman who
held his heart in her delicate hands.

Ahead David saw the flash of lights signaling an ambulance. He swerved to the side of the road before he
leaped out and sprinted across. His heart almost stopped
when he saw a small figure on the white stretcher.

"Susannah?"

"Davy!" Darla stood beside the ambulance. "We have
a baby," she said showing him the tiny bundle tucked
into Susannah's arms. "It's a girl."

"Grace," Susannah told him, her voice clear and her
eyes sparkling. "Her name is Grace, David. Because of
God's grace to me."

"Oh, Susannah." He bent and kissed her as his heart
lifted with thanksgiving. "I love you." He gazed down
at her and let the picture of mother and daughter frame
in his mind. "She's beautiful, Susannah. As beautiful
as you."

"We need to get them to the hospital now," one of
the EMTs said.

"Yes. Go ahead." David touched her cheek with his
knuckles, brushing one fingertip against the baby's velvet skin. "I'll see you at the hospital, Susannah." Then
he bent and repeated, for her ears alone, "I love you."

She opened her mouth but the attendants whisked her
away too quickly and he couldn't hear what she said.

"I helped get the baby, Davy! I helped." Darla danced
at his side, yanking on his arm in her excitement. "Su-

sannah said she couldn't ever have done it alone. I'm the first person Grace saw when she came in the world."

"You did really well, sis." He hugged her tightly. "I'm so proud of you."

"Me, too." She hugged him back but she couldn't stand still for more than a second. "Grace didn't cry at first. Susannah said she had to cry and she didn't so I prayed and said to God, 'God, can You make this baby cry?' And He did!"

"That's great, sweetie." He hugged her again. "You're quite a girl."

"I know."

While Darla related the events of the day, David glanced at the car Susannah had been in. He stopped Darla's story long enough to call a tow truck and his friends. Then Darla climbed into his car and they headed for the hospital.

Ecstatic over her role in the birth, Darla talked non-stop all the way. David heard little of it. He was too busy wondering how Susannah would react when the baby was adopted.

"Davy?"

"Yes?" He climbed out of his dark thoughts, noticing sadness creeping over Darla's face. "What's wrong?"

"Susannah's my sister, Davy. I don't want her or baby Grace to go away."

"Darla, honey, I explained to you about the adoption. Susannah wants another mommy to look after Grace." But Darla clamped her hands over her ears and refused to listen. She only dropped them when he stopped speaking.

"God made Susannah my sister," she said firmly. "Baby Grace is my family, too."

Nothing he could say could change her mind. But Darla didn't get angry and she didn't argue or yell.

When they got to the hospital she waited until he found Susannah's room.

"We must be very quiet when we see Susannah," he explained. "Don't ask her a lot of questions, okay?" He'd think of a way to explain it all later.

"I won't." Darla stopped a passing nurse. "Can you tell me where the babies are?" she asked.

"In the nursery." She pointed. "But only family can go down there. Are you family?"

"I'm the…aunt," Darla said proudly.

David winced. She was going to be so hurt when Grace went to another family. Maybe if he tried very hard, he could persuade Susannah to—

He pushed open her door and his heart stopped. Susannah lay still in the white bed. In her arms she cradled the baby. Both of them were sleeping.

"Kiss her, Davy."

There were times when Darla was absolutely right. This was one of them. So David leaned forward and pressed his lips against Susannah's.

"When will you wake up and love me?" he murmured.

She blinked. Then she lifted her incredible lashes and smiled.

"Right now. I love you, David." She lifted her head for his kiss.

"See? Sleeping Beauty. I told you, Davy." Darla smiled at Susannah. "Davy needs to listen to me more often."

"Yes, I do." He smoothed a hand over Susannah's glistening hair, needing to touch her, to reassure himself that he wasn't dreaming.

"I'll hold Grace while you talk about the wedding," Darla said. She sat in a chair and held out her arms. "I'm ready."

David glanced at Susannah who nodded and smiled. He carefully lifted the tiny child away from her mother, feeling awkward and stupid and clumsy, but oh, so blessed.

"Hello, Grace," he whispered. "I'd really like to marry your mother. And I'd love to be your daddy. Do you think that would work for you?"

When he touched her cheek with his finger, the sleeping child lifted a hand and closed her tiny pink fingers around his. Tears welled in his eyes.

Oh, Lord. His heart overflowed with thanksgiving at the love that raced through him for this precious child. This Easter baby.

He handed Grace to Darla. Then he returned to Susannah's side.

"Please marry me, Susannah. Let me be a part of your life, and of Grace's. Be a part of mine and Darla's. Nobody could be a better mother to Grace than you," he added.

"I don't know if you're right about that, David," she whispered, wrapping her small hand in his. "But I'm going to give motherhood my very best effort."

"Darla was right you know," she said.

"She usually is." David loved the way her hand fit into his—he adored Susannah Wells. "But about what, specifically?"

"I was Sleeping Beauty. Well, maybe not the beauty part but I was sleeping, because until I met you, I didn't know what real love was. There are so many facets to love, but I know now that it all begins with God's love. That makes everyone worthy of love."

"Yes, it does. I believe God led you to Darla and me, that it was He who placed love in my heart for you. So—" David dragged out the word "—does that mean you are going to marry me, Susannah Wells?"

"Yes, please," she said with a smile.

"Finally." He wrapped his arms around her and kissed her the way he'd been longing to for weeks.

"But not right away." Susannah leaned back, her arms still circled around his neck.

"But—" He frowned when she placed a finger across his lips.

"I need time, David. Time to understand what it means to be a child of God. Time to understand what being your wife will mean. Time to understand how to be a mother to Grace and a sister to Darla."

"I'll be in a retirement home by then," he teased. But he loved her all the more for her wisdom. "Okay then. While you're figuring that out, I'm going to learn how to be a father. My first lesson will involve a trip to the toy store."

"I think you can start learning how to be a daddy right now, Davy." Darla held the baby toward him. "Grace needs her diaper changed."

Epilogue

Four months later, Susannah and David's wedding day dawned hot and glorious in the Arizona desert.

"I don't want all the frills and frou frou," she'd told David. "I've realized that it's what's in the heart that matters. Choose whatever you like for our wedding." Then she'd returned to walking colicky Grace across the pool deck.

David, being David, had gone beyond anything Susannah could have imagined and as she stood inside his house—their house—on her wedding day, waiting for the music to begin, she couldn't believe what he'd done for her.

For starters, David had asked Hornby to work magic on the backyard. Roses climbed and burst and bloomed everywhere, their fragrance filling the air. White chairs with bows dotted the lush green grass and nestled near a fountain that spilled water over desert rocks and stones. Fronting the fountain stood a white filigree bower decorated in more roses and Susannah's favorite—limelight hydrangeas.

"Aren't you glad I persuaded you to buy this suit?" Connie whispered. "You look gorgeous, a perfectly dressed bride at her garden wedding."

"I only got into it because of all that swimming," Susannah whispered back. "I don't know what I'd have done without Darla to egg me on." But the truth was, the ivory shantung skirt and matching jacket looked stunning on her and she knew it.

She'd decided against a veil and chosen instead to weave a few bits of baby's breath through her upswept hair. Diamond hoops in her ears—David's wedding gift—were Susannah's only jewelry, aside from the beautiful yellow diamond solitaire on her ring finger.

"Are you ready, Susannah?" Connie asked.

"Yes." She was ready to marry her Prince Charming and begin the life God had given her.

Connie gave the signal and the soft melodious sounds of a wedding song filled the air. Darla went first, wearing her favorite red in a stylish sundress that showed her beauty. In her arms she carried Grace, decked out in a white frilly dress with red trim that displayed her chubby legs, and tiny feet clad in white ballet slippers. David's idea. He was going to spoil his daughter rotten, Susannah had realized.

Connie walked out of the house, her dress also red. And then all eyes turned to Susannah.

She was nervous at first. But then her gaze met David's.

This is the man God chose for me, she thought. *Because of God's grace I am worthy of love. I can give my heart to this wonderful man because I know that together we will share a future filled with joy and happiness. And love.*

She stepped confidently through the door and walked toward the man who'd taught her that love could grow to encompass everyone.

* * * * *

Get 4 FREE REWARDS!

We'll send you 2 FREE Books plus 2 FREE Mystery Gifts.

FREE Value Over $20

Both the **Love Inspired®** and **Love Inspired® Suspense** series feature compelling novels filled with inspirational romance, faith, forgiveness and hope.

YES! Please send me 2 FREE novels from the Love Inspired or Love Inspired Suspense series and my 2 FREE gifts (gifts are worth about $10 retail). After receiving them, if I don't wish to receive any more books, I can return the shipping statement marked "cancel." If I don't cancel, I will receive 6 brand-new Love Inspired Larger-Print books or Love Inspired Suspense Larger-Print books every month and be billed just $6.49 each in the U.S. or $6.74 each in Canada. That is a savings of at least 16% off the cover price. It's quite a bargain! Shipping and handling is just 50¢ per book in the U.S. and $1.25 per book in Canada.* I understand that accepting the 2 free books and gifts places me under no obligation to buy anything. I can always return a shipment and cancel at any time by calling the number below. The free books and gifts are mine to keep no matter what I decide.

Choose one: ☐ Love Inspired
Larger-Print
(122/322 IDN GRHK)

☐ Love Inspired Suspense
Larger-Print
(107/307 IDN GRHK)

Name (please print)

Address   Apt. #

City   State/Province   Zip/Postal Code

Email: Please check this box ☐ if you would like to receive newsletters and promotional emails from Harlequin Enterprises ULC and its affiliates. You can unsubscribe anytime.

Mail to the Harlequin Reader Service:
IN U.S.A.: P.O. Box 1341, Buffalo, NY 14240-8531
IN CANADA: P.O. Box 603, Fort Erie, Ontario L2A 5X3

Want to try 2 free books from another series! Call 1-800-873-8635 or visit www.ReaderService.com.

*Terms and prices subject to change without notice. Prices do not include sales taxes, which will be charged (if applicable) based on your state or country of residence. Canadian residents will be charged applicable taxes. Offer not valid in Quebec. This offer is limited to one order per household. Books received may not be as shown. Not valid for current subscribers to the Love Inspired or Love Inspired Suspense series. All orders subject to approval. Credit or debit balances in a customer's account(s) may be offset by any other outstanding balance owed by or to the customer. Please allow 4 to 6 weeks for delivery. Offer available while quantities last.

Your Privacy—Your information is being collected by Harlequin Enterprises ULC, operating as Harlequin Reader Service. For a complete summary of the information we collect, how we use this information and to whom it is disclosed, please visit our privacy notice located at corporate.harlequin.com/privacy-notice. From time to time we may also exchange your personal information with reputable third parties. If you wish to opt out of this sharing of your personal information, please visit readerservice.com/consumerschoice or call 1-800-873-8635. Notice to California Residents—Under California law, you have specific rights to control and access your data. For more information on these rights and how to exercise them, visit corporate.harlequin.com/california-privacy.

LIRLIS22R3